Praise for Sandra Byrd's

A Lady in Disguise

"With impeccable research and elegant writing, Sandra Byrd brings Victorian England to life in her latest novel, *A Lady in Disguise*. Readers of historical fiction will be delighted with the romance, mystery, and inspiration in this page-turning story, and they will be kept guessing until the end to see how the heroine will uncover the truth behind her father's death. Well done and highly recommended!"

—Carrie Turansky, the author of *A Refuge at Highland Hall*
and *Shine Like the Dawn*

"Sandra Byrd's talent for keeping readers on the edges of their seats once again shines throughout this well-written tale. Brimming with mysteries from the very first page, lovers of historical fiction and historical suspense will adore discovering the startling truths alongside the heroine in *A Lady in Disguise*."

—Dawn Crandall, author of *The Hesitant Heiress*

"Fans of historical Victorian and gothic romance will feel right at home in these tightly spun, suspenseful pages. Highly recommended!"

—Serena Chase, *USA Today's* Happily Ever After blog,
author of *The Ryn*

LADY

in

DISGUISE

A NOVEL

SANDRA BYRD

HOWARD BOOKS
AN IMPRINT OF SIMON & SCHUSTER, INC.

NEW YORK   NASHVILLE   LONDON   TORONTO   SYDNEY   NEW DELHI

Howard Books
An Imprint of Simon & Schuster, Inc.
1230 Avenue of the Americas
New York, NY 10020

First Howard Books trade paperback edition March 2017

HOWARD and colophon are trademarks of Simon & Schuster, Inc.

For information about special discounts for bulk purchases, please contact Simon & Schuster Special Sales at 1-866-506-1949 or business@simonandschuster.com.

The Simon & Schuster Speakers Bureau can bring authors to your live event. For more information or to book an event, contact the Simon & Schuster Speakers Bureau at 1-866-248-3049 or visit our website at www.simonspeakers.com.

Interior design by Jaime Putorti

Manufactured in the United States of America

10 9 8 7 6 5 4 3 2 1

Library of Congress Cataloging-in-Publication Data is available.

ISBN 978-1-4767-1793-7
ISBN 978-1-4767-1796-8 (ebook)

A
LADY
in
DISGUISE

CHAPTER ONE

HAMPSHIRE, ENGLAND
EARLY APRIL, 1883

I stood, that bleak day, in the graveyard in the village near Winton Park. The chapel's stone gargoyles, pitted and blinded by the elements, nonetheless mocked our mortality with their jeering grins. Mrs. W tarried beside me; it was only we two mourners. An awkward funeral had been held in London a few days earlier—*why had so few attended?*—and the interment was just as lonely and isolating.

Nearby, the grass over my mother's grave crept outward, erasing the decades-old rectangular spade edges. My grandmother's burial plot was a few years younger than Mamma's, and the grass atop it was sparse, thin, and blanched, like hair on an old woman's head. Grandfather's headstone looked like nothing so much as the king from a chess board. No grass grew near his. It was fittingly edged with gravel.

"Miss Young?" The vicar cleared his throat. "Are you ready?"

I nodded. Mrs. W took my elbow to steady me.

"The Lord is full of compassion and mercy, slow to anger and of great goodness.

"As a father is tender toward his children, so is the Lord tender to those that fear Him," the vicar softly began.

I knelt down, blinking back tears, and sifted the first handful of dirt onto my father's coffin. It mingled with a cold drizzle, black and white, dark and light, into a slurry. "Yes, you were tender to me and to all who knew you," I whispered.

I love you, Papa.

"We have entrusted our brother Andrew Young to God's mercy, and we now commit his body to the ground: earth to earth, ashes to ashes, dust to dust."

With that, the laborers began their work. I quickly turned away, but there was no blocking the sound of the first shuddering shovelful hitting the casket. I waited a moment for a sign of comfort: a dove flying in the distance, a sunbeam mysteriously piercing the clouds, a soothing song teasing forth in my mind.

I waited in vain.

We carefully picked our way out of the cemetery. It was slippery with moss, the only plant cunning enough to grow throughout the winter. An early-spring wind harried us forward, and we settled into the carriage and then returned to my crumbling country home. As we alighted I saw, in the distance, a man on horseback, stationary and watching.

"Who is that?" I asked the driver. *And why is he out at this hostile hour?*

"Why, that's Lord Lockwood, of course." The driver's voice reflected surprise. "He is your near neighbor and, er, a man of distinction in these parts. You have not met?"

"Not that I can recall, no." And yet, his name . . .

"His father, long passed, and your mother . . ." Mrs. W spoke softly, wanting to remind me, certainly, but not desirous of raising a topic that might seem indelicate.

Yes, then I recalled. Lord Lockwood the elder had courted my mother, the young Victoria Palmer. My grandfather had surprised everyone and allowed her to decline Lockwood's proposal. Certainly the old man had repented of that a half dozen years later when she married my papa instead.

Mamma. How I long for you.

Once inside the house we lingered in the Red Drawing Room, one of the few rooms in which the dust sheets had been hastily removed from the velvet furniture. The dark red flocked wallpaper made the room appear as though it were covered in bloodshot eyes; the pattern seemed to shift and follow me as I walked. Davidson, the caretaker, had seen to it that a fire was lit as soon as we'd arrived that morning.

There soon came a knock on the front door. Davidson moved faster than I'd expected for a man his age.

"Lord Lockwood!" Davidson's voice reflected deference as he opened the door. "Please . . ."

Mrs. W and I stood as the aforementioned man of distinction entered my home, a maid following behind him, the manservant next to her hefting a large wooden hamper.

Davidson seemed dumbstruck. I moved forward to greet my guest, out of my element but not wanting to reveal that. "I'm sorry there is no butler to properly announce you," I said. "We are not often here, of course." *And I don't employ a butler.*

Lockwood held my gaze with his own. It was strong and steady, but not impertinent. He stood straight, like a military man or a man in the police force . . . like Papa had been . . . I pushed away the sorrowful thought.

My guest removed his hat, which he handed to the manservant, and held out one gloved hand. "Thomas, Lord Lockwood," he said. "How do you do?"

"Miss Gillian Young. How do you do?" I replied. His rusty-brown hair tumbled in a slightly unruly manner, in direct contrast with his person, and I found that unexpectedly appealing.

"My mother sent a hamper." He indicated the manservant and his load.

"Truly considerate. How did she know we would be here?"

Davidson found his voice. "I told her, miss. She likes to know everything that is going on."

She did, did she?

I indicated the comestibles should be brought into the drawing room.

The maid set the tea, contained in a silver samovar, upon a creaking console table that was covered with tired blue and white delft tiles. Mrs. W, with a sniff toward Lord Lockwood, served. Lady Lockwood's bone china was very fine indeed.

"Your mother is too kind," I said. Lockwood appeared be-mused and a dry look passed between the maid and the man-servant.

"She is a"—Lockwood seemed to struggle to find the right word—"a purposeful woman. You don't remember meeting her, I take it?"

"No." I sipped my tea, which was still warm. "I don't think you and I have met before, either, have we?"

Lockwood took a perfunctory sip of his tea before setting it down on the side table. He had a presence and fitted—but only just—in the Queen Anne chair next to mine, its matching otto-man having been neatly pushed aside. His boots were impossibly clean for a man who had been riding in the wet and he emanated confidence and control.

"We haven't met per se," he replied. "But I remember you very well indeed."

I set my cup down in surprise. "From when, if I may ask?"

He stood, and indicated that I should do likewise. "May I?"

I rose, and he took my hand and led me to the tall, twisted oak staircase, once highly polished, now thirsty and cracked.

"Your grandparents held an annual ball. I was seventeen years old, down for the summer, an extraordinarily poor dancer and wishing to return to school with all speed. You and your parents attended, an unusual occurrence, I understand?"

I nodded and the memory of that evening eleven years earlier came back to me in a rush. In spite of the solemnity of the day, I found myself smiling. "We were all together, here for once." In spite of our rare visits, Winton had felt welcoming to me. I remembered Grandmamma patting my smooth hand with her liver-spotted one when Grandfather wasn't looking.

Lockwood smiled back and as he did his face infused with such warmth it was difficult to look away. I caught my breath and he continued. "Your grandparents greeted those arriving. I stood in the corner looking to make an early escape. Then—you walked down the stairs, grandly, as I recall, your blond hair awkwardly pulled back, wearing gaudy, bejeweled slippers a size or two too large. You tripped . . ."

I laughed, enchanted that he had remembered so many details. "I did. They were my mother's stage shoes. She was an actress."

"Yes," he said. "My own mother reminded me of that just today."

So you'll know, then, I thought, *that Mamma's father had shunned her for it, had little to do with her once she left for London and the stage, thought to be only for those of ill repute and easy morals. You know that the fact that she made a middle-class marriage is the reason we were rarely invited.*

I cleared my throat and continued. "The shoes were from a play she had just finished. My grandfather was horrified." I'd been thirteen years old, sashaying down that staircase. A quick movement of my grandmother's gloved hand had covered her grin but she couldn't hide the smile in her eyes.

"He may have been horrified," Lockwood acknowledged, his voice softening. "But I was truly charmed." He held my gaze for a moment, and then his face turned somber again. "I'm very sorry for your recent loss."

A veil slipped over me once more. "I, too."

We returned to the drawing room. "The house is yours now," he stated. But there was enough of a lift at the end to make me wonder if it was a question, instead.

I nodded. "It is."

"Would you like me to show you the property?"

My back flexed. How brash! It was not his to show.

"It is in critical need of repair," Lockwood continued. "A few years have passed since your grandmother died, and even then she was not able to care for it on her own. Your father was here six months ago . . ."

I nodded. "To store my mother's costume trunks."

He did not answer that, but continued, "And then perhaps a fortnight ago, again. His police colleague visited, too. A . . . Collingsworth?"

Mrs. W looked up, as surprised, I gathered, as was I. "My father was here, again? Recently?" I asked.

Lockwood nodded. "Yes. You did not know?"

"I did not." I'd thought Papa and I held no secrets.

Silence threaded its way through the room before Lockwood spoke again. "Perhaps your father was somewhat taken aback by the size of the property, and the maintenance and household commitments of a large country home and estate."

Was that a comment on Papa's social status, or simply an observation? It seemed oddly timed and did not address the conversation at hand.

Lockwood turned toward me. "I would be happy to escort you. Perhaps after the sleet relents?" He glanced out of the window.

Mrs. W took her brass watch necklace in hand, indicating the time.

"I'm sorry. I have every intention of exploring my house and the land, which I hold in affection and plan to restore to beautiful functionality as soon as I may. Winton Park is very dear to me indeed, as it was to my mother. But we have a train to meet." I held my head proudly. "I am a costume designer and a seamstress. I have work to return to meet my obligations."

Although now the heiress to Winton Park, I was also the daughter of a decidedly middle-class marriage. In addition to my theater work, I designed and sewed for a wealthy lady who was, I suspected, very much like his purposeful mother.

"May I be of service? Perhaps to have a look round and compile a list of what I see requires attention?" Lockwood asked. "I am mostly in London, tending to investments and other concerns. I could call on you."

His cordiality and helpfulness rebuked me; he had only intended to escort and assist. I did not need to look for disdain in every statement spoken. In truth, it was clear that maintenance and general upkeep had been long deferred. I had no idea where I would find the resources required, along with paying what would be considerable death duties. I lived by my needle. I

nodded, and stood, indicating that our time together was drawing to a close.

"That would be much appreciated. Thank you. I mean to do
well by Winton, for my mother's sake. She gave up this life"—I
used my arm to sweep around the house— "for my father. And
then she nearly lost her life giving birth to me."

At that, he winced, and I blushed. Oh dear. What an indelicate matter to mention to a man I hardly knew. Middle-class
indeed, Gillian!

We saw them out, and Davidson saw us, shortly thereafter, to
the hired carriage that would return us to the train station.

After boarding I looked out of the window as the train heaved
forward to gain momentum.

*Papa. Dearest Papa. Why were you here secretly two weeks ago
and with Inspector Collingsworth? Collingsworth had, to the best of
my knowledge, never been interested in nor welcomed at Winton
Park.*

CHAPTER TWO

LONDON

EARLY APRIL, 1883

It was dark when our next hired carriage left London's Victoria Station for the ten minutes' ride home. Mrs. W dozed, her ample bosom heaving with light snores, gray hair fringed and tucked under her bonnet. I wished I could sleep, too. It had been an exhausting day in an exhausting week since Papa had died. I appreciated her companionship and didn't wake her. If the jostles couldn't do it, no more would I.

We made our way down familiar streets toward Cheyne Gardens in Chelsea, where our townhouse was located. *My* house now, I thought with regret. Not ours.

The carriage slowed as we turned onto our street. I put a hand on Mrs. W to wake her. The sleet had stopped, but it was still pinching cold.

I paid the driver and as we approached the front door I saw that it was open. Very slightly, but unlocked and open just the same. It would be most unlike Bidwell, our manservant, to leave it ajar.

Mrs. W looked at me, hesitant, but I pressed on.

"Hello?" I pushed the door open and found that the hall and, indeed, the rooms were all dark. The smallest amount of light leaked up the stairs from the kitchen, a floor belowground. I made my way downstairs, where I found Bidwell and Louisa sitting at the small servants' table.

"He's here, miss, that man who knew your father." Louisa's voice trembled and she did not rise, as she normally would when I entered the room. "He told us to stay here and so we are."

An icy shock traveled through me. Someone was here.

Bidwell looked discomfited, too. "I don't want no trouble, miss. I'd have let him in if he'd asked. But he didn't." He lowered his voice. "I think he was here earlier, too, during the funeral, because I noticed just after that the lock had been scratched. I made nothing of it till now."

"Who is here?" I demanded, while also wondering if we should all quickly exit through the Area, the servants' entrance, for our safety. "Where is he now?"

Louisa pointed a finger upward. "Scared us to death, it did, when he broke in. Didn't expect to find us here, no doubt. Why would a policeman break in, I ask you, and one your father worked with, at that?"

"Inspector Collingsworth or Sergeant Roberts?"

"The young one," Louisa said, choking out the words.

Roberts. They had only worked together for six months or so. My father and Collingsworth had worked closely till latterly, when they had split to train younger officers as they were taken on.

Louisa nodded. "He was even digging around in the coal room."

"We've done nothing wrong!" Bidwell insisted. His old jaw trembled.

"No indeed." I marched up the stairway to summon strength I did not feel. My father's young protégé was here, in my home, un-invited. He had set my household quivering.

An unwelcome panic rose and I swallowed it back. What new grievance was being visited upon me?

I made my way to the ground floor and caught Roberts by the arm as he emerged from the library. "I beg your pardon, but this is my home. Exactly what are you doing here, and by whose leave?"

Roberts tugged himself free and turned to face me. He was perhaps a few years older than me. The very age, I'd imagine, of the suave Lord Lockwood.

"I'm investigating, Miss Young." He had the courtesy to take his hat off while addressing me, but his voice remained firm and unfriendly. His eyes darted.

"I'm just back from burying my father—who, by the way, was very good to you," I said, "to find my house turned upside down without permission." I heard the stealthy breath of the servants gathering on the back stairs, listening.

Roberts nodded. "I thought you were to return tomorrow and believed your servants would have gone with you, out of respect."

Caught in the act and admitting it.

"Why are you here, and on your own, in plain clothes?" I felt, rather than saw, Mrs. W move closer behind me, protectively.

"I've learnt, through another officer, that your father had been under suspicion and was the subject of an ongoing internal inves-tigation in the force."

"Under suspicion of what? My father? A man of long-standing integrity within the Metropolitan Police! A man who always took the time to return a single dropped coin rather than pocket it!"

"We're not talking a single coin, miss. It's been suspected that he was associating with and protecting criminal elements and profiting by it for giving protection from prosecution."

"Profiting by the protection of criminals?" My face flushed.

He nodded. "That's what's been discussed by higher-ups, that he's been protecting the criminal elite and their investments and colleagues as well as their, ah, feminine entertainments. Perhaps"—he looked downward—"sharing in those benefits."

From behind me, Mrs. W drew a sharp breath and I steadied myself by placing my hand on the mantelpiece nearby. The lamp sputtered.

"Involvement with unsavory women?" I could not bring myself to say the word *prostitutes*. No lady would use the word.

He nodded. "Unsavory and illegal situations all round, which is why I'm here. To look for evidence of any kind that might indict those participating with him. To discover who else might have been involved with him in covering up and facilitating crimes. I do not know how he was involved. But because of his odd behavior, because of whispers from police officers of long standing, I know that he was."

"Perhaps it was he who was investigating other wrongdoers," I offered hopefully.

"Perhaps," Roberts admitted, pulling himself straight, no longer shy about being caught in my house. "In which case, such evidence would clear him. But your father always—always—documented every suspicion, every contact, every bit of potential evidence for every case and investigation. I can find no such documents in our shared files, although I will continue to look. He was hiding something or not documenting it. Neither indicates anything good."

"You come alone with this ludicrous charge, you of all people, who should know his character, and are perfectly content to despoil my home."

His face grew sour. "And a very nice home it is, miss, if I may say so. Well beyond the reach of our officers. I don't think the superintendent himself lives so grandly."

My home *was* very lovely for our station in life. Doubt niggled.

"I wonder where he came by the money to buy such a grand place? Perhaps your toff grandfather gave it to him," Roberts suggested.

"Never!" Grandfather would not give my parents so much as a pound as a marriage settlement: marry beneath you and live with it, he'd said. Then I realized I had just added to Roberts's suspicions by doing away with a potentially reasonable explanation.

"My mother worked as an actress, and had some savings. When I became old enough, I contributed, too." Had Mamma's money been used to buy the townhouse? I didn't know. I would send a note to Mr. Pilchuck, Papa's solicitor, on the morrow, to ask him to clarify as he continued to sort through Papa's accounts.

Roberts looked skeptical. "I suppose that might have been enough."

"Do the other policemen know about these accusations?"

He nodded. "Some do. Inspector Collingsworth has commanded that the suspicions remain contained, he said, to protect your father's reputation if they proved untrue. People are careful not to wrongly accuse, but many believe it."

"Hence my father's ill-attended funeral." Shame burned at this new realization. "Do you believe my father was innocent?"

He kept his face impassive. "I hope so. But if not, and others were involved, I have a duty to investigate, not only because it involves criminal behavior, but because there are some"—he looked down again—"who are vulnerable and need protection." Roberts placed his hands, clasped, in front of him. "Did your father have a special place he kept confidential information?"

Now *I* kept my face impassive. Of course he did. I said nothing. "Do you have a warrant?"

He shook his head. "No one knows I am here. It's imperative that I find whatever notes he may have taken, miss, and deal with it as I see best. For your sake. For my sake. For the sake of others still involved."

I blinked and tried to absorb this new information.

"There is something they want, incriminating information of some kind, and they're not going to stop till they find it or believe it does not exist." Roberts looked terribly distressed for an experienced police officer. "I've been questioned," he continued, pacing now. "Repeatedly."

"Questioned by whom? And who are 'they'?"

He hesitated. I could tell he did not trust me. "The criminals."

"Members of the elite, ransacking my home? The only one ransacking my home, Sergeant Roberts, is a police officer."

He nodded knowingly and stared meaningfully into my eyes at those last words. "Yes. A police officer." His face flushed now, and his eyes grew brittle. "Your father was involved with some of them and they'll be as interested, or more, as I am, in acquiring any notes or evidence they may feel could expose them."

For all I knew, he himself was involved with the very evil men he spoke of—and sought to gather any evidence my father may have kept that mentioned him!

"Do you realize what sort of people we're dealing with here? They'll stop at nothing. Little people like us—you and me, Miss Young—are nothing for them to push aside . . . or push in front of a cart."

I gasped. "Are you saying Papa was murdered? That the runaway cart was no accident?"

Roberts looked down, his hands now in his pockets, his voice cool. "I said nothing, miss; in fact, if anyone asks me, I was only here to offer my condolences and see if you might need anything. If anyone asks you, I suggest you respond likewise. I'm likely to be followed from now on."

Mrs. W cleared her throat and we both turned to look at her. "I must speak up. What Sergeant Roberts is not telling you is that he came by yesterday evening, and I asked him to return for his search after the interment. He agreed to my request." She looked sharply at Roberts.

I turned back to the man and tilted my head.

"I couldn't take the risk that anything important would be hidden or destroyed," he answered simply.

"You've already committed a lie of omission. Why should I believe anything you say? Did you come earlier in the week? My man said the lock had been scratched during the funeral."

"I was among the few at your father's funeral, as you well know."

"I shall speak to Inspector Collingsworth of your irregular visit. He will see me immediately, I know." The house contracted in the cold, moaning and creaking as it did.

Roberts looked distinctly uncomfortable, as well he might. "Be very careful."

"Of Collingsworth?"

He shrugged. My head tingled. "You may leave, now, Sergeant Roberts."

"I have said I have not finished searching."

"I beg to differ." I walked toward the door, indicating that he should walk in that direction, too.

"I'll send for a locksmith to visit you this very night. I had no trouble with the lock," he said. "Nor will anyone else."

I looked at my dark hallway, door wide open, the cold wind gobbling up the warmth of the house. "Who else would want to break in?" My voice hushed to a whisper.

"There are evil people in this world," Roberts answered. "They don't always present themselves as such."

Maybe that was an unintended confession.

I kept my cares from my face, showed him the door, and true to his word, within an hour a locksmith came by to replace the broken lock. He handed two keys to me.

"Are these the only keys?" I asked.

"Why wouldn't they be?" came the reply. As he left, I couldn't help but wonder if he was going to deliver an additional key to Roberts. I would have it replaced again, and soon.

After sending Louisa to bed for the evening I sat in the drawing room with a late-night cup of tea, now gone cold, and Mrs. W.

"I'm sorry I didn't mention his request," she said. "I did not want to further upset you before the burial and had meant to tell you this evening, once home, so you might prepare."

"You don't believe him, do you?" I heard the plea for reassurance in my voice and hated it, but truth outs nonetheless.

She smiled gently. "Perhaps you should have a look around?"

I held my breath for a moment before exhaling. My head hurt from clenching my jaw. "I might find something that will clear him. That would be for the best."

She nodded, but her expression was dubious.

I sighed. "I suppose there is the possibility that he truly was working with bad people, that I did not know him as I thought I did."

That must be wrong. I desperately wished it to be.

"Perhaps," Mrs. W replied. Her lack of reassurance and terse replies breathed new life into the ashes of the night's anxieties.

She drained her cup and, with a creak of her knees, stood up. "If you should discover anything upsetting, do you think you can withstand it?"

The darkness deepened and settled round me. "I can. Mamma always said the truth would set us free."

She looked at me meaningfully. "Indeed. Good night, my dear." Mrs. W headed toward the stairs and to the third floor and her bedroom. She turned and looked at me. "Will you begin your search tonight?"

I nodded. "I must."

CHAPTER THREE

Perhaps my search would turn up nothing at all. I knew, though, that there must be a strong possibility. Roberts was young, but he surely understood that breaking into my house without cause would have severe repercussions if I decided to mention it to Inspector Collingsworth. Roberts had decided it was worth the risk.

I stood, knees wobbling, drew a shawl around me, and gave thought to where I should begin.

Like most policemen, my father had been cautious, maybe overly so. There were several secret cubbyholes in our home—the ones I knew of, anyway.

I turned on the gas lamp in the library. It flickered and I grew faint with the lamp's vapor or with the fear of what I might find, which of the two I knew not. I sat down on Papa's chair; it groaned as I reached my hand under the desk, feeling for the drawer. Once I located its cold brass catch I opened it and ran my hands along the rough-hewn drawer. Empty. Either Papa had not placed anything in it, or someone—Roberts or whoever had been here, if anyone had, during the funeral—had already found whatever was there and stolen it away. As I withdrew my hand I smelt the scent of the peculiar and costly spruce oil Papa had used on this desk and this desk alone. It mingled with the scent of his pipe tobacco, the one indulgence he'd allowed himself.

Behind me was a window, and the curtains, which had been kept closed, were now open. Had Roberts opened them? Was he, even now, peering through them to see if I might lead him to hiding spots? I steeled myself not to look toward it nor dash from the room in order to complete my task.

I opened all of the rest of the drawers in Papa's desk and found them empty. He used to keep his case files in there. Roberts was right: Papa had been a meticulous note taker and a man of unbreakable habits. Mamma had teased him about that because he'd only written her a few love letters in his life.

"Don't need to prove my love in court," he'd answer gruffly, and she'd laugh to let him know she was teasing, and he'd smile and laugh with her.

There was a scratching noise on the glass. It might have been branches, but I was too unnerved to walk toward the window and shut the curtains. Now that I had finished looking, I hurried from the room and pulled the door fast behind me.

Once in the drawing room, I lifted down the small portrait of Papa's mother, long since dead, and snapped off the false frame. There was another canvas behind it, but nothing was sandwiched between. I stood still for a moment but heard nothing but the rhythmic splatters of a dripping tap deep in the bowels of the house.

I then proceeded to make my way to Papa's large suite. He'd shared it with my mother when she'd been alive. I had not entered it since he died.

I pushed the door open and then closed it behind me. 'Twas unlikely any in the household would disturb me but I wanted to be alone. Alone with my memories, alone with my grief, alone with whatever I might discover.

The room still smelt of his shaving soap. The boar bristle brush rested in a silver holder on his bureau and I ran my hands over it, lovingly.

"What's that, Papa?" I ran into the room as he was preparing his toilette.

"My shaving gear, Gilly Girl," he replied. "Do you have whiskers that need taking care of?"

I giggled. "No, Papa. Girls don't have whiskers."

"Let me see, now." He took my chin in his big hand and pretended to examine it. Then he dusted the bristle brush against me.

"It tickles!"

"It does," he said. "No whiskers. I know one who has whiskers, though."

"You, Papa. You!"

He grinned at me and whisked his brush against the soap, releasing a spicy scent into the air.

"I do, it's true. And a certain rabbit, too."

"Yes! Do you have time to read to me before you leave?"

Mamma was performing, and Papa would soon release me to the care of Mrs. W. But he always made time for a story.

"That I do," he said. "But first, you recite a bit of it for me whilst I shave."

I used the back of my hand to wipe away my tears. I should only ever hear his voice in my head, and in my heart, henceforth. I ran my hand over his bristle brush once more; it tickled my hand. It would never be used again.

Next to the brush was a small stack of books: *Alice's Adventures*, then *Little Women*, which Mamma and I had read numerous times. The book was still rare in England, but an American actress friend had delivered a copy to Mamma as a gift. On top of the stack rested a copy of a Dickens novel Papa had said he'd meant to read; he was well read, too. I took the book in hand, as he had, wanting to touch something he had recently held. I flipped the book open, and as I did, something fluttered out.

A punched train ticket, used from Hampshire to London, not three weeks earlier, two weeks before his death. The ticket may have been a simple bookmark. Or Papa may have left it there to be found.

I tried to recall the day the ticket indicated. I remembered it because I had been repairing a torn gown for Lady Tolfee and consulting with her on new gowns for the forthcoming Season. Papa had put on his uniform, as always, and kissed me good-bye. He had said nothing of leaving town. It may have been an omission, or simply just not sharing the confidential nature of his work. Hampshire, however, did not fall under his jurisdiction and he did not like Winton Park, no doubt because he had been made to feel unwelcome. He'd often referred to it as Fortress Winton or "the castle from which he'd rescued the damsel in distress." Mamma. I smiled.

Across the room, in the panel of the big canopied bed, was the false cabinet that Papa had named the Rabbit-Hole after the one in *Alice's Adventures*. It blended in perfectly, and there were pillows propped against it. He'd said not even another policeman would know to look for one there. It was a family secret.

I recited once more from memory, softly. "She had never before seen a rabbit with either a waistcoat-pocket, or a watch to take out of it, and, burning with curiosity, she ran across the field after it, and was just in time to see it pop down a large rabbit-hole under the hedge.

"In another moment down went Alice after it, never once considering how in the world she was to get out again."

Down the hole I must go.

I reached my hand behind the bed and opened the cabinet's latch.

Once the door was open, I could see that there were, indeed, items within. I held my lamp closer to the cubbyhole.

A calling card. A stack of letters. A photograph. That was all.

I set the lamp nearby and began to examine each piece by the amber lamplight.

I quickly glanced at the photograph, feeling its draw, her eyes compelling me to connect with her though I did not recognize her. My heart quickened and, instead, I picked up the card. It had no calling name or address engraved upon it. It was of fine quality, much dearer than we could have afforded. There was an address scribbled on it, King Street, not very far from the theater district.

Perhaps this had been personal. If it had been case material, Papa most probably would have kept it with his case files at the division. *Unless he felt someone there could not be trusted, or that his files had been compromised.*

I put the card down because I could no longer avoid the eyes that followed me. I picked up her picture, drew it close in the waning light. I felt a curious sympathy for the young woman whose likeness had been dipped in sepia and now appeared before me.

She was beautiful. She was perhaps just shy of twenty, or maybe even younger. It was hard to tell, as she was all dressed up. No one of substance smiled in photographs. But this young woman smiled. What, or who, had made her so happy that she did not mind overlooking convention? Her clothing was well fitted, but the fabric was not of highest quality, nor was the stitching. I was well educated in such matters. She wore a pretty brooch. Why had she had this image taken?

I turned the photograph over, hoping for a name, date, or address. Alas, nothing had been scribbled on the back, and there was no studio name stamped upon it, which would direct someone to where the photo had been taken, either.

Who was she? And why had Papa kept her photo tucked among his treasures? *If you should discover anything upsetting, do you think you can withstand it?* I'd assured Mrs. W just an hour earlier that I could. Now I was not certain, not if the truth was sordid.

I set the beautiful young woman down on top of the small pile. She continued to stare. I turned the picture over, blinding her, muting her.

All that remained was a bundle of letters, lightly bound with one of my mother's hair ribbons. Papa had kept a locket with a curl of Mamma's hair tied in that same ribbon, the one she always favored, a rare silver blue, like her eyes, and mine. *Like a sapphire,* Papa had said, *shot through with silver.*

I'd buried that locket with him, clasped in his hands.

I loosened the letters and looked at them, one by one. Most had been posted early in their marriage, postmarked when Mamma had accompanied a traveling troupe for a short period, or even from before their marriage. I did not read them. They were too old to bear on the matter at hand, and, in any case, I did not have the heart to hear their voices. One letter, the final letter, was addressed to both Papa and me, written in Mamma's handwriting. Should I read it? It had been addressed to me, too, after all.

I held the letter for a moment; the broken red wax had been snapped, of course, when the letter had been opened and read. Mother's seal had closed the letter once; imprinted in that red was its mark. It was the same seal I now wore, our family signet ring. The ring had been passed, mother to daughter, for generations. Mother had never taken it off, as it had been the sole daily connection she'd had to her mother after having been nearly banished. I'd slipped the ring from her finger when she died and it had not left my hand since.

I unfolded the paper and a wave of nostalgia and grief swelled through me as I recognized her comforting, familiar hand. The note was short and addressed to "Drew." Only Mamma had called my father Drew rather than Andrew. My heart panged with longing for them both.

Dearest Drew and my little Gilly Girl,

I hope you are both well, and miss you desperately. I shall be home soon, and hope that you, Drew, will give our girl an extra kiss and squeeze each night till then.

Mother is doing as well as can be expected. I am glad I have stayed these extra few days to help sort through Father's belongings. We have had a chance to discuss Winton, too. She'll keep on the caretaker, cook, and maid, of course. I'll arrange for a nurse as well. There are resources enough to cover her expenses, but only for a few years.

The house is too big for one person, in truth. It is not necessary or even godly for anyone to have a home this size and no good has come of it. Knowing that, it is my intention to immediately donate the house to the Cause if and when it becomes mine, if that is your will as well, darling.

You know how given I am to the Cause and its ministries.
Perhaps then, good can finally come of Winton.
　　I shall be back to you both soon.
　　I remain, as ever,
　　Yours affectionately,
　　Vicky

I set the letter on the bed. The lamp flickered, winked, sputtered, and then went out.

I could not gather my thoughts; they were scattered by the
shock. My mother had intended Winton Park not for me, but for
the Cause! She had been deeply given to its Christian mission to
the poor and downtrodden, that I knew. The Cause had started as
a ministry to those poor and downtrodden in East London, feeding them and providing them with clothing. Soon, there were
speakers bringing the good news of the Gospel.

Mamma had volunteered there for many years, welcomed
by the underprivileged because as an actress she was also on
the outskirts of society and thought by many to be of base
morals because of it. Mamma, too, knew what it was like to be
shunned.

She'd spoken to the women aided by the Cause, loved and accepted them without reserve. She'd served meals and given rousing speeches. I had heard quite a few of those talks. As a girl, they
had bored me. As a woman, now, I was inspired. Mamma had
supported the Cause financially in small ways, which were, after
all, all that were available to us for many years.

Perhaps she'd known all along she planned to support them
magnificently in the end, with the resources only the donation of
Winton could bring.

Immediately, she'd said.

Why had she never told me? I had been young when she'd died. Perhaps Papa *had* disagreed. *If that is your will as well, darling.*

Perhaps he had intended me to make that decision with my future husband, as he and Mamma had always decided things together and the property remained in trust for me until I was married or aged five and twenty. *Or upon Papa's death.* I wiped a tear.

Maybe my father, so decisive much of the time, had faltered with this most significant request.

Had he faltered elsewhere?

I gathered the small bundle of ephemera: the letters, the calling card, the photo, and then slipped them into my linen pocket. I would keep them with me. Nothing within them could be of help to Roberts—could they be?—even if I were of a mind to help him. Currently, I was not. I turned my hand back to the letter.

Mamma, I shall, of course, do what you wanted with Winton.

I loved Winton, with its many rooms and pretty portraits of my forebears, and a wide lawn edged with a copse of trees. I'd always planned to restore it, to modernize it to my tastes while retaining the touch of those who had gone before. I thought, perhaps, I might live there, at least some of the time. I'd envisioned my children frolicking there in a way I'd not been welcomed to. I wanted to make it the happy home my mother had remembered from early in her life.

That was before she'd crossed her father, of course. I glanced down at the papers left by *my* father.

Who had he truly been, and what had he been involved with, and why had he died? Why had Mamma intended to leave her home, our family home, *my* home now, to the Cause? She had died, of course, before Grandmamma had, and the house had been placed in trust for me. Papa was the trustee.

Papa. Mamma. I was suddenly uncertain that I had truly known either of them. I grew anxious that if I pursued this further I would learn more than I'd expected and that things would never be the same. The realization nipped at my heels all the way to my bedchamber like the sly foxes in London's alleys.

I would not mention to anyone anything about what I'd found.

Late that night, I pulled out the bottom drawer of a bureau in my room, a drawer I had not looked in for perhaps five or six years, and pulled out the notebooks I'd stashed there. Most of them were clippings of her performances, reviews and acclaims and even the rare poor evaluation. She'd had Mrs. W clip and save those, too, to learn from. I ran my fingers lightly over the newspaper accounts, and stared at the pencil-drawn illustrations of her in costume.

Mamma. Mamma.

I set them aside and opened up the notebook in which the clippings from her charitable works had been gathered. Although she'd donated her time and fame regularly, she favored the Cause.

First was a clipping from the London *Evening Standard*.

Sir—will you allow us space to inform your many readers that we have just come into the possession of the People's Market and soup kitchen, attached? For a donation of 10s 6d we can supply 100 persons each with a basin of soup and bread. Tickets will be given away at the homes of the poor people by the missionaries and Bible women of the different religious denominations of the neighbourhood. Contributions will be gratefully received by the treasurer, NJ Powell, Esq., 101 Whitechapel High Street E.

I smiled as I recalled watching her serve up those basins of soup and bread.

I turned the pages and another clipping caught my eye.

We desire to correct the false assumption stated by one of your readers, and state, what has so frequently been stated before, that we have, for the past 15 years, acted as auditors of the books and accounts of this organization, and not only so, but that the books at headquarters are under our direct and continuous control. We go in at all periods of the year, ask for anything we think it may be right to have produced, examine the contents of the cash boxes, and see vouchers for all receipts and payments. The system for auditing these accounts is complete; at the end of each year a full and complete certified statement is printed and circulated among the subscribers and friends, and can be obtained by anyone on application at 101 Queen Victoria Street. Josiah Beddow and Son, Chartered Accountants.

Mamma had always been so proud that the Cause was open and forthcoming with its financial dealings. It was why, she'd said, she felt comfortable lending her name to their outreach.

I flipped the pages once more, ready to close the book, when an article with the word *theatre* in it caught my eye. It was dated just before her death.

On Monday last, about 400 supporters and friends of the Cause visited a site on King Street, to consider the establishment of the Theatrical Mission. Actors, actresses, and producers from London's many theatres will be instrumental in publicizing this ministry. A direct outreach of the

*missionary work undertaken by the Cause, the Theatrical
Mission will seek to provide a temporary respite and suitable training for those leaving professions in theatre and
who must pursue gainful employment elsewhere and otherwise. Upon establishment of the Theatrical Mission, sub-
scriptions will be gratefully received by Charles Owen,
Esq., Millwall and Blackheath, Secretary to the Commit-
tee.*

King Street, again: the spine of the entertainment district.

The next day, I wrestled over breakfast about what I should do
about Papa. Leave things be? But what if Roberts was actually
working in accord with someone who could do me harm? I
wanted to hear from Collingsworth that my father had been
under suspicion, or if he had been and was cleared. I wanted to
ask him about the runaway cart. I needed to know if it was, with
certainty, an accident.

I dressed and Mrs. W accompanied me to the Chelsea division headquarters. It was early in the day and somewhat quiet, but
the buzzing of police work was well under way.

"Good morning." I presented my card. "Miss Gillian Young,
Inspector Young's daughter."

I expected a word of condolence, but instead, he offered a thin
smile. "Yes, I know, Miss Young. How may I help?"

His attitude put me off balance. I looked around the station,
fronted by a cool blue gaslight that beckoned all who needed help
to come and receive it. The reserved faces around me offered no
such succor.

"I'd like to speak with Inspector Collingsworth."

The buzzing activity quieted. "He's not here at present."

"I'll wait," I replied.

"I'm afraid that's not possible. I'll let him know you called."

"Not possible? Why not possible?"

He stood up. His presence felt, somehow, intimidating. "Will you need an escort home?"

Mrs. W drew her breath in sharply. Were they throwing us out?

I stepped back, caught off guard. "No. No, we'll see ourselves out."

He tipped his helmet, politely, but his face was unfriendly.

Once on the street, I said, "He was told not to let me see the inspector."

Mrs. W nodded. "Distressingly, I must agree."

Collingsworth, who had unexplainably been to Winton Park of late, would never return my call. I knew it. Something was badly, perhaps dangerously, wrong.

CHAPTER FOUR

I'd been right. Collingsworth never called on or sent for me.

A week later I was bid come to the Theatre Royal Drury Lane, by Mr. Wilhelm, my employer of four years. I hoped for good news from this summons. Drury Lane was the most important theater in London. My mother had performed there, and it was dear to me. Most importantly I was, after all, on my own now and needed the continued work.

The Drury was the oldest theater in London still in active use; the queen visited regularly. I stepped through the foyer and into the cavernous theater itself. I had never overcome my awe of the place: plain seat or stately box, it mattered not. Each of the thousands of visitors enjoyed the same spectacle.

I stood in the empty foyer. A theater was an evening habitat; it was as eerie in the daytime, as dark and lonely and fearsome inside as a misty street was at night. I walked forward into the cavernous auditorium and sat in one of the tufted chairs. The quiet enveloped me. Then, I heard a noise.

Footsteps. I turned around, but saw no one. Wilhelm? The footsteps died away.

I stood and moved toward the stage to reassure and calm myself. Should I head toward the rooms behind stage? Perhaps Wilhelm was there. I did not relish walking back there alone at this time of day. The rooms may be empty. But if those had, indeed, been footsteps . . .

I took a deep breath and forced my mind to recall the joy of seeing my latest creations on that stage. What a pleasure that had been!

Oh. I heard more soft, measured footsteps. They seemed to be coming from the corridor behind the seating section to my right. Yes, someone was walking toward me, but unseen, in the corridor. I was certain of it.

"Hello?" I called out. As I did, the footsteps stopped. Surely if it were Wilhelm he would present himself. The theater was nearly black; I could only see shadows and shapes. The rich curtains draped all round and the heavy swag made the theater almost funereal, one colossal coffin holding only—me.

When I had been a girl, the stagehands would remind me and the other children about the skeleton of a man with a knife protruding from his chest. He'd been found when the theater had been remodeled some twenty years earlier. They'd tease me, "He comes from behind waiting to snatch up misbehaving little girls, you know."

"Mamma, is it true that there was a skeleton of a man murdered with a knife found at the Drury? And he wanders the halls looking for little girls who are misbehaving?"

Mamma drew near to me, her face bright with stage makeup, and kissed my cheek with her highly glossed lips, leaving a sticky residue. "He doesn't come for little girls, my dearest. Don't listen to such tales."

I kissed her back and sat back in my little chair in her dressing room. So it was true, then. There had been a skeleton with a knife. No one could know that he didn't come for little girls—not even Mamma. I slid my chair closer to hers and she reached down and stroked the top of my head while her wig was placed.

I'd lost myself in reverie till I felt a hand on my shoulder. I jumped and a little scream escaped my lips.

"Miss Young?"

I turned to face Wilhelm. I sighed in relief.

"I'm sorry I was late," he said. "I've just rushed in from the street. I needed to stop first, at the haberdashery."

So it hadn't been him walking in the corridor.

"No matter. I've spent the time thinking of the theater's legends, and of my mother . . . and of the costumes I've had the pleasure of sewing for you, and even upon some poor advice I had once received."

He cocked an eyebrow.

"I was told that if I were to sew for Drury Lane I could get away with a lower standard of workmanship. The stage was so large, the theater so substantial, that most viewers would not see lax workmanship from a distance."

"What was your response?" He stroked the left flank of his mustache, the furthest tendrils of which extended well beyond the fleshly limit of his cheek.

I grinned. "I told them that each bead and stitch mattered to me, yes, for the eye of the audience, but even more, for the mind of the actress."

He grinned back. "Truly?"

"Indeed! The costume is, of course, an object of delight for the viewers, but it is first the vehicle by which an actor is transformed into someone new: Juliet, a milkmaid, a pirate, a prince. I can transform anyone into anything."

"Splendid, Miss Young. Yes. How would you transform a lowly maid, overlooked by her betters, into Cinderella?"

My hand flew to my neck. I did not want to assume. I had never sewn for the principal leads before, only the pantomime children and lesser characters. "I've heard this year's pantomime is to be *Cinderella*," I began.

"It is indeed. Last year's pantomime, *Sindbad*, has not been received quite as Mr. Harris would have hoped."

I nodded. The reviews had run from scathing to tepid. Mr. Harris, the manager, had not been pleased. The principal designer had left for greener fields at Covent Garden.

"He is determined that all, from Queen to commoner, shall be enchanted with *Cinderella*. Nothing is to go awry. Will you undertake the commission, Miss Young? The gowns for Cinderella and several of her attending pantomime girls? They must be stunning beyond anything anyone has ever seen, and that is a tall order indeed, knowing the kinds of marvels Mr. Harris has helmed."

My eyes filled with tears; my heart thrilled with excitement. All I had worked for and dreamt of from the moment I'd known, as a girl, that I wanted to sew. It was coming true, now. "It would be an honor, sir. It is like I am Cinderella myself!" If I were to succeed, it remained understood but unstated, I would be considered one of a handful of principal designers and seamstresses working under Wilhelm in the following years, too. I calculated dates in my head. I could finish Lady Tolfee's gowns for the Season and then immediately begin on *Cinderella*.

"I'm delighted." Wilhelm stood. "I shall send along rough sketches, but I am leaving the creative vision to you. You let me know what you require—no expense is to be spared—and I shall see it delivered to your salon." At that, his face darkened a little. "You do engage adequate seamstresses to see this through?"

Not yet, I didn't. But I shouldn't let that stop me from reaching for the zenith of my calling, my passion. Because the theatrical performances sometimes required hundreds of costumes, individual seamstresses and those in their charge and employ worked from salons, mostly built into their homes, but sometimes in a shop, like my friend Sarah and her millinery shop. My salon was in my home, and I would see it expanded, and soon. I nodded. "I shall see it done perfectly, and the queen shall have no option but to knight Mr. Harris."

"Splendid." He lowered his voice and rested his hand on my shoulder in a protective fashion. "The stipend is generous and will include a small portion of the show's proceeds. I'm sorry about your father."

Wilhelm, son of a shipbuilder, understood what it was like to need to earn one's keep. "Thank you. I shan't let you down."

"I know that, my dear. That's why I chose you."

With that, he left the room. I waited till he had cleared the area entirely before racing up the aisle in sheer delight.

I had just been assigned the plum design role in all London! Now, to find seamstresses. It would be difficult, this time of year. The Season was under way and all the best seamstresses had already been engaged. I thought on the passage in Philippians that promised that God shall meet all of our needs. *Lord, please lead me to qualified seamstresses. Quickly!*

I exited the theater, and as I did, a policeman stationed outside caught and held my gaze and then touched his helmet with a wry smile.

Had he been the one lurking in the theater corridor? I had never seen a policeman stationed outside the Drury—especially in the morning. Perhaps a ghost didn't haunt the corridor, but someone had. I hurried away.

To conserve money, I did not hire another carriage. Instead, I began the long walk home; walking would help me think and plan the costumes. The day was cool but dry, and there were several routes I could take.

I thought, *Luck is with me this day.* I'd take a different route and return via King Street, a long, broad, and very popular thoroughfare. Perhaps I would even knock on the door of the address on Papa's card, which I had tucked into my bag.

Someone may answer, clear his name, and the day would become even more sublime!

I reached the house, confirmed the address on the card once more, and after slipping the card back into my pocket, walked up the steps. I sharply rapped the brass lion door knocker. I waited a minute, and when no one came to the door, I rapped it again. This time, someone opened.

"Yes?" He was middle-aged, well dressed, with a tuft of unruly white hair and a look in his eyes that was both wary and predatory at the same time. His eyes swiveled, reminding me of an owl. Just beyond him, I could see a most expensive oriental rug covering a highly polished floor. The smell of fine tobacco smoke drifted out, and I could hear the light tinkling of piano keys from somewhere deep within.

He cleared his throat.

Now I was there, I had no idea where to begin. "Hello," I said. "I had a friend who I thought lived here. I thought I'd call." Weak. But I had nothing else to offer.

"Your friend's name is . . . ?" he enquired.

"Miss Buttersley," I said, thinking quickly of a young seamstress I had known the Season before.

"No," he replied. He did not offer to be of assistance in any way. He looked me up and down and after having found me unsuitable for whatever purpose I was being evaluated, shut the door without a further word. Light, feminine voices could be heard from inside just before the lock snapped.

That was all. I stood there for a moment then made my way to the bottom of the steps and looked up and down the street. Just across the way, there were some poorly dressed men and women—one looked to be selling matches and another was shrieking that he would sell or sharpen knives. He appeared as someone well versed in their uses, too. I shivered.

Military men, forgotten, their uniforms in tatters, noses bulbous and red, loitered nearby on the edge of despair. A pair of police constables moved them along and, surprisingly, one caught and held my attention for a moment. Something passed between us. Did I know him? Or he, me?

When they left, I approached the knife hawker.

"Hello, sir," I began. He laughed and spat through the considerable open space in his gums.

"Sir." He laughed, with no mirth. "I don' think so."

"What is that"—I pointed to the house I'd just been at—"building?"

He glanced at it and then back to me. "I don't speak with toffs unless they're buying something," he said. "Not even their women, unless they're selling something." He laughed, and it was as vulgar as the meaning behind his statement.

I had never considered myself a toff; certainly those in the upper classes would never accept me as one of their own.

"But . . . ," I began. He turned his back on me and walked away.

I sighed, heavily. As I began to walk, a man appeared from nowhere and appeared to follow me. I picked up my pace; he did, too. The London fog had rolled in, blocking my ability to see who or what was nearby. The street appeared to be unusually quiet.

Another man popped out from a hidden crevice within the alley wall just feet away from me. I thought I could hear their breaths. Did they mean to rob me or . . . worse? They increased their pace. I could hear their footfalls on the uneven cobbles. I began to walk even more quickly, taking care not to catch my foot on those cobbles, causing a stumble. I looked to the left and right but no escape route appeared—the alley arteries could pose more danger than hope. I gathered my skirts in my hand and started to run.

Once out of the alleys and back on King Street, I continued walking quickly. I turned around and saw the two men following me still. Or were they? Could I be imagining it? The street was blocked just ahead. It looked as if there had been a terrible carriage accident, which often happened when the streets were darkened by the London Peculiar, a brew of smoke, fog, coal, and mist.

My father's death had been blamed on a cart accident. I did not have reason to question it then, but I did now.

The area was soon cleared for movement and I did not see the men who had been following me, if, indeed, they had been.

I looked at the addresses on the nearby buildings; though King Street was a broad trunk of a road, I was but a few blocks from the Theatrical Mission mentioned in Mamma's clippings.

I walked, breathing more easily now, and finally noted a lovely but nondescript building. It was the correct address, confirmed by the motto carved in stone over the entrance: BLESSED ARE THE POOR IN SPIRIT, FOR THEIRS IS THE KINGDOM OF HEAVEN. Matthew 5:3. *Perhaps if I would not have one answer today, I might seek another.*

A rough-hewn woman stood outside the front door.

"Hello," I said. "Is this the Theatrical Mission operated by the Cause?"

"Yes," she said. "We seek to give shelter, succor, the Gospel message, and hope to those who have been tossed out of the theater world." She looked at my fine outfit. "Likely you wouldn't know much of that."

"Oh," I said, glad to have a ready response this time. "But I do. I am a costume seamstress." She warmed a little. "And my mother was an actress who was very involved with the Cause. Her heart was to serve others. Her name was Mrs. Victoria Young. Have you heard of her?"

The woman shook her head no, but smiled. "My name is Mother Rachel. Do come in, if you like." I decided I did like and followed her inside, noting that the men who'd been following me melted away into the dirty haze that smothered the city.

Beyond the foyer was a proper sitting room, and beyond that much of the room had been turned into an extensive dining room. "We feed up to fifty at a time," she said. "Though not all of them live here. Upstairs, we have rooms, four or five to a room sometimes. And downstairs, the kitchen, and the workshops."

"Workshops?" I asked.

She nodded. "Come with me."

We made our way down the stairs and as we did, I saw to the left a mock kitchen, parlor, and bedroom set up in one large area. "They're training to be maids," Mother Rachel said.

Oh yes. The clipping had mentioned training former actors and actresses for new, viable professions. "They?" I asked. "Actresses?"

"Some are actresses," she said. "But mostly we care for the poor little pantomime waifs." Pantomimes had become the most popular offering of the London theatrical Season. They often included casts of one hundred, including child actors, and families from the lowest middle class all the way to the Queen's own loved the music, joking, and spectacular comedies based on fairy tales. Each Christmas season theaters competed to outdo each other, and themselves.

I tilted my head.

"We care for the children who are no longer hired for the spectacles—not young enough, sweet enough, or simply have outgrown their roles. The highborn love to see them onstage. Plan their Christmases around it, don't they? But once the little ones grow up into young men and young ladies, they don't want to be tainted by their presence."

"Surely not!" I protested. And yet, with Mamma's experience in the Cause, I didn't find it impossibly difficult to believe that even young actors and actresses would be shunned as those expected to have low morals.

She took me to another room, where several girls and women were head down over treadle sewing machines.

"See her?" she whispered, and pointed toward a young lady with red hair. "Hired as a nurse, after training, till they found out she'd once been an actress. Swiftly dismissed, I tell you. Twenty thousand working to perform each year, none of them wanted after they's through."

I did believe that. I'd heard the stories. "They like us like they like coal," Mamma had once said. "We keep them warm and happy, but they do not want to come too close lest we soot them."

What seemed to be a young boy—but in a dress?—approached me. Perhaps he was in costume. "Hello, miss."

If it truly was a boy, his voice had not yet broken.

"How do you do," I said. "What is your name?"

"My name is Ruby."

Ah, of course it was not a lad. Ruby grinned, and when she did she became lovely. She must have seen me eyeing her very short hair, which had led to my confusion.

"I sold my hair to buy myself some time for training and to find a situation."

Plainspoken, forward-looking, unflinchingly honest with herself.

"It's a pleasure, Ruby," I said. She tugged at my arm and brought me deep into the sewing room.

"This is my friend Charlotte." She pointed at a demure young woman sewing decent piecework on a machine. "And Mother Martha."

Mother Martha looked to be about fifty years old, but by her title I guessed that she'd shepherded and steered the pantomime children in one of the many theaters of London, earning the honorary title of mother as many in theater did. "How do you do?" I asked.

"How do you do?" she replied, perfectly properly. She held out her hand, and as I took it, I noticed it was sheathed in the most beautiful glove I had ever seen.

"The beading . . ." I barely got the words out. "Where did you find these?"

She smiled; she had lost several teeth. "I stitched them myself. Have you heard that old saying, miss, 'It took three kingdoms to make one glove: Spain to provide the kid, France to cut it out, and England to sew it'? I'm the sewing part, though I cut, too."

Suddenly, I could see Cinderella's ball gown remarkably sewn with rare beads and rare talent, something that would catch Drury Lane's light at every turn. I could not do it myself, nor could any woman I'd ever met bead as well as Mother Martha could. I must have her. I, and no one else.

"Are you looking for engagement, Mother Martha? I am in immediate need of seamstresses."

Even as I said it, though, I did not know how I could follow through. Yes, I needed her skills, but I could clearly not send pieces to her here, and anyway, I knew most missions only offered temporary housing. Ruby had alluded to as much. They had a new wave of those needing help approach them each month. Where would she live?

Mother Martha put her arm around Ruby. "I shan't leave my little friend."

Ah. I wondered if she was her real mother. "Do you sew, Ruby?"

She shook her head. "Not at all, miss. I've not talent for it, and I've tried."

That forthright honesty again. I could not afford to take on anyone who couldn't sew. But those beaded gloves . . .

"I can be a butterfly, miss." Ruby spread her wings and danced with unbelievable grace through the room. "I've played a ladybird." She crawled on the ground, screwing her face into a knot with pretended fear and frustration, imitating the red, black-spotted insect as she scuttled through the room. "I can be a gnome." Suddenly she appeared gnarled. "Or a fairy." She was light as sponge cake then. The room burst out in applause, and I joined them.

"Alas, I do not have need of a butterfly or a ladybird," I said. "Though I sincerely wish I did."

Ruby took my response in good cheer. "If you think of something I can do for you, miss, please return for me. I work hard. You can ask anyone."

"I shall." I did not know what she could do for me, or why she had so suddenly captured my heart. I could see why this mission would have been important to my mother. I'd been here less than an hour, and it was already important to me, somehow. I wouldn't displace my housemaid and cook, Louisa, and there was no indication the young girl would be any better at house-work and cookery than she was at sewing. I had no money to spare for anything but that which could help me fulfill my new sewing commission.

"I have but thirty days," Ruby called after me.

I followed Mother Rachel up the stairs and she held my hand tightly for a moment. "The girls have few options and sometimes do what they must to get by. Mother Martha, though she says she will not leave Ruby's side, is destined for a workhouse if a position cannot be found. Ruby is just a month or two beyond the legal age. There are plenty who would place them in working situations where men like them young and fresh and free from disease. Their runner comes round often, hanging about, promising and luring."

With dismay, I understood exactly what she meant. Girls may "consent" to relations with men when they were aged thirteen, not that any of them understood, in full, what they were consenting to. It was perhaps better, for a time, that beautiful Ruby had trans-formed herself into someone who looked like a young boy.

But her hair would quickly grow back.

CHAPTER FIVE

One afternoon in late April, when the season and the smoky fog still conspired to snuff the sunlight much too early, I decided I had waited long enough. I arrived, alone this time, at the Metropolitan Police Chelsea division my father had served in most of his career. I did not want Mrs. W to see me shamefully rejected once again, if, indeed, it came to that. I walked through the front door alone, damp and smudged, and approached the desk. I did not recognize the young constable manning it.

"Good afternoon." This time, I did not present my card. "I'm here once more to see Inspector Collingsworth."

"One moment." This officer smiled at me; how different from my last visit! He disappeared and in a few minutes returned not with the inspector but with his son, Francis Collingsworth.

"Francis!" I cried in pleasure at the appearance of the young man. "I mean, Constable Collingsworth." The son of my father's longtime friend had, as expected, followed in his father's footsteps. We had been friends since childhood, and it was a great relief and comfort to see him. "I hadn't expected you—I'd come to see your father—but this is a very happy mistake indeed!"

He took my hand in his own, and he embraced me, as long-time friends might do. "It's lovely to see you again, Gillian. Oh, I mean Miss Young." He blushed. "Come along. I shall take you to Father myself."

We walked down the narrow hallway, and passed several officers, many of whom I recognized, but some cast their eyes away from me, and toward Francis, who nodded as we passed. Soon, we arrived at the office of Inspector Collingsworth. I looked wistfully down the hallway, where Papa had once worked. Francis opened the office door and let me in.

"Father, Miss Young has come," he announced. Inspector Collingsworth looked up at me and a wave of surprise and perhaps distress crossed his face. He quickly replaced it with a smile, stood, and came forward to embrace me in his long, strong arms.

"Miss Young, I am so sorry I have not come to call. Florence was just chiding me today, saying we needed to make time for a call or to extend an invitation. She'll be well pleased to know you've called by."

He made no mention of my earlier call. Had he been told? I was certain he had been. No one would withhold information from an inspector.

Except, perhaps, Roberts. "I should be delighted," I replied.

"How may I help?" He got right to the point, in the manner of most officers I'd known.

"I've a bit of a concern," I admitted, fidgeting with the looped, bouclé yarn on my new scarf. "The day I returned from burying Papa, I arrived home to find Sergeant Roberts rummaging through our house."

He looked concerned, but not overly surprised. "Yes, I'd heard."

Now it was my turn to be surprised. Roberts had meant to keep that a secret. *I'm likely to be followed from now on,* he'd said. "It was most irregular, and truth be told," I continued, "frightening."

The inspector sat down behind his desk, across from me, but leaned forward. "Did he take anything from your house?"

I shook my head. "I don't think so."

He smiled. "He said he found nothing, and I've questioned him repeatedly of late."

That phrase. Roberts had said he'd been *questioned repeatedly.* Did Collingsworth believe Roberts was somehow involved, too, in dubious activities? Roberts had been Papa's final protégé.

Collingsworth nodded. "I've put a stop to it; I've put a stop to everything. He won't enter again, nor trouble you, nor make any enquiries. No one will. It was out of line for him to be there in the first place and he's been . . . disciplined."

My lungs tightened. "He said that Papa was, well, was under a cloud of suspicion of some kind." I lifted my eyes to his. "Is it true?"

"It's true he was under an internal investigation just before his death. I didn't see any reason to trouble you with it, as it's gone nowhere, now that he's passed on."

I nearly fainted. Confirmed, by someone who cared for him as a brother, and who would know!

I didn't want to know but I had to know. "Of what was he suspected?"

"I don't think the details will help, my dear. Crimes is all. I can't say that it was true or not, not at this point, though it didn't smell right. If so, the troubles died with him. All investigations into his crimes have been stopped, the case files are firmly closed and remain safely with me. There is, of course, no investigation into an accidental death. I've signed off on that myself."

"Are these accusations why so few attended his funeral?" He would have felt so shamed. But maybe he'd deserved to be shamed! No, I refused to believe that.

Collingsworth softened his voice just a little. "He was a smart man, Miss Young, who made a foolish and unwise decision toward the end, perhaps driven by greed or"—he looked down—"avarice. But that will not overshadow his many years of faithful service. It shall not be spoken of again. I am the guardian of his reputation and will see that all remains quiet. I promise you that."

Even if these "crimes" were not to be spoken of again, I was being told that they had occurred!

I needed to raise my other concern. "Sergeant Roberts mentioned that those who Papa might have been associated with could come for me."

He drew himself to his full height. "I've put the word out here and on the street that you are *my* concern and my concern alone now."

Then why hadn't he called on me to ensure I was all right?

He continued. "If you need anything at all, if you find something out of the ordinary, have any concerns, or are contacted by anyone, you come directly to *me* and me alone." He looked behind me and grinned. "Or to Francis, of course. In light of events, I've decided that it would be best if Francis looked after your interests. You'll want someone to protect you."

"Indeed. I'm always at your service," Francis spoke up.

"I shouldn't have a look around my house and see if there is anything of interest, of consideration to whatever Papa may have been . . . investigating?" I could not bring myself to say the crimes he was accused of being involved with. I did not, could not, believe that.

"Haven't you already looked through your house?" His question pierced. Would he know if I lied? Almost certainly. At least I could try to keep some secrets concealed.

"I have," I admitted. "I thoroughly searched and found love letters and novels from my girlhood. Papa's desk drawers were empty."

Collingsworth visibly relaxed. "It's in your best interest, in your father's best interest, in all our best interest, to let the dust settle. Let's let the man rest in peace now, shall we? It's the only right thing to do."

It did seem best. Papa was gone now. But I pressed on. "It's just, well, how could this be?"

He sighed and it was tinted with irritation. "My dear, if it will bring you some comfort, I will immediately tend to any new information that crosses my path." His voice grew insistent. "As for you—files or notes found anywhere, including your home, belong to the police and I expect them to be handed over to me, promptly and privately."

I gasped and a tear fell. I nodded. What was happening? Was he threatening me or insisting on upholding the integrity of his office?

He put a fatherly hand on mine. "The worst is behind you. You now realize that there are men in this world who think nothing at all of hurting a copper—or a lady, if she gets in their way. Do you understand? Let's not give them the chance."

He'd as good as admitted my father had been purposefully harmed.

The inspector turned to his son. "See her home now, will you? It's dark, and a young woman should not be out alone, unescorted."

Francis nodded, took me outside, and hired transport.

We passed a moment in silence in the moving carriage before Francis finally broke it. "I'm sorry about your father."

"His death? Or his reported involvement in crime?" I added sharply. I still could not believe it.

"Both," he said, quietly. He seemed embarrassed for me, and I repented of my tone. He was only trying to help.

"Francis . . ." I put my hand on his arm, as a friend might, and he looked at me oddly. "Do you know the exact place where the accident occurred? Where Papa . . . ?"

He nodded.

"I'd like to see it. I didn't think I could face seeing it earlier, but now . . . now I think I'm ready to. Could you instruct the driver to take me there?"

Now he rested his hand over mine. "Gillian, I'm not sure—"

"Please," I insisted. "It will bring me peace, I believe. I desperately, desperately need some peace."

He hesitated for a moment, and then spoke with the driver. We ventured into a worried area of town. The narrow streets were busy; wet cobbles now slick with new rain and horse muck. The lamps spread yellow warmth through the blackish fog. Cockfighting progressed down the dark lanes and alleys. Crowing and jeering and gobbled death screeches pierced the air and my heart. I hoped we could drive away from them with all speed.

Finally, the driver pulled up at one of those narrow alleys. It was off a main road, and twisted from it a bit, like a broken wheel spoke. "There." Francis pointed. "Against that far wall."

It was much too dangerous and dark for me to get out. I reached my hand out toward the area for a moment, as if trying to reach through space to the place where his soul had departed his body. "Papa," I whispered. I turned to Francis. "You're certain that this is the place?"

"I'm certain." He waited for a moment, and then ordered the driver to Cheyne Gardens. He rested his hand on mine again, and it was a comfort.

As the driver made his way out of the narrow artery I said, "To think of the poor who live here. I sorrow for them."

He smiled gently. "Mother was always impressed by your mother's kindness toward the poor," he continued. "She's running a bazaar this year, you know, to serve the parish poor. I believe your mother inspired her to charity work."

That lifted my spirits. I thought on my recent visit to the Theatrical Mission. "I'm considering involvement with a charity myself," I said. "It's located on King Street. The Theatrical Mission, for the cast-off pantomime children."

"It sounds like a wonderful match for you." He leaned across the carriage aisle, bringing his face closer to mine as we arrived at Cheyne Gardens.

"Thank you for seeing me home," I said. "It brings me great peace."

"I've been thinking of late. If you wouldn't mind, I should like to call on you in a more formal manner. If that would be pleasant for you."

Had Francis always felt this way about me? I hadn't thought so. He'd never seemed affectionate before.

"I'd very much appreciate a visit from you from time to time," I replied.

He did not let go of my hand. "I meant on a more personal basis, once your mourning has passed. Do give it some thought."

I could consider it. He was kind. I knew him well. Should there be more than that between a man and a woman before courting? I smiled, but did not answer him directly, and bid him a pleasant good night.

Later that night, I sat in the drawing room, sketching patterns for *Cinderella* to keep my mind on productive things. I could not sleep; I kept thinking of the dark alley where my beloved papa had lost his life. For variety, I drew Francis's face. Pleasant, kind, soft, and boyish.

Before I could stop my hand, I sketched Lord Lockwood. First I sketched him not smiling. Solemn and strong, commanding. Then I sketched him smiling.

I stared at him admiringly; I admit it! He was, there was no other way to put it, magnificent when he smiled. His jaw was more angular than Francis's was.

I played with those angles for a moment, and then, as I did, I thought, *The angles in that alley are wrong.*

I took a fresh sheet and sketched the alley as I remembered it, along with the dimensions of a typical cart. I well remembered how the road lay.

A cart could not have run away down that road and into that alley where it had supposedly hit and pinned Papa to death. The angles would not allow it. He had died there, I had seen no mis truth in Francis, I believed that. But his death had been no accident. No indeed.

CHAPTER SIX

Now that I suspected the cause of my father's death, it troubled me night and day, but I did not see anything I could do to clarify the matter that I had not already done. Inspector Collingsworth had made it clear there was no investigation under way, nor would there ever be one. No one but the police had seen Papa die and they would remain silent. My house had been scoured, and any clues, other than the handful of items found in the cubbyhole, were gone—if, indeed, they had ever existed.

One mercy was that Mamma had not lived to see his death. Thinking upon this made me yearn for her anew, and the next Sunday I told Mrs. W, "I should like to accompany you to services this morning." She looked at me in surprise. "Rather than my own services."

"Certainly, of course," she said. "Might I enquire why?"

"I do love my own church home, of course," I said, "but I feel the need to be close to my mother in some way today."

Mamma had always attended Sunday services at one or another of the missions throughout London led by the Cause, preferring their fiery speech, quick action, and, truth be told, regular women preachers. *You won't find them at your Anglican services,* she'd teased Papa, and she was right. Papa allowed her to do as she would, but continued to attend the parish church nearby. After Mamma passed on, I attended with him and grew to love worship and service there, too.

Papa. I do not see what else I may do with the information at hand. But this I promise you: I will keep looking. And if something presents itself, a clue I might follow to clear your name, I will do so to the uttermost. I promise. Even if it means I may find out the worst.

Even if it risks your own life? I did not know where that thought came from.

The hackney cab could barely squeeze down the narrow brick alleyways; it reminded me of trying to assist actresses who had grown thick with bread and beer into costumes they'd fit a year earlier. With relief, we popped out onto a wide thoroughfare and in front of the hall used by the Cause for their meetings.

The Cause met all across London. Indeed, it had spread like a cure in the past decades. First drawn to helping the least of these, as Jesus might have, the ministers also now reached out to alcoholics, opium addicts, prostitutes, and . . . actresses. It did not matter if one had a never-trimmed beard or a lace-trimmed bonnet, one was welcomed at the Cause.

Mamma had told me that her father refused to speak of the matter, but Grandmamma had once, but only once, accompanied her to a meeting. She refused to look anyone in the eye lest they strike up a conversation, but on the way back to London had said, "That was lively, dear." It had been her first and last word on the topic, and Grandfather had not allowed her to visit London again.

Soon after, Mamma died. We'd had her funeral held at one of the Cause meetinghouses. Grandmamma was too unwell to attend. Of course, Mamma was buried at the chapel in the village near Winton. Papa had even wanted it so. I'd then buried him next to her, as he would have wanted.

I sat on one of the hard benches and although the sermon was rousing, my mind wandered. It would not focus on the words being enthusiastically delivered but quietly centered on the phrase I'd seen above the Theatrical Mission. *Blessed are the poor in spirit, for theirs is the kingdom of heaven.*

I had read that verse before in Saint Matthew, but it had never struck me as it did just then. I knew one should never accuse the Lord, especially in church. As Ruby's stubbled skull passed through my mind I couldn't help but remind Him, gently, *I have hopes that they will have a kingdom in heaven, Lord, because You have not provided much to them in this kingdom here on earth.*

There was no response but a forbearing silence.

I am grateful for Your forbearance and love, Lord. Please help me understand what to do and how to move forward to please You and to do good as my mother surely would have.

And, I added, *my father, too.* Why did I feel less confident in that?

I felt, suddenly, that God would show me, and I felt bathed in undeserved sunlight. Saint Matthew threaded through my heart and mind.

After the service I was greeted by many, including Mrs. Finley, who had been particularly inspirational to my mother as they'd worked together in the East End slums. "It's good to see you, my dear," she commented. "I often think of your dear mother."

I was delighted to hear someone speak of Mamma. "As do I."

"I know she had great ambitions for you," she said.

"As a seamstress?" Mamma had always encouraged my designs, that was true.

"As a soldier," Mrs. Finley responded. "Remember what General Booth has said, 'All my best men are women.'" She giggled, and so did Mrs. W, and I caught their enthusiasm and laughed with them. Mrs. Finley took my face in her hands and kissed each cheek, softly, before we parted ways.

We walked home in silence, and I thought of the many good things the hundreds of missions throughout the city achieved. Like the Theatrical Mission, and my girls. Mother Rachel did what she could, but there was one of her and so many pantomime children who became too old to work.

What lay ahead for Ruby? She had no skills that were in demand, but there were certainly men of no conscience and low purpose who would take more of her person than just her hair if given the chance. I knew that.

Ruby can't sew, I prayed in silence.

Is anything too hard for the Lord? came the response.

I knew the proper response was a trumpeted, faith-filled *No*, but the one I believed was, *I hope not.*

The next early afternoon I sat in the spring sunshine, taking a moment midway through the day to review some fashion magazines for inspiration. On the pile were some Christian publications, too. I paged through them, folding the corners of pieces I wanted to read later, and came to one speaking of the workhouses that had practically enslaved children some years back. Lord Shaftesbury, a man known for his charity as well as his title, was quoting Saint Matthew: *"And the King shall answer and say unto them, Verily I say unto you, Inasmuch as ye have done it unto one of the least of these my brethren, ye have done it unto me."*

Saint Matthew had been whispered to me, and I'd taken note now twice. I felt the certainty of conviction. I set Bidwell to work and asked that he hire a man for the next day. We were going to make changes.

"What's going on?" Mrs. W asked. Men lifted furniture up and down the stairs, jostling them here and there, biting back strong language as the narrow staircases impeded their progress. Louisa threw a look that implied she did not appreciate her coordinated routine being thrown off by the doings, but she said nothing. I paid her generously, an annual amount of twenty-five pounds, which was about the cost of a woman's simple dress. But Louisa mainly worked for her room and board; if I dismissed her, she would have nowhere to go. I would never do that.

"I'm moving the household about," I declared gently but firmly, and she sniffed but carried on. "I am expanding my sewing salon, in light of my new commission."

The first step was to move everything from the third floor, where my sewing salon was currently situated, upstairs to the fourth. In a well-to-do household, the many maids would have slept on the fourth floor, but as we had only Louisa, I could now put the extra space to good use. The windows allowed in ample light, there were gaslights for long evenings, there was space to move about, and I could run a table along the length of one room. I would order two more treadle machines, on credit if need be, and place them in opposing corners.

Mrs. W rounded the corner with me, huffing up the narrow passage. "We can fit four or five of us in here, easily," I said.

"All well and good," she replied. "But there are not four or five who can sew."

"Not yet."

"If it's all right with you, I'd like you to move into my chamber on the second floor, where you'll have more space and privacy, and then I'll move into Mamma and Papa's room." A dart of pain shot through me, but I knew they'd approve. Papa had had Mamma's costumes stored at Winton Park some months earlier so I could have room for my salon.

I'd feel closer to them in their bedroom, too, as the comfort of their things might encourage me forward into a future without them.

"That's fine, dear, but what do you mean to do here, then?"

"I mean to bring on a seamstress . . . and apprentices."

"To live here?" She looked bewildered. "We had not discussed that." Now I was too old for a guardian, she acted as chaperone and household manager. She often forgot she was not, in fact, the decision maker.

I nodded and reminded her about my new commission for the *Cinderella* gowns, which she had been very proud to hear about. "No need for discussion; I have decided. I cannot do all of this alone. Papa would approve."

"Would he, now?" she asked, her lips tightened skeptically.

"He would," I said. "Whatever do you mean?" She had, of late, been rather cool when Papa's name was brought into discussion.

"I just meant you have Lady Tolfee's gowns to sew," Mrs. W sniffed. She did not like me "hiring myself out" to the titled.

No society lady ordered her gowns in advance, wanting to wait until the last possible minute not only to judge what was in current fashion but also to try, as best she might, to ascertain and then avoid anything that might look like another woman's dresses. It was why they commissioned designers, after all.

Most patronesses insisted upon nearly immediate delivery for the April-to-mid-August Season. We worked twelve- or sixteen-hour days to make this happen—sometimes it was exciting, often it was dull as dusting.

"Yes, I have Lady Tolfee's sewing to do, and I cannot allow this remarkable opportunity to pass. If all goes as I plan, I shan't have to worry about income again. I will be a principal designer! Imagine that."

She smiled and we headed downstairs and once in the parlor, we took tea. I began with news I knew would make Mrs. W glad.

"Constable Collingsworth has asked to call upon me."

"Delightful!" She had always liked him. "Have you responded?"

I shook my head. "Not yet. I shan't give him a formal answer, but if he asks to accompany me somewhere, I shall go out with him, at least once or twice."

After a biscuit, I explained the rest of my plan to her. "Are you familiar with the Theatrical Mission?"

"Yes, yes, of course. The one on King Street. Established by the Cause. Your mother spoke of it before . . ."

I nodded. "Before her death. Mamma always wanted me to be involved in the Cause," I began.

She nodded vigorously. "She did."

"And yet, while I admired her zeal, I did not share it. But now that I've I met the young girls, really, who've worked so close to me—I may have sewn some of their very garments!—I find I can no longer turn my head and my heart. I can't get them out of my mind. I, too, want to help, especially if it means being a part of the Theatrical Mission. That is very close to my heart."

Mrs. W nodded once more. "The girls at the Theatrical Mission can sew, then? Well enough to help you?"

I fidgeted. "Two can." Mother Martha and Charlotte. On the other hand, Ruby . . .

She raised an eyebrow. "And do you know anything else about them?"

I shifted to the other side of the chair. "No." I hadn't thought of that. "But hadn't Louisa been a stranger when we'd taken her into our house?"

"A stranger with references," Mrs. W reminded me.

"Mother Rachel will vouch for them," I said.

"And who shall vouch for Mother Rachel?" Mrs. W sniffed, but softly. "I shall make enquiries within the Cause."

"Thank you!" I reached over and touched the back of her hand. She was not given to physical displays of affection. I'd learnt that when, as a child, I'd tried to embrace her as I would Mamma and Mrs. W had recoiled.

Do not take it to heart, Mamma had reassured me. *It's her way of being.*

I stood up. "I . . . I should like you to enquire with all speed."

"The dresses?" she asked. "You must begin sewing."

I nodded. "Yes, absolutely, and well . . . there are those who would like to see Ruby and Charlotte, too, I'm certain, in the East End."

Mrs. W looked queryingly at me. "Whatever do you mean?"

"In houses of ill repute. Ruby is already past the consenting age of thirteen." She would certainly understand my meaning.

"I meant, what do you mean by East End?"

"The area where that kind of dark activity transpires."

Mrs. W laughed, but there was no delight in it. "My dear, I'm sorry, but there are just as many evil abodes here on the West End."

I shook my head. "A few, maybe. But just as many?"

She nodded. "But of course. Those pretending to be and do good, angels of darkness parading as light. Some start out that way and some, just like those angels, start in goodness and then are tempted and fall. Oh yes. There are plenty of evildoers right here . . . and also in the fine country houses of Hampshire. That kind of wickedness just has practiced manners and is better-dressed."

CHAPTER SEVEN

A few days later we arrived on King Street. Mother Rachel was happy to see us and invited us into the parlor. Then she called Mother Martha and Ruby up to sit with us.

Mother Martha sat in her chair comfortably. Ruby perched on the edge and held herself in place by the tips of her toes. I held back a smile. Ten years earlier, *I* might have tried not to slip off a silk brocade.

"I have need of some help in my household," I began. "Sewing and, well, other activities as may be needed."

"What activities?" Ruby asked.

I had no answer for that. "I have not yet determined that," I said. "Sewing primarily."

Ruby spoke again. "Perhaps you should take Charlotte and not me," she said. "She's extremely clever with the needle. Mother Martha says so." Mother Martha nodded her agreement while drawing closer to Ruby. She wore her exquisitely beaded gloves and I knew she would do wonderful work in my salon. I also knew from our past encounter that I could not take her without also taking her charge: she would not leave Ruby behind.

"Perhaps Charlotte can come along as well as you," I said to Ruby. "I can teach you to do the broad cutting required. You won't need to sew. Just cut. Will you try?"

She smiled and jumped up. "I'll try! Miss, can I go and get Charlotte and see if she'd like to come? She'll be ever so glad. I know it."

I stood and spoke softly. "You may speak with her, but you don't need to fetch her now. If she'd like to come along, she's welcome, and I'll come to collect all three of you two days hence. You and your things."

Ruby grinned. "It'll be an easy load. We don't have any 'things'!"

True to my word, just as May was breaking I came to collect the girls. Mrs. W chatted easily with Mother Martha, who seemed to be of an age with her. It was difficult to tell. Like herbs in a pestle, life steadily ground out the essence of those who did not have access to comforts. I showed them the kitchens, and the lower floor, though they would have little cause to be down there. They would not likely be in the parlor or library, nor even the dining area, too often. At least not till the sewing was caught up and I was already behind on Lady Tolfee's next gown.

"And this is your floor!" I exclaimed.

"Our floor?" Charlotte spun like a ballerina, taking it all in.

I grinned. "You and Ruby shall share this room." I pushed open a door, and in the small room were two beds, each up against a wall, with two small dressers separating them. "You each have your own dresser."

"We've naught to put in them," Ruby said.

"You soon shall," I promised. "Aside from room and board, there will be a little stipend of your own. And, I am promised a small stake in the show's proceeds. If you sew and sew well, I shall share that with you all as well."

Ruby and Charlotte clapped their hands and then clasped them together.

"Look!" Charlotte said, pointing to her bed. "We have our own blankets! I've not had one since my ma passed on."

Mrs. W caught my eye and I hers. How very little it takes to care for someone; how very much I had taken for granted.

Mrs. W spoke up. "As has been said before and is the rule here: The Lord may care for the birds of the air, but he does not drop food into their nests. Each of us must carry part of the load."

"We will!" Ruby said.

"We will!" Charlotte, she of few words, echoed.

I showed Mother Martha her small room, adjoining the girls', and the table at which they would take their meals. Louisa stood on the stairway between the second and third floors.

"Yes?" I asked her.

"You've a letter just delivered," she replied.

"From whom?"

Louisa glanced at the letter. "I don't know, miss. It didn't come by post, it came by messenger. He said he'd wait for a response if you don't mind. He's waiting at the curb."

I glanced out of the window; a fine carriage lingered.

She handed it to me, and as she did, I turned it over and saw that the back had been stamped in gold, with an "L" firmly embossed in the center.

I glanced at Mrs. W, who pursed her lips. She, too, had guessed who the sender was.

Lord Lockwood.

Inelegantly, I slit the note open with my finger and unfolded it, then read. "He has some information about the state of affairs at Winton, and wonders if he might call and share his news." I wrinkled my forehead. "He says he will bring his mother?"

Mrs. W pursed her lips. "I suppose he is not certain if someone will be here to chaperone you."

"Ah, yes, how thoughtful," I said. "He may not know you live with me."

I turned toward Louisa. "Please tell his man that he and Lady Lockwood are welcome to call any afternoon during calling hours."

She smiled. "I shall. I'll make fresh biscuits every day this week, too."

"Thank you." I grinned. "It's very much appreciated."

That night, the girls were settled in their new beds, tittering quietly together till a late hour, when they finally quieted and slept. Mrs. W had slipped away early; she almost always took a sleeping draught. The household staff, of course, had long since retired. I sat in the parlor, reading a fashion magazine alongside the preliminary sketches I was making for the Cinderella gowns, when I heard the faintest knock at the door.

Tap tap. Tap.

It was nothing. It was late. It was the wind.

Then, three times, rhythmically. *Tap. Tap. Tap.* Rougher now. Knuckles on the door.

I turned down the lamp and stood up, legs shaking. If it had been only me I'd have run up the stairs. But I had the girls to think of now, too.

Tap. Tap. Tap. Insistent. Then fists nearly beating.

I tiptoed toward the door and stood just on the other side of it. I glanced at the lock: brass polished. New. The lock that I'd had replaced after my conversation with Roberts.

Tap. Tap. Tap. Tap. Softly again now. *"Miss Young . . . ?"*

I jumped back and my hair stood on end. It was a man's voice! Should I run? I did not have the voice to scream—my voice would not work at my command.

"Who is there?" I was finally able to ask, my warbling escaping the lump of fear in my throat.

"Do not open the door."

I most certainly would not! "Why are you here at this hour?"

"Do not go back to King Street, Miss Young," came the man's insistent voice. It sounded familiar, but it was so soft-spoken I could not be sure who it was. It was hauntingly insistent, slightly threatening.

"I have business at the Theatrical Mission," I said with more courage than I felt. "And will not be dissuaded."

"Do not go back to King Street. I have it on good account that it was not only the Mission you've been calling upon. It's dangerous for you . . . and for the others, those girls you took in. They may well find themselves in residence there. Perhaps you'd end up somewhere unsavory as well."

I recalled locking eyes with the policeman when I had knocked on the King Street door the day my Drury Lane commission had been given. Had that officer known me? Been following me? Perhaps it was the men who'd harried me all the way to my sanctuary at the Mission.

"Who are you, and have you been stalking me?" In spite of the flex of prickles hastening up my spine, I did want to know what this man had to say.

"I prefer to think of it as protection," he said. "Not stalking." He had lowered his voice, and I bent near it to hear. "Others are more interested in stalking. Stalking prey."

My chest contracted and I could not draw a deep breath. I used up the half breath on a short question. "How did you know it was me?" I held my hand to my throat to steady the tremble in my voice, an old theater trick.

"You have a very distinctive scarf," he said. "It's not difficult to find you. Do not go back to King Street. Stop making enquiries. Let things lie and all shall be well with you. If not . . . they'll show you they mean business. Wait for it."

For emphasis, he slammed his fist against or kicked the door—I did not know which. The door violently shuddered and I was not certain if he was trying to break in. I fell back and swallowed a scream so as not to worry the girls.

Nothing more happened. After a few moments, I heard footsteps on the concrete stairs, and I summoned the courage to peep from behind the curtain. A man in an overcoat much too heavy for late spring and with an upturned collar hurried away. By the time he'd reached the street he'd vaporized into the night mists and I could see no more.

I shakily checked the locks once more, and the catches on the windows, before retiring to bed. I lay there, sharply awake, for hours. He'd threatened my life. He'd implied he could have the girls placed somewhere unwelcoming, or dangerous—whatever that King Street property held.

In the morning, I would have Bidwell burn my new bouclé scarf in the rubbish bin.

CHAPTER EIGHT

MAY, 1883

Each day, just before calling hours, Louisa made sure the parlor shone. I changed from my work dress into my best dress day after day and waited, reading, breathing in the delicious smell of fresh biscuits wafting from the kitchen while time passed. After calling hours, I put my work dress back on and returned to the salon to sew with Mother Martha and the girls, putting the final touches on a gown I would soon deliver to Lady Tolfee.

One Thursday our awaited guests finally arrived. Bidwell, though hardly a butler, showed them into the parlor. "Your guests, miss," he said.

I moved forward and could not hold back a smile when I saw Lord Lockwood. I do not know why the smile came so readily, but it did, and he returned it warmly. His mother, however, did not smile. I cooled my enthusiasm toward her accordingly.

"You must be Lady Lockwood. How do you do?" I held forth my hand. As soon as I did, I realized I should have allowed Lord Lockwood to introduce us.

"As there is no one employed to properly announce our arrival, yes, I am Dowager Lady Lockwood," she said. "How do you do?"

Dowager? Was Lord Lockwood married, then? It would only be upon his taking a wife that his mother would have used that title.

"Please, do sit down." I led the way toward a little quartet of chairs centered by a table we'd use for tea things.

Lady Lockwood limped into the room. I did not stare, of course, but I was surprised to see her disadvantaged, as it was not how I'd envisioned her. Lord Lockwood took his mother's arm and helped her, but she held herself at a stiff reserve and seemed irritated with his attempts. I rushed to indicate that she should sit in the most comfortable of the chairs, and she did though it engulfed her. Louisa brought tea and set it down among us. Mrs. W served.

"Mrs. Woodmore, my mother's companion and my chaperone," I said by way of introduction. "She, too, is originally from Hampshire."

Lady Lockwood lifted her head. "From which family?"

Not from which town, but from which family.

"You wouldn't know them." Mrs. W finished pouring and set herself, quietly but firmly, across from the Dowager.

"No, I suspect not." Lady Lockwood raised her cup to her lips. "I received your gracious note of thanks for having sent over the tea at your father's interment."

I nodded.

"Good china," she continued. "Your mother's?"

"Yes," I said, pleased by the compliment. The tart citrus scent of the bergamot in the tea soothed me, as it always did. "You'd met her?"

She did not look away. "Oh yes. Lord Lockwood"—she glanced at her son—"my late husband, that is, ensured that we'd met. I met your father, too, a pleasant, middle-class sort of man. Seemed out of his element," she continued, "at Winton Park."

I had nothing to hide. "He was urban. Sophisticated, and he didn't feel he needed to hide in the country. London was home, for Mamma, too." *There. Take that.* As soon as I'd said it, though, I felt shamed. Parrying like this did not bring me nor my parents honor.

"About Winton," Lord Lockwood began, withdrawing what seemed to be a small leather notebook from his case.

Then the Dowager Lady smiled. "Ah. Winton Park. A beauty. The house, while in desperate need of attention, is magnificent, though perhaps small. And the grounds—the trees, the stream, the geese upon the green. Lovely place, a veritable work of art—though one in need of repair. I can't imagine why your mother ever left."

"It does need quite a few things." Lord Lockwood opened his notebook and drew near to me so we could both see the page. I did not look him in the eye but concentrated downward. I could not avoid the enticing scent of his cologne; I recognized it—Australian sandalwood. Warm, creamy, woody, spicy. His clothes were perfectly tailored.

"Miss Young?" he said.

"Oh, yes," I replied, blushing.

"The repairs, inside and out. Many of them."

As I glanced down at the book again, I heard a knock upon the door. I stood and opened it and then stepped back. Mother Martha led the way into the room, her clothes clean but worn, and Ruby and Charlotte followed behind her. Ruby had a small linen napkin with bits of bread in it.

"Off to the Mission?" I asked.

Mother Martha nodded. "If it's still all right by you. I thought I'd ask."

"It is," I said. "Ruby . . . what is in that linen?"

"Bread crumbs, miss. For the little pigeons."

I smiled. "Have a care feeding them. They'll soon decamp to our doorsteps. Some might consider them pests, and if you feed them, they'll stay."

She grinned. "Some might consider us pests, too, miss. But you're feeding us."

I laughed. "Off with you, then." They left, and I turned back to my guests. "Please forgive me. My new seamstresses, by way of the Theatrical Mission. I've been offered a commission for the *Cinderella* gowns at Drury Lane this coming Christmas."

"Congratulations," Lord Lockwood said. "That's an achievement. I'm quite fond of the theater."

"Did your mother used to perform at the Theatre Royal?" Lady Lockwood enquired.

"She did," I answered. "For the Queen."

"Nell Gwyn performed there, too, I believe," Lady Lockwood said.

"My word!" Mrs. W burst out.

At this, I stood. I could not let this go unaddressed, no matter how ill-mannered I may appear. I had no need to speak, however.

Lord Lockwood stood and took his mother's arm. "I'm sorry, Mamma is feeling unwell, that is clear. It's best I take her home. I'll leave my notebook with you, Miss Young. Thank you for your kind hospitality."

Lady Lockwood looked as though she was about to say something more, but her son silenced her with a look and I saw them out myself before returning to the parlor.

"Well, I never!" Mrs. W said. "But I can't say as I'm surprised. Nell Gwyn, indeed."

I sighed and drained my now-cold tea. It had been a terrible insult to compare my mother, an actress but respectably married, to Nell Gwyn, an actress and King Charles's strumpet two hundred years earlier. "It's what they all think of actresses," I said. "Which is why Ruby and Charlotte were in such a precarious position."

Mrs. W pottered about indignantly as she saw the tea things cleared. I took the brown leather notebook in hand and began to turn page after discouraging page of neat notes on the repairs, replacements, and impossibly costly restorations Winton required. At the moment, I had just enough resources to tend to my small London flock and undertake the expenses incurred by Cheyne Gardens. I could not, under any imaginable stretch, underwrite the costly repairs and modernizations Lord Lockwood had listed.

I sent a second note to Papa's solicitor, Mr. Pilchuck, to ask when I might visit him and get my accounts clear and in mind. He'd not yet responded to the first note I'd sent so I used slightly sharper words, reminding him that it was up to me now to tend to my accounts and, as it was, he was in my employ and I expected to be treated accordingly.

The following Tuesday the girls and I were all in the salon, sewing. I was, conveniently, nearly the exact size of Lady Tolfee and her daughter, and I was draped in bits and pieces of the garments I was putting together for her ahead of our meeting the following week. I had strips of cloth down each arm and one around my waist, like a sash. My hair was in disarray as pieces of cloth that would be delivered to the milliner had been placed there to see if the colors went well together. I held the hat feather between my teeth, which made it difficult to speak when my guest appeared at the door to the salon.

I opened my mouth to speak, and the feather drifted ignominiously to the floor as if being released from a beak. "Lord Lockwood!" He stepped into the room and took his hat off. His hair, that rusty brown, was quite unlike the regular brown or blond of most men of my acquaintance.

From behind him stepped Louisa. "Lord Lockwood, Miss Young." She dipped a proud curtsey.

I hid a smile. "Thank you, Louisa."

"Still playing dressing up, I see?" Lord Lockwood teased. "I'll have you know I dance much better than I did the last time I saw you in costume, when you were about the age of these young ladies. I shall have to prove it to you sometime."

I laughed. "No, alas, no time for play. I have a gown to make, and quickly. Although I adore dancing, I am not among the ladies you are likely to partner; it's far more likely that I dress them. Please, let me see you to the parlor downstairs. Mrs. W is out for the moment, as we were not expecting guests, but I could have Louisa make some tea."

He held his hand up. "If you don't mind, I'm curious to see what you are about here. I'm a member of the Garrick and most interested in theater."

The Garrick, I well knew, was the gentlemen's club dedicated to the arts. Mr. Garrick himself had acted, after all, at Drury Lane, and had taken a special interest in the costumes.

"At the moment, we are working on gowns for the Season and not the theater. Lady Tolfee's gowns, in particular. My patroness."

He nodded. "I know them well. Lord Tolfee, in any case."

I was not going to leave my girls out. "Allow me to make proper introductions. These are my young seamstress apprentices, Miss Charlotte and Miss Ruby."

"Nice to meet you," each said, kindly, though it was not the proper phrase.

"How do you do?" Lord Lockwood asked. I was so pleased he did not flinch nor stare at Ruby's skull.

"And my master beader, Mother Martha."

"How do you do?" she asked properly.

"How do you do?" he responded.

"Lord Lockwood," I said to them all. The room was quiet. They had more than likely never met anyone titled, and I highly doubted the present viscount had ever been introduced to previously employed pantomime girls.

"Now that you say it, 'Lord Lockwood' sounds so stuffy," he proclaimed.

"It's your name," I protested.

"I do have a nickname." He smiled at the girls. His friendliness was unexpected and very welcome indeed.

"A nickname?" Ruby asked, unaware that she should not ask. "What is it?"

"Lumpy. Lumpy Lockwood."

I turned to him, mouth agape. "What? Why?" And why had he just admitted to it?

He drew himself up and began a dramatic recitation.

"There is a curious boy, whose name / Is Lumpy Loggerhead; / His greatest joy is, oh for shame! / To spend his time in bed. They fit with gongs alarum clocks / That make your blood run chill: / And they encourage crowing cocks / Beneath his window-sill."

Charlotte, who rarely spoke, broke out in laughter. And then Ruby drew herself up, young actress that she was, and chimed in.

"In vain the gongs,—his eyes are shut,— / In vain the cocks do crow; / Empty on him a water-butt, / And he will say, 'Hallo!' But only in a drowsy style, / And in a second more, / He sleeps—and oh! to see him smile, / And oh! to hear him snore!"

"Ruby!" I said. "You know the poem!"

"Of course, miss. I've been in the theater my whole life."

Lord Lockwood continued.

"He seems to carry, all day long, / Sleep in his very shape; / And, though you may be brisk and strong, / You often want to gape / when Lumpy Loggerhead comes near, / Whose bed is all his joy; / How glad I am he is not here, / That very sleepy boy!"

At that, Mother Martha began clapping, and Charlotte and I joined her. Ruby and Lord Lockwood bowed toward one another, and Ruby grinned.

I turned and saw Mrs. W, now returned and standing at the top of the stairway looking decidedly unamused. "I've prepared a proper tea for our guest," she said. "Come along."

I indicated that the seamstresses should continue with their work. "We should proceed downstairs," I whispered to Lord Lockwood. "Lest I vex my chaperone further."

My feet were light on the steps. I hadn't laughed so since Papa had died.

Tea awaited in the parlor. Mrs. W served, then hovered nearby.

"I must know whence your nickname came," I began. "I would not ask if you had not introduced the topic. But you have, and I must say, you delivered those lines very well."

"I was assigned the poem to memorize in school, as I was always the last out of bed. It was supposed to have made me repent, and I suppose it has, as I work hard and tend more to duty than rest now." He blushed, which I found charming. "I do not know why I shared it just then, perhaps because your home seems happy. I've not told anyone else."

"It was lovely of you to share it with me and my girls," I said. Had it been good manners or a good heart? "Thank you. I did not expect you today."

"I wanted to return and apologize for Mother," Lord Lockwood began. "She would have come herself, but she's returned to Hampshire to see her doctor. You did say I might come any day during calling hours."

"You're very welcome," I said. "I was simply surprised."

"She's not well. Arthritis, and it affects her, I'm sorry to say. She was frightfully rude. You knew, of course, that my father had proposed to be married to your mother, when they were both young?"

I nodded.

"That did not come to pass, of course, but Father spoke of your mother very often, and in the most flattering tones. I don't think Mother ever got over my father's constant comparison of her with your mother. He did not stop even when Mother asked him to let the subject rest."

Ah. Yes. But I could hardly be held to account for that, understandable as it may be. "Thank you for your many notes on Winton Park. I have had Mrs. W copy them into my notebook, so I might return yours to you."

"No, I'm happy for you to keep it. You may find that you need to add to it, I'm sorry to say. Your grandfather did not tend to the estate as he might have in his later years, and he kept Davidson on out of loyalty, but his strength fails him, too. It's quite the costly proposition, Miss Young. You should know that."

I had realized that, after having read his notes again and again. I simply could not afford to make even the simplest round of repairs to the property.

"Have you thought about selling Winton Park?" he pressed. "Or considered other options, such that they may be?"

I looked up sharply. Was this the cause of his call? The purpose to his friendliness? To bring me round to sell my family home to him? His mother clearly coveted it. Perhaps because it was beautiful. Perhaps because it had been my mother's, and now something Mamma had loved and been denied could be wholly possessed by Dowager Lady Lockwood. What other options did he think there might be?

"Winton Park is dear to me, very dear, but I am, of course, considering all options," I said slowly. I had said nothing about donating the property to anyone. Surely he could not know about the letter? I had just barely read it for the first time myself. Had my mother possibly mentioned something like that when Grandmamma had died, and she'd been at Winton? Or Papa, to Lord Lockwood, when he'd been there of late?

I had nothing but my sewing salon and my homes, and now, with the *Cinderella* commission and Lady Tolfee's patronage, I might just be able to barely take care of both. But not if the repairs were too costly. I could not underwrite major renovations.

"I'd be happy to look after things for a month or two until you return to Winton and get things properly assessed," he said.

"Thank you. There will be no need to go inside, but if you note something on the property, please let me know." My resistance to his supposed kindness strengthened.

"My father, though passed, and I would have it no other way. It's a welcome duty to care for a neighbor." He smiled and seemed warm and natural again. "You seem to understand duty, Miss

Young. It was charitable of you to take those girls in and apprentice them."

"Not a duty, Lord Lockwood. A pleasure, and wisdom, too, I
think. They have . . . mostly . . . been a great help to me. I hope
I have been to them, too. I wish I could take on more girls but I
cannot just now. I can do for one, or two, what I cannot do for
many. Is that not so?"

He softened and set his cup down quietly. "It is so, Miss
Young, and so aptly put. Very selfless of you."

I smiled at him. "Oh, it's not quite as selfless as it may
seem. I am passionate about my designs and I will do whatever
it takes to see them shine." I took a bit of a jellied biscuit and
then spoke again. "Which is why I am exceedingly enthusiastic
about my appointment to design this year's *Cinderella* costumes at Drury Lane. Are you passionate about anything, Lord
Lockwood?"

I caught the shocked look that crossed Mrs. W's face, from
the foyer, where she tarried with her correspondence. Oh my!
One did not speak of *passions* with a man.

"I meant, do you have interests?" I smoothly corrected.

He suppressed a smile. "I'm enthusiastic about my investments," he said.

I pursed my lips and said nothing. He seemed uncomfortable
in the silence and spoke up again.

"I'm very close to my brother." His face softened. "He was
wounded in the Boer War and is unable to provide for himself and
his wife. I shall see that they never want, no matter the cost."

"Better!" I commended. Whyever was I being so forward with
this man? I said nothing more.

"Fencing," he finally admitted. "I love fencing and make time
for it, though I often feel regret for those hours wasted in pleasure

when I might be working toward something meaningful for others."

I rewarded him with a smile. "But no! Fencing is noble sport and one my father very much enjoyed watching."

Mrs. W cleared her throat; calling hours were nearly over.

"I must return to my salon." I stood and kept my face much steadier than the flip-flops my heart was doing inside. "Thank you so much for calling and please do convey my kindest regards to your mother. Please let me know if you notice anything unusual at Winton. I do appreciate your concern."

He put his hat on and took my hand in his. "I shall. Please let me know if I can be of service in any other way, as you consider your options."

I withdrew my hand, gently, but firmly. "I shall."

As I sewed that evening, I reflected upon him. He was such a mixture. Hard man of the City investments. Titled. Landed. And yet—he'd tease with the girls and me, own up to a silly nickname, and seemed genuinely interested in helping me. Wasn't he?

And then. That sandalwood. *And oh, to see him smile!*

I finished working on my sewing and turned down the lamplight. I thought I heard footsteps on the entryway. Bidwell was still fussing about in the coal room so I asked him to check outside and I went with him.

"I see no one, miss. No one on the street, neither."

"Does that look like a muddy footprint?" I asked, pointing to a light impression on the stairwell.

"Er, no, miss. I don't see nothing." He looked at me as if I had taken leave of my senses. Perhaps I had. I summoned up my authority.

"Thank you, Bidwell. That will be all."

We went back inside, and once there, I sat in the sitting room with the lamp down. I *knew* I had heard something, someone. Or was I perhaps imagining it and allowing my fears to become outsized?

Nonsense. Anyone would be frightened and cautious if they had concerns about the cause of their father's death and someone strange *had* appeared, whispering threats and warnings outside their front door.

I retired for the evening, into my new room, sitting on the bed and finally opening the cubbyhole within the headboard once more. I set aside the love letters, though they grew most compelling. I didn't know why. Perhaps because Mamma and I had had little time to discuss the affections of a man and a woman before she'd died? I had been younger, and not yet interested in a man in that way.

Was I now? Perhaps. But which man? At least one was clearly interested in me, though I was not sure he was the one to whom I would return like affections.

I picked up the letter Mamma had written to Papa and me. *What should I do with Winton?* I prayed. *I want to honor my mother's wishes, and she had been deeply devoted to the Cause.* Now, with the Theatrical Mission, I was, too. And yet Papa had not spoken of my giving the property to the Cause once I came of age to receive it. Perhaps he was waiting for me to marry, or turn five and twenty? He'd grudged them Mamma's death, but I'd never seen Papa fail to carry out her wishes. Perhaps nothing had ever pained him as much as that had.

I reviewed the card upon which was scrawled the King Street address. It had a clear meaning. If it had been nothing of consequence, I would not have been warned away. I must find a way to learn with certainty what was happening at that address. I shivered at the risk to myself, to the girls. I read the address over and over in my head, memorizing it, in case the card should somehow disappear.

Did I believe that my home, even my very bedchamber, could be breached again?

Yes.

I picked up the photo; the girl stared at me. Smiling, but empty, somehow. Was she smiling now, right this moment, in real life? Where was she? Who was she and why had Papa kept her photograph? Was she even still . . . alive?

What a macabre thought! I took the photo and slipped it into the finely embroidered linen pocket I always wore deep beneath my dresses. I did not want to lose the photograph. And yet I also felt uneasy with it so close to my person: because it might taint me or because we would grow closer, mysteriously, than I wished, I did not know.

Mamma, Papa. I want to understand, and I desperately need you each to be whom I believed you to be.

I changed into my nightgown and glanced at the stack of precious books still resting on the dresser. *I should have Mother Martha read* Little Women *to the girls, in the late afternoons.* The girls in the book often chattered together while sewing. It would give Mother Martha's gnarled hands a rest, too.

I picked up the Dickens book, *The Mystery of Edwin Drood*, and lifted the train stub out. My eyes caught a phrase on the page where Papa had slipped the train ticket:

> *Circumstances may accumulate so strongly even against an innocent man, that, directed, sharpened, and pointed, they may slay him.*

CHAPTER NINE

Lady Tolfee sent an embossed card instructing me to be at her residence promptly at noon the following Monday. I would take Mother Martha with me so she could measure Lady Tolfee's hands for a new set of gloves. I walked up the flights to the sewing room where Charlotte was hard at work pumping the treadle machine, and Ruby was single-mindedly cutting fabric, roughly, slowly. The scissors seemed an awkward fit for her; for me, they felt like a natural extension of my hand. I hardly sensed them there anymore.

"Mother Martha and I will be gone for some hours. Do you have all you need to continue working?" I asked.

"Yes, miss," Charlotte answered, then bent over her work again.

I picked up the copy of *Little Women*; Mother Martha had laid the book facedown at the page where she'd stopped reading. I well remembered this section and read it aloud.

"Meg's high-heeled slippers were dreadfully tight, and hurt her, though she would not own it, and Jo's nineteen hair-pins all seemed stuck straight into her head, which was not exactly comfortable; but, dear me, let us be elegant or die."

Ruby pretended to stick hair-pins in her head, and Charlotte, encouraged to join in the fun, pretended to totter on high-heeled slippers before sitting down at her machine once more.

"You laugh, my girl, but it's a good thing Lady Tolfee insists on being elegant, or the lot of us would be on the street," I teased. My affection for them swelled. I would have enjoyed helping any young girls in need but . . . theater girls, as I was . . . we were of one cloth!

"Yes, miss, I know. We will work hard." Charlotte looked up, blinked her eyes, which I knew grew cloudy from long hours examining close seams.

Tolfee House, in St. James, was stunning; the May sun illuminated the lime-washed stone exterior; the house commanded an entire corner of the block. I knew from my years designing for Lady Tolfee that the home, all told, had seventeen bedrooms, fourteen reception rooms, and a conservatory. It was anchored by one of the grandest ballrooms in London, perhaps seventy-five feet long and connecting with a magnificent picture gallery, decorated in gilt, like the hall of mirrors at Versailles. Lady Tolfee meant to keep the pride of place in that ballroom, and it was my commission to ensure she did.

We alighted and made our way to the door, where her butler showed us in; her lady's maid, whom I rather liked, showed us up to Lady Tolfee's suite.

She sat on a chaise, her combing jacket pulled around her shoulders to protect her hair whilst we measured her and then decided on gowns for the Season.

"Lady Tolfee," I said, walking into the room. She stood to put me at ease, and then looked toward Mother Martha.

"Mother Martha," I said, "please meet my patroness, Lady Tolfee. Lady Tolfee, my master beader, Mother Martha. She'll be measuring your hands for the new gloves, and beading them in such manner as London has not yet seen!"

Lady Tolfee graciously extended her hand, and Mother Martha, hers, in return. Mother Martha's hands were covered with a set of her beaded gloves. Lady Tolfee's eyes widened in admiration, and then she turned to smile at me.

"I've heard you've been awarded the commission for the *Cinderella* gowns," she said as we walked toward her dressing dais.

I grinned. "There is little you do not know." My having been chosen would reflect well on her.

She laughed, and when she did, she reminded me for a moment only of my mother, with whom she would have been of an age. "This is true. Lord Tolfee and I delight in our arts patronage, so we are often the first to be told. I mentioned to several friends that you were designing for me as well this Season, and reassured them that you were exclusively mine." She locked eyes with me. "Is that still true?"

I could afford to lock eyes with her but not to lock horns. As of now, she kept me fully employed. Perhaps after *Cinderella* . . . "Of course," I said. "My expenses will have risen, of course. I have my home in Hampshire to think of now."

"Do not concern yourself with rising expenses," she said. "I shall ensure that is taken care of. Congratulations on your new country home. Winton Park? What an interesting turn of events for you."

I smiled, warily, hearing the bite in her compliment; the highborn did not like to see anyone raised to their orbit. "Yes, Lady Tolfee. I was there, just recently, burying my father."

She took my hand in hers. "I'm so sorry, my dear."

I wrapped my tape round her while we talked. "My near neighbor, Lord Lockwood, has said he'll keep an eye on it till I can visit again. He's mentioned you. Or Lord Tolfee, in any case."

She turned round on the dais at my nudge. "Oh yes. We know the family well. He'll be in attendance at several events this Season. Kind man." She glanced down at me. "Very attractive."

In spite of my efforts, I blushed. Caught! She smiled at me, but it felt empty.

"Very keen on investments, sharp mind. Has a special interest in land. His wife's family has significant holdings."

My hand froze. "His wife?"

Stella, her lady's maid, knocked. "Tea brought up?"

Lady Tolfee shook her head. "No, dear, not with the fabrics about." She turned back to me. "She's dead now, of course, poor mouse, some years past. Died not a year after they married. Of course, that was long enough, one would imagine, for him to have buttoned up the rights to her land and other holdings. Lord Lockwood was very happy to have arranged such a prosperous marriage for his son. He had a title; she'd had the land."

I pretended to concentrate on the measurements, but my mind reeled. *His wife was dead. She'd inherited a lot of land.*

"But I don't bother myself with such things, and, I'd imagine, neither do you. The Vernissage, Miss Young?"

I shook my head clear, opened my sketchbook, and brought the conversation back to her question. "Yes," I said. "I have an idea I hope you'll like, as it's already under way." Vernissage, or Varnishing Day, was the opening of the Royal Academy of Arts for the Summer Exhibition. Lord and Lady Tolfee were principal patrons of the Academy, and as such acted as hosts of the event. Varnishing Day was so named because the artists would place final touches on their pieces, or, indeed, varnish the oils, in front of the oh-so-exclusive invitees. I could not let her down.

"As Mr. Robinson is just now publishing his book *The English Flower Garden* to bright acclaim, I thought of a light-green silk gown with embroidered flowers and vines. Then Mother Martha"—I glanced toward my dearest find—"can embroider beads which shall shine in the evening lights like stars over your country garden. It's very 'of the moment.' Impressionistic."

"Delightful, dear. A perfect idea. Spare no expense."

Although I sometimes envied the women I sewed for their freedom with their purses, I did not mind in the least their ability to provide me with the best materials, and I did my best to transform them into the dazzling, but tasteful, spectacles they desired to be.

We remeasured Lady Tolfee's daughter for a gown, too. She would not look toward her mother, nor did she speak. I would ensure her dress was stunning, but not as stunning as her mother's dress, which I knew without it being spoken is what Lady Tolfee would prefer. In fact, it was already under way. Within the hour, the butler showed us out, and Mother Martha and I were on our way to Drury Lane.

"Are you weary?" I asked her.

"Not at all, please do not worry about me," she reassured.

"I've a few items I need to leave at the theater. Would you like to come in and see the inside?"

She nodded. "Yes. But it is not new to me, I've been there many times over the years."

I had no idea she'd worked with the pantomime children at my own theater!

The opera *Esmeralda* was just ending its run and a youth revival was about to begin. I had promised to sew a few small pieces as a donation, the least I could do. I left them for Wilhelm and then headed back out of the theater. I noticed that Mother Martha tarried beside one of the dressing rooms.

"Are you all right?" I called. When she did not come toward me, I returned toward her. Then I noticed which room she was standing in front of. The wiggery!

"Yes! Why had I not thought of this?"

She smiled widely. "You have the same idea."

"Ruby!"

I quickly returned to Wilhelm's workshop. "May I take a wig? To borrow? And perhaps some strands of hair to fashion a few more?" In case the original style did not suit, we would have something to work with.

"I will be driven out of business by the greed of my principal designer and seamstress!" he said.

I caught my breath. He'd called me his principal designer and seamstress. Already! And not a stitch had yet been sewn for *Cinderella*. Some may have used that to ease off, but not I. The vote of confidence would drive me to perfection. "I shan't if you prefer . . ." I said.

He grinned. "Nothing too costly, please. And whatever you do, do not cover your lovely flaxen hair."

"It's not for me," I said. "But thank you. Thank you!"

Once home, Mother Martha and I could barely control ourselves from racing up the steps. Ruby hunched over yards of fabric, her little scalp looking like nothing so much as a smooth field with young wheat waving as her head bobbed.

I looked at Mother Martha. It had been her idea, after all.

"Go ahead," she encouraged.

"Ruby, stand in front of the dressing mirror, if you will," I said.

She looked at me wonderingly but did as I'd asked. I pulled the wig out of a linen bag and settled it on her head just so.

She turned and looked into the mirror, and when she did, she smiled. "I'm a real lady!"

I gasped. Mrs. W gasped. Ruby was stunningly beautiful. I looked once more at Mother Martha, who nodded knowingly. It *had* been a blessing that Ruby had cut her hair before one of the men looking for young women had found her and offered the "life of leisure" they so readily lied about.

"You are beautiful," I said. She took the bag from my hand and looked at the other hair swatches. She put a few on my head, and I curtseyed in jest.

Everyone broke out in laughter. When it quieted, Ruby spoke up. "Miss, with those on, you look like one of them watercress sellers near Covent Garden."

"'Cool! Fresh! Picked this mornin'!'" I teased, and they laughed. We soon got on with our work on Lady Tolfee's gown.

But Ruby had given me an idea.

I would not ask questions. Nell Gwyn, the lowborn orange seller who had captured the heart of the King, would.

CHAPTER TEN

In the early evening I let it be known that I preferred not to be disturbed and that I would have Louisa send supper upstairs to the rest of them. I waited till things had grown quiet and then I changed into an old dress, one that barely fit, was stained, and that I had planned to have torn into rags. I snatched some hair extensions and other strands from the drawers upstairs where we had left them after returning from Drury Lane and placed them under a well-worn bonnet, so that I appeared to have dark brown hair. I left my gloves off. For once, my hands, rough and red from working with cloth and needle, would not have to be hidden. Instead, they would help me disguise myself accordingly.

I went downstairs through the kitchen and snatched a basket used to carry flowers along with some oranges from the larder. If only Lady Lockwood could see me now! I looked the part. I had clearly been followed and noticed at King Street; I would not go out through my front door. Instead, I stopped by the coal room and smudged myself and my clothing, just a little. Then I exited through the Area, used exclusively by servants and sellers.

I walked down the darkening street, which was filled with a toxic blur of coal smoke, fog, and disdain. Many women curled a lip in disgust when I finally came into view. Men leered at me and the carriage drivers did not seem to care that they came too close to me, splattering my hem with filthy puddle water. No one nodded a pleasantry. I was unsettled: at best I was ignored, at worst, reviled.

I had become unsuitable, and their disdain and revulsion reverberated through me. *I* liked myself less, at that moment, a sentiment I did not understand and was not proud of. *The apparel oft proclaims the man.*

Yes, I had wrought a costumer's profession from Shakespeare's truth.

I eventually made my way through the smoky haze of dusk toward alleys that splayed out like grubby fingers from the palm that was the thoroughfare. I positioned myself just a few row houses away from the King Street house on Papa's card, just down the alley. There were sweets sellers and cigarette hawkers crying their trade, gasping in the filthy air, coughing out the smoke, shouting out once more. They hovered near the streets that would bring people to the theaters, and people were lying rough against the wall, passed out from fatigue or drink.

"Ouch! Who? No!" I cried. An arm reached out and grabbed my waist, pulling me toward him. I smelt him before I saw him: the knife seller who had been positioned directly across from the house last time I'd been here. I stood next to him, holding out my orange basket as I imagined an orange seller might.

"Who are ye, lovely lass? I've not seen ye here before," he said, leaning in to try to kiss me, which, fortunately, he did not.

He did not recognize me as the "toff's woman," then.

I wriggled away, revolted. "Selling oranges, sir. And looking for a friend. I think she lived there." I pointed to the neat house among the other neat houses on King Street.

"That house, then." He looked wary, but I shifted my oranges to remind him, hopefully, that I was one of them.

I fished in my linen pocket and withdrew the picture. "Here." He looked at my hands and nodded. Then he took the picture in his own. He was missing fingers on each hand. Knife injuries, perhaps.

"I seen her. We sees everything and everyone, watching from the shadows. They think we don't, but we do. Her? She's gone now. Hasn't seen her for months. She's gone."

"Gone?" My heart beat in my throat.

He shrugged. "There's plenty others. You want to work there?" He cackled and spit, his spittle tobacco brown. "The toffs and their protectors, they likes 'em a little younger than you are, so I'se thinking you wouldn't be their type. Yer my type, though." He drew close and breathed on me; I nearly fainted from the fetid mothball breath that passed through his rotting teeth.

I drew away. "Younger women, then?" The voice that had whispered at my door had suggested Ruby and Charlotte might be snatched and brought here if I didn't quit sleuthing.

"Course. They're supposed ta be clean. It don't matter to me if yer poxed." He tried to paw at my dress. "It'll matter to them, though."

I stepped aside. "I've got to sell these." I hurried away from him, throwing a glance at the King Street house.

A brothel. A brothel for young, clean women, and the woman in the picture I'd found in Papa's cupboard, near the address, had been there.

How young?

I once more hurried down the street. A well-dressed man reached toward my orange basket, his grasp coming uncomfortably near my person. I put the basket down on the pavement and crossed my arms over my chest, protectively, fighting the impulse to retch.

Passersby avoided me on the street, stepping aside as they would from horse muck. I understood, just in part, what it felt like to be reviled and unprotected, like so many women were. I understood in a fresh and personal manner why my mother had been so defensive of them, her drive to help them find safe places to sleep and eat and work. I recognized, just a little, the despair a woman must feel when she understands she has no other means to provide for herself.

And Papa. He must have been working to protect those girls somehow.

Mustn't he have? Perhaps he was guiding them to the Cause, like Mamma may have done.

But he hadn't shown any interest in the Cause after her death, blaming them, I knew, for the typhus that she caught tending the poor. If he had only been helping, why had Papa kept a photograph, then, as a treasure? And why only of the one young woman? A young woman who could not be traced because the studio name remained unstamped, unusually, on the photograph itself. My dinner threatened to reappear.

The knife seller's comment haunted me. I withdrew the picture and looked at her. *She's gone,* he'd said. *She's gone.*

I picked up my basket and started out again. The streets were dark and uneasy, and I was at risk dressed as I was and walking alone. People seemed to appear and then disappear in the dark, foggy haze. By the time I could make clear the figure of any who came near me it would be too late to learn if they were found to be friend or foe. What had seemed like a good idea and perhaps an adventure of a kind at home now seemed foolhardy and upsetting. I had learnt nothing that advanced my knowledge but plenty that had deepened my anguish.

And now, my person was at risk. I heard footsteps closing in. Someone was definitely following me.

My chest heaved as I tried to draw a clean breath through the dark miasma of coal smoke and mist. Fear further squeezed my lungs. The men who had, I dared assume, killed my father would not regret harming me if they could. Did they wonder how I knew about King Street? Did they believe it implied I knew much, much more than I did?

I dared not turn around, but slowed my step, and the man did, too. I could not ignore it any longer. I gathered what little courage I had from the four corners of my mind and turned around, bracing myself to confront whoever stalked me.

He ran smack into me at my sudden stop. "Excuse me, miss."

It was the lamplighter. I nearly cried.

The streetlights, which had not yet all been converted to electricity, were being lit one by one like eyes opening one at a time. As the lamplighter moved his way down the road, I wished, once more, for the blessed relief that the darkness of ignorance can bring.

What good could come of further enquiry? Much harm and sorrow could, that I knew; Collingsworth and Roberts had both said so.

I rounded the corner to Cheyne Gardens and ran toward its safety. Once inside, I closed the front door, leaning against it to catch my breath, thinking back to the danger I'd just escaped outside the brothel and the girls who had not escaped but were trapped within.

Please, Papa. Had you been helping them somehow? You must have been. It's the only explanation.

It was certainly the only explanation I could live with, and so I settled upon it.

The trip to King Street had given me courage to call directly upon Mr. Pilchuck. He had ignored my two notes, and I very much needed to know where my accounts stood and that I was financially secure. The following morning, I took Mrs. W with me and presented myself to Mr. Pilchuck's assistant at his office in the City.

His assistant was most dismissive. "You do not have an appointment?" His words were as drawn out as his lean frame.

"Not for lack of trying," I insisted.

He knocked on Mr. Pilchuck's door, went in, and spoke with him. Both men appeared in the front office, and I expected to be escorted back. Instead, Mr. Pilchuck came forward into the greeting area.

"Miss Young," he said. "What a surprise."

"I was worried that perhaps my letters had gone astray," I said, rather accusingly.

"Not at all, my dear," he said, his voice thick with condescension. I shouldn't have been surprised if he'd leaned over and patted my head. "Probate takes time, and I have many other clients—well-placed clients with important investments."

I understood. The fees I'd pay him would be negligible. "I am concerned about my house, my accounts," I said.

He drew near me. "Your house in London, and your house in trust, are both securely held. You have not much more than that, you understand. Your father was a police officer."

I sighed a relief. Cheyne Gardens was mine. "And then I have additional questions," I began, but he held up his hand.

"Patience, Miss Young, although I know that is often in short supply in the fairer sex. Lord Tennerton is about to arrive. Please post your questions to me, and I shall send for you when I have your affairs settled." He turned to his assistant, who moved to show us out without a farewell.

Once on the street, Mrs. W sniffed her indignation.

"Well, at least both houses are secure," I said.

There was an unusually long pause.

"Indeed," finally came her response.

CHAPTER ELEVEN

The next day Lord Lockwood sent a note round asking if he could call the following Wednesday. I was unaccountably eager to see him, but I did have a few items I needed to deliver to Drury Lane that day. I hoped he would call early.

He did. As Bidwell was occupied with a water leak in the scullery, Mrs. W opened the door and was clearly not pleased to see Lockwood. She stood in his way, rather, so that it would be difficult to proceed to the parlor.

"Lord Lockwood, please, come into the parlor," I said. "I've had some tea freshly prepared." After a sip of his tea, he did not drink it again.

"Is it not prepared to your tastes?" I asked.

"Tea rarely is. I've grown fond of the brisk strength of Turkish coffee. Your tea is prepared perfectly well, Miss Young. Do not concern yourself."

It was for him to bring up the topic of his visit and I waited. I looked at him directly and he did not turn away from me. His eyes, a shade close to the rusted brown of his hair and close-shaved beard, were warm and I couldn't help but notice a few tiny freckles on the skin near the corner of his left eye, which gave a boyish feel to his otherwise firmly masculine face.

He cleared his throat, and I focused. He smiled. He *knew* I'd been examining him and I felt a blush rise. "I stopped by to ask if you'd like me to have my groundskeeper repair your fences. The park's deer are breaking through and are, I'm sorry to say, somewhat of a nuisance. After he treats my fields this spring, I could have him tend to them."

I nodded my agreement. "I have no plans to do anything in terms of the land at Winton Park. I understand the grounds and the house both need considerable attention. The carriage house and kitchens are in grave disrepair, I know. They will need my first attentions."

If I can afford to provide what they need, I thought.

"Thank you, Lord Lockwood. Please have the invoice remitted to Davidson and I shall see it attended to."

He smiled. "I will let you know myself."

"It was kind of you to come all the way to London to let me know." I thought I should make it clear that he owed me nothing, he being so duty bound. "But a note would suffice in future, as I do not want to put you to trouble."

"Oh, it is no trouble. I am in London for a few days with my brother and his wife, to see a medical specialist, and on a theater errand."

"I hope your brother is well," I said.

"I hope he will be after this visit," Lockwood replied, and I could see love for his brother in his eyes. "He fought while I merely wished to, but as first son, I could not. My family duties precluded me, but I shall see to it that his carrying out *his* duty denies him nothing beyond what he's already lost."

We made small talk for a moment, and though I did not want our interlude to end and it did not seem that he did, either, I knew

I had to make my deliveries. "Thank you for your attentiveness to Winton and to me. But I'm afraid I must depart for Drury Lane; I have some items to deliver ahead of this evening's performance."

He stood, then, and spoke, his voice infused with a restrained enthusiasm. "I'm on my way to the Lyceum Theatre for an hour or two of sword training of the actors in *Henry V*."

"Oh, I adore Shakespeare, and in particular *Henry V*!"

"May I offer you a lift to Drury Lane so you won't need a hired carriage?" His voice was hopeful. "And then you could perhaps see something for yourself of what is going on at the Lyceum? Your competitor?" He grinned.

I remained silent, and he spoke up again, softly. "You'd asked after what I had . . . passion for. You could view it yourself." His voice grew personal. "You're the only one who's ever asked."

Mrs. W shook her head disapprovingly in a manner I'd long come to read as *Do be sensible, dear*.

"Why, yes, that is a fine idea." I would not turn down the opportunity to offer a kindness in light of all he'd done for me. Mrs. W's face soured and she sighed with resignation.

Why did she not like the man? Had it to do with his father, somehow, or just her long-standing dislike of titled men?

I gathered the soft leather bag in which I kept smallish costume pieces that needed transport—they would be fogged and sooted if not wrapped well—and told Mrs. W not to wait on supper for my return.

I followed Lord Lockwood to his very fine coach and he held a hand out to help lift me in. I placed my hand in his, and he wrapped his gloved fingers around mine, protectively. I was glad for my gloves, then, the soft leather hiding my rough skin. I slipped a little on the step and reached out for his shoulder to steady myself.

When I rested my hand there, a thrill ran up through my arm and into my chest. I knew he felt something, too, because he unexpectedly looked in my eyes.

"Are you all right?" he asked.

"Quite so," I responded, and he grinned. We were off, and about thirty minutes later we arrived at Drury Lane.

He waited while I ran the bags in to one of Wilhelm's dressers and then I returned with all speed. Lockwood kept a beautifully wrought carriage clock in his coach, so I knew he was a man who valued punctuality.

Within a few moments, we were at the Lyceum. "I'd always loved theater." He held his hand out for me to alight from the coach as he spoke. "But mostly as an observer. It grew increasingly difficult for me to enjoy the fencing scenes prominent in so many performances." He let go of my hand and held up his walking stick. "The actors were clearly not trained; they would shake their swords this way and that, lunging inelegantly, or waving it around like a conductor leading an orchestra."

"*Quelle horreur!*" I said, and laughed.

He laughed with me. "I have found a calling of sorts. A way by which I might return the favor to actors for the many hours of enjoyment they've provided to me. To properly train them with the sword, as surely many in their audience would know the difference between rightly and wrongly wielded weapons."

"How rewarding! I, too, know the joy of seeing my handiwork on the stage."

"If I train with them, over and over, it allows the movements to become almost second nature. That way, when they are concentrating on something else, for example, their lines, or if a mishap should come along, the arm will move in the right direction without the actor even having to think about it. I repeat a stroke so many times that when I am fencing I can focus on tactic and strategy knowing my arm will do what it has been trained to do by repetition."

"Sewing is like that, too," I said.

He nodded and settled me into a soft chair in a box halfway up stage left. "Do you have a good view?"

"I can see well enough from here. Thank you."

He left me in the box and within a few minutes I watched him begin to train two actors for a duel. He guided them gently but firmly, and even to my untrained eye I could see how authentic they became with less than an hour of his instruction. Like me, he used his skills to ensure that the actors became the characters, and the characters then quickened to life for the audience. He returned to me within an hour, reddened, without his jacket or waistcoat, radiating masculinity.

For a relished moment I was quite undone.

"Well done, Lord Lockwood." I clapped lightly. "It's not often I have the view from a box. But the greater pleasure was seeing you at work with the men."

He grinned and sat next to me. "My barrister and good friend Henry Colmore Dunn quotes the master when he says, 'To be a good fencer, the great point is to know how to defend and ward off the blows that the enemy gives. Always beware the unexpected stroke.' I find that all to be true in life as well as with the sword in my hand."

"Do you have enemies, Lord Lockwood?"

"I do, Miss Young." He sat next to me. "So do you. We all do."

He did not elaborate, but my mind went, for a moment, to Roberts's warning.

I turned back to Lord Lockwood. "Between this training and your presentation of Lumpy Loggerhead, perhaps you should join the actors someday."

"Perhaps!" He laughed but was clearly pleased. "I learn lines when I train with them, and I was quite a little thespian at school."

"I learn lines in dress rehearsals, too." I had never felt so comfortable with a man. I did not inhabit his titled world, but clearly, in theater, he inhabited mine.

He drew near to me. His breathing had slowed and his voice took on a low, intimate timbre. "Are you familiar with the lines from *Henry V*?" The theater was empty but for the two of us. Mrs. W would not approve. I should have stood up and made for the door. I did not.

"Yes, I do. Very well indeed. I have seen many performances with my mother, and have assisted with costumes as well."

He held my gaze. He was close enough now that I could see the individual lashes that curved upward like the curl of hair on his collar. He did not move away, and I would not be first to do so, either. Then, he spoke lines, as Henry V.

"Fair Katherine, and most fair, will you vouchsafe to teach a soldier terms such as will enter at a lady's ear, and plead his love-suit to her gentle heart?"

My heart thrust against my chest; 'twas the most famous passage in the play. Dare I respond as Katherine, the woman who would one day be Henry's queen, had? Before I could temper myself, I replied, "Your Majesty shall mock at me. I cannot speak your England."

He no longer displayed a boyish grin but instead the steady look of a man on a mission. "Lovely Katherine, if you will love me well with your French heart, I'm happy to hear you confess it in broken English." He lowered his voice before continuing: "Do you like me, Kate?"

Was he asking me, Gillian Young? Or was he speaking to Kate as Henry V? Yes, yes, Kate liked Henry very well indeed. Did Gillian like this man? I kept my face impassive, I hoped, but I knew the truth. Gillian did like the man—perhaps, ultimately, to her disadvantage.

I knew the next lines well; I also knew where this passage inevitably led, and I did not know if I wanted to go there. Well, that was untrue. I knew I did.

I proceeded.

"*Pardonnez-moi*, I cannot tell what is 'like me.'" What exactly did he mean? Like him as a neighbor? As a friend? As a woman?

He leaned even closer to me; I inhaled the heady-woody-musky deep of the sandalwood and felt his breath as he spoke. It melted me within and without. "An angel is like you, Kate, and you are like an angel."

He could not speak to me thus as Lord Lockwood: not use my first name, not come so close. He could not express sentiments like that to a woman to whom he was not promised or to whom he had not declared himself.

He could, though, as Henry.

Was he caught up in the passion of his fencing and the play, merely acting? Was I? I thought back on Mrs. W, who did not trust him. But she did not trust any titled man. What did he want with Winton Park? Did he care for me, for myself? Or did he think because I was not of his class I was easy prey and readily available? Did he hope to show me how expensive Winton would be so I'd realize I must sell?

"The tongues of men are full of deceit," I said. As Katherine. As Gillian.

He said nothing; I had perhaps broken the moment. If I had, it was for the best. The line was spoken, true.

He did not step out of character. "Upon that, I kiss your hand . . ."

He lifted my hand to his lips and kissed it. As he did, an inde-scribable pleasure sizzled through me. I held my breath for a moment and allowed my eyes to close but for a second and then withdrew my hand. I should not have spoken the next line; I *would* not have spoken the next line as Gillian, Miss Young. But as an actress, perhaps a liberty might be taken.

"I can't allow you to lower yourself by kissing my hand . . ."

"Then I will kiss your lips, Kate."

He made no move, awaiting my response as a gentleman would, but I could tell he wished to by the forward tilt of his body.

I considered, then stood and spoke softly. "It is not the custom for French maidens to kiss before they are married."

He took it no further and put a foot or two of distance be-tween us, purposefully breaking the crackling connection. "You have beautiful eyes, Miss Young," he said. "Sapphire blue, with a brightness to them."

"They are my mother's eyes."

"No, Miss Young," he disagreed. "They are entirely your own. I will see you home."

The moment had passed, perhaps for good. I was not yet cer-tain if I regretted that, but I did not regret that it had happened.

The next day, I found Ruby at the table where the fabric was laid out for cutting.

Instantly, I knew something was wrong. I held a sleeve in my hand. I picked up the other.

"Ohhh." A low moan escaped my lips.

"What's the trouble, miss?" Ruby asked. "Are they not right?"

No, no, they were not right at all. Not only were they two different sizes but one clearly would be too small even for Lady Tolfee's thin frame.

"Ruby, have you cut on the skirts?"

"Yes, miss!" She ran to the cupboard and brought out several rounded disks of cut fabric. I had given her the dimensions, and she could read numbers. Still, by looking at them, I knew they were wrong. Not only wrong, but so wrong that I would have to buy more of the watered silk—if I could find it in time. Our financial margin in the project would completely disappear.

I did not want her to see my agony. My forehead broke out in a plague of sweat, which I could not let drip on the fabric. Charlotte kept her head down; a natural seamstress, she more than likely knew what was wrong. I also did not want Ruby to see me recut the pieces.

"You've been working very hard," I said. "Would you and Charlotte like to run down to the Mission this afternoon? I've looked at the calendar, and it's the day the speakers come to encourage the young ladies. Perhaps you'll even know someone there, as many will attend, and it's sure to be a rousing talk."

"Yes, thank you, miss!" The two of them raced to their room to change into the clean, nondescript outfits I'd bought them when they'd started working for me, and Ruby made sure her wig was affixed underneath her bonnet.

While they were gone, I unrolled the remainder of the green silk.

"Can I help you cut?" Mother Martha asked.

"No, thank you." I trusted no one but myself. I could not afford another error, not today with this dress, nor, truth be told, in the future.

Ruby had not taken to sewing, not even to the broad cutting. I could not afford to keep her endlessly. I could not afford to continue to replace fabric. I would have her try her hand at dipping the many dramatic layers of ombré fabric, which I suspected she could do. But I had little need for that year in and year out. This one Season, thankfully, I did, for one dress. And then?

I hoped she would not ruin it, good intentions or no.

Several hours later, as the late-spring sun began to set, I heard a giggling hubbub out of the window. I peeked outside. Ruby and Charlotte were returning, Ruby with a bouquet of flowers in her hand. They held hands as a young man, who had clearly been accompanying them, tipped his hat and then ran off.

They tumbled up the stairs. "Guess what, miss?" Ruby's eyes shone. "I met the most wonderful young man. He stopped me as we and the other girls were coming out of the Mission—picked me out specially of them all, he did, didn't he, Charlotte?"

Charlotte dutifully nodded.

"He gave me a posy—my first ever, miss! He said there were situations waiting for young ladies such as myself, in lovely houses where we would be an ornament—an ornament, imagine that! And all we'd have to do is keep the place dusted and such."

I gaped in horror. My mind quickly flew back to the whispered warning at my door, and the threat of the King Street brothel for the girls and the promise that I'd be shown someone meant business and I should quit sleuthing. Was this lad attached to that whisperer and his threat somehow? Had I been recognized dressed as Nell Gwyn? I needed to learn more if I could, and I knew how to do it. A visit to see Roberts. "What did you say?"

"I said nothing, miss. Not yet."

I drew her near me. She sparkled with life.

"Those boys mean no good," I said. "And I have made a grave error in letting you come home, escorted by a young man and no chaperone."

"But you came home escorted by a man with no chaperone not long ago," she said.

"How do you know that?" I demanded.

"You're not the only one who watches out the window, miss," she said, and then laughed. I laughed with her because I did not want to frighten her. I pulled Ruby close to me for just a moment, and as I did, I caught Mother Martha's eye. She nodded slightly. She'd had the same idea I did.

"Regardless of what I do, I'd prefer you not keep his company. Not whilst in my employ. I am a woman grown. You are not." She arced a little against that. "Mother Martha will accompany you where you may need to go. Truthfully, we will have very little time for social events while the Season is under way."

Her smile dissolved.

I did not remove the posy from her, but I wanted to. The flowers suddenly seemed funereal.

CHAPTER TWELVE

A few days later I took the Metropolitan Railway as far as I could, and a bridge, then I walked the rest of the way to Sergeant Roberts's house. The streets were rough and some parts of them were filthy. The fog was far denser near the river, and I could see no more than two feet in front of me as I walked. It cleared a bit as I walked further on; the thoroughfares were gritty here, and vagrants clotted up against the brick buildings like carbuncles on rough skin. I walked briskly and did not make eye contact. It was the middle of the day, and yet I was chilled.

Several times I thought I felt rather than saw someone behind me; I tingled with the unmistakable sensation one has when one is being watched. However, when I built up the courage to turn around and look, no one was behind me. Perhaps he had dropped a few feet behind, out of sight in the dreary iron-tinted fog. Perhaps I had imagined things; I felt that not only could I not trust those around me, I could now not even trust my own intuitions.

It was time to let things go, after this visit. I did not want to lose my mind or my life! Papa would have wanted neither, but I felt I owed it to him, and to Ruby and Charlotte, to try once more to see if I could sort out Papa's death and somehow, some way, protect us all at the same time.

Papa had told me once that Roberts lived on Neptune Street—I'd remembered the odd name. I found the small terraced house at the far end of the circled court upon which several small houses stood. Passersby eyed me, clearly not one of their own, as I walked to the door and knocked. A face looked out from behind a small curtained window. A moment later, a woman opened the door.

"You must be Mrs. Roberts." I extended my hand. "I am Miss Gillian Young, the daughter of Inspector Andrew Young, and I am hoping that your husband, Sergeant Roberts, might be home?"

"No, he's not here, sorry," she said, and was about to close the door in my face when I heard a man call out.

"Wait."

A moment later, Sergeant Roberts appeared, wary, and dressed in street clothes. "Come in," he said, and his wife, sullen, backed away.

I did not trust this man. I did not know whom to trust—doubts had even sprouted in the fertile faith I had in my dear parents.

"Miss Young?" He showed me to a small sofa, and I sat down.

"I've come to call, to ask . . . Well, you were looking for information which might clear my father. Notes which might tell of others involved in the crime, anything that might clear the criminals and bring protection to the rest of us. Have you located any such evidence?"

He shook his head. "I've tried mightily hard to find anything, something. I've looked at the division, I've looked at your house, as you know, though I suspect someone was there well before me."

Alarm rose. "At my house?"

He nodded. "Perhaps during the funeral. I've heard rumors at the division. They might have missed something, though."

They did, I thought. *The cubbyhole Papa had so cleverly carved into the bed. And if they were rumors he'd heard at the division, that must mean it had been the police.*

"Have you come across anything?" he pressed.

"I have nothing for you," I answered. I must be cautious.

"Collingsworth is pressuring me. He knows your father took detailed notes and did not break that habit in twenty years of policing. I must give him something, and so I shall. I'll write down notes indicating some of the officers who may have been involved, and a highborn name your father and I discussed, just to get him to leave me be. That should be enough."

I looked at him wonderingly. "Will we all be safe then? If you tell him Papa and you discussed it, and this time you wrote it down? Because I am afraid that someone is not only following and threatening me, but the girls I care for."

He nodded. "I hope and believe that if I give him something, and he believes that's the whole of it, he will leave off unless further provoked—and you and me, we don't do that. They won't want to stir up a ruckus. As long as I stop asking questions, and you stop making enquiries . . ."

I blushed.

He nodded. "Yes, I've been warned. And in turn I warn you, Miss Young, out of respect for your late father. Do not ask questions on your own; it is not safe. I've heard you visited King Street."

The policeman who had locked eyes with me? That had not been Roberts, of that I was certain. "Don't trust anyone," he said.

"Not even you, Sergeant Roberts?" I asked.

He stood then, and I thought he was going to show me to the door, but instead, he walked to his wife and she withdrew an envelope from her linen pocket, which was beautifully embroidered. She handed it to him.

"This is yours," he said.

I took it in hand. "Where did you get it?"

He did not answer that directly, but instead said, "You will know to trust me, won't you, when you see that I've seen this safely returned to you. Please let me, and me alone, know if you come upon anything informative."

I walked to his door, tucking the letter deep in my own linen pocket, hidden beneath my skirts. "You could have delivered this letter the night you came to whisper at my door."

He looked confused.

"A short while ago when you refused to come in but spoke with me through the door."

He opened his own door. "You must leave. It is not good for you to remain here. That was not me who visited you," he said. "Which is further reason for you to take heed of my warnings. Beware. And good day."

A short distance from his house I was stopped by a police officer.

"Hullo, miss. If you'll just wait a moment," he said.

I kept walking. He followed me and grabbed my arm, jerking me to a stop. "I asked you to wait a minute," he said.

"Who are you?" I demanded. I looked at his uniform and noted the absence of a division letter and personal warrant number, which would have identified him.

"If you don't mind, I'll just have a look through your handbag."

"Certainly not! Do you have cause and permission for such a search?"

The officer took my handbag, and when I refused to let go pressed firmly on my fingers till they released their grip. "Indeed I do," he said with a grin.

He riffled through the contents, seeing nothing but my personal items and some money, and handed it back to me. "That will be all," he said. "Watch out for runaway carts and such on the way home."

I whirled, and he challenged me with a look and tutting finger and went on his way.

Had he just admitted that the runaway cart that had killed Papa had not been an accident? He clearly knew who I was.

The letter remained safely under my dress. I was so glad that Mrs. Roberts had also kept the letter hidden in her dress where it could not be found by a search of their home, which had in turn prompted me, perhaps unconsciously, to keep it folded safely away in my own.

I would read it at home.

I walked across the bridge to the north side, and decided to walk home to clear my head some.

I pulled my shawl tightly around me. Melancholy dogged my every step. I passed some highborn gentlemen's clubs and my stomach roiled. There they were, not a care in the world, laughing and filled with pleasure because they felt their wealth and position protected them. Perhaps it did. They used others, like the young woman whose photo remained in my linen pocket, for what they would, and then those young women were "gone." What kind of hearts, if any, were tucked under those fine waistcoats?

I walked farther, past the Theatrical Mission, and was struck anew at the hypocrisy—this time, my own.

I had not called on the Mission offering to help others, though it had ended that way. I'd called hoping to find someone, some young seamstresses, whom I could use to further my own goals, my sewing, so dear to me.

And whilst I was thinking of the highborn, why hadn't Mamma said anything further about Winton Park? Or had she, to Papa, and he'd kept that to himself? It would be another secret in what was beginning to look like a line of them.

No. I did not believe it. I truly did not. Perhaps the letter would shed light on this. I clutched it, under my dress, and quickened my pace toward home.

I sat by lamplight and opened the letter. It had been dated the day before he'd died and seemed to be quickly scrawled. I had guessed, of course, that Roberts had taken this the night he'd searched my home. Or had he found it in the division files?

Dearest Gilly Girl,

His use of my nickname pricked my heart afresh.

> *In case something happens to me, which a policeman must always think upon, know that I loved you and your mother well.*

Another scratching at my window. I had forgotten to close the curtains. I took a deep breath and made my way to the window, keeping my eyes to the side, focusing on the window frame and not the pane. I could not bring myself to look out; my heart trembled. And then I took courage. I yanked the curtains fully open. Sitting on the ledge was one of Ruby's pigeons, staring at me.

I laughed. Little lovely thing.

I returned to the bed and kept reading.

You shall be well provided for; our homes will hold both memories and treasures for you and, of course, you have your skills as an excellent seamstress. I shall always remember you both as my little girl playing at dressing up, then a capable grown woman sewing beautiful costumes for others who played at dressing up, like your dear Mamma. Marry well, someone you trust and love without reserve, a man who can rescue you, my little 'damsel in distress,' should you need it. Fear not.

Yours always and ever,

Papa

A last note, to give me courage should I have to travel alone, which I now must. A love letter of sorts . . . to me, like he'd written to Mamma when they were to be parted. I lingered on his other words. How much he loved Mamma and me. I should marry someone I love and trust without reserve.

I would not be afraid.

I climbed under the coverlet and blew the lamp out, but kept the letter in my hand. I had nothing further to follow, at the moment, but I could not back off if further evidence appeared that might lead me to clear his name. I just could not. Papa had been the man I'd thought he was, and he'd admonished me, in his last days, to not be afraid.

I whispered words from *Julius Caesar*, one of Papa's favorite plays, as Portia, a woman, was called forth to courage. "Think you I am no stronger than my sex, / Being so father'd . . ."

I would not be afraid. For him, and for me. No more playing at dressing up. I'd put on my armor instead.

CHAPTER THIRTEEN

Not long after, on the last day of May, I was tending the flower boxes outside my home, myself, when Francis—that is, Constable Collingsworth—strolled up.

"Constable Collingsworth! How delighted I am to see you." I nestled the last pansy in the box. I loved spring, the season of new life. The little plants, small as they were, would soon blossom into a profusion of vibrant beauty. I pulled off my gardening gloves, confident and comfortable that Francis would not be put off by the sight of my working hands. "I'm delighted you've come to share this fine afternoon with me."

He did not join in the merriment; his face remained gray and grim, very unlike his usual cheerful countenance. My merriment fell away.

"What is the matter?" I asked. He would not come calling unannounced and with such a dire look for no cause. I hoped he and his family were well.

"Can we go inside?" he asked.

I nodded, and we went to the parlor. I waved Louisa away. I did not care for tea, and Francis did not look as if he did, either.

"I'll get straight to it." He took my hand in his own. "I wanted you to hear it from me. Roberts is dead."

My heart dropped. "Dead? Sergeant Roberts? How, and when?" I grew cold at the core. Did I want the honest answer, and truly, would I get the truth even if I did? I nearly said, *But I just saw him!* and stopped myself as he looked at me with sharp interest.

"He was knifed," he replied. "Approaching vagrants can often mean dirty business. One turned on him and on some of the others who were with him."

Knifed. Dead. I'd just seen him. Had I withheld evidence from him, things I'd come across in the cubbyhole, that might have saved him? I was pained at the thought.

"Were . . . Were there others killed?" I asked.

Francis shook his head. "No. Just Roberts, and perhaps some of the alley dwellers, too. I'm not sure, as that was not reported to me."

"Who told you?" I asked.

"Father," he said. "But everyone knows now. We all mourn when an officer is down. And as Father put me in charge of you, I thought you might like to know."

"Because he was my father's partner?"

Francis nodded. "Among other reasons."

What other reasons? Did he know I'd visited Roberts? I did not want to tip my hand by asking, but I must be cautious. I remembered the officer who had searched me when I'd left the Robertses' home. "Has this . . . Has Roberts's death anything to do with my father's death?"

He pursed his lips. "I don't think so, but of course, we can't ever be sure because we don't know who the culprits were. By the time we arrived on the scene everyone else had fled."

* * *

"Of course you must attend the funeral. It is the right thing to do." Mrs. W joined us the next evening when we sewed by lamplight to have Lady Tolfee's dresses ready in time. I had set aside the *Cinderella* gowns, for now, and focused on the ones for the Season, as it was immediately at hand.

"Yes, I think I must," I said. "Out of respect for my father and Mrs. Roberts." And, perhaps, I thought I might have a few questions that could be answered.

But was a funeral a place to ask questions? Even if posed they may never be answered.

"Yes, it's the right thing to do," she agreed. "I will write to them for you and say you'll be there." She turned back to her correspondence, continuing to speak as she did. "My sister's husband is ill. When he dies, I shall visit her."

"I'm so sorry," I said. "To my regret, I did not even realize you had a sister." Had she ever mentioned her? I had not thought she had any family at all, and that was why my mother had offered Mrs. W a permanent position so many years earlier—to save her, like I'd done for Mother Martha, from the workhouse. "You may feel free to leave sooner, if you like, to assist her at this difficult time."

Mrs. W shook her head. "After he dies, yes. Thank you, dear, I should like to see her then. It has been quite a long time; she's not been to London in a decade."

I didn't recall Mrs. W ever having visited her sister; long ago, perhaps. Like all girls, I hadn't paid much attention to the adults around me.

* * *

The day before Sergeant Roberts's funeral, I decided to have the girls join me at the dining table for the midday meal. Ruby had told me that neither of them had ever sat at a proper table, nor had been taught how to hold their cutlery, fold a napkin, or make pleasant conversation. It was something I could do for them as we looked toward their futures and bring a bit of brightness to a dark week.

"Oh, miss," Charlotte said as she approached the room. She curtseyed to me, which I found charming.

"Please, have a seat, Miss Ruby and Miss Charlotte."

They giggled but did as I'd requested.

Louisa had set the table with our fine china, edged in blue. The drinking glasses were blue, too. My mother had loved blue tableware, though she'd told me her mother had wondered if it was a bit dramatic.

Like Mamma! I'd thought. Dramatically perfect. I thought upon what china and glassware I might like when I started a family of my own. My own tastes weren't quite the same as Mamma's. Perhaps I'd like cut glass, and maybe china edged in holly berries, simple, elegant lines. It would be a waste, though, to buy new when these served perfectly well. I knew what Mrs. W would say . . . I'd better not be wasteful.

"Miss Young?" Louisa's voice interrupted me. The girls were looking at me wonderingly, too.

"I'm so sorry." I sat down. "You may proceed."

I'd requested a luncheon that was more elaborate than we normally would have eaten, just for the opportunity to use the utensils. I had admonished myself to only offer five tips for this meal, so as not to overwhelm them. After the Season, there would be time for more. But I knew it would build their confidence, and show them that they had a proper life to look toward.

Charlotte slurped her clear gravy soup in a noisy glug. Should I chide her? I did not, which Ruby took as approval, and slurped hers even more loudly, not willing to be outdone. "Perhaps a silent sipping, like so, is more appropriate." I showed them how to hold the spoon, dip it forward into the soup so it would not dribble, and drink it quietly.

They each did so, and then made their way through a small meat course of roasted guinea fowl with Spanish rice, followed by an ice.

"Sweet ice!" Ruby said.

"Blackberry," I affirmed.

After the meal, they came and dipped a curtsey, as though I were the Queen herself. I didn't correct them, not then; I would later. I wanted to end on a sweet note in every way.

Louisa cleared the table, and I was about to return to the salon when a note arrived. Bidwell brought it to me.

"Didn't come by the post, Miss Young. Some young urchin delivers it an' then runs away."

"Thank you." I stood by the front window for the light. I slit open the envelope and instead of a letter falling out, a portion of the Scripture—an entire page of the Bible—was folded up inside. I took it out. Most of the words had been darkened by pencil, leaving only a few words remaining. It was from Saint Matthew, chapter eight: *"Let the dead bury their dead."*

Saint Matthew again.

"Has the post arrived, then?" Mrs. W came into the room.

"No, no. Not yet," I said, holding the page close to me.

"Someone is reading my magazines before they are delivered," she fussed. "They are bent and have been mishandled and always arrive a day or two late." She sighed. "I'll ensure your mourning dress is pressed. And mine, too, if you'd like me to accompany you."

Should I attend, still? Someone had sent this dire warning in a most inappropriate manner. Why? To warn me away, of course. Because perhaps I should learn something there.

"I'll attend, of course, out of respect for Papa, but you needn't come," I said. "Constable Collingsworth said if I attended he would see me home."

"A fine idea." She beamed. "I'll see to pressing, then."

I folded the paper and took it to my room with me; then I secured it deep inside Alice's hole, the upside-down world where everything that made no sense belonged.

I was glad to be alone as we pulled up to the church, as I was not then required to cover my open shock. There, outside the church, stood four black horses, draped in velvet, with a cart behind them. There were plenty of police guarding the entrance. I nodded at one or two I recognized; they did not acknowledge me. Two mourning mutes stood behind the hearse. Unusually, they did not even smell of gin.

Once inside, I found the room to be filled, mainly with officers in uniform. This was in direct contrast to the desolate funeral for my father, an inspector. His had been so sparsely attended that the songs of the chorister, a lad whose voice had not yet broken, had bounced mournfully off the cold stone walls, echoing throughout the empty room.

They must not suspect him as they had Papa. Or Inspector Collingsworth had commanded they attend, or both.

The widow sat in the front row, clutching a baby who seemed to consider the crowd with a combination of fright and curiosity. Mrs. Roberts was surrounded by two older women—perhaps her mother and her mother-in-law?—and several officers. Several rows in front of me sat Inspector Collingsworth, and his son, Francis. Francis looked around once or twice, and when he spied me, he smiled gently. I knew he would see to me after the proceedings.

The vicar's service was punctuated only by the occasional fitting wail of Roberts's young child. Afterward, the mourners gathered to pay their respects to the widow before filing out after the coffin.

I recognized one officer, someone who had worked many years with Papa. I made my way to him.

"Miss Young." Guardedness glazed his eyes, but they also filled with friendliness and warmth. He smiled kindly, but backed away.

"I'm delighted to see you, though the occasion is sad," I said, moving toward him again. "I missed seeing you at Papa's funeral . . . I'd hoped to ask you about that, and about Papa."

"Good day, Miss Young." He abruptly severed our conversation, though I saw regret cross his face first.

As I moved on, I realized: his voice! It was the voice of the man who had whispered warnings through the door to me. Was he truly trying to help me or . . . was he dark, too? He turned back and recognized my sudden understanding—I could see it in his eyes—nodded briefly, and then walked away from me. I turned toward another man, a sergeant my father had trained and who had once visited our home. He didn't offer a look to me before making his way toward the door.

I felt a hand on my elbow. I turned to the warm face of Constable Collingsworth.

"They won't talk with you, Miss Young. They've been instructed not to and they'll obey to a man. My father's told you he handled it, and he's told them, too. It's best. I admire your loyalty to your father—loyalty is the most important value a person can carry—but in this case, it's misplaced and risky."

I nodded, which seemed to set him at ease. I felt like crying, and could, here and now, without note because it would be assumed that I was mourning the deceased. In truth, my tears were for my papa and myself and the confusion that his life should have ended so ignominiously. Francis touched me gently. "The line is long and you are tired. Let me return you home."

I nodded, thankful for his kindness.

The next day, I repented of not having stayed to offer my condolences. Roberts had been so kind to me, so loyal to Papa. I would visit his widow and let her know how grieved I was. Even if her house was being watched, it would be natural for me to call. Perhaps she would have some news—or papers—to share?

I arrived in early afternoon. "I hope I am not too early to call," I said. "I sorrowed of leaving yesterday before sharing my condolences. I'm very sorry, and thankful that at the end of my father's life he was led by a man such as your husband was."

She let me into the house, reluctantly. "They just left. Good it was that I gave you that letter earlier."

"Who is 'they'? The 'they' that searched your house?" I tried to keep the alarm from my voice.

She looked at me, scared. "Isn't that typical? To look for official materials and such? They mentioned your father by name when they were here."

Typical for your family and mine, maybe, but not for most officers. "They searched our house, too," I replied.

She exhaled.

I hoped I could help her in some way. "I am a seamstress and am looking for women to do piecework. I couldn't help but notice that your linen pocket was so very nicely done. Would you be interested in piecework?"

She smiled weakly for a moment. "Thank you for the compliment, miss, but given all the trouble since your father died, I would rather not."

"Can I help in some other way?"

She stood up. "They made it clear that my police widow pension was going to be given me at their . . . direction?"

"Discretion?" I offered.

"Yes. 'Make no trouble' is what the word meant, however you say it. I understood that much, miss. I have a young boy to care for and no man. That pension will be welcome and I can't have it interfered with by association with trouble."

"I understand, Mrs. Roberts," I said. Trouble, meaning me, associated with Papa, still.

"I'm glad you do, Miss Young." She headed toward the door. "This will be good-bye, then."

I nodded and bid her good day. She did not answer, and I could not blame her. I would not call upon her again. Now that both officers were dead and Roberts had, I assumed, provided the dummy list to Collingsworth, I suspected that the pressure on me would ease off. Nonetheless, it was likely that for a time Mrs. Roberts and I would both be watched.

CHAPTER FOURTEEN

The next morning, I received an invitation to the Collingsworths' home. I had been expecting Mrs. Collingsworth to extend an invitation much earlier, since her husband had mentioned it, but the timing, now Roberts was dead, was suspect to me.

I replied affirmatively and then sent a note to Davidson to let him know that I would visit Winton Park immediately, having all but the final beading done on Lady Tolfee's Vernissage gown. I meant to look round the "castle" and see if I could find anything that Papa might have hidden when he was there just before his death; he had referenced it in his final letter, after all, obliquely. Had Inspector Collingsworth accompanied Papa every time he'd visited? I would ask.

I sewed in the morning while Mother Martha read to us from my mother's rare and dear book. I shed a tear or two, though I tried to hide them, when she reached the part in *Little Women* quoting the girls' mother.

"The love, respect, and confidence of my children was the sweetest reward I could receive for my efforts to be the woman I would have them copy," she read, and I dabbed my eyes. I wanted to be my own woman. And yet, I wanted to copy the woman I loved and admired, too.

"Are you feeling well, miss? I feel sad sometimes when I thinks about me mum, too, though I doubt she often thinks of me," Ruby said, and then came and patted me on the shoulder. "Haven't seen her since I stopped bringing money." I reached over and hugged her, for her and for me.

Perhaps we could all use an outing. "Would you girls like to accompany me to the shops?" I asked. "I will stop by and select some supplies for our sewing, as well as a gift for Mrs. Collingsworth."

"Would you like me to make a pair of gloves for Lady Lockwood?" Mother Martha offered. "As a gift for her."

"That won't be necessary," Mrs. W said.

"That is most generous!" I contradicted her. It was for me to decide. I did not even know if I would see Lady Lockwood whilst I was in Hampshire, but perhaps. "You have not measured her hands, though."

Mother Martha smiled. "I saw her the day she took tea in your parlor. I can make the gloves exactly."

I grinned. I could measure most by size, too, having sewn for many and having a natural dressmaker's eye. But gloves were a much more difficult project to judge. I had not, I knew, been sewing as long as Mother Martha must have been.

Mrs. W declined to accompany us; another headache. Mother Martha preferred to read. The girls and I chose a parasol and took to the shops along Regent Street; the baby birds cheeped and peeped us along the way. First we visited a haberdashery shop, where I bought buttons and beads and a beautiful pincushion that swung from a gold chain for Mrs. Collingsworth. Then it was off to the milliner, who was a friend.

"Girls, please meet my friend Miss Sarah Gordon. She runs the shop with her mother."

The girls exclaimed over the hats, barely daring to touch them. Sarah let them wander round her shop and we saw, in the back, a wiggery. I let Ruby peek into it.

"Can I try one on, then?" she asked, and Sarah nodded her agreement.

First Ruby tried on a ginger wig with elaborate loops that made her look sunny and social and then she tried on a long dark-brown wig that made her look sophisticated.

"Come along, Charlotte," she encouraged. I closed my eyes and prayed that the wigs would not be damaged; I could not afford to replace them. But the girls had so little opportunity for fun. Charlotte pulled on a gray wig. Ruby used her hands to make a few loops and curls, even pulling a pin out of her own wig to hold it up, and pronounced Charlotte "Old!" Charlotte bent over like an elderly lady, mincing around the store.

We all broke into giggles, but I was impressed beyond measure with Ruby's quick hand in fixing the hair and I thought, by her look, that Sarah was, too. I placed an order for Lady Tolfee's hats; Sarah already had her head size from earlier orders. As we left, she handed a new hat to me.

"I shouldn't!" I said. And yet, I thought to my visits just ahead. It was a beautiful hat, sky blue with clouds of cream roses and a storm of purple plumed feathers to match.

"You can sew something for me at the end of the Season." Sarah urged it on me. "Go on, take it."

"Take it!" Ruby urged. I nodded, delighted; Sarah wrapped it in a paper, and then we were off.

"Home now?" Ruby seemed disappointed.

"Not yet," I said. "We're off to take tea." The gift of gloves for Lady Lockwood had given me an idea.

"Oooh," Ruby responded, "I've never been to take tea."

We arrived at a Turkish shop I knew; I enjoyed bringing the girls along and was delighted I could combine two purposes into one. I'd forgotten the simple pleasure of visiting with others at a coffee or tea house, which I did often before and after the Season. I should endeavor to meet with my friends, once more, and enjoy myself, come autumn. "First, I'm going to buy some ground Turkish coffee," I said. "Then I shall order tea and tea cakes for us. Why don't you two find a table for us to sit at?"

Charlotte spoke up, quite soberly. "I'd prefer to try Turkish coffee if I may, Miss Young."

I laughed aloud. Charlotte rarely requested anything. "You may indeed, my brave girl." I had two coffee drinkers in my life now. My heart skipped a beat.

Was he truly in my life?

I purchased the finest Turkish coffee beans in stock and had them placed in a costly hammered copper container. We sat on tufted chairs beneath French chandeliers that were blazing elegantly, even at midday, while suspended from the high ceilings. The brick walls were lined with brass containers and curiosities, glass apothecary containers holding sweets that could be purchased. The serving girl soon brought our treats.

"Why didn't Mrs. W want to come, miss? She seems not to be very happy, if you ask me, and if you don't mind my saying," Ruby said as she picked her teacup up by the handle and immediately slurped it all down. I stopped her from pouring the milk pitcher's contents into her cup entirely.

"I don't know," I said.

"How did she come to live with you? Did you find her, like us, at the Mission?" Charlotte asked. I smiled. Such an innocent.

"No, she was a friend of my mother. I kept her with me after Mamma died. She's a kind of a chaperone, I suppose. She's my godmother."

"Ooh, a godmother. The pantomimes always have fairy godmothers, like Cinderella, right, miss?"

I nodded. "That's right."

"Only I thought fairy godmothers smiled more," Ruby pointed out.

"Most do," I agreed. "But she's not a fairy. Her duties, when I was a child, were to help direct me closer to God and His will. Perhaps we should stop and buy her some fairy dust to sprinkle over her just to lighten her mood now I can make my own decisions!"

"I wish I had a fairy godmother," Ruby said. I smiled but said nothing. The table jiggled, and I thought perhaps Charlotte had lightly kicked her from under the table. Charlotte was coming into her own.

"*You* are a kind of fairy godmother," I said as we finished our tea.

They looked at me, heads cocked in question.

"To the pigeons, of course," I said, to which they laughed in innocence and delight, filling my heart with affection.

On the way home I realized, with a start, that Mrs. W would not be able to accompany me to Winton. I could not leave Mother Martha and the girls at home alone with no one in charge; certainly not Louisa and Bidwell. What if someone broke in again, a possibility I did not even want to raise with Mrs. W? What if someone came to call? Mrs. W would have to remain, which meant I would be alone in that vast, desolate house . . . but with Lockwood just over the hill.

. . .

Constable Collingsworth came to escort me to his home. I had put on a new dress and my purple plumed hat, along with a pair of ivory gloves. Mrs. W conversed with him in the parlor until I came down to greet him. The floor above me went quiet. I suspected the girls were eavesdropping. I couldn't blame them. I would have been, too.

"Constable Collingsworth." I held out my hand.

His eyes reflected his admiration as he took it in his own. "Miss Young. You look lovely."

I looked him in the eye and smiled, and he smiled back. We had crossed some boundary, the one from childhood friends to adults, whatever that may hold, and there would be no return.

Although the distance between our homes was considerable, we walked, and I was glad of that. Collingsworth held his elbow out, and I slipped my hand into it, and we walked companionably.

"How does your sewing proceed?" he asked.

"At the moment, wonderfully," I said. "I'm putting the finishing touches to a dress for Lady Tolfee. She's to open the Royal Academy of Arts Summer Exhibition following the Vernissage," I said.

He looked bewildered. "I've never been to that museum, or heard of that kind of thing."

"It's a part of the Season, parties and balls and events and such. I've chosen a dress that is to do with Impressionism."

He did not answer. I thought maybe he was unfamiliar with Impressionism but did not want to say.

"It's also about a gardening book," I quickly added, hoping to set him at ease. "One that showcases English flowers, in particular."

He relaxed. "Oh, Mother is always pottering about her veg patch. You should mention that book to her. Now it's June, she's out planting more in the back. Father has told her that soon, when we move into the new house on Berry Street, we shall have an even larger house and a larger garden for her to plant in. She's quite thrilled." He smiled at me. "Though I expect I shall not be living with them by then, so I don't know why they would need a larger home."

"You plan to move?" I asked. We passed one of the brass Salvation Army bands, and I slowed. "Do you mind if we listen for a moment? Have we time?"

He nodded. "Certainly. To answer your question, yes, I hope to have moved into my own home by next year. Father has indicated that I am likely to be promoted to sergeant." He smiled once more.

"Congratulations!" The band played a rousing tune and Collingsworth seemed to enjoy himself. He did not have his uniform on today, and the pink of his cheeks and the close-shaved blond mutton chops made him look younger than when he was dressed for the force.

We began to move toward his house again. "Wasn't your father a sergeant when he married your mother?" he asked.

I took a slow breath. I thought I now saw where this was headed. "Yes, yes, he was," I replied.

"They seemed very happy, in spite of . . . how it all ended for your father." He stopped, seemingly having realized that he had introduced a difficult topic into a sunny day. "Perhaps her death . . . well, you know how upsetting that can be to some people. Causes them to lose their bearings and head in another direction."

"They were very happy indeed," I said. "But I do not believe Papa's bearings were lost." We made small talk about the weather and church functions and the duties of the policeman on the street till we arrived at their tidy, but small, home.

If my home was lovely, and it was, and Mrs. Roberts's was small and cramped, the Collingsworth home fell somewhere in the middle. Plain, but pretty, a brick house on a lane that did not have mews but did not have vagrants loafing about, either. It was neatly cut and held together with freshly pointed mortar; it rather put me in mind of a layer cake. I wondered where their new home would be located, and if the inspector had been investing toward that future, as my papa always had.

"My dear." Mrs. Collingsworth opened the door; her home smelt of roast and potatoes with the slightest sweet tint hovering round the edges of the room, which suggested a delightful pudding to follow it all. She took me into a warm embrace and until she did I had not realized how I longed for a mother's touch. I embraced her warmly in return. She held me at arm's length. "Getting on all right, then?"

I nodded. "I am, such as I can be due to the circumstances."

She looked a little wan herself, and I noticed she had a rash on her wrists, beneath her short gloves, that looked as though it extended to her palms.

"Caroline will serve dinner if we take our seats." She indicated that we should follow her into the small dining room. I hoped we hadn't tarried long and delayed her meal.

Inspector Collingsworth looked over at me; he seemed to look me over long and hard. It was uncomfortable.

The food was served, and after he said a blessing the inspector carved the roast joint for us.

It was silent for a moment. "Constable Collingsworth tells me that you're leading a charity bazaar," I said. "I'm most interested in hearing about it."

Mrs. Collingsworth looked delighted. "Please say you'll attend. The funds raised will go toward the poor. I've been sewing for months to ensure I have something proper to donate."

"I would love to attend. Just let me know the time and place. I understand sewing for months, believe me! I've been sewing for Lady Tolfee, for the Season, and I'm soon to begin work on the costumes for *Cinderella*, which is my most important commission to date—it means all for my future if I succeed and utter disaster if I do not! I should have liked to have sewn for the opera held at Drury Lane, *Esmeralda*. It was magnificent."

Mrs. Collingsworth shook her head a little. "I'm not familiar."

"It was based on *The Hunchback of Notre-Dame*." My comment was received in silence; I do not think the family approved of theater.

Francis cleared his throat. "Miss Young is involved in her own charity work," he bridged the gap. "And it includes her sewing."

Inspector Collingsworth forked a large piece of roast and said nothing, but his wife spoke up. "Do tell us!"

"Well," I said. "I've taken on a master beader and two apprentices. I don't mind saying I've grown close to the girls. I found them at the Theatrical Mission, on King Street."

Mrs. Collingsworth cooed, but the inspector set down his fork and looked at me. "King Street?"

I nodded. "Yes. It's the Theatrical Mission."

"Ah," he said, and dug into his meat again. "I'd heard some noise that you were visiting King Street again, asking questions, and I said to meself, no, no, that can't be right. If she had any questions about anything she'd come to Francis or to me, as she said she would." He chewed and swallowed before looking at us each, one by one.

A cold wave traveled through me. How had he heard that I'd been asking questions on King Street—and why should he care?

"I had no idea someone would be speaking to you of me," I replied, and took a tiny bite of potato though my appetite had fled and been replaced with anger tinted with a little fear.

"You know how it is. We all look after those we care about. Your father is gone, and I feel it's my responsibility to look after you in a way. Like you're a . . . daughter of sorts. Your father and me, we were like brothers." He looked at Francis and broke out in a grin. Francis smiled softly and looked at me. I looked to the table for a moment. Francis had clearly not thought King Street would turn into an issue, or he would not have raised the subject of the Theatrical Mission.

Or was that precisely why he'd raised it? To bring it into the open?

"Just like you look after those young girls, what were their names? Ruby and Charlotte?" the inspector said. "We all tend to the people we care about."

How did he know the girls' names? "That's true," I said. "I'm very glad for the ways you've cared for our family. Lord Lockwood, my neighbor at Winton Park, has told me you accompanied Papa on a visit there."

I deliberately did not mention when that visit was made.

"Some months ago, yes," Inspector Collingsworth said. "Your father had not told you?"

He had me there. I shook my head.

"Then he didn't like you to know," he said. "Which is the way of men. I understand you've inherited that grand house, then?"

"Yes, I have."

"Will you move there, dear? I shouldn't like to be all alone in such a huge house." Mrs. Collingsworth shivered.

I laughed. "If I moved there, I wouldn't be all alone, have no fear."

The inspector grinned at that and looked at Francis. "That's very true, very true. You'd need just the right set of people to help you manage it all, enjoy it with you." He set his utensils down, and

I guessed from the way the family responded we were all to do likewise. "I'm sure, properly guided, you'll do quite well."

I nodded uncomfortably, and Mrs. Collingsworth called for a lovely Bakewell pudding to be brought to table. Afterward, the inspector said to his son, "Francis, join me for a pipeful?"

Francis nodded. "Please, sit with Mother for a while and catch up on lady things. I'll be back to accompany you home in a short while."

Mrs. Collingsworth's maid cleared the table, and we retired to the sitting room. I handed her the pincushion ball on a chain, which she could clasp to her waist if she wished.

"See?" I opened it. "You can place buttons in the center if you like. It's as much an adornment as it is useful to us seamstresses." We did have that in common. My mother, bless her, had not sewn much.

She cracked the ball open, like an egg, and saw the cavity. "That is wonderful." Her eyes looked tired and anxious. I hoped the men would soon return so I could leave, and she could rest.

"Do come along to the bazaar," she said. "It would mean so much to have you there. I don't have a daughter, you know."

That was the second mention of the word *daughter* in one evening. "I shall, I promise. Maybe I could bring along my apprentices? I keep them so busy they have only the rare occasion out."

"Of course," Mrs. Collingsworth said. "And here are the men."

Inspector and Constable Collingsworth returned to the room, trailing thick pipe smoke behind them. I put on my coat and my new feathered hat and said my farewells.

As he left me at my door, a short while later, Constable Collingsworth rested his hand on my arm. I flexed it, a little, rather than yielding and softening.

"Be careful in all you do," he said. "You've no brother, no father, no husband to care for you. I should like to step in as pro-

tector if you've ever need of or
can."

I was not sure what tha
tion he may just have had
plore the topic further just
his father's intensity and
scared me a little.

"May I call on you?"
knob.

I wasn't ready to dismiss him entirely. H
and was a good man. And yet, there was little else betwee
Perhaps I had not given him enough of a chance.

"An evening to St. James for the music might be lovely, sometime," I said. "After I return from Hampshire."

He looked alert. "I've heard, from Father, that it's a beautiful
house."

I nodded. "It is."

"Perhaps I could visit sometime?" He smiled. "You could show
me round. We could bring Mother to chaperone."

This was an odd line of thought. Had he ever expressed interest in Winton before? I didn't think so.

"You intend going? Soon? Alone?" Francis continued. "I could
accompany you or send someone along with you if you like."

"Why, yes, I intend to go, very soon, actually. It is my home,
and I have staff there, thank you. I've informed them I'll be arriving, alone."

I fully intended to go unaccompanied. I did not want my
handbag searched as I left.

CHAPTER FIFTEEN

WINTON PARK, HAMPSHIRE

JUNE, 1883

When I caught the train to Hampshire I noticed a man standing near me, following me, first with his person and then with his eyes. I took the first class coach compartment, as I was traveling alone and it was safer; he parted ways with me then. When I departed the train, he did, too, though only one or two others did at our station. They had people waiting for them; I did not. I intended to hire a carriage.

The strange man did not take a hired carriage; in fact, when he saw me get in one he returned to the station and stood in the waiting room on the side where those returning to London awaited the next train, which was very odd indeed. Perhaps he had merely forgotten something of importance in London, and had no connection whatsoever with me. After the dinner at the Collingsworths', Francis's declared intentions, and Roberts's untimely death, I hoped I was no longer being followed.

Perhaps hope was not wise. I had a fleeting thought: Would I have to rid myself of Sarah's beautiful and distinctive hat as I had my bouclé scarf?

The day was glorious and sunny though already tilting toward dusk when I arrived at my country home. My fingertips tingled as I thought it—it was *my* country home. The home my grandfather had banished my mother from, but one I had made quiet hopes and plans for each time we'd visited. It was vast and done up like a powdered lady, dressed in exquisite finery that now, sadly, had gone to moths. I paid the driver and then proceeded to walk up. I had but a small bag to carry and wanted to take in the land, the house, the outbuildings, everything that Winton encompassed.

Before the driver departed, I asked him a single question. "Which way is the property of Lord Lockwood?"

He pointed west. "You'll mean Darington, then. It's the largest estate in these parts, miss, and we are not short of them hereabouts. He makes it his business, if he can, to enlarge his acreage each year. Successfully, too, I may say."

I nodded, and he reddened a bit and hurried off, perhaps realizing that he'd been bordering on hedgerow gossip.

The drive was made of crushed rock the color of sand; I walked down one of the wheel ruts, as it was smoother and easier for my heeled boots to navigate. In the distance, Winton beckoned me forward. Its brick front was real, and not a façade. It was guarded by Tuscan columns, straight and tall. To the left of the main house were the empty stables and the unused carriage house, where the footmen had slept in better days. A gate hung ajar, like a dangling broken arm. To the right was the building that housed the kitchens, the laundry, and some storage areas. I had found it curious, as a girl, that the kitchens were disconnected from the house.

"The smells," Mamma had told me. "That way, the household does not need to smell the food cooking or meat roasting or bread baking, or the nip of the lye when the laundry is being done." Before dinner the following night she'd shown me down to those kitchens—a visit that had not been well received—to explain how the food was loaded onto the wooden delivery carts, heated with coal. The carts were wheeled through the underground passages to the Servery, where they would be organized and delivered to the dining room.

Dishes, once used, were returned in like manner: I remembered a footman saving all the uneaten ices after they'd been collected from the table; we'd eaten them together, sneakily, he and I. I'd stood in that basement passage for a moment; one small cutout in the ground above framed in iron and shaped cheerfully, like a daisy, allowed fresh air and light, but also rain and ice, to fall through and then upon the heads, for better or worse, of the delivering servants.

I approached the house itself. Some of the stones slumped like Atlas's shoulders, no longer able to bear their burden. I could see that better in the bright light of summer than I had at Papa's burial. The lawns were infested with weeds that had capitalized on the weaknesses of the grass and boldly claimed vast swaths of territory. A rabbit hobbled here and there in the distance, which brought a smile.

But for them, there was no sign of life whatsoever. Desolate. Lonely. I could resuscitate her, bring the house back to cheerful life.

If I had more money. A flush of fear passed through me. Had . . . Had Papa been thinking that as well? Could he have been tempted not by money for himself, but to save my estate?

No. Never. And he knew, in any case, that I would likely give it away.

I approached the front door and knocked. *This is ridiculous. I'm at my own house, and there is no butler; I shall just walk in.* I opened the front door, which was unlocked.

Once inside the staircase hall, I called out, "Hello? David-son?"

I set my bag down and began to walk through the rooms. I started with the largest, the Saloon. That most formal of the reception rooms opened onto the green that led toward Lock-wood's property, Darington Hall, though it was so far away that should I scream at the top of my lungs no one there would be able to hear me.

I laughed nervously. Why should I be thinking of screaming?

The dust covers were still on the furniture, ghostly; they lifted and trembled in the wind, which crept in through the door I'd left open. The ceiling was blue like the sky, with gilt ribs running from each wall to the center circle, also gilt, and from which hung a French chandelier. None of the candles were placed in sockets, so it looked like a beautiful mouth without any teeth, dark, rotted, and not right.

To the right was the Red Drawing Room, with its red flocked wallpaper and delicately plastered ceilings. Last time I'd been in that room, after Papa's burial, I'd been with Lord Lockwood. It, too, was shrouded once more. I walked to the Little Parlor.

The wraps had been removed from the furniture, and the wood had been newly polished, yes, it had. I drew a finger across a table and it came back clean. A fresh set of tea trios rested nearby; the setting was for two. I picked up a cup. It had no trace of dust, either.

Empty houses were dusty tombs, indeed. Who had—very re-cently—set these here? "Hello?" I called once more. Nothing.

I passed the Stone Hall, where Grandpapa had withdrawn with the other men to smoke. The smell from their cigars and pipes remained, perhaps in the oriental carpets, which looked as though they had not been recently beaten.

Then I arrived at the Dining Room. It, too, had been freshened afore my arrival. The table was polished and set for one. The candelabra in the middle of the table had fresh tapers. I ran my finger round the edge of a dish, and then, I heard a noise. Footsteps.

"Who is there?"

They did not sound like the heavy fall of a man's shoes. In fact, the sound rather put me in mind of the felt shoes actors wore behind the stage so as not to cause thumps on the wood during a performance.

"Who is there?" I insisted as a fright ran through my chest. I turned toward the hallway and a woman appeared like an apparition. She looked to be about forty years old and was dressed in a maid's uniform of black and white.

"It is I, Miss Young. My name is Ruth. I am one of Lady Lockwood's maids."

I exhaled. "Thank you, Ruth. But what are you doing here?" At that, I heard the heavier footfall of a man, one heavy step alternating with a limping light one. Davidson.

"I'm delighted to see you home, miss," he said to me, not wincing at all when using the word *home*, which made me smile. "Lady Lockwood thought you would need a maid for your days at home, seeing as there is only me now."

I spoke gently, but certainly, to the old man. "How did Lady Lockwood know I was coming?"

"Why, I told her, Miss Young," he replied, as if there had been no other choice. Perhaps there had not been. She lived nearby; I had been here but a dozen times in my life. "She'll be by tomorrow," he said, "for tea."

"I'll come by to prepare it, miss," Ruth said. "I'll bring the Grey's tea. I remember your father preferred it."

My heart double-beat. "When did you serve tea to my father?"

She dipped her head.

"Did you serve tea to my father?" I asked once more.

"I may have misremembered," was all she would admit to. "Please, miss, do not mention this to Lady Lockwood."

Ah, yes. Lady Lockwood. My emotions were tangled. Why did she want to see me? What would we speak of? But then, she was, after all, Lord Lockwood's mother. I had developed a compelling interest in the man, perhaps too quickly, perhaps too deeply. But I wanted to make a good impression.

"You won't be spending the night, then?" I asked Ruth.

She shivered. "No, miss. I was not asked to do that. And I should not prefer to. It's dark and empty here. But I'll tend to your supper before I leave."

I nodded. "That's fine."

"The house looks well cared for," I said to Davidson, wanting to encourage what must be a lonely old man.

"Your father pays me well," he said. "And I do my best."

My father? Ah. He must have mistaken me for Mamma. Or . . . perhaps not.

Davidson brought my bags upstairs while I gathered my thoughts in the Little Parlor. That was where Grandmamma had sat, when she was old, and stroked her spaniels for their comfort and hers. I remember visiting her once or twice after the old man was gone, with Mamma. Her mind was not clear, nor were her eyes, but her smile had been.

Later that night, after a dinner of well-sauced cold meat and fresh bread, Davidson saw himself down to the small Steward's Hall, near the old Beer Cellar, where he stayed. It was many floors away from my room, and though there was a bell system for summoning help, he was deaf enough that I doubt he could have heard them chime, let alone my distant shout.

Again that fear. Why did I think I'd need to shout?

The house was blackness itself, surrounded by blackness outdoors, on all sides. I took a lamp with me and rounded the stairs.

I settled into the big bed, alone in the Tapestry Room. The posts of the bed rattled, and I knew they would have to be replaced. Lord Lockwood had mentioned that all the chandeliers would need to be reattached—no small task indeed. I hoped one should not crash down before it could be tended to. When would I have funds to tend to a chore such as that? There were perhaps thirty chandeliers in all.

The room smelt dead, as though the air had not circulated for some time, and it likely had not, but the bedsheets were clean. I supposed I should be thankful for Lady Lockwood's kindness. I did not appreciate her knowing every move I made in the country. I did not appreciate Inspector Collingsworth knowing every move I made in the city.

Perhaps he knew every move I made in the country, too, if it had been his man who had followed me. If not his man, then whose?

Francis, came a thought. *Francis's man.*

In truth, the walls were closing in around me in every direction and I had no idea whom to trust.

I could not sleep. I got up and opened every cabinet in the room to see if Papa might have stored something in any of them. Had that been why he had come to Winton just a few weeks before his death? I did not know. They were empty.

Perhaps the punched train ticket had not even been Papa's.

I wandered, quickly and quietly, down the hall to the Flower Room, Mamma's childhood bedroom. I noted, right away, that the clock on the mantel perfectly matched Lord Lockwood's carriage clock.

Mamma's picture was on the wall; she looked like me, or perhaps I like her. I held my lamp up. She was not smiling, and I barely recognized her. Mamma had always smiled, even up till the end when Papa climbed into their big bed and held her till he handed her, gently, to the angels who came to carry her to her waiting savior.

I reached into my linen pocket and fingered the photograph of the smiling young woman. I would ask Davidson, next day, if he'd seen her with my father, here at Winton.

I pray Davidson had not seen her, I believe Father had not brought her here, but I must ask nonetheless. Papa had long been a widower. He could have had a rendezvous of sorts here at Winton without anyone in London knowing.

I stood for a moment. The night was silent but for the croaking frogs in the park lawns outside. The vastness of the house closed in on me. I did not believe in ghosts, of course, but I sensed the memories, somehow, of what had transpired in Winton over the hundreds of years. It simply felt different from my new house in Cheyne Gardens, which the three of us had been the first to occupy.

Winton had been passed along, one inheritor after the other, hand over hand like men pulling a rope, to continuing generations. What had been the hopes and dreams, the desolation and fears of those who had lived here before me? Would I be letting them all down to give it away?

The frogs went silent.

I opened the black japanned cupboard in Mamma's room; it was etched with red peonies. Could Papa have placed anything here? It was a hidden cabinet, of a sort, the sort we'd had at home in London.

It was empty. I closed the door and glanced at the bedside table, on which still rested a pressed flower book with notes by Mamma and some of her friends. I blew the dust off it and opened it; it had probably been left as it matched the theme of the room. I smiled at her girlish delight; Mamma had chosen to press and annotate both unusual and unworthy flowers, whereas her friends, including Barbara—Mrs. W!—had pressed traditional roses and made notes to their findings.

I looked through the rest of the room. Nothing. I'd complete a search of the upstairs the next morning before Lady Lockwood came to call for tea. *I wonder what she has in mind?*

I walked down the hallways, the doors to the rooms were closed. I dared not go in them so late at night. It was dark. I had but one light and no idea how long the oil would last.

I returned to the Tapestry Room and looked out of the window. Far in the distance, through a veil of trees, night lights flickered. Darington.

Was Lord Lockwood here or in London?

I closed my eyes, and when I did, I saw him draw near me. *Then I will kiss your lips, Kate.*

He reached toward me and did just that. I became entangled in the scent of sandalwood and reached an arm around his neck, entangling us further and kissing him back.

In the morning, the breakfast table was laid before I arrived downstairs. Ruth had already been there. Davidson waited by the front door, in a worn leather chair. I hoped he should not feel it was necessary for him to remain there for the duration of my visit. But he had been carrying out his duties since long before my birth and I was not going to instruct him.

I did come close to him before taking my meal, though. I withdrew the photograph from my linen pocket.

"Davidson, if I may ask a question. Have you ever seen this young lady or someone like her?"

He took the picture in hand and then brought it close to his eyes, and then held it as far away as his arm would stretch.

"I don't know about her, but yes, yes, this *kind* of girl is familiar to me."

"What does that mean, 'this kind of girl,' and when did you last see one?"

He looked embarrassed. "Your father would sometimes bring them kind in through the basement passages, miss."

My father!

"Through the downstairs, that's right," he continued to muse, "so none could see. There weren't as many of us there then, you know. But I saw. I and Mrs. Abbot."

Mrs. Abbot had been the housekeeper, who had been dead many years.

"My father, Davidson? Andrew Young?"

He looked confused. "No, miss. Lord Palmer, of course."

I sighed, just a little. He had confused me with my mother again and perhaps was misremembering much more.

Davidson nodded toward the dining room. "Lady Lockwood will be here to see you soon. She's not been back since we buried your father, you know."

Now he seemed to know who I was again.

"Speaking of Lady Lockwood, has Lord Lockwood been here since my father has died?"

He looked confused. Perhaps I should see to getting him some help; I would make a note of that. Then he shook his head clear. "No, Miss Young. He distinctly told me that you'd asked him to look at the outside but not inside again and that I was to tell him if anything needed to be tended to. Captain Lockwood, though, he comes round often, to check on me."

I'd wandered, room to room, and thought how beautifully the place could be restored, tidied, filled with laughter and love. Circulating fresh air, one might say, in a new way.

But who had Davidson referenced? "Captain Lockwood?"

"Lord Lockwood's younger brother." He lowered his voice. "The one that was maimed . . ."

I nodded and replied softly, "Thank you, Davidson."

I finished breakfast, and after, whilst waiting for Lady Lockwood to call, explored the main floor.

I went from room to room, peeking under dust sheets, looking to see if any portraits had been recently moved, but I could see no recognition that anything had been disturbed by Papa hiding something.

Perhaps he had not hidden anything at all, and I had misinterpreted his last letter, wanting something to be there that was not. He may have been wishing me love and luck, and reminding me of his affections, as any father would. He'd clearly known, however, that his life was at risk.

And it had been. The runaway cart had, it seemed, been deliberately loosed or pushed, if it had been a cart at all. Andrew Roberts was dead, too.

By the time I'd finished my exploration of the main floor, it was time to greet Dowager Lady Lockwood.

Ruth showed her in, and I stood to greet her. "Lady Lockwood. How do you do?"

"How do you do, Miss Young," she said. "I hope Ruth has been of some help."

I showed her to the seat that faced the window, and Ruth stood nearby to serve tea.

"I could not have asked for a kinder gesture from you, nor a more gracious attendant." At that, Ruth served the tea.

We made small talk for a moment or two—she had seen and enjoyed *Esmeralda*, and her younger son and daughter-in-law had accompanied her—and then she came round to her target.

"Do you intend to keep Winton Park, Miss Young?" She set her teacup down and bit into a biscuit, one of her own cook's making, I imagined.

"What else would I do with it, Lady Lockwood?" I took a sip of my tea, hand steady.

"You might consider it a part of your dowry," she said.

I hid my surprise. Whyever would she be thinking of my dowry and marriage? My heart skipped a beat.

"My mother did not bring a dowry to her marriage," I said. "I do not expect to have to, either."

But maybe, for the right man . . .

She frowned, but then nodded and continued. "I suppose as you'll certainly marry someone middle class you won't need a dowry. I had thought you might want to sell Winton." She shrugged. "It's a large home, in need of much attention and repair. I know you are mostly in London and are not a part of a set that would need or desire a country house."

My face reddened, but I stood and walked toward the window to cool it off before answering her. She was right. I could not afford to modernize or even maintain Winton Park on my seamstress income, which was barely enough, at the moment, to support the London property. "I'm giving serious consideration to donating Winton Park to the Cause."

Her teacup clattered. "Donate? To an organization for the . . ."—I knew she searched for a socially acceptable word— "underserved?"

Now our positions were equaled again; I returned to my chair. "Yes. It is what my mother wanted. In the end, Winton was hers to do with as she pleased."

She looked me in the eye. "Your mother would *never* have given Winton Park away, and it is now yours to do with as you wish." For a moment, the certainty of her conviction shook me. Then I realized, she was not given to generosity herself and would not understand the kind of woman my mother had been.

"Exactly. It's best for me to decide."

"But your father . . . ," she began.

I raised an eyebrow. "My father?"

She shook her head a little and took her teacup in hand; Ruth had warmed it with a refill. "As you've said, it's for you to decide."

She'd clearly had an insight that she was not sharing.

A minute of awkward silence ticked by. "I brought a gift for Lord Lockwood."

Her eyebrow raised and her face hardened. "That was not necessary."

I handed it to her. "To thank him for his kindness in looking after the property. I thought I might see him this visit, but I return to London tomorrow." And I'd had no real excuse other than the plan to show up at the front door with the gift, knocking like a schoolgirl.

"I'll see he gets it." She handed it to Ruth. I wondered if she would see it delivered to him or if it would go straight to the wastebin.

"I have one for you, too." I reached for a second wrapped package.

"For me?" She seemed genuinely surprised.

"Yes. I thought maybe we would have occasion to see one another during my visit." I held back a wry grin.

She gently unwrapped the package and took out the pair of exquisite gloves, soft ivory calfskin with pearl beads. "Oh my," she said. "They are lovely. They are . . . art."

Unexpectedly, she took off her gloves and slipped them on. "They are a perfect fit. Remarkable! Without even measuring me." I could barely focus on what she was saying, though, so surprised was I that her hands were red and rough, pricked by pins and sliced through by thread.

My astonishment must have been evident because she genuinely smiled and said, "You are not the only woman who sews, Miss Young."

CHAPTER SIXTEEN

The next morning, I worked my way through the many rooms in the house, one by one, floor by floor. The furniture was draped and drifted with dust; it did not appear as though any had been disturbed in quite some time before I approached. I found nothing, not even in the desk in the library. Papa had seen to it that the official papers had been archived with Mr. Pilchuck; he was careful about such records. I should have to see to them now.

I finally arrived in the basement, much to Davidson's dismay. "What are you looking for, Miss Palmer?" he asked, confusing me with my mother once more. "I can help you. You know your father will be most distressed if he finds you belowstairs."

I spoke softly to calm him. "I'm just taking inventory." I had an idea. "I wonder . . . have there been any others in the house lately, people who are not family or staff?"

"Just that copper Lord Palmer doesn't like." He sniffed.

Papa!

"What was he doing here?"

Davidson looked at me, pointedly. "You'd know better than I, Miss Victoria."

Dear me. I was not Victoria. Was he referring to Papa or to Inspector Collingsworth as having been here of late?

The next room was where Mamma's trunks were stored. It was more of a large closet, really, with one small window but two large doors that pulled open from the outside. In earlier days it had held extra kitchen linens, and the room and doors had been built to accommodate large laundry carts. Perhaps that was why Papa had stored Mamma's costumes here when he'd made space for my sewing salon. The cases would fit through the double doors, and the room was exceedingly dry.

I pulled the left door handle, and it opened outward; it was unlocked. Just inside was the costume repair kit, a sewing cabinet of sorts: the hodgepodge of drawers held scissors and needles, some threads, ribbon, felt for her stage shoes, and a variety of pieces for fixing her hair. I pocketed one of her pincushions, for fondness, and placed it into my linen pocket. Once dropped in, I felt it shift. Did it rest uneasily with the photograph I always carried?

I'd propped the door open, which let in a little more light than the small, dirty-paned window did, but it was filtered, and the air was saturated with motes that clouded my vision.

Each wall was lined with two trunks as tall as a man and thrice as heavy. I undid one leather strap and pushed open the case. It held an emerald gown, hanging; the gown had been given to Mamma as a gift for her role in *The Merry Wives of Windsor*; she'd played Anne. I reached in for the dress, but it felt as though it might crumble beneath my fingers. I slipped my arm through one sleeve. *Dearest Gillian*, I chided myself, *will you never stop wearing your mother's clothes, and be your own woman instead?* As the dress was grimy with age and punctured by a few moth holes, I dared not do more lest it fall apart on me, and gently eased my arm out. I could not lose one of her treasures. Soon I would take it, and the others, and use all of my skills to beautifully restore them.

I looked at the floor of the trunk, and in each of the pockets that lined the trunk's walls, where accessories sometimes were stored. Nothing but the gown.

I worked my way down the trunks, looking for false floors, finding one or two that held nothing but shoes beneath them.

The fourth trunk down brought the day's first laugh. A dress of aubergine and the matching shoes that I had worn the night Lord Lockwood had first seen me in Winton's Staircase Hall! I took them out, their faded blue ribbons encircling my arms. I considered taking the shoes with me, but then could not, for the moment, separate them from their dress. They were twinned and belonged together.

Nothing in the right trunk pockets but a playbill, for *Rapunzel*, crisp and yellow with age, tucked into the trunk with the Rapunzel costume. The long blond braids were severed and awkwardly tied around the waist of the dress. I felt bad. They had been chosen to perfectly match Mamma's hair and had been shorn, likely, from someone who had needed to sell her hair.

I thought of Ruby and grinned and then grimaced. What would come of her if something should happen to me?

I left the room and closed the door tightly behind me.

No notes from Papa. It had only been a hunch, of course, based on a train ticket, but it had proved wrong.

Next, the hallway from the kitchen to the Servery. It was in terrible disrepair and as I pushed open the larder scores of black beetles escaped, racing over my feet; I could feel them scramble across the silk of my slippers. I dared not move for fear of stepping on one of them, until one began to crawl up my dress, and then a dozen clawed their way up my petticoat, clasping me with their six feet, scanning me with their antennae. I screamed and shook them free and struggled to shut the larder door again.

Lord Lockwood had mentioned that the pipes in the kitchen were in desperate need of repair; they probably entered through those decayed pipes. I fled the kitchen, closed the door that led to the house so they could not proceed inside, and stood in the hallway catching my breath and trying to forestall retching. In five minutes, I moved to the laundry rooms, just to be thorough, but found nothing but more beetles.

Papa, the least you could have done was see to it that the house was properly maintained. I knew money from my trust was available for such things. Papa had never felt comfortable with Winton—out of his league, he'd said—and rather than face it head-on, he'd let it crumble. Left it for *me* to deal with.

I walked upstairs to find Davidson waiting for me. "Lord Lockwood is here." His smile released a baker's dozen folds among his wrinkles.

I stepped into the Little Parlor, which was glorious and gold-gilted in the early-summer sun. Lockwood rose. "Miss Young."

I came near, and as I did warmth and joy ran through me. "Lord Lockwood, how pleasant, and unexpected, to see you." My heart raced. Unexpected, yes, but certainly not unwelcome.

I remonstrated with myself. *Isn't that why you'd sent a gift, hoping he'd return the call to thank you?*

I blushed, and he grinned. *He must know, too.*

"I came to thank you for the Turkish coffee," he said. "It is the finest I've ever had. You'll have to share the name of the shop where you purchased it."

I opened my mouth to offer the name of the proprietor but

realized that would forestall my needing to take him there . . . if I so chose. "You're very welcome," I said.

"My mother was delighted with the gloves." His voice was soft. "It was a truly kind thing to do."

"The gifts were my pleasure. I was delighted to learn she sews."

He walked up to me, close to me, and lowered his voice while holding my gaze. "I hope to offer you a ride to the train station. I'd planned to return to London just ahead of the Vernissage. I've changed my plans so I will return to London early. Today. With you." He smiled and it lit my world.

I smiled back. "Thank you." I didn't move nor look away, nor did he, till Davidson interrupted the moment. "Your bags are in the carriage, miss."

Lockwood held out his arm to me. "Shall we?"

He told his driver to take the long way to the station, and on the way pointed out all the local landmarks, and waved in a friendly manner to the villagers we passed, who seemed to hold him with genuine affection.

"I should tell you about the time I got lost," he said. "And they had to rescue me, delivering me on muleback to my father who was not at all pleased to learn my horse had bolted and the work-ingmen had to break their day to return me."

He told the story, and when he was done, I was giggling. I told him of how I once crawled beneath one of the stages, hoping to spy on my mother, but was trapped there, with my cat, who mewled off and on for all five acts, requiring the actors to speak loudly and cover up the noise. I had no pudding for a month after that event. "But it had been worth it," I said.

"My adventure had been, too," he agreed, and we smiled a bonding kind of smile.

I fastened my hat and shook my head a little to fluff the feathers. A strange look flittered across his face.

"Turkish tobacco." He bent toward the hat Sarah had made for me and sniffed. "Yes, it's a distinctive and rare blend, one very recently, and exclusively, acquired by a man in the City of London Club. Trades in Turkish goods, invests in tin mines in Singapore. Set for life, really."

I took the hat in hand. "The new fabric and feather must have captured and held the scent."

He nodded, and looked strangely at me.

As we made our way to the train platform, I thought, *The only people who have smoked near my person, while I wore this hat, were Francis and his father. Surely they could not be good friends with someone at Lord Lockwood's club.*

Could they be?

The train trip was pleasant—we laughed and discussed our favorite plays and he told me about his school days and I regaled him with entertaining tidbits about Miss Genevieve's Day School for Young Ladies and how Miss Genevieve had not only encouraged my profession, but influenced my hopes for the future. When the train arrived in London we stood on the platform together. I did not want to say good-bye. I did not think he wanted to, either, because we stood together not moving nor speaking, affection and attraction thick between us.

"Would you . . . would you like me to show you the shop where I purchased your Turkish coffee?" I asked.

His face lit. "Yes, what a splendid idea. My new driver will be waiting outside the station."

His beautiful carriage was, indeed, waiting. I was surprised to see that for as polished as the carriage was, his new driver was rough. He looked worn by the elements and I noticed he had only one hand. Unusual for a driver.

Once I told the driver the name of the shop, and we were settled in the back of the carriage, and our bags put on board, Lockwood turned to quietly address me. He must have noted my surprise. "He was begging outside of one of my gentlemen's clubs. Former military. Honorably wounded."

"What a lovely gesture." I was genuinely touched.

"Do for one what you cannot do for many, isn't that right, Miss Young? I believe the Lord has His eye on the downtrodden but he desires us to join Him in His important work. 'He that giveth unto the poor shall not lack: but he that hideth his eyes shall have many a curse.'"

"Proverbs," I said, and I nodded as he took my hand in his, moved that he'd remembered my saying that about helping one, if not many.

"Precisely."

We soon arrived at the coffee shop, and after securing us a table by a window, Lockwood asked, "Do you mind if I order for us both?"

I shook my head. "I'm delighted by surprises," I said. "And I rarely get to enjoy any."

He went to the counter and then returned and sat across from me. The rain sluiced down the outside of the window, a direct contrast to the cheerful room and the warmth easily circulating between the two of us.

"I hope to start a charity of some kind for wounded veterans," he said. "As Viscount, I cannot do my bit in the way I would have preferred, with the troops, but this is something I can do."

Our coffee was delivered to the table in brass and glass cups, looking like nothing so much as deeply muddy water. "We're to drink this?" I enquired politely. It was twice as dark and thick as the one Charlotte had enjoyed.

"We are." He smiled and placed two lumps of natural sugar in my cup with the tiny gold tongs. "I hope to make things sweeter for you," he said, looking in my eyes as he said it, a promise, really.

What could he mean? When the tea cakes were brought, I served him and picked up the thread of our conversation. "I, too, have been thinking of a charity, one for the pantomime children."

"Like your apprentices." He poured himself a second coffee with the steadiest of hands.

My own were already shaking as if I'd had a pot of tea to myself.

"Would you like some more?" he asked.

I laughed. "No, I suspect I shall already have difficulty sewing a straight line for some time."

He laughed with me. "Your charity sounds delightful."

We spent an hour talking of *Cinderella*, and theater and music.

"How did it come by that your mother became an actress?" he asked. His voice did not reflect disdain.

"The traveling troupes," I said. "Year after year, my grandfather hired a grand troupe to perform on his vast lawn for the benefit of his friends and peers. He did not know that my mother was secretly, delightedly, dressing up in costume and practicing lines. One year when they came, she returned to London with them. My own father loved theater, and music," I said. "That is how they met."

"My father did not appreciate either theater or music." Lord Lockwood's voice grew both sad and firm. "There was not much he enjoyed."

"You did not . . . enjoy a companionable relationship?"

"No," he said.

"Pity," I responded. "My papa was wonderful."

He took my hand in his own but the look on his face was not really one of sympathy alone. It was, perhaps, also one of concern. Or disdain? Perhaps, or perhaps it was one of covering up.

"Did you know my father?" I asked. I had the feeling he must, but I did not know how.

"A little," was his only answer. He looked away, ending that portion of the conversation.

We talked comfortably for a few more minutes, and then he led me to the glass apothecary jars filled with sweets. "Which do you prefer?"

"Oh, Ruby and Charlotte would love the jellies," I answered.

He took my arm firmly in his own. "Which would you prefer?" he asked once more. "The gift is not for the young ladies, deserving as they may be. It is for *you*."

I smiled; no one had purchased sweets for me since I was a girl and Papa had taken me to a sweet shop.

I pointed out a few I knew I'd enjoy. "And these"—I indicated a few odd-looking candies—"because they are altogether new and untested."

"Ah, there's the thing, my daring Miss Young." He went to fetch the shopkeeper, and as he did, I relished the phrase once, twice, thrice. *My* Miss Young. His!

He returned with six or seven large bags. "I shall never eat all of these," I said, and then laughed.

"I want them to last," he said softly. "So you'll think of me each day."

I nodded and ran my finger down the back of his hand. "I shall. With or without a reminder."

His driver came round to the front, and Lord Lockwood told him to head toward Cheyne Gardens.

"I do so appreciate the sweets," I said. "But I am certain they cannot make up for the bitter news I shared with your mother. I wanted to be the one to tell her."

"That you are considering donating Winton Park to the Cause."

Anger rose in my chest. I should have known. His mother had already shared *my* news. "Yes. It was my mother's clear wish."

"Understandable, then," he said, but a strange look—doubt, perhaps, or the suppression of knowledge—flickered across his eyes and brow. "It is certainly a weighty decision, and not one to be lightly, or quickly, undertaken. There are other options. A sale."

"Are you trying to dissuade me?" I asked. Had he come with me, then, this day, to plead his case as a potential purchaser? His substantial holdings in the area, which, as the carriage driver had told me, Lockwood increased each year, were not enough land to satisfy him?

"I trust you know your mind, Miss Young. I would not seek to persuade you, or anyone, against your will and better judgment."

"I think your mother has a concern that someone unsuitable will move in." We rounded the corner down my street.

He nodded. "Yes." At least the man was honest.

"I think she would find *me* unsuitable," I said.

He came close and took my hands in his own. "She may at that, Miss Lockwood. But I do not find you unsuitable in the least."

For a moment, I wondered what he should have said if I'd changed the word *unsuitable* for *undesirable*. I did not want to remove my hands, and I wished his motives to be personal and unmixed. As I moved to get out of the carriage, I bumped the feather on my hat against the doorframe and wondered once more about that Turkish tobacco. I just did not know. It seemed to me that once I had understood nearly everything about everyone, but now I understood almost nothing about everyone I knew and had known.

Lockwood saw me to the door of my home, and while our gazes lingered, he did not kiss me good night.

CHAPTER SEVENTEEN

The next morning, I found Mrs. W in a flurry, and I could tell she'd been crying. Had I ever seen her cry before? I could not remember. She held a letter toward me. "My sister's husband has died and she's asked me to come after the burial. I'd like to go. But I cannot leave you alone, my dear. However will you manage without me?"

"But of course, you must go. Mother Martha is here. And you'll be back soon." I did not want to tell her I could manage quite well without her, not at this delicate moment.

She lightened. "Yes, that's true."

"And," I reminded her, "I'm a woman grown, and not of the class which requires a constant chaperone."

At that, she agreed. "The Cause . . . I've promised to give the sermon this week."

"I shall let them know you've been called away. Surely Mrs. Finley can step in."

She took a deep breath. I'd never seen her so out of order. "Yes, that will do. As long as the text is covered properly, and I can't be certain of that without being there. But . . . thank you, my dear. I shall be gone a few weeks. I'm finally looking forward to time spent with my sister."

It seemed an odd sentiment, but I had no sister so perhaps I did not understand. Within a day she had taken her leave.

The post that had been delivered while I was at Hampshire waited for me. A letter from Mr. Pilchuck informed that while it would take him till the close of July to sort out all the financial and legal details, he wanted to reassure me that any death duties and immediate expenses had been paid with money set aside by my father. Mr. Pilchuck had already transferred ownership of Winton Park to my name.

As Mrs. W was not at home, I jotted off a note to Mr. Pilchuck, thanking him for his attention and asking him for a small favor: Might he look into the ownership of the house on King Street? I desired to know who owned it, and since when. Had it any licenses? Mr. Pilchuck had told me to write if I had further questions, after all.

Then, I took a few hours to unpack my bags from Hampshire, placing my mother's pressed flower book in the sitting room, on the console, a place where it could be readily seen but also protected from the rolling in of the tea trolley. My clothes I gave to Louisa to have the visiting laundress care for, and then I returned to the salon to view Lady Tolfee's gowns, taking my mother's pincushion with me.

Once upstairs, Ruby insisted I take a seat. "Charlotte and Mother Martha did most of the work, and I know they are too modest to show you, so I will!" She brought the Impressionist gown out first, for Lady Tolfee.

I clapped with delight. "Simply stunning!" I had seen the pieces, of course, but Mother Martha had finished beading the starry bodice and Charlotte had sewn the pieces together. All that remained for me was finishing up the embroidery, which I would do that very day.

Next, Ruby brought out the sky blue silk gown that we'd made for Lady Tolfee's daughter, Mary. Mother Martha had beaded tiny crystals all over so it, too, would stand out, just not quite as much as Lady Tolfee's. I smiled.

"I am so pleased and proud of you all. This calls for a celebration. A few weeks hence, a friend of my mother's has invited me to a charity, and we shall all attend."

Now Ruby clapped *her* hands and Charlotte looked supremely pleased; Mother Martha looked pleased, too, but I suspected it was because the girls were so happy.

"And," I continued, "you shall each have something to spend whichever way you so choose."

Even *Charlotte* clapped now. It was unlikely that either of them had had pin money before; most pantomime actresses had to turn their money over to their parents. Ruby's comments reminded me, though, that there was little for her to do here because I could not entrust her with the fabric, or the sewing. For now, I had her measuring and sorting but could not afford to keep her for that. I may even have to hire another seamstress. One who could sew. But could I keep Ruby on, then?

Mother Martha picked up *Little Women* and read a few pages, as she did now and again, while we finished our projects. I listened, but didn't hear, lost in my work for a time. Suddenly, though, my ears and heart prickled at the same time.

"'I want to do something splendid . . . something heroic or wonderful that won't be forgotten after I'm dead,'" she read. "'I don't know what, but I'm on the watch for it, and mean to astonish you all someday.'"

I set my sewing down. Everyone else was deep in their work and didn't seem to notice. *Little Women* was my and Mamma's book. Winton was ours, shared, too.

Yes. I want to do something heroic and wonderful that won't be forgotten after I'm dead.

I picked up my needle again, and as I plied it, a disheartening proposition threaded itself through my heart and mind.

Donate Winton.

A few days later, I told Louisa not to hold dinner for me as I had a delivery to make to Drury Lane. I took a carriage to the theater and then ran the pieces in, handing them, but not the bag with Lady Tolfee's gown, to one of the dressers, but he grabbed my arm as I went to leave.

"Wilhelm wants to speak with you." His voice was firm and unfriendly, and it unsettled me.

I sat in one of the unused dressing rooms, waiting, the theater commotion burbling around me. Normally it was a soothing sound, but not today. Could I have done something wrong? Perhaps I was to have returned the wigs I'd given Ruby. I should see to that right away.

Wilhelm came in and sat next to me. "Miss Young."

"Yes, sir, I waited when I heard you wanted to speak with me. I'm just finishing the sketches for *Cinderella*. You'll love them, I promise. Would you like me to run them by you before I begin sewing?"

He shook his head. "No, dear, I know your designs will be fine. I mean to speak with you about . . . the police."

"The police?" My voice was shrill, I knew. I needed to keep it low. I swallowed. "My father was an officer," I said by way of feeble explanation.

He nodded. "A few officers stopped by yesterday. Wanted to know if you kept an office of sorts here, anywhere you might keep or store things, and if so, they'd like to search them. Said an officer who'd worked with your father had died and they had not found all of his notes, but believed you might have them. I told them nothing was kept here; you sewed at your salon with those in your employ, like other seamstresses in the theater industry, and they seemed comfortable with that."

A throbbing began in my skull. "Thank you. I . . . don't know what they'd be looking for. I am not involved in anything unsavory."

"I trust you, Gillian. But when the police visit, it upsets everyone. Changes the mood behind the stage, in the green room, before curtain time. Even our guests . . ." He moved his arm expansively. "They come for entertainment and to forget the cares of the world for a few hours."

"I understand," I said.

"I'm relieved to know you feel that is the end of the matter." He took my hand in his own and squeezed it. "I shall have the materials you've requested for *Cinderella* delivered soon."

I smiled. "Thank you, sir."

He smiled back. "Thank me with dresses that will make Harris gasp."

"I shall," I promised.

Shaken, I made my way to the street. Nearby was the neighborhood police division. I had to know what was going on before my livelihood was threatened for good.

A carriage pulled up just as I stepped toward the street. I got in as it had begun to rain.

"Metropolitan Police Division," I said. The driver, a clean-cut man, smiled, perhaps a bit impudently, and took off. We arrived a few minutes later, and he tipped his helmet to me. "Would you like me to wait?" His grin seemed saucy somehow.

"No, thank you," I said. I would get another carriage.

I walked into the division, and asked to speak with any inspector. I told them my name and that I was the daughter of Inspector Andrew Young. I didn't know if they'd have heard of him, his not having worked here, but the name seemed to prompt recognition. The man at the desk left, and then came back.

"The inspector says to tell you he's busy just now."

"Can someone please tell me why someone from your division was at the Theatre Royal asking about me? My name," I repeated, "is Miss Gillian Young."

He disappeared again and then returned. "Inspector says no one was sent after you, miss, at Drury Lane." He peered at me. "What division did your father work at?" His face grew hard.

Suddenly, I felt I should not say. It would get back to Collingsworth. And, I suddenly realized, it was not perhaps this division who had been sent to enquire. It was Chelsea—where Papa and Roberts had worked. Roberts's scheme to leave a dummy list had not erased the risk!

"Never mind." I turned and quickly left.

I took another carriage, but by the time I returned home I was slick with damp anyway—and from anxiety, and fear.

The evening of the Vernissage ball I arrived just a bit late. I hurried up the stairs; Lady Tolfee was in her dressing room, tapping her finger on the dressing table. Her hair was already done, and her lady's maid stood, idly, nearby.

"I'm sorry," I said as I arrived in her suite. "Here, this shall take but a minute." I pulled her dress out of her garment bag.

I noted the delight on her face, and only at that moment felt relief myself. A beautiful gown covers a multitude of sins, as far as

Lady Tolfee was concerned. I always tended to Lady Tolfee dressing in her gowns, in case there was a hem that needed adjusting
or a button firming up.

"Shall we call Lady Mary?" I asked, referring to her eldest
daughter. I had the lady's maid remove the sky blue dress from the
bag.

"She shan't be attending," she replied coolly.

"Oh . . . I'm sorry she's unwell. She can perhaps save the dress
for another event?"

"No, dear, she's not unwell. We had a little discussion, and I
told her if she was not thankful for the opportunities afforded to
her, then someone else would be." She eyed me. "You're just her
size, aren't you?"

Cold washed over me. "Yes, but . . . perhaps it won't fit in any
case."

"Come, now. Every woman knows the size of other women,
and this will fit you beautifully. Even I know that."

She was right. It would.

"I think it would be a lark for you to attend," she said, as I'd expected. "You're an heiress now, of a great country property, which
makes you eminently suitable for an event, especially as my guest.
None will cross me. Lord Palmer was your grandfather, and I shall
introduce you as such. Yes, this is a splendid idea."

Her maid began moving toward me, to help me change, I assumed. Had she just come across this idea? It seemed unlikely. I did
not know if she was trying to punish Lady Mary for the unspoken
indiscretion by having her replaced by "the help," or promote me,
somehow, for some reason. Or both. There were jewels at the ready,
and ivory loose slippers that could be tightened by laces to fit.

As her maid did my hair, I recognized that I depended upon
her good graces and patronage, and so I would attend this post-

Vernissage ball as her guest, dressed in a crystal-crusted gown of blue silk.

It is but one night, I reminded myself. I smiled and thought about how I'd just chastised myself for still wearing my mother's costumes. *Yes, I can play a role for one night.*

Lockwood, I knew, would also be in attendance.

An hour in, though, the pleasure had begun to fray at the edges. I was not truly Lord Palmer's granddaughter in a way he would ever have acknowledged, and I might not even be heiress to that qualifying country house for long. I felt like a fraud, the granddaughter of Lord Palmer here, but not the daughter of Inspector Andrew Young. And yet . . . I was both, wasn't I?

My fevered thoughts broke when I felt a hand on my arm, and another one reach around me in a familiar manner. I turned. "Lord Lockwood."

He looked very fine indeed in tie and tails, and there were quite a few glances our way. I held no illusions—they were looking at him and wondering who I was. He grinned at me. "I am delighted beyond words that you are in attendance and would not have arrived late had I known," he said. "May I have the honor of a dance?"

I nodded, and he led me to the center of the room where a waltz was about to begin. The checkered wood parquet floor tiles gleamed under the blazing crystal chandeliers, and the orchestra struck up a beguiling Strauss. A young woman looked at us, bewildered. I suspected Lockwood's name had been on her card for this dance.

"I had not expected to see you here." He turned me from her view. "I did not know that you . . ."

"Mingled with this social set?" I asked.

"Yes," he said. "But not because you are not worthy. I am just used to seeing, well, none other than married women, the dowagers, and the debs. You are none of the three."

"I do feel a bit out of place; I had not expected to be here myself."

He raised an eyebrow inviting me to say more. I would, but not for a moment. First, I wanted to relish the feel of his one hand engulfing mine, protectively, possessively, almost, and the other resting intimately against my back. The warmth from it emanated through my gown and reverberated within my entire body. It was an entirely new and welcome sensation.

"You are a fine dancer," I said. "You have come a long way since your awkward boyhood days."

He laughed. "For a woman who does not often dance, by her own admission, you float in my arms."

I smiled. "We have Miss Genevieve's Day School for Young Ladies to thank for that. I love dancing, to lose myself in the music, in the warmth, in the rhythm . . ." *In the arms of a man I want to dance with,* I ended silently. I hadn't met one before him. "I would dance every night if I could."

Ah, Miss Genevieve. You'd be proud to see me here tonight. Mrs. W had worked hard to find me a place in the school; it had been a triumph when I'd been accepted.

"Lady Tolfee invited me as her guest," I said, finishing my explanation as to why I was, unexpectedly, in attendance.

"And you'd had a dress ready? As a seamstress, that is understandable."

"Oh, no. I could never afford this dress on my own, not even the material. It's been lent to me; Lady Tolfee commissioned it for her daughter, who has been banished for some reason."

He nodded. "I've heard Lady Mary has fallen from her mother's favor."

"Something I hope not to do," I admitted. "And so I am here. The dress shall be returned to Lady Mary. No matter. I am not of this world."

The music stopped, and normally, we would have parted ways. I could not imagine that he had not filled up the cards of many young debs and perhaps a few dowagers. In fact, one beautiful woman was looking our way insistently. He turned so I would face her, and not he. She glared at me and then walked toward Lady Tolfee.

"Is everything so black and white to you, Miss Young?" The question was honestly, but not rudely, put. "Not of *this* world, definitely of *that*? Do you consider where you want to be, regardless of the world to which you believe you have been assigned?"

I was taken aback. "I suppose you're right," I said, thinking of my mother, thinking of myself. "It is not always so clear."

"Good, then we agree." He drew nearer to me than he would have had to, and whispered in my ear, which tingled as it received his welcome words and, just barely, his lips against the ridge of it. "Even in a borrowed gown, you are the most beautiful woman in this room. It's why all eyes are on you—not because you don't belong, but because you are compelling."

I blushed. "I do not know what to say." I did not. It was not often I was at a loss for words, but by his smile, this man seemed to relish that he had put me in such a position, though gently.

"Say you'll attend a fencing exhibition. Colmore Dunn and I are going to spar. You said your father enjoyed the sport. Surely he would approve."

Francis Collingsworth had invoked my father recently, too.

Lockwood turned me on the dance floor. We fit perfectly. I

allowed myself to melt into his arm. "He did," I agreed. "And he would."

"You seemed to enjoy our time together with Henry V," he continued. A tease crept across his face.

I would not let him win all. "I enjoyed watching you train actors, certainly," I said. I would not own to my relishing our exchange of lines.

He laughed. "I don't remember it quite that way, myself. He looked at me deeply; I willingly fell into the intimacy of it. "Always trying to keep the upper hand. You are a fencer, Miss Young, at heart. I should not like to spar with you." He put his index finger up and held it out like a sword. I put mine up, too, and crossed his, as though we were sparring. He smiled and curled his finger around mine possessively for a moment. I caught my breath.

"Someday, I truly shall test your recollections of *Henry V.*" He let my finger slip away. "I'll send round information on the exhibition so you may put it on your calendar."

"When the dates arrive, I shall see if I may fit it in," I said, allowing a little sparkle to my voice. "Thank you for thinking of me."

He bowed, the dance over, and drew near to me before moving toward his next dance partner and whispered once more, his lips close enough to read.

"I think of you constantly, Miss Young."

I danced with a few other men, and while I found the conversations engaging and the manners kind, I was not taken with any of them in the way I had been with Lord Lockwood. The conversations revolved around politics of the day and hunting; neither topic interested me. Lord Lockwood was never alone, each dance brought a new woman, clinging to him. I felt an unreasonable despair, for a moment. Then I thought of them as clinging beetles, and it raised my spirits somewhat.

I went to thank my hostess, but she was engaged with other guests. I left via the servants' entrance, hailing a hired carriage from the fleet of them that tarried nearby. The night was thick with the coal fog that hung like an unwelcome apparition and made for heavy breathing. I could just barely make out the outlines of a row of carriages waiting to return guests to their homes. The fourth in line pulled forward; odd, as the first would normally have pulled toward me.

I stepped toward the door; I could not make out the features of the driver until he came round to open it for me.

"You again?" Horrified, I could barely squeeze out the words.

CHAPTER EIGHTEEN

It was the same driver who had taken me to the police division hours earlier. There were hundreds, perhaps a thousand, hired carriages in London, too many for this kind of coincidence.

"Cheyne Gardens," I said.

"Yes, I know where you live," he said, grinning, and then closed the door behind me before I could hop out to safety. "But we're not going there."

A flush of fear coursed through me and I nearly cried in panic. Who was he? How did he know where I lived? How had he arranged to be my driver, twice?

Most important, where was he taking me now? I could not escape a carriage driving at this speed without hurting myself.

Lord, protect me. I do not know what to do.

He drove through the night like a madman, the carriage barely escaping hitting other carriages and, once or twice, a pedestrian. I wondered if I would die in a runaway carriage as Papa had died by a "runaway" cart. Had this man been the driver then, too?

I prayed that he would go too far and would catch the atten-

tion of a police officer, but that was not to be. He never stopped—
if he had, I should have risked all and jumped out.

I crossed my arms in front of my chest to tamp the panic, and
it worked. *I must keep my mind alert.* He drove out of the West
End, heading east, toward the City, where Lockwood had offices
for his investments, as did Mr. Pilchuck. We passed the Tower of
London; I, too, was very much a prisoner. The fog had settled all
around us again and I could not see where we were headed, but
east, yes. East. Toward Wapping and the London Docks? I had
heard of young women being kidnapped and shipped abroad. Was
this what he had planned?

The scent of the brackish river was a hint and I could hear the
creaking of large ships as they wavered in the water. The fog lifted,
as there was little coal smoke weighing it down.

Yes, the dock. He slowed now, knowing, I was certain, that I
dared not get out. I looked out of the carriage window and saw a
trio of men, coarse and drunk, who called out vulgar sentiments
when they glimpsed my face. I pulled back from the window.

The driver pulled up to a ship. "Care to visit a foreign port?"
He barked a laugh.

"Certainly not."

"It would be easy to arrange," he promised. "You'd be just as
much a treasure in the right hands as the ivory, spices, coffee, and
cocoa that come through."

I could see that it would be easy to arrange for my disappear-
ance now, or later. Unless I remained in my own home and never
took transport again it would be simple to kidnap me once more. I
could not remain cloistered and work—or live! To whom could I
turn? The police? I did not know who was trustworthy and who
was not any longer.

"Return me to my home," I insisted. Should I take a chance and step out of the carriage? I reached for the handle, and as I did, he chucked the horses and took off again. Slowly at first, so I could still hear him speak.

"I will, this time, missy. But don't be poking around new police divisions asking questions or making enquiries, or you shan't find me as forbearing. If you learn anything new, you know to whom you should deliver that information. Otherwise, leave well enough alone. The dead are dead. You do not want to join them nor end up in a distant port."

I held my breath all the way back to Cheyne Gardens, not really knowing if he would take me home or not. Finally, the carriage did stop in front of my house. I had not told him which house it was; I had not needed to.

He came round and opened my door, making a big display of bowing. "Be careful, Miss Young. London is not safe for an unprotected lady. Nor is the contented countryside of Hampshire."

"Who do you work for?"

"Myself," he answered slyly. "Doesn't everyone?"

Shaking, I walked up my front steps. I reached my key into the lock, half expecting it to be unlocked, but it was not.

I entered the hallway and walked into the sitting room. I noticed immediately that my mother's flower book—new to the environs— had been moved and that it was open, facedown, on the console.

Someone had been looking through it. Were they still here? I stood motionless, but heard nothing. Perhaps he, or they, were standing still as well. Had my kidnapper had a twofold purpose? To warn me off, and to keep me away whilst someone searched my home?

After some minutes, I quietly looked about.

The console drawers were ajar and I looked through them, quickly. Nothing had been removed.

I walked to Mrs. W's room and cracked the door open. Nothing seemed open or disturbed, so I closed the door behind me and moved on.

Heart in my throat, room by room, I found nothing was askew until I reached my bedroom. There, the books had been moved on my dresser and the drawers all opened. The cubbyhole was blessedly closed and its contents remained intact.

I smelt Turkish tobacco, which prickled my mind into attentiveness.

Whoever had come and likely gone had been looking for something—probably something I may have just returned home with from Hampshire. The timing was right, and I'd been home but a few days. Whoever searched knew that Mrs. W was not here and that I would be gone that night.

A horrifying thought crossed my mind and I nearly fainted in fear. The girls!

My legs jellied as I raced up the stairs. I knocked quietly on Ruby and Charlotte's door. Neither answered, so I quietly pushed it open to find them both peacefully asleep in their beds. I stared for a minute and thought I saw Ruby's eyes blink. Was she awake, and did not want me to know? Had she been looking out the windows as she'd admitted to doing?

No matter. Heaving with relief, I closed their door and knocked on Mother Martha's. After a moment, she called out a muffled, "Yes?"

"Are you all right?" I asked. "Is everything fine?"

"Quite all right, miss," she said. "Do you need my help?"

I wished she could help. I did not wish to scare her. "No, thank you," I said. "I shall see you tomorrow."

I walked downstairs and then all the way to the basement. The door to the Area was unlocked. I did not know if it had been pried, or if Louisa or Bidwell was in the habit of leaving it unlocked. I would remind them, on the morrow, to lock it. But neither would admit to having left it unlocked for fear of reprisal.

I worried that if I alerted anyone to another break-in, my staff might leave my service.

Mrs. W returned to us the following week, considerably cheered, and I was glad for her company; it made me feel safe. I had decided, for all of us, to leave well enough alone now, as Papa was gone and I had the girls and myself to think of. No more incidents had occurred, and I'd had the locks changed once more.

I kissed Mrs. W on both cheeks. "You need to visit the country more often," I said. "You're humming with life!"

"You shan't get rid of me," she said. "You need me. The visit did me more good than I could have imagined. The old goat has been buried for good, and has gone to the hot place he deserves."

I pursed my lips at her lively and entirely unexpected irreligious description.

As she put her things away, I busied myself in the sitting room, waiting to hear if she'd say that her things had been gone through. But she didn't, so I guessed that they hadn't.

"Constable Collingsworth is calling on me Sunday afternoon, after church, to take me to hear the music in the park," I told her. "Do you feel it's quite all right for me to attend with him, alone?"

Mrs. W nodded. "You'll be outside, and in a public place, so, yes. He'll pick you up and see you home?"

I nodded. So it was, Sunday afternoon, that Francis came to fetch me.

I wore a light summer bonnet and a cotton gown. One of my favorites, it was sprigged with roses and made me feel young and free.

"If you don't mind my saying, I am pleased and proud to accompany such a beautiful lady," Francis said as we left the house and started for Hyde Park, about a thirty minutes' walk right up Exhibition Road.

"Thank you, Constable Collingsworth," I said, happy to be with a man I felt comfortable with.

"That'll be Sergeant, now, Miss Young," he said, his face pinking with pride and pleasure.

"Well done!" I said. "I did not know."

"Father just told me," he said. "It changes things for me, more financial security, future and prospects stable." I knew what he was driving at. I had no answer for him.

The park was filled to the edges on the beautiful early-summer day. Some were on horses, some were in carriages pulled by horses, but most were like Francis and me, on foot.

A variety of bands played, including some string quartets, which I loved. Little birds pecked around the ground, plucking, plying, and pulling earthworms, but their songs were silenced. I understood. Who could compete with the beautiful music reverberating from all quarters? "It puts me in mind to dance!"

"I'll be glad to watch, but I don't dance," Francis said. He must have noticed my disappointment, because he next said, "But I do have an idea for fun. Come along!"

"All right."

He took me by the hand toward an artist who had set up an easel under a large spreading oak. "Oil portrait?" the artist asked, hopefully.

I looked wonderingly at Constable, no, Sergeant Collingsworth.

"Perhaps a sketch?" he asked. "Of the young lady." Francis pointed toward me.

"Oh, no," I said. "How about one of you?"

He smiled widely. "I'm delighted you would want one." He turned back to the artist. "One of each. I'll have one sketched of you that I shall keep, and one of me, for you!"

"I can't." I put my hand up in protest.

"I insist," he said more firmly than I had ever heard him speak before. It would not do to get into an argument in public, so I dipped my head in acquiescence.

The artist sketched us on little cards, quickly, and so accurately I could not believe it. Soon, he was finished and presented both cards to Francis with a flourish. I slipped mine into my linen pocket, which was empty but for the photograph. I should have brought some money, too, so I might have offered to pay for the sketches.

Francis reached inside his jacket pocket to remove some money to pay for it. I could see a stash of white, folded papers in there, too; it was a thick stack. He looked at me, flushed, and then quickly closed his jacket pocket.

After paying, he took the sketches and we began to walk home. "You saw the folded stack of papers in my jacket."

I nodded. No sense denying it. I would have made nothing of it if he hadn't flushed.

"I didn't want the day spoiled," he said. "But I meant to give these to you today, in any case." He opened his pocket again. A pipe almost dropped to the ground, but he caught it in time. "New." He winked. "A gift from Father upon my promotion."

Faintly, but presently, drifted the scent of the Turkish tobacco. I kept my eyes to the ground till I was certain I'd hidden my surprise. I would think upon that later. I looked up at Francis. He brought me to a bench just on the edge of Hyde Park.

"Father has finished looking into your father's case."

Papa was a case. I wanted to cry.

"The only thing remaining to return to you are these." He reached back into his pocket and pulled out a stash of certificates. I looked at them, one by one, and as I riffled through them, they emitted the distinctive odors of lemon pine oil and Papa's tobacco. I leaned in and sniffed them. They had been in his desk drawer recently enough to have retained the scent.

Francis looked at me oddly. "You're smelling them?"

I nodded. "They smell like my father's desk drawer. Where did they come from?" I asked. They looked to be mostly investment certificates, a hundred shares in this, a thousand in that.

Collingsworth pursed his lips. "I couldn't say. We're not the kind of people who invest in companies . . . simple coppers and all that."

I looked at him sharply, understanding the implication. "My father may have invested money my mother earned. How did you acquire these?"

He shrugged his shoulders. "Oh. Father found them when clearing out your father's case files." He reached back into his pocket. "Then, there's this."

He handed over a receipt, made to Papa. It was for . . . one thousand pounds? I inhaled sharply. That was a colossal sum. I could not ignore this. Where had it come from?

The risk, Gillian. The risk! The docks! Do not pry or enquire.

"Thank you." My voice quivered, and I knew Collingsworth heard it, too. "I shall return them to Father's desk drawer and then ask . . . shall ask Mr. Pilchuck, my father's solicitor, to look into all this when I see him."

Francis took my hand in his own. "I shan't say this but once more, Gillian." He used my Christian name, and not in the way he had as a child, but to a woman, a woman he may have been in love with. "I beg you to let this matter go. Father did not give me all the details, but he did share enough for me to know that your father was involved with trouble, fraud, and perhaps . . . women. High-placed people who have much to protect often have no scruples about so doing. Father has assured me there is solid, written evidence of wrongdoing somewhere, and I believe him."

"But Francis, there still are avenues to pursue, though granted, they have nearly come to an end. It's my father we're talking about. I can't let it go."

"Look at what happened to Roberts," he said softly.

I tilted my head. "Killed by vagrants?"

He unblinkingly stared to convey the truth that his lips would not. "That's what was said."

The docks. The girls. But . . . dearest Papa had spent his entire life helping others. Hadn't he?

"I understand. 'Killed by vagrants,' like a 'runaway cart.'" I reached for my linen pocket, into which I could tuck the certificates. As I tried to arrange them within, the newly sketched portrait of Francis and the photograph of the young woman I had pulled from Papa's secret cubbyhole spilled out onto the ground.

"Here, let me help." Francis bent down to pick up the fallen pictures, and as he did, he gasped and went white.

"What is it?" I asked.

He stared at the photograph but for a moment longer before handing it back to me. "Do you know her?" His voice was sharp and angry. "Do you?" he insisted.

How should I answer? Why would I be carrying a photograph of someone I did not know? I hoped I'd be forgiven a half-truth.

"No, I do not know her. I found her photograph while tidying my house and decided I'd sew a dress like this one. I carry it till I can sketch the idea. Do *you* know her?" I asked. He seemed flustered, and then turned to me, firmly, having recovered his police persona.

"I think it's best if I return you home," he said with firm finality, his eyes uncharacteristically angry and hard. "And no. I do not know who that young woman is."

But I thought that he did. I also knew he would admit it to no one.

CHAPTER NINETEEN

The next week, Mrs. Collingsworth's fancy fair was held.

"Here." I handed ten shillings to each girl. They stared at the coins as if they were golden eggs laid by a goose.

"Ten shillings?" Charlotte spoke first. Ruby just stared at them in her palm, her eyes round.

"Earrings . . . ," she whispered almost to herself. "With little drop jewels and clasps that will screw into my earlobes."

"A lovely idea," I agreed. It was a lot of money, I knew, but they had been working very hard, and we had many late nights, poked fingers, and strained eyes ahead of us.

"Buy something for yourself, and you'll also do a bit of good for the charity," I said. "All of the money from selling the fancies will go toward the underserved." Mrs. Collingsworth had told me that the proceeds were to benefit The Guild of the Poor Brave Things—children who had been crippled.

"Just think," Ruby said. "Only a few months ago, we were the underserved. Now we're not, miss, due to you."

Charlotte spoke up. "Our fairy godmother." The girls twittered, and I could not have been more pleased.

We walked to the hall, which had been let for the occasion. The hall had once been an infirmary, first for the war wounded, then for women who had lost their sanity. Perhaps because I had so much death and uncertainty in my life, I felt that I could sense the lost souls and harried spirits of those who had died here.

Come, now, Gillian. Get ahold of yourself. Fancies about souls and spirits, indeed. I did not want morose thoughts infiltrating my sunny feelings this day, a pleasant interlude. And yet, I could not shake free from a sense of impending doom. It clung to me, tightly about the neck, covering me in full, like an unwelcome wool shawl on a hot day, which that day most certainly was. After my wild dockside ride and Francis's odd reaction, who would have blamed me?

The booths were mostly staffed with young women, and therefore, there were plenty of young men hanging about. Bazaars were often safe places for young men and women to flirt.

I watched as some young gentlemen bought fancies—handkerchiefs and beaded bracelets and such—and then handed them right back to the girls staffing the booths, as gifts.

Charlotte was drawn to the booth that sold silk slippers. "Miss Young, if I bought many of these, I could sew beautiful designs on them and then sell them next year, for a price, which may help the others."

I drew her close to me in a side embrace. "That is a lovely thought, Charlotte. If you wish to do that, you may. Be sure to find something you fancy for yourself, though," I said.

Ruby and I walked toward the end of the hall where Mrs. Collingsworth directed.

"Miss Young!" She clasped my hands in her own and as she did, I noticed a faint tremor. "I am so grateful you made time to attend."

"I shouldn't have missed it for anything, Mrs. Collingsworth. The hall is simply lovely." She had seen to it that it was garlanded in lace and greenery, and the booths had been draped with pretty white linens. A small band played quietly from the garden in the back.

"My dear. Perhaps you could donate next year? I know it's a busy Season for you, sewing for the society matrons and all. Something little, perhaps."

I smiled. "I should be delighted. My apprentice Charlotte may even be able to embroider some slippers."

Mrs. Collingsworth smiled. "I'd best be off and tend to the till. Do say you'll come by for dinner again soon? Inspector Collingsworth and I adore having you around." She grinned slyly. "Francis does, too. But that goes without saying."

I muttered a polite thank-you, and she left.

"Ruby," I began as I turned around. But Ruby had wandered away. I looked through the hall. I caught the eye of Inspector Collingsworth, and he tipped a hat to me and smiled broadly. I ducked my head just a little and smiled back. A spontaneous wave of fear rolled through me.

Was Francis here as well? I had not heard from him since our day in the park.

I walked to the garden area and found Ruby deep in conversation with a young man. I recognized him as the one who had followed her home from the Theatrical Mission weeks ago and given her a posy.

"What I want isn't for sale here," he said, his voice sliding into a leer.

"What would that be?" Ruby asked. She clearly enjoyed flirting with this young man, who looked to be about eighteen years old, but she could not have had any idea what he might be after.

"I'd start with a lock of your hair," he said.

"Will you donate the money to the poor?" she asked.

"Of course I would," he said. She laughed. I'd had enough.

Was this an innocent flirtation? Someone from among the men Mother Rachel had mentioned? Or, more ominously, someone sent to lure Ruby to King Street as had been threatened?

"Ruby." I came up behind her. She jumped, nearly spilling the lemon ice I suspected she had not purchased for herself. As I did, Mother Martha appeared from behind me. She, too, must have spied what had been about to transpire.

"Might I have a word with you?" I asked my young charge.

Ruby nodded, reluctantly, not wanting to be seen as a child in front of the young man. I remembered that feeling, too. But this man meant her no good, I felt, and apparently Mother Martha agreed.

"I'll see to him!" Mother Martha marched after the young man, forcing him to hurry ahead of her. She followed him out toward the street and closed that gate behind them.

I led Ruby to a bench. "You mustn't speak with him again. How did he even know you'd be here?"

She shrugged, sullen. "I suppose he followed us here," she finally said.

"Have you spoken with him again, since he gave you the posy?" She nodded. "But only through the window."

I took her hands in mine, but she abruptly withdrew them.

"I'm sorry," I said. "I did not mean to treat you as a child."

She softened. "It's all right, miss. He said I am beautiful."

"And you are," I said. "But he means you no good. I understand men like that. He will say what he needs to in order to get you to do what he likes. He likely does not have connections with fine houses that you could . . . be a maid in. Those kind of boys work for men who would rather have you work in a very bad manner."

She turned to me. "How do you know that? He said he'd already placed our friend Bridget in just such a house, and she's going to live in France, miss. France! Maybe he knows the truth, and you do not."

I spied Inspector Collingsworth walking toward me.

I turned back to Ruby. "I know I am right and he's wrong because my father was a copper, that's why." *Who was, I hoped, doing good when he died. I could hardly tell her the rest.*

She seemed to accept that. "Maybe. Still. I'm going to ask Mother Rachel about Bridget."

"It's hard, I know," I continued. "None of us wants to see the truth of what is right in front of us, do they? But for our protection, we must not sugar-coat the truth. We must have the courage to see people for what they are."

"Do you do that, miss? *Always?* Even if it's about something you really, really want? Like visiting Paris?"

I couldn't tell if she was asking or challenging. "I try to, always," I said. "I think that's the best we can do. I try to seek the truth, even if it's not something I wish, initially, to know the truth about. I hold you in great affection, Ruby, and want only the best for you. But if there is some other situation you should prefer to pursue, I cannot stop you, nor would I. You have a will of your own."

She nodded. "I know, miss. I appreciate all you've done for me. I'd like to stay with you, at least for now." She leaned into me for an embrace, and I melted into it. We began to make our way through the hall again and saw Inspector Collingsworth laughing, his teeth glistening like a fox's.

"I don't like him, miss," Ruby whispered to me as we left.

I didn't like him anymore, either.

CHAPTER TWENTY

It was like Christmas, except that it was June. The first batch of materials for the *Cinderella* gowns arrived. First, the plain fabrics. Well, plain for theater. I made sure everyone washed her hands and then we unrolled bolt after bolt. There was a simple blue cotton, and then a red, for Cinderella's maid costume, with a bolt of bright white for her apron. I had just the hat in mind and would ask Sarah if she could come up with something bright and beautiful that could be seen from the farthest reaches of the theater.

A few days later, Cinderella's ball gown material arrived. I had planned for an ivory dress with beautiful gold brocade. Mother Martha would stitch gold beads all over it. It would be bridal and beautiful, as was befitting Cinderella.

The slippers came, too, white silk. "Charlotte, would you like to embroider these?"

"Oh, yes, miss. I can hardly believe you would trust me with that."

I told her I would use a pencil to draw very lightly the design on the slippers once she had practiced the design on a sampler and showed it to me. Mother Martha was already sorting through and sighing over the gold and pearl beads.

Ruby stood by, expectantly. "And me, miss?"

I swallowed. I thought. I prayed. "Could you help me with the fabric for Lady Tolfee's gown for the Silver and Gold Ball? It's a very important project. I have an idea for fabric dipping, and you're awfully good at that."

She grinned. "Sure I can. What will it be?"

"I'll call upon her tomorrow to be certain, but I have an idea. Then, my girl, I shall let you know. Our fingers will have to fly— the dress will be due in two weeks! Till then, please organize our cupboards and cabinets."

An hour later, we reacted with shock when a new young lady suddenly appeared in the salon. "What? Do you not recognize me?"

"Ruby!" Charlotte burst out. She had made a new wig out of the stray pieces I'd brought from Drury Lane and then changed her gown.

"It's almost like magic!" I said.

Ruby beamed, delighted, I knew, to have discovered a talent of her own. "Mother Martha remembered a few things I'd done in pantomime and suggested I might have a talent with the hair pieces and, well, I guess she was right!"

Right indeed. I should think upon this after we were finished sewing *Cinderella*.

I'd thought all of the fabric had arrived but soon came another delivery. It was addressed to me, no return address, but arrived with a note saying it was for me, personally.

Oh, Wilhelm. All was forgiven, and his long years in theater costume, and as my mother's friend, helped him to know exactly what would please me.

The fabric was a light-silver silk that caught and reflected the light upon every fold. It had been overstitched with lilies. "Whatever should I use this for?" I asked Mrs. W, who had taken the delivery. "I don't know that I shall ever be invited to an event which would require fabric as grand as this."

It was almost as beautiful as the fabric for Cinderella's ball gown, which had cost Mr. Harris, the theater manager, a fortune.

"Come," Mrs. W said. "Let's have tea."

Louisa brought tea to us in the drawing room. The tea was lukewarm, which did not meet with Mrs. W's approval, but did with mine, as the day was insufferably warm. The girls had propped open the windows upstairs—at my bidding. The young man had not returned after Mother Martha's stern rebuke.

"The lilies on the fabric . . . ," I said. "They put me in mind of something." I spied my mother's pressed flower book on the console. "Ah, yes! Mamma's book. How did you meet Mamma?"

"We lived near one another in Hampshire, of course, and although we were not of the same social set, I had met her a time or two at charity events. I was already deeply devoted to the Cause and had reason to mention it to her. Later, when she was in London, we met again at an event in the East End, for the ministry; in the early days, the meetings and speeches were primarily held in unused theaters and she was around the theaters often. From then on, we were friends."

Mrs. W smiled and continued. "Sometimes, when she needed to flee the city for a time, we would take the train to the country for the fresh air it provided, even visiting Winton Park a time or two, though your grandfather would not see her. I well remember searching for field flowers with her and then pressing them. We had a wooden press, and we'd screw the plates together as firmly as we could, right in the field, to keep them fresh. Next day, we'd place them in our books and make notes before returning to London, leaving the book at Winton for the next time."

I opened the book and spied a simple flower. "Daisies?"

Mrs. W smiled. "Oh yes. Victoria would not see a flower go unrecognized for its commonality or a lowly position. At first, in our book, she put it ahead of the rose. I switched it later, though, just because it seemed proper that the wild flower should come after the cultivated."

I touched the daisy, pressed into the page, knowing my mother's hand had touched it, too.

Mamma and I sat on the lawn at Winton. I turned my new patent leather shoes this way and that so they would catch the sun. Mamma had not wanted to be inside, where Grandfather had begun a new argument. Maybe I could cheer her.

I picked a daisy. "Let's play He Loves Me, He Loves Me Not, Mamma."

She laughed at me and plucked a daisy for me from the ground. It was small and delicate. "In French, the game is called Effeuiller la Marguerite, or 'Pluck the Daisy.'"

"Oh! That sounds painful," I said.

"So let's not pluck them," she answered. "We'll count instead." She touched the petals one by one. "He loves me, he loves me, he loves me, he loves me."

I swatted at her. "Mamma! That is not how you play the game. Even I know that."

"Do not marry a man if you are not sure he loves you for your-self alone, dearest little daisy," she said. "Never a man about whom you even think, for a moment, he loves me not."

"I miss her." I brushed away a tear.

"So do I," Mrs. W said. Her eyes welled.

I turned the page of the flower book and noticed that Mrs. W had written next to the rose; it had been her flower selection.

"That was how our friendship worked. Victoria was flighty and spontaneous, impulsive and sometimes slack with the details but always decisive. I was there to help her see those good intentions through."

"And so you came to live with us?" Hadn't she ever wanted to marry? I dared not ask for hurting her and breaching protocol, which she would most certainly rebuke me for, though gently.

"I did," she said. "When my position as a companion ended upon the death of the elderly woman I looked after, I came to your home and took care of the household events and also her correspondence, responding to the many admirers who would write after seeing her perform. I took care of the duties she would mean to tend to and your father kept me on after she died, at her insistence, I am sure, as she knew I had nowhere to go. She was extremely generous."

I wondered why she could not have gone to her sister's, but did not ask, lest she think I regretted having her live with us.

I turned the page and found the pressed lilies; Mrs. W had written some notes here, too, and a reference to Scripture.

"I wish I had a generous heart like Mamma's," I said.

"You do," Mrs. W said. "There *is* something you could do if you like. Perhaps it is a holy suggestion, brought about by the discussion of lilies and"—she pointed to the page—"the Scripture."

I tilted my head. "What is that?"

She began to quote Saint Matthew. "And why take ye thought for raiment? Consider the lilies of the field, how they grow; they toil not, neither do they spin: And yet I say unto you, That even Solomon in all his glory was not arrayed like one of these. Wherefore, if God so clothe the grass of the field, which today is, and tomorrow is cast into the oven, shall he not much more clothe you, O ye of little faith?"

I looked at the beautiful silver lily fabric that had just been delivered. "But seek ye first the kingdom of God, and His righteousness; and all these things shall be added unto you."

She nodded. "You could sell the fabric—to Lady Tolfee, for example. And give the proceeds to the poor, if you like."

Blessed are the poor in spirit, for theirs is the kingdom of heaven. It was written above the door of the Theatrical Mission. I cast my eyes down. What if I *didn't* like to give it away? I, who toiled in those fields all day every day for other women, purposeful women, women with unlimited purses, had never owned such a beautiful piece of fabric for myself.

"I only suggest it because you said you wished you had a heart like hers."

I had said that. But I did not want to sell the fabric.

"It is quite possibly the right thing to do," she repeated before sipping her tea. She was subtly pressuring me again. When I was a girl she'd forcibly pried pennies from my little hands to give away to the poor. She'd insisted I read my Scriptures before I read my novels. I would have given my pence and read my Scriptures first anyway but because she forced me, the pleasure, the meaning, was stolen. It became her compulsion and not my spirit that had given.

And yet, though my heart was heavy, I suspected she was correct. "You're right," I said. "I won't even need to ask her. She'd covet this material upon first sight." I carried the material upstairs and began cutting the design I'd already had in mind. At bedtime, I heard the girls giggling in their room, and that cheered me. I would give the proceeds to the Theatrical Mission.

I thought about the gowns I'd been designing, and about Cinderella—maid to princess, toiler turned beloved. Would it ever be my turn? I rubbed cream onto my raw hands and slipped my sleeping gloves on them, hoping they, and I, would not be red and angry in the morn.

The following Monday I asked Louisa if she could bring lunch upstairs for us so we would not have to slow down. It was full steam ahead if we were to finish Lady Tolfee's dress by the Silver and Gold Ball.

"Yes, Miss Young. I can bring up some egg sandwiches for you and the girls. A letter came for you, too."

"Mrs. W usually handles the post," I said, wondering why Louisa had this time.

"'Twas not by post," she replied.

Louisa handed an envelope to me; my name was not handwritten but had somehow been crudely typeset.

A feather of fear waved through me. Through the lightweight white envelope, I could see a page that had been mostly blacked out.

"Thank you, Louisa; that will be all." I smiled weakly and waved her away. My fingers trembled as I opened it. Another page of the Gospel of St. Matthew, torn from the Bible and mostly blacked out. What kind of brute desecrated Scripture?

"But whosoever hath not, from him shall be taken away even that he hath."

CHAPTER TWENTY-ONE

JULY, 1883

Mother Martha placed Lady Tolfee's new white gloves with silver beading on top of the gown I had in my leather garment transport bag. I was always hesitant when taking a hired carriage, but I could not bring the gowns to Tolfee House on foot. Lady Tolfee waited for me in her dressing room. Like a magician pulling a rabbit from a cap, I withdrew the beautiful silver gown from my bag.

"Oh, goodness gracious . . ." Lady Tolfee fingered it as though it was a treasure, a work of art. "Wherever did you come upon this, Miss Young?"

"I knew it would suit you perfectly," I answered. "And as it's silver, and the ball is Silver and Gold, it must have been meant for you."

My heart hurt like a medallion pressing too firmly against the base of my ribcage. I wished I'd kept the fabric.

Her lady's maid helped her into it and then I took in a tiny tuck or two, so it fit her perfectly.

"It's beautiful, dear." I showed her the invoice; I'd added 15 percent, as all the proceeds were going to charity. She barely blinked. "Have it delivered to my husband's man."

I would. With all speed.

"How comes Winton Park?" she asked as her lady's maid finished her hair.

"In need of some maintenance, but the lady is as grand as ever," I said. "I'm proud."

"As you should be," she said. "Listen, dear, Mary and I have reconciled ourselves, but as you've no mother, heaven rest her, I feel I should take you under wing a little. Lord Tolfee and I are holding one more ball this season . . ."

"The Twin Ball," I said. I'd known already, of course, and had been planning for it.

"Yes." She looked at me through her reflection in the mirror. "I'd like you to come. You might meet someone . . . you never know."

I've already met two someones, I wanted to tell her. Of course, she would only find one of them suitable—Francis. In the manner of things, Lady Tolfee would most probably feel a viscount was beyond my current station.

"I couldn't, really," I said.

"But I insist!" she said. "Just this once. Now, what kind of design had you in mind? I've just been telling Lady Amberley how boring and unimaginative it is to purchase gowns from Worth like everyone else. I'd much prefer you. I trust your designing eye implicitly."

"Oh, thank you!" I said. To be compared to the House of Worth, in any way, by a lady of her stature. It was unbelievable. "I thought you may like to go as Fire and Ice?" The Twin Ball was a favorite of each Season; costumes were designed so that half exhibited one thing, and the other half its opposite. "I could dip the fabric ombré, so the flames will seem to climb, and the ice descend, melting as it gets closer to the fire."

"Yes, dear, perfect. Plan to come early and bring your costume, too. If need be, I shall add to your stipend so you may have the resources available."

After having sewn for her for so many years, I knew her measurements perfectly, allowing her to forgo many fittings. She turned from me and I said nothing more. I had no intention of attending another ball, and even if I had decided to attend I most certainly would not expect her to pay for my gown. Now, what I decided to charge her for the Fire and Ice gown, that would be another matter. Mr. Worth's creations were very dear indeed. Perhaps I should raise my fees, and take on another apprentice, or even a full-fledged seamstress!

Lady Tolfee went to meet her husband and greet her guests. After tidying up, I took my bags and descended the servants' stairway. There was music in the ballroom, already. I stood by one of the false serving doors that staff used to deliver champagne, wine, and water. There was a window, partially obscured and hidden by design from the ballroom, by which servers may keep an eye on the festivities in case one were needed. I stood there for a moment; no one could see me from the ballroom, and I was ignored from the inside, as I was not truly staff and they had other duties to attend to.

The room was already half filled. I willed myself to have some self-control, to not scan the room looking for one man, one particular man alone.

But I did. I relented, overcome by the desire to see him. I spied him laughing with a young woman, sharing *that smile* with her and her alone. She was a deb, surely, and not a dowager, a deb with a dowry, no doubt, and property, perhaps. A short time later, he led her to the dance floor, and I watched them then, too.

Yes, I was very much like Cinderella, with my mop and rags, watching from the outside. I was more like my girls than I cared to think. I did not belong in this world, but behind stairs. And sometimes I did not belong there.

The dance ended and I swore that Lockwood turned and looked directly at me. I did not turn away because I did not think that he could see through the glass that was lightly tinted on the outside to match the wallpaper.

His words, the last time we were at a ball together, challenged me.

Is everything so black and white to you, Miss Young? Not of this *world, definitely of* that? *Do you consider where you want to be, re-gardless of the world to which you believe you have been assigned?*

He turned toward Lady Tolfee, so beautiful in her silver gown with her silver hair, and walked briskly toward her. He seemed to be asking her a question with intent. *Could he be asking about me? Oh, Gillian, truly. You are likely not in his mind.*

I think of you constantly, Miss Young, he'd said. Had he been telling the truth?

He walked away, looking angry. Angry? I wondered why.

I took my bag and finished walking outside to the hired carriages. I'd decided two things.

I would stop, right now, at the Theatrical Mission and tell Mother Rachel that I would be making a very large donation within the month when Lady Tolfee's invoice was paid.

And I would attend the Twin Ball. As Cinderella, my two costume halves would be Princess and Maid.

I walked to the street to hail a carriage. There was a line of them, and the third from the back came forward. I held my breath.

Why the third?

Every time I got into a carriage now, I hesitated just a little. In fact, I refused to get into one until I saw the face of the driver. He did not come out to let me in. I held my breath and walked round to the front of the carriage. "Hello?" I asked.

"Oh, sorry, miss." It was not the man who'd stalked me; I exhaled and he came to help me in. I should let go of my fears. It was never the man who had stalked me anymore; perhaps those who had pursued me had realized that I had nothing left to investigate as far as Papa was concerned and had left me be after searching my home.

That made me both happy—I felt safe—and sad. I could not reclaim his reputation and he'd been murdered. Who but I was left to right what was wrong?

"Please tarry," I asked the driver as he pulled up to the Mission. "I'll be but ten minutes and then I would like you to take me to Cheyne Gardens, please."

He agreed, and I made my way up the stairs. Mother Rachel had just finished serving soup, and the house was quiet.

"I hope I'm not interrupting," I said. "I could come back . . ."

"No, dear, that's fine," she said. "It's late."

I nodded. "It is, and I shan't stay. But I have good news, and I wanted to share it right away. I've received a commission—one which paid very handsomely, but for which I had little cost. I want to donate it all to you."

When I told her the amount, she started crying and pulled her stained apron up to her face. Then I started crying, and suddenly I did not care at all about the silver gown.

"It's too much, my dear. You've already taken on Ruby and Charlotte. I can help many more with that amount. Where would you like it spent?"

I thought. "As you wish, except . . . for the purchase of a treadle machine. To help one more girl. To prepare one more for a productive, and safe, life."

"It shall be as you say," she said. She walked me back to the door; I could see the carriage waiting.

I had just gone through to the steps when I turned. "Oh. The girls were asking about a friend of theirs . . . a Bridget?"

Her face grew sad. "She's gone. To France, with some men . . . a pretty little thing."

She did not need to say any more.

The day was hot and as I buckled myself into my many layers, I wished, just once, for the simplicity of the clothing I'd worn as a child. Everything had been simpler then, but I was no longer a child.

Lord Lockwood and his friend Colmore Dunn and Colmore Dunn's wife were to arrive shortly and then we'd be off to the fencing exhibition.

"You're sure you'll be fine, then?" Mrs. W asked as she pottered about the parlor.

"Of course. I trust Lord Lockwood implicitly." An uninvited waver crossed through my voice. Mrs. W, so sharply attuned, caught my eye. "And Mrs. Colmore Dunn will attend with us as well," I said.

She nodded. I had not yet told her I planned to attend a second society ball.

When the carriage arrived, I could hear laughter from inside it through my open window, and I smiled. An outing would be pleasant. The city was not as crowded, now that Parliament would close within a month or so and the Season was beginning to wind down.

Lord Lockwood arrived on my doorstep. I let Bidwell open the door. It would not do to show my enthusiasm by opening it myself!

I took my parasol, very glad indeed that Sarah had insisted I buy a new summer hat of light blue that set off my hair and my eyes, and we were off.

"I'm truly enthused that you're attending." Lockwood led me protectively as we walked from my door to the carriage. "The exhibition hall will be crowded; we hope to encourage those who might consider the sport for future Olympic events."

"I'll be there to cheer you on," I said, and was rewarded with a large, spontaneous smile. His face warmed and his eyes crinkled at the corners and then softened again, bringing out those small freckles. I had a momentary impulse to reach up and touch them, but did not.

"I thought fencing, and duels, were only for women and war?"

He laughed aloud. "Is there anything else that matters? No, Miss Young. Fencing is for honor, justice, and faith. Those three values mean the most to me, and I could not live a life without them." Lockwood opened the carriage door and introduced me to his friends.

Mrs. Colmore Dunn was pleasant and progressive, and I very much enjoyed her conversation. "Please, call me Matilda," she said. "And your Christian name is . . . ?"

"Gillian," I answered.

"I hear you work," she said. I flinched, wondering if a barrage of some sort was about to erupt from her forthright self. "Good. I am a novelist, and in my spare time, I work for women's suffrage. Perhaps you'd like to join me in some volunteer campaigning?"

I thought that was an idea I would very much like to consider, but she continued without giving me space to say much and I was happy to listen. Her husband seemed polite enough, but said very little. He looked at me, oddly, once or twice. The first time I passed it off to his wondering about me. Had Lord Lockwood often brought ladies to view their exhibitions? Perhaps not and Colmore Dunn found me a novelty.

The second time he stared at me I looked at him wonderingly. He smiled and looked away. There had been something there, though. I knew it.

The journey from Cheyne Gardens to Islington took a pleasant hour. Lockwood made good conversation when Mrs. Colmore Dunn did not interrupt him and smiled at me from time to time, but we had little to say. I think he had nerves ahead of the exhibition. He certainly fidgeted now and again, and I hadn't seen him do that before.

We arrived at a large country home with a brick exhibition hall on the side grounds. "They are great fencing enthusiasts, and had the building converted from an outbuilding," Colmore Dunn told me.

The grounds were beautifully kept. *I could re-create this sort of garden at Winton,* I thought. Fountains and a Roman garden, walking paths strewn with crushed rock specifically formulated— perhaps even dusted—to catch the sunlight.

"What a lovely green!" I pointed at the beautiful lawn between the house and the exhibition building. "Perfect for bowls."

"Do you enjoy lawn bowls?" Lockwood asked.

I nodded. "I do. But as you can imagine, there is no space for it in London, and my grandfather did not want us bowling on the green at Winton Park during the occasional summer visit. He did not want the grass torn up." What he might say about the current state of disrepair of Winton's lawns, I couldn't tell. Perhaps, if I kept the house, I could repair the lawns and let my children enjoy a game and even a somersault on the green softness.

We alighted and the carriage pulled away. The men went to put their fencing costumes on while Mrs. Colmore Dunn took me in hand and led me to the viewing area.

The first group of fencers came out, and I watched politely, trying to understand what the movements were, and while I can't say I understood much, I did see the intensity, the skill, the valor, and the manliness that poured into each exchange.

The third pair to duel was Lockwood and Colmore Dunn. I should not have recognized them if Matilda hadn't told me. "You'll notice they each wear an iron fencing mask fronted with tight wire—it's up to each man to inspect his to ensure there are not spaces for a blade to slip through."

"Goodness gracious! It would be easy to be maimed," I said.

She nodded. "If they're not paying attention. A stout leather jacket covers them from neck to waist, and below that a protective apron is draped," she said. "Underneath it all, Lockwood wears a plastron, though most men do not unless they are teaching. Afterward, you must ask him about it." She smiled wryly.

A plastron? That was a decorative part of many bodices. I'd had Mother Martha repair the beads on one of mine. I did not know men wore such things.

They stood facing one another, tips of swords touching, and then Lockwood made a move, wrenching his tip away, and made to thrust it toward his friend and barrister. I wondered if his legal fees would go up if he beat him! Back and forth they sparred, and Lockwood tapped his friend on the wrist, indicating that he could have cut him if he'd wanted to. Colmore Dunn backed away a little, and Lockwood opened his arms wide as if to say, *Come and get me.*

Colmore Dunn did. He moved forward in advance but then feinted and switched tactics, taking Lockwood by surprise. He touched him on the neck, indicating that he could have killed him there. Lockwood backed away, seeming to regroup and think through his strategy. Within seconds, he seemed to have found one.

He backed around and made as if he were moving left, but moved right, and Colmore Dunn did not move quickly enough. Lockwood placed the tip of his sword in the middle of his opponent's chest.

"Touché!" Colmore Dunn called out, indicating that he'd been touched, would have been killed, and relinquished to his opponent.

The crowd clapped wildly, I among them.

It was thrilling. He was thrilling. I was breathless.

After the other pairs had performed, the men came to speak with us, still in their fencing leathers, which made them seem even more masculine than did their everyday attire.

"Bravo!" I said as Lockwood approached me. The Colmore Dunns wandered off to speak with other friends. "I am suitably impressed."

He grinned. "I'm so glad you watched. In days past, the victor could demand a favor from his lady. A ribbon or something to tie to his sword."

His lady. My heart pounded.

"You shall have to ask her, then," I said. "When you see her next."

He burst out laughing. "You delight me, Miss Young."

I felt quite elated from emotion and while it was not unwelcome, I was aware that we were in public and in no way formally connected to one another. I changed the subject. "Matilda has said I should ask you about your plastron?" I hoped I was not stepping into some jest.

He sat down on the bench near me and unbuttoned his jacket. I was bewildered and my heart raced, involuntarily. What was he doing? He saw my discomfort and smiled, taking what seemed to be an ironic pleasure in it.

Once the jacket was undone, he spoke and pointed to the thick padding beneath it. Right over his heart was . . . a heart. Stamped in red. "The plastron is to protect the heart, Miss Young. You see, it protects my heart from getting pierced."

It was a tender, revealing sentiment. "A woman would find that useful as well." I was certainly not going to introduce the word *bodice* into the conversation. "I find I might have need of that very thing."

He took my hand in his for a moment and kissed the back of it. "Each and every one of us does." Then he buttoned up his jacket. "As you have no ribbon to award me, I shall ask a different indulgence."

Was he speaking of blue ribbons, such as one awarded a winner, or the favor a man might ask of *his lady*?

"What would that be?" I asked.

"Come with me, and my brother and his wife, to see *Henry V*. The performance will be followed by a benefit dinner at my club, and I know Jamie and Lisbeth will see you are a civilizing influence upon me. Say yes, Miss Young. Please."

I said yes. Perhaps I shouldn't have. But I did, and it made me happy to have done so. It would have been the perfect ending to a perfect day if only he hadn't enquired about my plans for Winton on the way back to London.

CHAPTER TWENTY-TWO

JULY, 1883

I sat with the girls, sewing, contented to be in their company on that hot summer's day. We were nearing the end of the sewing for the Twin Ball, and the costume they were most excited about, of course, was mine, especially when I'd explained to them that we'd give Cinderella a test run and practice some stitches on my Twin Ball gown. I told them how proud I was of them, and I was.

"We want your dress to be the most beautiful one," Charlotte said.

Mother Martha had been reading from *Little Women*; then she switched, of a sudden, to Scripture. I had not seen her do that before, but the girls did not seem troubled. She opened it up straightaway to a passage and read aloud:

"He that diligently seeketh good procureth favour: but he that seeketh mischief, it shall come unto him."

And then she closed the Bible without comment. What had she meant? Or had her mind simply gone? She was getting older, after all.

"Mother Martha, would you like to rest awhile? The beading is nearly done," I said.

"Oh, no, dear. I am fine," she responded.

The first part of the Scripture passage gave me pause for thought. Winton, which I had for many years thought to look forward to living in, was becoming a burden of its own. I had no idea if Lord Lockwood had any interest in me outside of the property itself, either as a sale or, in my more fanciful daydreams, a dowry. Inspector Collingsworth and even Francis had seemed unhealthily interested in it. Perhaps they knew it would all come to Francis, too, should we marry.

Of greatest importance were Mamma's expressly stated wishes.

I'd memorized the letter's passage. *The house is too big for one person, in truth. It is not necessary or even godly for anyone to have a home this size and no good has come of it. Knowing that, it is my intention to immediately donate the house to the Cause if and when it becomes mine.*

What exactly had she known in order to know with certainty that no good could come of it? More than I, likely. Had it been cursed somehow? Did it hold horrible memories she had not shared? And I did want to be godly, as my mother had seen it, after all.

I thought of Francis, so earnest, and yet there was nothing that pulled me to him. What pulled him to me? Tradition and expectation? His father? Winton?

And then, Lord Lockwood. I was pulled to him, as they say, as the Tideway to the Thames. And yet, as Mamma had said, *Do not marry a man if you are not sure he loves you for yourself alone, dearest little daisy. Never a man about whom you even think, for a moment, he loves me not.*

I am your dearest little daisy, Mamma, I thought. *I wish you were here, and then all of this would make sense and be put right.*

But she was not, so I had to make my way through alone.

I looked at Ruby, who did not wear a wig on this hot day, her short hair pulled back in an adorable queue. And at Charlotte, who never put a stitch wrong. There were others in this difficult world who also needed my help.

I admired Matilda, writing her novels and working for the vote for women. She had not inherited wealth or a grand home or any of that, and she was happy making her own way. She'd complimented me on my profession. Lady Tolfee had compared me to Mr. Worth, for goodness' sake. I did not need to inherit a life, either.

And yet, I truly loved Winton. It had been Mamma's. I could make it the warm place she and I had always wanted it to be, full of love and giggles and not strife and struggles. But Mamma had clearly other plans for the house. I would honor them.

After months of consideration, I was now resolute. Before I could change my mind I marched downstairs. "Mrs. W?" I called into the sitting room.

"Yes, dear?" She set her reading down on her lap and took off her spectacles.

I walked in but did not sit down. "I have not discussed this with you before, but . . . I have spent a considerable time thinking about this, and as the trust has now placed the property in my name, I have decided to donate Winton Park to the Cause."

Her book clattered to the floor. "In truth? In faith!"

I nodded firmly. "I am sure. Please write a note to the head-quarters, East End, and tell them I shall come and sign the appropriate papers soon if it suits them."

Her eyes welled with tears and she hugged me . . . a first. "I shall do exactly that; Victoria would certainly have approved."

. . .

Mrs. W accompanied me to the East End, of course. I rarely visited anymore. I knew my mother had caught typhus working among the poor there and I'd had a little phobia about catching it myself. Mrs. W, apparently of sterner stock, was rarely ill and worked among the poor every week.

The streets stank of gin and rubbish stewing in the summer sun. There were mothers walking with their children, trying to keep them clean, tidy, and orderly in a very disordered situation. I admired their determination. Many of the women who found themselves in East End brothels had been actresses or had been pushed aside by their parents, or misled into a life of vulgar servitude. I pitied them. But for circumstance, it could have been my Ruby, my Charlotte. My mother.

Me.

When we arrived, Mrs. W was treated like a sister, a mother, almost a celebrity. She was as much the star in this arena as my mother had been on the stage. The building in which the office was located was actually a large hall, mostly used for Sunday and Wednesday meetings. There were also a few dormitories for women to shelter themselves for a time and a kitchen and dining room, with rough wood tables stretching end to end. I remembered running around them as a girl, with the children the Cause served. I went upstairs to meet the Director while Mrs. W fussed with her friends downstairs.

The Director, a godly man whom I had first met as a thirteen-year-old girl the year before my mother had died, spoke kindly to me. I explained the situation: my mother had left instructions for Winton Park to be donated.

"Are you certain this is what you'd like to do, Miss Young?"

Less to tend to, less to fear losing, I supposed. After swallowing hard and blinking back tears, I nodded. "It's what my mother wanted." He said nothing, waiting for me to continue. "It's what I want, too," I said. "I'm very given to the work you're doing with the Theatrical Mission on King Street. It has become very dear to me, and I wish to see its work continue." He'd been waiting to hear that.

"Do you want us to attach any restrictions to the property?"

I thought of Lady Lockwood and her fear of unsuitables moving in, and smiled.

"No, there are no restrictions. You may use the property however you feel it may be put to best service for the Cause. Except, whatever arrangements you may make, I would like Davidson, our estate manager, generously pensioned from the proceeds. My mother would have wanted that." I grinned. Who would now spy for Lady Lockwood?

"Yes, Miss Young. I shall see to that myself. I will also ensure there is plenty of time for you to reclaim whatever sentimental objects you may wish to keep. We'll be in contact about that."

I signed the documents and the transaction was complete.

I collected Mrs. W, and we got into a carriage to return home. As the driver slowly made his way down the streets, I pitied and was filled with compassion for the poor wretches who lived there. Man, woman, child, all were in filthy clothes, some leaning or lying against brick buildings that must be heated like ovens in the summer's sun. A clutch of little boys sat on a stoop like fledgling chicks, their trousers much too short for their thin legs. Farther down the road, a woman stood outside a public hall, already loud with drunken rowdies, hoping to sell whatever bruised fruit she had left in her basket. Whether it was for throwing or for eating, I did not know. The bloody smell of the tanneries was carried, somehow, on the wind. I held my linen kerchief to my nose.

I told Mrs. W to take a carriage home, as I wanted to stop by the Theatrical Mission. I didn't know why, but I wanted to be near Mother Rachel. I arrived just in time to help her serve Mrs. Beeton's Nourishing Soup.

I kept a smile on my face as I served the girls, and as Mother Rachel showed me the treadle machine she'd purchased with Lady Tolfee's silver gown money, which the girls were so proud of.

Later, though, as I helped tidy up the dishes, the tears came, and they would not stop. Mother Rachel asked no questions but took me in her large, soft arms.

My house. My dream. My mother, my father. All gone.

The night we were to see *Henry V*, Lord Lockwood showed up punctually—of course, his carriage clock would not let him down. For a moment, I thought about the partner clock in Winton Park and was sad. Perhaps I should take it? Had his father given it to my mother? I purposefully set the melancholy aside. I would not allow anything to impinge upon my excitement for the evening ahead.

Lockwood's brother and his brother's wife waited in the landau, a larger model than the carriage he'd earlier collected me in, but his new driver handled it quite well, and waved at me, friendly. The top was open, as the night was glorious and warm, but a light breeze teased us, and I was glad Ruby had fast-secured my hair.

"Miss Gillian Young, my brother, Captain James Lockwood."

"How do you do?" I asked. His brother was perhaps my age, and still had a pinch of baby fat around his cheeks that made him look rather jolly.

"How do you do?" he replied.

"And his wife, Mrs. Lisbeth Lockwood."

"How do you do?" she said. "Please call me Lisbeth!" Her hair was a tumble of ginger curls, and she looked as jolly as her husband. My dressmaker's eye told me that she might, just barely, be with child. We chatted comfortably along the way; I took by her conversation that she had married her husband before the military service in which he had sustained his wounds.

The driver took us to the Lyceum with all speed. We arrived ahead of the crowd so that Lord Lockwood could deliver a faux sword to one of the actors.

Captain Lockwood did not walk well or quickly so we took our time disembarking from the carriage. That gave me time to view the beautiful Lyceum Theatre in its full.

We walked up the few steps, Lord Lockwood helping his brother, and then into the foyer. The room was covered with gold-flecked wallpaper; the carpets were red, and the lamps glowed already, though it was only early dusk.

As we reached the door, I heard the cries of the sweets seller, the meat seller, the cigarette seller, and wondered where they slept at night.

"Come along." Lisbeth took my arm as she saw my face dim. "Do not be dour; this will be a night of good fun."

I smiled again. I suspected that life was difficult for her and her husband, with his wounds and their complete dependence on his older brother for his maintenance. All properties went to the oldest brother in titled families, of course, but many of the other resources were also divided according to his will. It did my heart good to see Lord Lockwood speaking to his brother so kindly.

We got them settled into a comfortable box very near the lower floor, and then Lockwood leaned toward me. "Come with me to deliver the sword?" His eyes twinkled with promised fun.

"Oh, yes!" I excused myself and Lisbeth winked. I winked back and squeezed her hand as I passed by.

We made our way through the labyrinthine passages backstage. A few actors recognized Lord Lockwood and waved to him as we passed, calling out a greeting. He waved back—with his right hand; the sword was in a sword-belt. With his left, he held on to mine, which I did not mind in the least.

Once backstage, he delivered the new sword and safety blade, and then we began toward our seats once more. I knew as many of the backstage crew as he did. I had lived backstage all my life.

I took the teasing calls of "Traitor!"—to Drury Lane, that is—in good spirits. One actor, who had indicated his interest in me, asked if I'd be by again soon, or if he could come to call. I waved at him brightly but did not have time to answer as Lockwood firmly led me away. Because we had tarried to talk, we did not make it through the passage before the first act began.

"Come." Lord Lockwood pulled me into a cozy room aside the backstage. We could hear all that was going on but were hidden by a thick velvet curtain barely restrained by gold cords. We stood there, waiting till we could dash on ahead of the second act.

"I cannot hear the lines at all!" I said. Drat.

Young ladies do not use such language, filtered through my mind, and I smiled. *Yes, Mamma.*

"You smile?" Lord Lockwood asked. He was very close to me in the tiny space, close enough that I could count the freckles in the constellation near his eye, the freckles that I, unaccountably, adored.

"It's just that I cannot hear the lines." I wanted to reach up and touch the tendrils of hair that rested against his starched, white, upturned collar, above his tie.

"Let's recite them, then." He took both my hands in his and the warmth of his hands seeped into mine. They were a comfortable fit; an intimacy passed through us like a tidal current. I had a suspicion he did not mean the lines from Act One.

I nodded and held his gaze as he softly spoke Henry's lines.

"Lovely Katherine, if you will love me well with your French heart, I'm happy to hear you confess it in broken English. Do you like me, Kate?"

What did I want him to know, and was I even certain of my feelings? "I do."

"An angel is like you, Kate, and you are like an angel." He drew nearer to me. "Could you love me?"

I must know. "Do you speak as Henry or as Lord Lockwood?"

He smiled but even doing so did not lose his intensity. "As Thomas."

I whispered, "Thomas. I do not yet know."

He raised one of my gloved hands to his lips. I was particularly thankful that Mother Martha had used a thin skin for this pair, as I could feel him press gently against it.

"I can't allow you to lower yourself by kissing the hand of one of your humble servants." I urged him toward the response I desired. He did not disappoint.

"Then I will kiss your lips, Kate." He waited, as he'd done the first time.

I nodded and he leaned forward and kissed me gently. His lips lingered longer than I'd expected and it felt better than as I'd imagined during my dream at Winton Park. I fell down an entirely new, and welcome, rabbit-hole. His heady-woody-lovely sandalwood enveloped me even as he pulled away as things grew more urgent. I leaned forward and kissed him back and then pulled away while holding his gaze and my breath.

"I've long waited for that," he whispered.

"I, too. I shan't forget it, ever."

He smiled and ran his thumb along my jawline. "Do not fear. I shan't allow it to be forgotten."

I looked down for a moment to compose myself, and then we returned to our seats ahead of the second act. Neither Captain nor Mrs. Lockwood asked us to explain. Thomas looked flushed, and so did I; I could feel the heat in my face. I avoided catching his eye, but we were both wrapped in the gauze of that kiss. When the play came to the fifth act, and the words were spoken, a delightful emotional tension bonded us. He felt it, too. I sensed it.

After the play, we drove to his club for the benefit dinner being held. Normally, gentlemen's clubs did not admit ladies—in fact, the Garrick, where he also held membership, admitted ladies under no circumstances. Other clubs did for benefit events. This was one such evening.

Lord Shaftesbury, Seventh Earl of the same, hosted this event and so nearly everyone was in attendance and prepared to, as was said, do their bit for the charity. He was widely loved and admired for his charity work on behalf of the poor. Thanks to my sewing skills and the fact that I was allowed to retain the overrun fabric from the gowns commissioned me, I was dressed as finely as any woman there. "I am seriously delinquent in the jewels department," I whispered to Mrs. Lockwood.

"As am I," she said. "But for my wedding ring, and I rather doubt among these baubles that would count for much."

Lord Lockwood introduced me to everyone as Lord Palmer's granddaughter, and when I could, I politely spoke up and said I was also the daughter of Inspector Andrew Young, lately passed. I thought Lockwood quelled a smile, but I would not have half of me dismissed to push forward the other. I noticed odd and off looks sent my way once in a while; sometimes a man or two stared. I couldn't help but wonder if it was due to my class. Certainly, I could not be told apart. Perhaps it had been the mention of my father? Did they know my mother was among the actresses they would have enjoyed seeing perform, but would not have invited to the benefit?

I also could smell, very faintly but definitely, the rare and expensive Turkish tobacco Lockwood had scented on my feather. That same tobacco the Collingsworths had been smoking.

There were also several young ladies present who preened in front of Thomas and were not pleased to see me. By their glances, I surmised that they considered me a novelty and a passing fancy.

Was I?

Lord and Lady Tolfee were in attendance and she was most gracious and warm, introducing me to a friend or two of hers and her husband. "I shall look forward to seeing you soon," she said.

The Twin Ball, I knew she meant. I had not told her of my Cinderella gown. Would people imagine that I thought of it to represent myself, or was just nodding toward this year's pantomime?

I had not told anyone that I had donated Winton Park and that I was no longer heiress of a grand country estate. I would, soon enough. Life would turn normal. Later this very evening I would return to Cheyne Gardens and pick up my sewing again with my red, rough hands.

Thomas and I stood apart from the others, talking intimately to each other about books we'd read and our favorite childhood memories. Captain Lockwood joined in with a few funny memories from their boyhood and Lisbeth smiled and chatted with me about her girlhood, which sounded rather like the one my mother experienced. She patted her abdomen once or twice; I caught her and smiled warmly, and she blushed.

When it came time to eat, I sat across from Lord Lockwood, and whenever he could he lifted his eyes to me and did not look away, or he lifted his wineglass to his lips and nodded in my direction. I blushed the first time. The second time, I answered him in like manner.

Please, please, I prayed silently as we ate. *Don't let midnight ever arrive.*

CHAPTER TWENTY-THREE

LATE JULY, EARLY AUGUST, 1883

Thomas returned to Hampshire to assist his mother with the midsummer managing of their agricultural holdings and other duties as required of the lord of the area. He told me he would return for Lady Tolfee's Twin Ball. "And then, we shall talk," he promised.

"Haven't we talked?" I asked the night he'd dropped me off at my door.

"Not really," he'd said with a gentle smile. Captain Lockwood and Lisbeth had waited in the carriage for him; and Mrs. W was on the other side of the door so he'd simply kissed my gloved hand, letting his lips linger while we looked into one another's eyes, and bid me good night.

The next week found me aflutter. I had finally been summoned to meet with Papa's solicitor, Mr. Pilchuck. I removed the investment certificates and receipt that Francis had passed along to me from the desk in Father's study. I looked at each one—they were made out to Papa as owner and signed by a company representative—and placed them into a long leather envelope. I hoped that Mr. Pilchuck would be able to look them over and confirm that all the companies were in good standing and had been long and honorably associated with Papa's investments. They were important, and I would sort out why.

I remembered Francis's unspoken accusation against Papa and the investment certificates, that he had not come by the money cleanly. I did not know. I also had come to the tentative conclusion that Inspector Collingsworth was involved in dirty deeds of some sort himself.

Had Papa been, too, partners in misdeed as well as on the force? Was Collingsworth taking care to cover for Papa so both their indiscretions and, perhaps, illegal activity would not come to light? Or, had Papa uncovered Collingsworth's misdoings?

A sorrowful thought pressed against me. Was Francis involved, too? *I can protect you like no one else can,* he'd said. Just what had he meant?

I joined Ruby on the front porch. "They're going to grow fat, you know, under this kind of over generosity." She shook a few more bread crumbs toward the juvenile pigeons. "It may be time they found their own food."

She smiled at me, brilliantly beautiful now her hair was nearly grown in and she was under the care of people who loved her. "It's as much for me as for them, miss."

My heart squeezed. I understood. I should not like to see her leave when that time came.

"I must be gone for most of the day, but Mother Martha will oversee your work," I said, the day heating up as the hour marched on.

"Will we be working on the *Cinderella* dresses?" she asked. A fissure of anxiety ran through me. We must get started on the costumes, but the Twin Ball dresses were not complete.

"No, the Twin Ball dresses," I said. I sighed. "I should not have agreed to go. We would then have Lady Tolfee and Lady Mary's dresses completed by now."

Ruby put her hand on my arm. "It's most important to us, miss, that you go. It's why we're working so cheerfully. To see you go and have a wonderful time. It'll almost be like we're there with you." She returned to the sewing salon, and I prepared myself for my visit with Mr. Pilchuck. Mrs. W would accompany me to his office.

Midafternoon, the hired carriage delivered us to his offices in the City of London, where all financial transactions occurred. Mrs. W remained in the reception room whilst I accompanied Mr. Pilchuck's secretary, a tall, thin, dour man, back. He knocked on the door. "Miss Young, sir."

The door was pushed open and I walked into the room. I expected Pilchuck to stand and greet me. He did not stand. He simply motioned for me to have a seat across from his desk.

"Miss Young," he began. "While normally it would take me six months or so to sort through the postmortem accounts of a client, I have, of late, accelerated this to bring the matter to a complete close."

His tone was so far removed from the fatherly tenor of the last visit. I held the leather envelope containing the investment certificates to my side.

"I had certainly expected to hear from you sooner. Fortunately, I am a woman with an income and was able to provide for myself, in however tenuous a manner, whilst I waited for your tardy response."

He nodded, but did not acknowledge my admonishment.

"First," he continued, "I must tell you that I received notification that Winton Park has been fully, legally, and completely transferred from you to the Cause." He pushed a paper toward me; I scanned it quickly and nodded. He placed it into the top of a large stack of towering boxes, hastily arranged, it seemed, near his desk.

"Some fathers would not have wanted their daughters to have given away such a large property. Your father had never mentioned it to me, and I must remind you that I find this a perhaps foolhardy thing to have done."

A flutter of doubt. Had I done what Mamma had wanted but not what Papa would have wanted?

"Some husbands would not take kindly to understanding that their wives had given away valuable property before the marriage. That money could also have served as a dowry." Mr. Pilchuck looked down his nose at me, with a mixture of disgust and fear. Why?

"The property was mine to do with as I pleased."

"The Cause is a worthy organization," he not-quite-agreed.

His first kind words. I smiled. "Thank you."

Pilchuck handed over a stack of papers. "You'll find all of the details on your father's accounts herein. There are two bank statements, information on his few investments. You've just reminded me that you sew for a living."

It sounded so . . . desperate. "I do."

"Good. After death duties were paid and some other invoices and accounts he had outstanding, there is just a bit left over from that sale of some arable acreage between Winton Park and the neighboring estate, but not much more."

"Sale of arable acreage?" The hair on the back of my neck rose to attention. "I had not heard of this."

"Oh yes," he said. "Six months or so before his death. The trust allowed the trustee to make such a sale if it were for the benefit of the trustee or the property." He mentioned the exact sum on the receipt I had found in Papa's papers, and I withdrew it from the envelope and handed it to him.

He looked at the receipt. "Yes. Via barrister H. A. Colmore Dunn."

Colemore Dunn! *Thomas's* barrister, and friend. Colmore Dunn had not mentioned this to me. Perhaps it wouldn't have been polite.

Perhaps he'd been told not to.

Yes, yes, Dunn's name was on the receipt. I supposed I hadn't put them together because the first half of his surname had been left off.

"Who was the purchaser?" My hands trembled, and I kept them held together, in my lap, to steady them. Even before he answered I knew the answer. A fact that had been deliberately hidden from me.

"Viscount Lockwood," he said. "Your father hadn't told you?"

I shook my head.

"Perhaps he didn't want to burden you with the details, my dear," he said. "You're a woman, after all. Gentlemen of all classes do not discuss their financial dealings with, or in the company of, women. I only do now as you have no one attached to you with whom I might discuss this. It was well within his rights to sell some property to finance your ongoing maintenance."

I reeled. Thomas had bought some of my land and had not even told me, not during any of our discussions about Winton Park! Worse, Papa had not told me!

One comforting thought crept forth—my father could not have been the recipient of a steady flow of ill-gotten gains if he had needed to sell some of Winton Park's acreage to pay the death duties or maintenance on either property.

"I am well able to manage my accounts," I said. "About my written enquiry. The King Street property."

His face blanched. "Yes. As an especial favor to you, and because you are a young woman alone, I made some enquiries. I'm sorry to say that was a grave mistake on my part, and perhaps yours. Within a few days of floating the query down some legal and professional channels, some . . . gentlemen . . . arrived at my office. They informed me in no uncertain terms that it was privately held property. That people, meaning myself, Miss Young, should not be concerned with ownership or activities of property to which they had no attachment. Or else."

He'd been frightened off?

"They next asked me how long you'd owned your house in Cheyne Gardens, and if I knew how your parents had come by the funds to purchase it."

I swallowed. Were they coming next for Cheyne Gardens? "And your answer was?" I did not even know the answer to their question. No one had shared information about the family finances, of course, with me then or at any other time.

"I replied I did not know where the funds for the original purpose had come from. I had not handled that transaction, mostly just those associated with your trust, as I had worked with Lord Palmer, your grandfather. I was not your father's solicitor long; I understood him not to need one. I primarily handled affairs related to the trust and your grandfather's papers." He glanced at the stack of boxes. "Out of regard to your grandfather, I did not mention the recent sale of acreage with its proceeds returning to your father."

He continued. "Those visitors indicated that it might be better for me if I severed our professional relationship."

I stood, shocked. Then I sat down again.

"I told them that my relationship had been primarily with Lord Palmer, and now the trust was closed I need have no further dealings with anyone in your family, nor you."

"I'm stunned," I said.

He lowered his voice and looked at me with regret. "I cannot have anyone alarm my other clients, Miss Young. Many of them work in the financial districts of the City, where these men came from. Should word get round that I am a solicitor who pokes his nose where it need not be poked . . ." He lifted his hands and shrugged as if to say, *What could I do?* "They made it clear."

He pointed to the stack of boxes astride his desk. "You'll take these home. It's all the papers from your grandfather, and a few from your father, which I have kept safe and secure. I have not looked through them of late . . . I do not want to."

Nor did I.

"I suggest you keep them somewhere secure," he said. "Will that be all? You'd mentioned you had further enquiry?"

My hand sweat onto the leather envelope, which I clasped so tightly I had no sensations in my fingertips. I could not, by any means, show these certificates to him now. What if they should prove to be unlawful somehow, or if Collingsworth had proved a false friend and had planted something nefarious within the stack of my father's legitimate investments? I would, of course, have to work this all out and then take action. But not immediately. And not with Pilchuck.

Whom could I trust? Papa had not told me of this sale. Nor had Thomas.

"No," I responded. "That will be all. What do I owe you for your fees?"

He waved his hand. "In light of your generous donation to the Cause, I will waive my fees."

How very Christian of him, just after he'd cut me adrift, with, as he'd stated, no protector.

I returned to the carriage, where Mrs. W asked if things had gone well. I said yes, but she must have wondered because Pilchuck's associate roughly deposited the boxes into the carriage. Once we were home I had Bidwell bring them into the study. Mrs. W did not enquire further; she had always been discreet. But I'd noticed that she had rarely spoken of Papa since his death, and when she did, it was with a cool tone.

I placed Papa's investment certificates back into his desk drawer—for the moment—and spent hours and hours looking through the boxes for something that might prove Papa's innocence. Some of the notes he must have taken about the case he'd been working on when he died—the ones that had stirred his enemies and mine, long after his death, to intimidate Mr. Pilchuck—must remain.

I found nothing.

One day soon after, I packed my garment bag with some of the near-finished pieces for Lady Tolfee's Fire and Ice gown and commissioned the hired driver to Tolfee House. Lady Tolfee had summoned me—I thought perhaps so she could begin to match her accessories with the fabric.

Ruby helped me fold the fabric. "She is going to be in an admirable shock when she sees the fabric you helped me with. It looks like flames climbing the skirt!"

"Thank you, miss," Ruby said. "But now that's done . . . what do you have next for me? I cannot cut. I cannot sew."

I nodded. "I'll find something. Do not fear."

I arrived at Lady Tolfee's dressing room. Her lady's maid, normally so friendly to me, would not meet my eye. She dipped to her mistress and, oddly, left the room.

I brought my case near. "I do believe you will love this. I've brought the skirt and a sleeve so you'll be able to match your jewelry and shoes."

I pulled one piece after the other out of the bag, and she cooed. "Just beautiful, stunning, really. Whatever shall I do without you?"

"What do you mean?" My heart beat faster, and I allowed the skirt to slip from my hand.

She sat near me. "Lord Tolfee has heard, well, that your father was involved in some reprehensible situations."

"Where did he hear of that? And I assure you, it's not true in the least," I said. If I lost her commission, I would not be able to care for myself, Cheyne Gardens, and the girls. At least not unless Wilhelm and Mr. Harris could assure I'd remain a principal designer and seamstress, a position I had not even been assured of at this point.

"Oh, you know how men are, dear. They gossip worse than women, really, and this has become a particular line of conversation in the past few weeks," she said, pointedly.

Since the benefit dinner at the club? Since the enquiry Mr. Pilchuck had made in the City? Both?

"I don't know what to say."

"When I pointed out to Lord Tolfee that you were, anyway, an heiress in your own right, he rebuked me and said you have donated Winton Park in its entirety. I told him I cannot believe that . . ."

She waited for me to contradict her. "I did donate Winton to the Cause. It had been my mother's wish."

"Generous, but perhaps unfortunate." She came closer. "Listen, my dear. If it were up to me, I would have no qualms. But I have no right or will to cross Lord Tolfee and he says he finds the entire matter distasteful."

She put the sleeve and the skirt back into the garment bag. "I do hope you'll still attend the Twin Ball, as my guest, though Lord Tolfee might object, if he knew in advance. I know you must have been working on your costume, and it would be a pity to let it go to waste."

I thought, perhaps I should sell it, as I may very well be in need of the resources, and soon. "I'll give it consideration."

"I insist," she said. First I was the tool she'd used to punish Mary, now she'd use me to punish her husband, if I agreed.

I smiled at her, brightly. The one redeeming fact of this situation was that she was no longer in any position to insist upon anything from me. Now that I knew I'd lost her commission and affections, I did not want to attend. Now that I knew that Thomas had withheld telling me of his purchase of some of my property—why?—I felt uncertain about seeing him, too.

"I'll be back with your gown in enough time to dress," I replied. "Will that be all?"

She nodded and looked as though she were going to lean toward me, to touch my arm or for a brief, lady's embrace. I moved backward, out of her reach. She did not rebuke me. She did, on some level, understand.

I walked home, not wanting to risk an odd carriage driver right now and to save my pence. When I arrived, all could tell that my mood was diminished.

"Did she not like the fabric, miss?" Ruby asked.

"Oh, no, she loved it," I said. "She was very pleased with it."

"Then what is it?" Charlotte asked, and Mother Martha leaned forward, too, to hear my response.

"It's just that, well, I am not certain any longer if I shall be attending the Twin Ball." I looked toward the dressing dummy; the girls had been working on my gown in my absence.

"Why not, miss? Isn't that posh man you are in love with going?" Ruby asked.

"Ruby!" I used my best outrage voice. "I am not in love, and in any case, I have no idea if he will be attending or not. Although . . . I suspect he will."

"Were you . . . disinvited, miss?" Charlotte asked.

I shook my head. "No. It's just complicated." I put on a smile. "Let's not worry, shall we? In the meantime, I should like to take the Cinderella pantomime costume along to Drury Lane and show Wilhelm. Is it at hand?"

Charlotte proudly brought out the gown we'd all been working on, including Mother Martha's stunning beading. "Mother Martha has been teaching me to bead," she said, holding up a glove.

"Charlotte! That is well done!" I couldn't believe how good a seamstress she'd become in such a short period. She had the gift.

Charlotte blushed and smiled.

"Is all well, dear?" Mrs. W pulled me aside.

I shook my head. "Lord Tolfee has decided that I should not continue making dresses for his wife. She protested, but to no avail."

Mrs. W's face went hard, and then she took my hand. "To the theater, then. They can be trusted."

Yes. I took the costume and then took a carriage to Drury Lane. Hired carriages were an expense I needed to watch more carefully now, but it was important I keep in Wilhelm's good graces. Perhaps I could ask him if there was additional work this Season.

No. I'd best stun him with my current commission so he'd offer even more work to me the following Season. Once word got round Lady Tolfee's friends that she'd dismissed me, it would be unlikely that they would commission me.

The theater was a hive and while everyone buzzed around, I went to the back and found some pantomime dressers. Wilhelm and a bevy of actresses exclaimed with delight over the gown and told me how they were looking forward to the reveal of the costumes for Cinderella herself. It was a relief. More often than not, they found complaint with final costumes, till it came time to leave them behind when the show closed; then suddenly they found they could not do without them.

Reassured, I left them to their work on the current production and walked into the theater itself.

It was dark; the lights were not lit, of course, during the day. I sat in one of the theater boxes, a box very much like the one I had recently shared with Thomas and Captain Lockwood and Lisbeth.

The stage curtains rustled, but no one came out. The ceiling creaked and then crackled again. I imagined the actors who had been on that stage, who had played people who lived and died, and had lived and died themselves.

I heard steps in the corridor behind the boxes. I waited, and they seemed to stop right behind me. I held my breath. Was I imagining being followed again?

I stood and hurried out into the waning afternoon light. I walked, and as I came near the Lyceum, I stopped. My heart clutched. Thomas? Had he come back to bring additional fencing materials?

I would speak with him. I'd ask him about the purchase of my land, and gently ask him to account for his silence in the matter. He likely had a good answer.

I hoped he would.

I was about to call out to him, but he protectively put his arm around a very young lady and helped her into his carriage. My mouth opened and my heart closed; I wanted to close my eyes, too, but I found I could not.

The young woman was exceptionally pretty. She smiled up at him, admiringly, trustingly, and he smiled back at her with that smile that had melted my heart. He spoke to her gently. An iron mantle of despair burdened my shoulders, crushing my spirit.

Perhaps it meant nothing. Perhaps she was but a friend. And yet . . . the tenderness with which he had gazed upon her. I waited till they left and then walked home, to clear my mind, via King Street, making a point not to look at the high-end brothel filled with the too-young.

Papa. What had you been doing there? I do not understand.

I thought of Thomas, buying my land, escorting that pretty young girl.

I recalled Lady Tolfee's easy dismissal.

I am bereft, Lord. I have no protector. No one but You, and You seem very far away indeed.

I recalled a line in *Othello* and whispered it as I rounded the corner toward home. "But I will wear my heart upon my sleeve, For daws to peck at."

Unlike Thomas, who had taken proper precautions for life, I had not worn a plastron, and my heart was now pierced clear through.

I went to bed early that night, hoping for the respite of dreamlessness. It was not to be.

A rush of footsteps could be heard clattering down the stairs, and then came a crash against my door, a banging, persisting knock.

"Who is it?" I called out, jumping up and pulling my robe around me. I opened the door.

"Miss!" Charlotte burst out. "Ruby—she's gone!"

CHAPTER TWENTY-FOUR

"Gone?" In spite of the still-warm summer night, a feverish chill trembled through me. "Gone where? When?"

Charlotte put her face into her hands and began to cry.

"I thought I heard a noise, but then I didn't wake properly. Something kept plucking at my heart, though, and finally, I did wake up, and then I looked over, and Ruby was not in her bed. Her blankets were all pulled up neat-like. Then I came down to get you."

I ran up to their room; Ruby's clothes were still in her drawer. I ran back downstairs, Charlotte trailing behind me. The door was unlocked. "Did she meet someone?" I asked Charlotte. "Did she mention wanting to leave with anyone?" That young man ran through my mind, but there had been no word of him since the charity bazaar.

Charlotte sniffled. "She did say she wanted to walk along the park next to the river, miss. Last time we rode by it in the carriage."

The Chelsea Embankment. I threw on a dress and half buttoned my boots.

"I think Mother Martha is gone, too," Charlotte called after me. "I looked in her room an' didn't see her, neither."

Right now, I had no time to worry about a woman grown, much as I cared for her. Perhaps she was with Ruby. The only man nearby was Bidwell and if I were even able to quickly wake him his age would slow me down. I fled out the front door.

The night was stale and motionless, which amplified the sound of my boots hitting the cobbles. The streets were empty but for the prowling of animals that magically appeared when I was but a foot or two away from them; the smothering fog made it impossible to see clearly unless I was directly under a streetlamp.

Someone cried in the distance. As I got closer to the river, the smoked soot blanched to fog and lifted from the streets like a specter, twistedly following me like a ghost. Two drunks appeared out of the ether; when they saw me, they reached for me, catcalled, and nearly caught the hem of my shawl, which would have allowed them to pull me toward them.

My heart squeezed with fear but I pressed on for Ruby's sake.

I picked up the pace, but because my boots were half unbuttoned, I wrenched my ankle and had to slow down. The night fog hid me, I'd thought. But soon my pursuers closed in and I forced myself to pick up the pace, fear as well as the loose boots making it difficult to walk steadily.

"Well, isn't that a bit of luck?" one called to the other. In spite of the pain, I kept walking. Would they follow me to the Embankment? What if Ruby was not there? What if she was and these two louts apprehended both of us?

One shouted lewdly, but his inebriation made it impossible for him to keep up. Reaching for me again, he lost his balance and fell hard into the gutter. I passed an alley and a shadow moved. I heard a clawing, and more shadows, and then a fox, no two, appeared. One arched his back when he saw me, and lifted a paw, grinning, and then turned toward the other, inviting mischief.

I did not know if running would cause more attention, so I slowed my pace to a quick walk.

Please, Lord, let Ruby be well. Let me find her. Let her be here because if she is not here, I do not know where she might be.

I reached the park that bordered the Thames, which quietly lapped against the Embankment. A man and a woman slumped together against a tree, but no one else.

I walked to the right and then turned back and went the other way. Fifteen minutes later, I saw her, sitting on a bench, dead center, alone. A lit lamp flickered a halo above her tilted head.

Ruby.

I pressed my balled fists to my eyes in relief and held back the tears so I would not distress her. I'd thought someone had made off with her and was overwhelmed with thankfulness that they had not. I quickly, but calmly, walked toward her. She was alone; wherever Mother Martha had gone, it was not here. I should have to reproach her, too, for leaving at night. Had this been a habit?

I was in nothing so much as a hurry to return to the safety of home, but I remembered a time when I had happened upon a wounded bird once, as a child. In my rush to pick her up she'd fluttered away from me in fear to a place in the hedgerow where I could not reach or help her.

I approached Ruby from the side. "May I sit next to you?"

She jumped, afraid, perhaps, and then once she saw it was me, looked anxious of a reproach. She reclaimed her catlike indifference and shrugged. "No one else will."

I sat down next to her. "What do you mean?"

She pointed toward a rough, large, intimidating man sitting on the bench near us. His bowler hat was pulled down so I could not see his eyes, but by the alertness with which he held his head, he was clearly not asleep. "At first, some young men came and sat by me for a moment, asking my name and such. But then that man looked at them, and they left. The man sat down on the other bench"—she pointed toward it—"and no one has come my way since."

I looked around; it was true. There was a large perimeter of emptiness around her though there were animals and a few vagrants prowling other parts of the Embankment. I positioned myself in between the man and Ruby and turned my back to him, to protect her from his sight in case he, himself, had bad intentions.

"'Tis for the best," I said. I wanted to rush home immediately, out of this dark and sinister park filled with ne'er-do-wells and drunkards and desperates with nothing to lose. *To rush Ruby might be to lose her.*

Her gloom stayed settled round her like London's melancholic fog. "I knew you would say that, miss."

I held back a smile. "It is not safe here. You should not have come."

"I could not sleep."

"We have a parlor."

She shook her head. "I feel cooped up, miss. And . . . sad. I could not sleep."

I should have expected they would feel cooped up. Of course! They were but girls and I had not given them much time of late for rest or for play. When we were safely home, in the morning, I should explain a bit more frankly how and from whom the girls were at risk.

"We shall come to the park tomorrow . . . when it is daylight. And I promise to make more time for amusements. I'm sorry."

She lifted her head. "I just got . . . Well, it just got too much, miss. Every time something good seems like it's going to happen, why, then it don't. There's more fun in the theater—yes, it was hard work, but we had fun, too. Now all we do is sew for people who don't have to do anything difficult—rich people and actresses. My fingers hurt and so do Charlotte's, though she'd never say so. Sometimes we're bored. Then finally, we all sew on the gown for you to go to the posh ball, and after all that, you're not going to go. You said we were to have a bright future, miss. But if even you don't have a bright future, then how can we hope to?"

I sat quietly for a moment. She was right. I hadn't given them a good example. They—and I—had worked very hard on that dress. It may well be my last chance to attend such an event. I would go, for them, and for me.

I could not deny that I wanted to speak with Thomas. He'd promised, after all, that we'd talk.

"Whoever said I was not attending that ball?" I said brightly.

"You, miss."

"Well, I said I was not sure. But now I am sure. Of course I'm going to attend! I shall even see if I might sneak home some sweets in my garment bag for the lot of you."

She looked up at me. "Really?"

I nodded. "Really. We all have to work—and you'll have to trust me when I tell you that those living a life with riches aren't always blessed with happiness. *You* have a bright future. I shall see to it myself. I promise."

She kicked the ground. An owl hooted. I sensed people lurking nearby. "I can't sew, miss, and we both know it."

Yes, we did.

She looked at me head-on for a full minute, her green eyes searching my blue, looking for honesty, fidelity, and commitment,

I knew. Then she nodded. "I believe you, miss. I have a bright future."

I took her by the hand. "Let's return home now. We'll come tomorrow, with Charlotte and Mother Martha and Mrs. W. We'll buy a bag of bread crumbs for the pigeons." She brightened and put her arm around my waist and I put mine around hers; we began to hurry home. At the catcalling of a distant man, I think even she began to feel nervous. She picked up her pace, and I did, too, praying for protection.

"We'll buy an ice for you, one for Charlotte . . . and one for Mrs. W!" I kept up the cheery chatter to counterbalance the fear as we stepped down the dark cobblestones. The lamps were fewer and farther between now.

The foxes fell out of the alley and slunk behind us.

"Does Mrs. W eat ices, then?" Ruby glanced toward their glittering eyes and sharp teeth.

I did not know. "We shall find out." I refused to look at the animals. It might engage them. I sensed them behind us now. It put me in mind of Little Red Riding Hood.

"*Little Red Cap, just where does your grandmother live?*"

"*Her house is a good quarter hour from here in the woods, under the three large oak trees. There's a hedge of hazel bushes there. You must know the place," said Little Red Cap.*

The wolf thought to himself, "Now that sweet young thing is a tasty bite for me. She will taste even better than the old woman. You must be sly, and you can catch them both."

We began to run and I quickly opened the door, pulling Ruby inside, and closing it fast behind us.

We panted for a full minute, then collapsed in the parlor. I looked at her and she at me. We were safe now and burst into exhausted giggles of relief. Mrs. W appeared, her unkempt hair barely restrained by a sleeping cap; she looked just like Little Red's grandmother, which set me off laughing again.

"Never mind. All's well now. We'll have an outing to the park tomorrow."

I helped Ruby and Charlotte upstairs, and as I did, I knocked on Mother Martha's door.

"Yes?" She called out, her voice thick with sleep.

"Are you quite well?" I asked.

"Quite well, thank you," she said.

Charlotte turned toward me at the sound of Mother Martha's voice coming from her room. The girl seemed unsettled and confused. "I'm sorry, miss. I must have been mistaken. I was certain she was gone."

Next afternoon, we walked back to the Embankment, and before we reached the ice seller we came to a little gathering of girls and women, holding hands and dancing in joy in front of an organ grinder. His long, rough beard protected his sun-browned face, his two little boys idled beside him, learning his trade.

We stood for a moment, clapping. Two little girls, one in a straw hat, one in a blue felt bowler, led the way, lifting their skirts prettily in time with the music. Then one of the grown women in a blue dress with a red underskirt that looked just like our Cinderella's maid costume took Ruby by the hand to invite her to dance, and then Ruby took me. Mother Martha and Mrs. W joined in, and we whirled with them all. A policeman, one who looked very smart in his uniform, his buttons polished, his hat firm and the flap in front carefully folded, grinned at us, watching, protecting, allowing all to enjoy and seeing no mischief was worked.

Papa had once been like that.

I looked toward the bench where Ruby's protector had been stationed the night before. It was empty.

After a few minutes, the tune ended, and we all laughed and danced. I gave the grinder a few pence for his music. "Perhaps you should attend the Mission more often with Mother Martha," I said. "It might be enjoyable."

Ruby looked at her toes, and Charlotte spoke up. "No, miss. I mean, we like the service on Sunday and all, and when the speaker comes that's just for girls but, well, that's enough for us till we're old, I think." Even Mrs. W held back a smile.

After an hour, we were ready to return to Cheyne Gardens. We had sewing to do. Very soon, Sergeant Collingsworth was coming to call. I should soon have to tell him we would be nothing more than friends, as I did not want to mislead him. But I did not wish to anger him or turn him against me, either.

CHAPTER TWENTY-FIVE

I'd had such a delightful time on the Embankment with my household that when Francis came to call, I asked him if we might walk along it, too. He was delighted and I was glad for another activity we could comfortably share.

"Mother would like us to pop round for tea after," he said. "If that's all right with you?"

I nodded, but wondered what he, or they, had in mind.

His face was drawn, and his normally pink complexion pale: odd, for midsummer. "Are you quite well?" I asked. "We could postpone this to another day if you like."

He shook his head and put my hand inside his elbow, comfortably, as we strolled. "It's been a little taxing lately," he said.

"On the force?" I asked.

He nodded. "And at home as well." His eyes darted away, and he would not look at me for a moment. I did not press it just then.

"Have you met with your father's solicitor?" he asked. We walked close to the water, and a little girl stood nearby selling posies. He bought one for me, which was awfully sweet. I put my nose in the center of a rose and inhaled its sweet scent.

"I have," I answered as we continued. I would not tell him how I'd been dismissed, nor why. Is that why he'd asked? Had he been put up to it somehow? Instead, I changed the subject. "I should tell you . . . I have donated my property at Winton Park to the Cause."

He full stopped. "You have?"

I nodded. "It was what my mother wanted."

Francis took a moment to shake his head clear. "You should have kept it. That was not wise."

Who was he to offer such stringent condemnation of my freely made decision with my own property?

He returned to the earlier topic. "Was your solicitor able to answer your questions about your father's investment certificates?"

Now, I did not want to lie, but I was not going to answer forthrightly, either. I had no trust of Francis's father and did not know where Francis stood on these matters, either. We passed a pottery seller, his wares displayed on a ladder that leaned against a brick building. Further down, the organ grinder and his two sons were playing for tips.

"I intend to make further enquiries about all the certificates with my friend Viscount Lockwood, who is heavily involved in investments, in the City," I said. "I will see this through to a clear answer."

"Your *friend*," Francis said.

I did not answer. I was not to be held to account by a childhood friend whose father may or may not have turned my father astray.

The day grew cool and clouds blew across our conversation. We turned in the direction toward his home. Mrs. Collingsworth already had the kettle on in the back; I could hear it.

"I'm delighted you've come," she said to me. "Go on, Francis. Join your father in the garden for a pipeful."

He smiled at me, and I smiled back, warmly, to reassure him that his mother was in good hands in his absence.

Mrs. Collingsworth brought out some chocolate biscuits. "These are really quite good," I said. "Do you mind if I take another?"

"I'd be delighted!"

We talked for a few minutes about the success of her charity bazaar and then she brought the conversation round to how good a friend my mother had been to her.

I hadn't recalled them being overly friendly but did not want to contradict.

"I think she, and I, had hopes that you and Francis, well . . ." She let the sentence drift off and blushed, the first time any color had flushed her face since my arrival.

I smiled and nodded but said nothing. She coughed a little, which then turned into a fit, and then waved her linen to excuse herself. I nodded. "Yes, yes, please take care of yourself. I'll be fine right here."

She left, and I sipped my tea and looked around the parlor. There were no novels or magazines, but one newspaper. I read the first page:

> *Parliament will recess without further motions made on the Criminal Law Amendment Act, an Act to provide further provision for the Protection of Women and Girls, the suppression of brothels, and other motivations, such as transporting girls and young women to the Continent for "immoral purposes." The House of Lords, led by Lord Granville, formed a select committee to investigate and confirm an increase in child prostitution and white slavery.*
>
> *After reviewing the facts, the House of Lords made recommendations for this bill, which would include raising*

the age of consent to sixteen years from age thirteen, as well as introduced further and more stringent criminal penalties for sexual offenses. The bill easily passed the House of Lords but was dropped by the House of Commons. It will be reintroduced.

My poor girls. Was there to be no justice?

I set the paper down and looked for comfort. Here was a family Bible on a side table, and another one propped oddly in a tiny bookshelf.

I reached for it, to page through it and pass the time till Mrs. Collingsworth returned. I turned to the Psalms first. The printing was unusual, different. But I'd seen it before. Where?

I held my breath. I knew where I'd seen that.

I prayed that no one would enter the room before I had a chance to flip through the pages.

Oh no. Oh no. The book of Saint Matthew, chapter eight, had been removed from the Bible. I remembered the first warning I had received, from that very chapter. *Let the dead bury their dead.*

I flipped forward a few pages. I could hear the men returning. Yes, Saint Matthew, chapter thirteen, was also missing. *But whosoever hath not, from him shall be taken away even that he hath.*

Which Collingsworth had sent them to me?

I quickly replaced the book on the shelf, and within fifteen seconds, Inspector and Sergeant Collingsworth walked in. They looked uneasy together; Francis looked paler than ever.

"Where's Mum?" he asked.

"She felt a little unwell," I replied, my heart still pounding at my discovery. "Is there something else I can do?"

"I'll tend to her, son, and you take Miss Young home," his father said. Francis agreed.

We walked; it was a lovely summer evening, and the cries of children playing outside filled the air. A light breeze ruffled round my bonnet, which I was glad for. I had grown overheated in the Collingsworths' sitting room. The missing pages of the Bible kept flitting through my mind, and it made my situation with Francis even more uncomfortable.

"Gillian . . . ," Francis began. His voice sounded both intimate and tentative at once.

I tilted my head toward him.

"You mentioned that viscount today, and it reminded me, well . . . I should like to court you seriously, exclusively. With an eye toward something more in the future."

I was relieved that he had raised the topic, as I could not let this go further; I did not have those kinds of feelings for him and I felt entirely unsafe in his family home. "You are a good man," I began. He held his hand up to silence me.

"Hear me out. I would treat you with affection and respect; I would not stand in the way of your work. We have a background in common, and we are comfortable with one another."

All of that was true, and I nodded.

"The world is a dark place; no one knows that better than a copper, or"—he looked at me—"the daughter of an officer."

"Has something started up again?" I asked. I thought back to my conversation with Mr. Pilchuck.

"We can make a dark situation light together. I can protect you, Gillian, like none other. It would be a delight and a privilege to do so." He continued. "My mother loves you. Please . . . just think it over. For me."

We'd nearly arrived at Cheyne Gardens. I sighed. "I will think it over, for you, Francis. In earnest, I will."

He smiled. "Thank you. You'll soon see it's best." He stood

there, and I wondered if he was going to try to kiss me. I backed away, just a little, and he smiled, briefly, and left.

I stood by the door and watched him return the way we'd come.

What did I feel for Francis? Before this had all come about I had always considered him to be a good man, but I did not daydream of him. I did not think about pressing my lips against his, or how I could make him laugh or catch him out with a parry. I had not considered what our children might look like, his and mine.

I had with Thomas.

I did not want to ask him about the young lady in the carriage. I did not want to ask him why he had purchased my land and not told me, because everything I'd hoped for and dreamt of with him might suddenly collapse.

Perhaps Francis, then . . . and yet, no. Francis and I could not talk about theater together. I did not love him. And, importantly, he had said his mother loved me, but he had not said he did.

"Do not marry a man if you are not sure he loves you for your-self alone, dearest little daisy," Mamma said. *"Never a man about whom you think, even for a moment, he loves me not."*

Did Thomas love me?

The next morning, I awoke realizing there was little time for introspection because the Twin Ball would be held the next day. But we did take a fast moment to play Old Maid first, relaxing a bit ahead of the long night; I was attentive to the girls' needs now. They had purchased a card set at the charity bazaar. Ruby was worried about this particular game.

"Shall we invite her, miss?" she asked. "Will she be hurt?"

"Will whom be hurt by what?" came a steady voice from behind.

Ruby and I looked at one another wide-eyed as Mrs. W appeared from nowhere.

"Cards, ma'am, if you'd like."

Mrs. W looked at the deck, and I saw both tenderness and pain as she recognized what Ruby had been trying to protect her from.

"I think I've won this game already," she said with a light laugh. I was shocked. I had never seen her . . . *jolly*. She was more interested in *righteous*.

"There is the game Old Bachelor," Mrs. W said. "If you truly cared for my feelings, you'd consider a purchase of that next bazaar."

I could not contain my surprise. What had happened to my solemn chaperone and old Auntie these past months since, well, since her sister's husband had died? She'd become light.

Ruby delighted at the parry and we played a game or two before returning to our work.

I'd had Bidwell install some metal rails to the beams on the fourth floor. From one of them hung Lady Tolfee's Fire and Ice gown; it was stunning and original, exactly what she'd requested. If I had to lose her commission, I was proud to have designed this as my last gown for her.

Lady Mary's gown was also beautiful; she had wanted to be Sun and Moon, and her dress would spin, like a clock, from noon to midnight as she twirled. Mary could show herself as sunny to one man if she approached from the left, or mysterious to another, if she approached from the right. I whispered a little prayer over her dress. She needed someone to care for her, too.

Those dresses now hung from the rails—the summer heat was such that I would not have to press them before placing them in the garment bag, though Lady Tolfee's lady's maid might render some assistance once I arrived at Tolfee House.

"Come, now," Ruby instructed me. "Sit here." She pointed to a chair in the middle of the room. "I'm going to style your hair with some inserts and jewels and such."

I obeyed and the girls giggled. Ruby twisted and pulled and curlicued my hair. She held up a hand mirror.

I adored what I saw in the reflection. "Oh, Ruby! This is absolutely wonderful. Will you be able to do it again before the ball?"

"Of course," she said.

I realized with a pang that I should speak with Sarah about Ruby; perhaps, after the Season and after the dresses were readied for the pantomime, Ruby might apprentice with Sarah. The thought of losing her hurt my heart.

Mother Martha cleared her throat and began to read from *Little Women.* "But that autumn the serpent got into Meg's paradise, and tempted her, like many a modern Eve, not with apples, but with dress." She looked at us, and we laughed.

"It's not autumn!" I declared.

"Put on the dress, please, miss," Charlotte said.

Gladly!

I slipped into the dress with Mother Martha's help, and the girls sighed.

"Oh, it's . . . it's perfect," Charlotte said. "Even the Maid side is perfect."

"It's my first masquerade ball as attendee," I said. "I've never had my own disguise before—imagine that!"

"We've all been around masquerades our entire lives," Mother Martha stated.

Well, I guessed that to be true. She'd been in theater, too.

She continued somewhat strangely, her voice almost warning. "Pride can masquerade as standards; control can masquerade as a concern. Self-righteousness masquerades as religion."

The room was silent with that unexpected truth. I stepped on the dressing dais and looked in the mirror. The room was quiet with a holy hush. The left of me was costumed as the young daughter left without a protector—no loving father to watch over her. She worked hard and hoped for the best.

The right side of me was a fairy tale, gauzy water-kissed fabric that rolled and curled like a frothy wave every which way I turned, perfectly accented by crystal beads. I turned toward Mother Martha for approval.

"You're beautiful," she said. I held back the tears. It was almost the voice of my mother. Almost.

"It's interesting." I tried to bring the conversation back to where I could control my feelings. "Women at these balls are always told how beautiful they are, but in truth, it's the hair and the jewels and the gowns and the shoes that have been made by rough hands, hands like ours, hands that struggle to put food in our mouths and find a blanket to sleep under that make them beautiful. Lady Tolfee shall not be pleased if I up-stage her."

"But you will," Mother Martha answered. "Because it's not her night. It's yours."

"Mine?"

She reached for *Little Women* and read out a passage: "Love is a great beautifier."

I gasped. "I am not in love!"

"Yes you are, yes you are!" the girls shouted. "You are!"

CHAPTER TWENTY-SIX

I arrived on time at Tolfee House. I raced up the back stairs—fitting, I thought, for a woman who would be half maid that night. But I'd enter the ball by the front stairs. I suppressed a smile.

"My dear! How shall I do without you?" Lady Tolfee asked, and her lady's maid and I helped her into her Fire and Ice gown. *Better than I'd fare without her,* I thought. There was no doubt she would be the stunning center of attention. She put me, just a little, in mind of Cinderella's stepmother with her overbearing manner.

"I shall miss dressing you," I whispered to Lady Mary as I helped fasten her gown.

"And I shall miss you." She took my hand for a moment. "I know what it's like to be on Mother's dark side."

After they had left, I helped myself into my gown, because I had lost Lady Tolfee's favor. I had lost her lady's maid's favor as well. But Ruby had done my hair perfectly, and I'd had it held with a scarf till I arrived. It was a beautiful swirl of blond. Mother Martha had crocheted me a fine net studded with crystal beads, and they caught the light everywhere. I knew I would make an impression. There was only one person I cared to impress. I made my way down the back staircase, and then walked into the ball-room. The murmurs started immediately.

"Perhaps she should have dressed half as a copper and half as a criminal," someone whispered cruelly behind my back. "Seems like it would have been easy enough to puzzle out that costume." The voice was a woman's. I did not receive a warm welcome from many others; they had, apparently, been informed of my father's troubles, or considered me otherwise ill-suited for present company. I turned and smiled at her. She smiled, thinly, and slunk away.

I turned back and then I saw him. His hair curled over the collar of his costume, which I could not completely make out. Within a moment, he took my hand. "Lord Lockwood," I said.

He grinned. "If you're not going to call me Lumpy, then perhaps Thomas will do."

I echoed the sentiment he'd expressed months ago, quietly. "Thomas will most certainly do."

He swept me into his arms, possessively, and we joined a dance just about to begin. I wanted to melt into his arms without reserve. But there were unresolved concerns. I held back just a little.

"That is a magnificent gown," he said. "The fabric is lovely. I was so disappointed to see the fabric I'd gifted to you appear on Lady Tolfee for the Silver and Gold Ball."

I nearly tripped. "You'd sent that?"

He smoothly kept me in the dance. His hand on my back fitted perfectly, like the hand of a musician caressing the neck of a cello. We were two pieces, a flawless fit. "Yes."

"Why didn't you tell me?" I asked. "I should never have parted with it."

The orchestra played, and the music expanded through the room and then exhaled outward—the windows and great doors had all been opened to the street to let in the breeze.

"I knew the gift was too dear for a man to gift to a lady he was not formally attached to. And yet it was so beautiful; your hair is so blond it may be spun silver. I wanted you to have it. I wanted you to love it, and wear it, and to see you in it."

I sighed. "I did love it. I'd wanted to keep it. I suppose I should have followed my instincts and done so. Mrs. W convinced me I should sell it and donate the profits."

His hand flexed. "It was Judas who said the perfume used to anoint Christ should have been sold and the money given to the poor."

I pondered this truth for a moment, till he spoke again, quietly.

"I'm sorry you had to hear that comment about your father," he said. "Just before I came to take you from the foot of the stairs."

"My costume," I said. "You overheard." He nodded. The dance was nearly over.

"I had heard the rumors, of course, but would not engage in gossip with you about something so hurtful. Has anyone spoken about it of late?"

"The son of . . . my father's inspector friend has. He feels as though, well, as though he should protect me."

Thomas grimaced. At the idea of another man protecting me? Or because he felt I needed protection? "I see. If there was nothing there to prove, then it will die down again. In time, people will forget."

The music stopped, and I pulled away from him. "Do you believe he was guilty?"

He held my gaze. "Do you?"

Did I? I slowly shook my head. I did not want him to think ill of Papa, either. But I needed help. "I do not believe my father was guilty. But I admit I do not know for certain." I did not tell him, of course, but that was the first night I had left the picture of the smiling young woman at home in the bedroom cubbyhole. I hadn't wanted her company or reminder.

"I've followed every lead presented that might clear his name. I've made enquiries about something bad happening on King Street, which my father was involved with in some manner. My solicitor shut me down. Should I pursue it?"

His face grew hard. "Do nothing to put yourself at risk," he said.

"I won't," I said. *Think you I am no stronger than my sex / Being so father'd* . . . I knew I'd follow whatever leads might bring me to clearing my father's name. We were in the midst of the crowd again, so I lowered my voice.

"There is one other path I might pursue. I have some certificates, investment certificates, of Father's. Could you, would you look at them sometime and let me know if you believe them to be, well, legitimate? I know you are familiar with such things."

"Yes, of course. As the Season is concluding and Jamie's medical treatments are completed for a few months, I'd planned to leave London tomorrow. Duty, not passion, calls." He grinned at me. "I will return by Monday, the twenty-fourth of September, when I have some transactions to conclude. Will that be soon enough?

"Certainly. Thank you." I had an overwhelming amount of sewing to do and could not imagine there would be any reason to press the case sooner; Collingsworth had already viewed and returned them. I wanted to have the answer, and then again I did not. There was a reason, after all, that Inspector Collingsworth had taken, and then held, the certificates, a reason I could not discern by reading them.

It was time for us to change dance partners. I danced with a portly man who was dressed half hawk, half dove. I complimented him on his costume. He complimented me on mine, and he said with many of the matrons present he felt more mouse than hawk, and we laughed. We danced near a couple, and I noticed a huge ruby ring on that man's forefinger; I'd seen it before. Where?

Oh, yes. At the dinner at Thomas's club.

My next partner, too, was pleasant and funny. He had the dramatic happy/sad hypocrite masks on.

"What a clever costume," I said.

He looked at me and grinned. "I'm the only honest man here tonight, aren't I?" He made me laugh, and when he asked me for a second dance, I agreed. We discussed theater and politics and potato soup, which he was unaccountably fond of, and then the music ended. He looked as though he was going to ask me for a third dance, but Thomas came and tapped the man's shoulder and held his hand out to me. He looked warily at my admirer and I hid a smile.

"Lockwood," the man said, somewhat coolly.

"Moreworth," Thomas answered and nodded before he whisked me away. "I could have come half as Prince Charming, half as a shoe shine, had I known you would be dressed like this," Thomas said, his voice softer now. "So we'd match." His costume was half king and half commoner, sewn straight down the middle, front and back, fabrics carefully selected and skillfully merged to convey the theme but be attractive, still. I'd thought it wasn't as clever as it might be until I saw the V on the kingly half. Then I applauded the homage.

"Henry V," I whispered.

He bowed his head. "I hoped you'd be pleased."

"I am indeed." I enjoyed his happy company so much just then, I could not bear to think of bringing up his purchase of the acreage at Winton. What did it matter? The property was gone anyway.

It would not matter . . . if I had not wanted a future with the man. But if I did then I had to know his heart was honest. That had not been proved.

I must ask.

I sat the next dance out, watching from the sidelines as the young woman who had so coolly assessed me at the club dinner danced with Thomas. Lady Tolfee danced with a man who was half chimney sweep and half broom, his black hair held straight up from his head like bristles.

It was almost like being at the theater. A fat man was dressed in costume, left half sewn to represent capital, rich with gilt, while his right-hand side depicted labor and a poor man's threads. A particularly prickly matron appeared as angel from the front, but when she walked past you could see her costume depicted devil from behind. I thought about costumes and masquerades. Perhaps we all wore one, even in plain dress.

I remembered what Mrs. W had told me when I'd shared my shock at the high-end brothels in the West End.

Those pretending to be and do good, angels of darkness parading as light. Some start out that way and some, just like those angels, start in goodness and then are tempted and fall. Oh yes. There are plenty of evildoers right here . . . and also in the fine country houses of Hampshire. That kind of wickedness just has practiced manners and is better-dressed.

Thomas came to claim me to dance . . . again. Eyebrows were raised; I cared not.

His hand went round me again, and I wished for it never to be removed. When it was over, he bowed to me, and then said, "Let's repair to the gardens so we can talk."

Ah, yes, the promised talk. I had a few topics I wanted to discuss as well: the purchase of my acreage and the identity of the young lady I'd seen him escort into the carriage in front of the Lyceum.

In the center of the property was a courtyard square with plants and chairs and statues, a garden of sorts. There were other groups and couples mingling, and Thomas found us a quiet corner with a bench.

"I'm so glad you came tonight," he said. "Else I'd have found another way for us to speak before I depart London."

"I am, too."

He took my hands in his own. "I'm sure you've heard I was married," he began. It was, I admitted, a difficult way to begin a conversation.

"Yes," I said. "And she's passed away. I'm very sorry."

"I am, too," he said. He looked at his hands holding mine. "She was a good woman. A young woman. We didn't know each other well, of course, but that is how these things are done. We'd met a few times, and I found her pleasant, and she, me. Her family had land and other capital resources; I, of course, have a title, an established family, and resources of my own. Our fathers decided . . ." He shrugged. "And we acquiesced. We were young, and knew no other way."

I nodded, not wanting to interrupt. An undercurrent of laughter filtered up and clashed into a brackish blend with the gentle string instruments playing inside.

"She was kind enough, though we shared no interests, and shortly after our marriage she became with child. When it came time for the baby to be born she knew something was wrong. She sent for me at the end and pled with me to care for the child no matter what my feelings had been for her. I replied, of course I would, horrified and brimming with regret that my lack of warmth would have been so obvious, and the last thing on her mind as she neared her death. She wished me peace and happiness, joy and the truest of loves. And then, she died."

His face contracted a little, and I thought he was going to cry, but after a moment, he regained himself. "Our child died, too."

Ah. So this was the cause of the wince when I'd mentioned at our first meeting that Mamma had nearly died giving birth to me. I reached over, so I held both his hands in mine. "I'm so very sorry for your loss, what a devastating heart blow. I wish there were more that I could do, but I can say I understand that kind of pain, having lost my own parents."

"I gave back her land, you know." Thomas looked into the distance, reassuring himself as much as telling me, it seemed. "To her family."

I understood. "You realized then that you loved her, and you couldn't bear to have it near you."

He shook his head. "Quite the opposite. I knew I did not love her as I should have, could I have done it over. I would not profit from her death. Father was not pleased. But it would have been, at best, unchristian and unsportsmanlike. I hadn't paid for it but had received it anyway, and it was mine to do with what I pleased. If the child had lived, of course, I would have kept the property and passed it along to her as it was her due—" He stopped abruptly and blushed.

Which is, I knew he was thinking, exactly what my mother did not want to do with me and Winton Park; rather than have me inherit it, she'd planned to give it away if it had come to her first. In spite of myself I felt a little knob of irritation and the subtle rebuke.

"But the greatest regret I have is knowing that I loved the child more than I loved its mother. Marianne will never know the kind of true love that she wished for me. I'd feel guilty enjoying what she can never now have. One doesn't marry for love alone. Not in our circle."

"My mother did," I said quietly, and he flinched. I hadn't meant it to be a subtle rebuke of its own to parry the one he'd offered about keeping the property for his child. Just a way of keeping my mother and father with me, as I remembered them, and perhaps an indication of the differences in our upbringing. "But I completely understand that's not how it is, for the most part."

Thomas waited until a group of people who had come near moved away. "I have worked tirelessly since that day to do right by people, to be honorable, to do my duty by all. I have distanced myself from those who carouse and plunder or lie or make light of life so I can redeem myself in some way for the love I could not offer her. It is, perhaps, why I feel so drawn to help Shaftesbury and his causes."

Lord Shaftesbury, I knew, was present at the Twin Ball as well—I'd just seen him in the garden, looking toward us before disappearing into the house again. He looked very old.

"Has working for charitable causes helped you find that peace and joy, the happiness and love?"

He smiled, and his face warmed brilliantly again; I recalled the day I'd met him, truly, the day we buried Papa, and his smile had melted me then, as now.

"Miss Young," he started.

"Gillian," I said softly.

"Gillian," he said. "Gillian. I have said it in my head and my heart—and in the solitude of my chamber—but to say it aloud to you! Yes, Gillian, that is the most wonderful thing. I have found all of those things, not through duty . . . but with you."

With me!

He'd also said his class did not marry for love.

Ah! My heart sank. He had not mentioned marriage.

"*You* bring me peace and joy and delight and interesting conversation. I laugh again, now, and I hope I bring you laughter, too."

"You do," I said. "You are, decidedly, everything I had hoped for in a . . ." I could not say husband! And yet I did not want my feelings to go unacknowledged, as he had so openly shared his. I continued, ". . . a man, but did not know that till we met." I said no more as someone came by and stopped to speak quietly to Thomas; he nodded and then said he'd be in shortly, before turning back to me.

Marry well, someone you trust and love without reserve, a man who can rescue you, my little damsel in distress, should you need it, Papa had said. Did I trust Thomas? Would he prove honest? There was only one way to learn.

"I must ask. Did you buy some acreage from my father when he visited with Inspector Collingsworth?"

Thomas's face wrinkled with confusion. "Your father never came to Hampshire with Collingsworth that I know of."

"But you'd said, when I buried Papa, that he had."

Thomas shook his head. "No, I said they'd both been there. But not at the same time. Your father came and yes, he did sell some acreage from your trust to me, the arable land."

"The arable land. That which I could have farmed to provide income for Winton's upkeep."

His firm gaze held. "Yes. He was not working it anyway and I could put it to good use and he, for some reason, needed the funds. Then he came again just shortly before he died and a few days after that visit Collingsworth came."

"How did you know?" I asked.

"Davidson told my mother," he said.

Ugh. His mother. But why had Collingsworth come on his own? He must have thought Papa had left something at Winton, something he wanted, and would secret away if he could.

"I should have told you about the acreage," Thomas continued. "I'm sorry. I didn't because, well, your father hadn't told you. I thought it was a confidence and I wanted to keep the confidence and honor him in that way. I sensed your father was keeping secrets of some kind; it was an awkward meeting at the end. With all that has been said since . . . I hope you understand that I had good intentions. I knew you'd learn when the paperwork for the trust was completed."

I nodded. That was plausible.

A crowd of people filtered onto the portico now; it must be near midnight when supper would be served. Our hostess was calling everyone inside.

Thomas looked at me intently. "There is something you should know, and I'd like you to hear it from me. I have purchased Winton Park."

CHAPTER TWENTY-SEVEN

I sharply inhaled. "Already? It's only been signed over to the Cause nigh on two months."

He nodded. "My land agent knew I was interested and he let them know. I paid ten percent more than the asking price as soon as it became available, to honor your mother's wishes as well as my mother's wishes."

My stomach clenched. Well, what had I expected when I turned the property over? That it would not be sold? The sale had done what my mother had wanted it to do: fund the Cause. It just seemed that he'd lain waiting for it, ready to pounce at the first moment.

I turned toward Thomas. Perhaps . . . perhaps he'd had me in mind all along. I spoke softly. "Why had it been so important to you to buy Winton? Because it was the neighboring property . . . ?" I left the sentence hopefully open-ended.

He nodded. "Yes, of course. My mother has long wanted it."

His mother. Again! He'd not had me in mind, but her. Of course she wanted it. She coveted anything that had belonged to Mamma, and now she had it. She could walk right in now and take down Mamma's portrait and reclaim the matching carriage clock and everything else. My face must have shown my anger because he stopped talking and put his arm around me, which I shrugged off.

"Gillian. Is something wrong? Do you wish I had not been the one to buy it? I thought . . ."

I did not know what to think. All the men I thought so highly of had thoroughly confused me. I was glad he had it, I supposed. But not his mother! I spoke without thinking. "I'm uncertain of what I feel, Lord Lockwood. Perhaps, with your mother desiring Winton, you might have lightly exaggerated the expenses, such that they were, required for modernization and repair in order to sway my opinion."

He stood up, recoiled by my use of his formal title, and, I supposed, my accusation, and moved away from me. Lady Mary came to greet us. "Come now, Miss Young, Lord Lockwood. It's time for supper." She looked at us, happily, and said, "You might still be seated together." Then she must have noticed the looks on our faces. "Or not." She scurried away.

"I apologize for whatever I said or did that upset you and however I may have comported myself that could bring about a charge of misdeed or mistruth," Thomas said. "I did not know you preferred that I not purchase the house." He sounded hurt. How could he have known? I nodded. It was better, after all, that it had gone to someone who loved it. It was just, well . . .

His mother. I suppose, tucked deeply in my hurt heart, I'd hoped he was going to say he'd purchased it for me, not her. What a childish desire, Gillian! He certainly seemed to be telling the truth about the repair expenses; Papa had said the house was crumbling, too. His manner grew distant.

Still coiled in disappointment, confusion, and loss, I said, "I do not think I shall remain for supper." Yes, indeed, Cinderella would flee just ahead of midnight.

He looked angry and hurt. "Perhaps that's just as well. I have made a commitment to speak with Lord Shaftesbury this evening. But could I please have my driver take you home? I'm concerned for your safety."

I nodded. "I would very much appreciate that." Part of me wished he would try to cajole me into a further conversation, but on the whole, I grudgingly admired that he let me to my own emotions and did not try to direct me against my will.

He escorted me to the front and called for his carriage; he did not lean forward to kiss me good night. If he had, I would have gladly accepted and it may have broken the tension between us. I, foolishly, did not offer an olive branch, either, upon which a dove of peace might have landed.

"Good evening, Miss Young." His voice broke just a little. My heart did, too.

The carriage, driven by the army veteran Thomas had rescued from outside the gentlemen's club, chucked the horses and we departed. By the time I was home I was filled with regrets. My bitterness was the spoiled fruit of pride.

I regretted not feeling cheered that someone kind had purchased my family home, and telling him so.

I regretted the implication that he had overstated the repair costs, and yet, I was still not sure he'd proved true.

I regretted not staying for supper, the time that might have allowed the unexpected wound to heal and the matter happily resolve.

I regretted causing that heart-pierce in a man who had let his guard down with me.

I hadn't even brought home the sweets I'd promised to the girls.

I went into my room, took off the Cinderella gown, and slipped into a dressing gown before climbing under the sheets. I opened the hidden cupboard behind my bed and pulled out all of the papers.

First, the letter from Mamma regarding Winton. *I did as you'd asked, Mamma. I hope you are pleased. Thomas is a good man. I do not know what you thought of his mother, but I pray she will treat your home with care.*

I set aside the letters between her and Papa for a moment.

The photograph of the young woman. I felt almost guilty having left her at home. Her glance looked to me now not to be happy, but pleading. The smile of a woman who has been told to smile. I saw, now, that the smile did not extend to her eyes. As I locked eyes with her, I knew I must still try to find her, help her, somehow.

But how?

I fingered the punched train stub. Thomas said that Papa had visited Winton just before his death, and then, just after, Inspector Collingsworth had come. I'd come to believe that at least one Collingsworth was mixed up in something evil and wrong. Had Papa been a partner in crime as well as in crime fighting? I did not believe so, otherwise, why would Collingsworth have come on his own?

The inspector was looking for something. Something that would prove him guilty, and that he wished to do away with. But I had searched Winton.

So had he. Had he found it and spirited it away before I arrived?

No. Because then there would have been no reason to have had me followed, or had my house searched.

Was Francis involved, too? Perhaps. I hoped not. But perhaps.

I looked at the love letters between my parents. Surely they'd known, by saving them, they would fall to me someday. These letters, in truth, were what I had come looking for this late night. I spent an hour reading their voices, their humor, their hopes and dreams and declarations of love.

Then I turned the lamp off and lay there in owl-like alertness, filled with yearning and the pain of an epiphany that could, perhaps, no longer be responded to.

Thomas. Are you who I think you are?

My girls are right. I am in love.

The girls had noticed that I was less enthusiastic in the days that followed, but I told them I was tired, and I was. I had an unquiet mind. I needed to write to Thomas and then to Francis, Sergeant Collingsworth. I felt overwhelmed and waited a few days to begin to make sure I wasn't speaking hastily, writing something I might later regret.

I could have chosen a life with Francis; he was a kind and good man, attractive. It was perfectly acceptable and most probably what was expected of me. I smiled a little, wryly, just as, perhaps, my mother had been expected to marry Thomas's father. But I was not in love with Francis, and I doubted that he was in love with me. Being in love would probably not even have crossed his mind. It wasn't necessarily a requirement in his world, either, to marry for love. Duty, suitability, companionship, yes. Love, if one was lucky, came later, after marriage.

It had come sooner for me, before marriage, which was most unlucky indeed.

I looked out the window. It looked like the bakery cart was, once more, rolling down my street. They often did, once or twice a day, to sell their wares at the Embankment. But this cart had gone down the street perhaps five or six times that I had noticed.

"Ruby?" I called her downstairs.

"Yes, miss?" She bounded down and stood before me.

"Have you noticed anything odd as you've looked out the window?"

"I'm not skiving off, miss, I'm working hard."

I smiled. "Yes. But on your breaks, when you look out the window?"

She nodded. "A bakery cart, back and forth, back and forth. And sometimes a rat catcher, which is odd, miss, because they do not normally work in the daylight, do they? And these are new men now, not the usuals."

I shook my head. "No, rat catchers do not work during the day. Thank you." Were they spies?

She returned to the sewing, and I wrote a note to Francis, asking if he could call on me the next week during calling hours; I would tell him in person. First I needed to get a little ahead on the sewing; I'd been asked to assist with last-minute costumes for *A Sailor and His Lass* because one of the other seamstresses had become ill. We were sewing the forest fairies costumes for *Cinderella* as well. We could get them all done, but only if nothing went wrong. Without Lady Tolfee's continuing patronage I could not say no to the new theater work.

I sealed the note to Francis with my mother's ring and then set it for the postman.

Next, I wrote a note to Thomas. I was certain by then of what I wanted to say.

Dearest Thomas,

I would like to beg your forgiveness for my quick tongue and unpardonably bad manners at Tolfee House. I believe that the shock of learning that my home, which I had long cherished the idea of seeing come to life under happier circumstances, had already been sold put me off balance. I especially regret the implication that you had been duplicitous in the expenses for Winton Park.

No, I regret it all.

The continuing strain and tension over my father's situation caused me to act in an uncaring manner. Please call on me at your convenience, or write if you prefer. If you do not, I will understand that matters have concluded between us due to my rash actions and words, and wish you the very best henceforth.

I meant every word when I said you were all I'd hoped for.

I remain Yours Truly,
Gillian

I'd thought of addressing him as Lumpy just to tease and bring back the playfulness, but did not presume.

I sealed it with red wax and my signet ring before addressing it to be delivered to Darington, as he'd said he was leaving London. I prayed he would receive it within a day and respond warmly.

No, I prayed he would return to me with all speed.

The first day possible, Sergeant Collingsworth came calling at teatime.

I'd asked Mrs. W to let him in. I did not look forward to speaking with him.

I went downstairs and as I greeted him, Mrs. W disappeared into her room and closed the door, leaving us to our privacy.

He stood in the hallway. "Gillian, it is a delight to see you." He'd taken his hat off; some of his color had returned, and I thought what a handsome man he was, especially in his uniform. He carried an official leather pouch with him. I glanced at it. He looked nervous.

"I cannot stay long; I'm sorry," he said. "I am to return to duty in a short while. I wanted to come by quickly, though, and not let any more time elapse after having received your note. I can return in a day or two. Perhaps we might take tea at a shop? Or we could visit the park?"

As I was about to show him from the foyer into the parlor, I noticed a man was standing on my steps. "Has someone come with you?" I asked.

He smiled. "Oh, yes. Jones. We work closely now, good chap. Senior sergeant helping me learn the next step. He's waiting whilst we have a chat."

I looked out the window, and as I did, Sergeant Jones turned to look at me. He did, and tipped his hat, and grinned.

I stumbled. Jones laughed mockingly, silent to our ears, through the closed door. Francis could not see his face.

"Gillian, are you quite all right?"

I could barely stand, but I did. "Yes, yes, I, well, I shall get our tea. Please, give me five minutes."

I stumbled down the stairs to the kitchens, gasping as I did. Louisa was not in attendance, for which I was glad.

Disgust and terror overcame me. Sergeant Jones had been the carriage driver who had kidnapped me and taken me, threateningly, to the docks! He'd come today to taunt me. I knew it. Did Francis know?

I steadied myself; the flesh on my upper arms trembled and grew cold; I could not stop them shaking.

Things had not died away, as Thomas had said they might. As I'd hoped they would. They had suddenly become even worse.

I breathed calmly for two or three minutes, then went to find Louisa. I instructed her to make the tea and bring it upstairs. After a minute or two more, I returned to Francis. He had moved to the parlor. I did not look out the window, at my front porch.

"Are you quite well?" Francis asked. "I'm sorry . . . I cannot stay but for a moment more, so I'll miss tea." His ear tips were now red and he would not meet my gaze. *Why not?*

"Yes," I said. "I wish this didn't have to be rushed but, well, I think it's best to be straightforward. I have been thinking and praying and I've come to the conclusion that it would be best all round if you and I remained as friends."

I'd said it. He fidgeted.

"I'm very sorry to hear that," he said. "Perhaps a few more weeks of consideration might change your mind."

I shook my head. "No, Francis. You are a dear, dear man. I respect you and know there is a woman perfectly suited to you. But I am not her."

His face flashed with an emotion I could not completely discern. Anger? Fear? Embarrassment? All three?

"So it's to be the viscount, then?" He glanced deep in my house, past me. Why?

"I hadn't said that," I replied.

"But you will see him again?" Francis insisted. I had no compulsion to answer him, but I did anyway, out of respect for the many years of our companionship. Plus, if he was involved in the troubles with my father, I thought my association with Thomas, no matter how tenuous, might provide me some protection.

"Yes," I answered firmly. "Yes, I will. Soon."

He nodded. "I see I won't need to come back to take you to the park, then."

"No, thank you," I replied. "But I hope that our paths will cross again."

"Oh, they will. You can be certain of that."

A noise clattered behind me; my back was to the staircase. I turned and saw young feet scamper up the stairway. Ruby, and perhaps Charlotte, had been eavesdropping.

Francis had seen them, too. "I hope it goes well for all of you." He put his helmet back on his head.

Had that been a threat? It felt like one.

"Good day, Miss Young. I can let myself out."

Normally, I may have protested, but I had no desire to see Sergeant Jones again, and so I let Francis go.

Within a minute of his pulling the door closed behind him, Mrs. W opened the door to her room and joined me in the hall.

"Don't worry, miss. We'll take you to the park," Charlotte said. "You needn't wait for him to come and take you."

"We don't like his father anyway," Ruby agreed. "And that copper he came with today. I've seen him before somewhere. Maybe from the window. I can't recall."

I looked at her sharply. "He's been here recently?"

"I don't remember when, miss. But I've seen him from the window.

Ah, yes. My young spy.

"Back to work with you, then," I said, shooing them to their duties. I sent Mrs. W to fetch Bidwell. Then I sent Bidwell to fetch the locksmith once again. This time, I had a most expensive lock installed that would be very difficult indeed to breach. I gave one key to Mrs. W and kept one for myself. Both would be needed to unlock the door.

Each day I eagerly awaited the post, but no letter came from Thomas. It certainly had been long enough for a letter to reach him in Hampshire and then return to me. He had, perhaps, decided that, as things were awkward and cool between us, and he'd secured Winton for his mother, it was best to move on. Perhaps it had been a lovely interlude and nothing more. The thought saddened me.

One afternoon Mrs. W opened the door and began a conversation. I looked at the clock on the cabinet in the salon—yes, it was calling hours! I stood on the dressing dais in front of the mirror and adjusted my hair and dress. The girls did not look up at me, but they also had not asked me any questions since the ball. There had been no mention of being in love. I suspect my face and mannerisms, and the fact that Thomas had not called again, had conveyed my disappointment.

I walked downstairs to find, not Thomas, but Mrs. Finley, my mother's friend from the Cause.

"Mrs. Finley!" I went forward and greeted her warmly. "Please, come into the sitting room. I'm delighted to see you."

Mrs. Finley looked at Mrs. W, who nodded and smiled. "I had asked Barbara if I might call."

"You are welcome anytime!" I said. Mrs. W bustled off to ask Louisa to prepare treats and sweets for our guest.

Mrs. Finley sat near me and folded her hands in her lap. "I do want to say, dear, how pleasantly shocked I was to hear that you'd donated your home to the Cause. The effects of that rippled across all who knew your mother. Barbara has proudly made it known to all, and of course, the funds will do a great deal to help the less fortunate for a decade or longer."

I smiled and hoped my mixed feelings would not express themselves in my voice or on my face. "It's what my mother wanted. I'm sure she'd be gratified."

Mrs. Finley nodded. "You've heard it's been sold already. There were quite a number of interested bidders. I'm happy to say it went to a good family who paid a premium."

"Yes, I'd heard," I said dryly.

"The papers have not yet been completed, but the estate will be fully transferred by the third week of September. They'd like the property to be available to them then. There are many repairs to be made before the weather arrives."

The third week of September, when Thomas had said he must return to London to conclude a transaction. This, then, among other things, perhaps, was his reason for returning then.

Mrs. Finley continued. "I was sent to speak with you because, well, your mother and I had been great friends."

Mrs. W brought the tea and settled it between us. "Stay, please," I insisted. She was much more a part of the Cause than I, and great friends with Mrs. Finley. She smiled and poured for us.

"You do have personal belongings there, is that right?" Mrs. Finley said. "Things you will want to retain for yourself, mementos and such? We understood that the home was to be sold with the furnishing intact."

"Yes on both counts," I said. I'd sold it intact not only because it had made it more valuable but also I did not have room for more furnishings and, well, it seemed sad to split the house from its mementos and furniture. "I do, however, want my mother's costumes and such."

"Would you like to travel to get the things you'd like?" she asked. "Or, the family has suggested if you preferred to spare yourself the trouble, you could make a list, deliver it to me, and they will see everything you request shipped to London."

He did not want me to come there; then he'd have to see me.

"Perhaps that would be best," I said, crushed as the reality of the ending of our relationship came sharply clear. "I'll ensure that I get the list to you soon."

"Fine, dear." With the business at hand out of the way, we enjoyed our tea and biscuits, and Mrs. Finley left, promising to return for a visit soon.

As she left, a delivered note came from Drury Lane. I'd been summoned.

CHAPTER TWENTY-EIGHT

SEPTEMBER, 1883

"Miss Young." Wilhelm held out papery hands, the mark of an older man, and enveloped my smooth ones within them. "Come, let's have a seat." He led me to a box, which was costumed in its way—upholstered in soft midnight-blue velvet and painted in rococo swirls of gold and blue. "It will be more private here, for talking."

I'd thought we would go behind the stage where the production members were hard at work, or belowstairs to the open wardrobe room where we seamstresses would soon gather from our salons, bringing the costumes with us so we may finish up the fittings and final details on the actual actors and actresses ahead of the dress rehearsal for *A Sailor and His Lass*.

It did not bode well that he wanted to speak to me in private. I thought on my loss of Lady Tolfee's gowns and pushed the panic down. He must somehow be convinced of my worth!

I pulled one of the forest fairies pantomime costumes out of my bag. "I'm very happy with how these have turned out—I tried to design elfin and darling." I held the bright sash I'd made for each child. "These will tie together with the costume Cinderella would wear in the forest." I giggled, and he looked alarmed. "I'm sorry," I said. "I just thought it funny, 'tied' together."

He smiled wanly. I must sound hysterical. I was approaching hysterical!

"My apprentice Charlotte has made little green slippers, soled in felt for silence," I said after quieting my voice. I held one toward him.

He looked at it, and then me, fondly. "You're doing well, Miss Young. But . . . the police have just been back for another visit." He sighed.

"What?" My pitch rose again.

"A Sergeant Jones."

"What did he want?"

Wilhelm grimaced. "He asked if you kept regular hours here. The dresser told him you would be back next week and the week after, in the afternoons, for fittings and such if he cared to see you, but were here only occasionally otherwise."

Oh dear. I could not avoid those fittings; it was a critical part of my commission. But I did not want to have a public confrontation with Jones at the place of my employ.

"I'll speak with someone about it," I said.

"Can they not speak with you at home? Surely they know where you live."

Yes, yes, they did. They were making it difficult for me, isolating me, intimidating me.

"They do."

"You understand, Gillian, I have a certain fondness for you. Your mother and I were very good friends and you are like a daughter to me in some ways. But I cannot risk my position here, either. Mr. Harris won't have these kinds of disturbances, and regular visits from the Metropolitan Police do not make for a festive atmosphere. We can't alienate our paying guests with a suggestion of wrongdoing. It disturbs the staff as well."

"Yes. I know. I shall attend to this matter."

"It doesn't look good. Soon, people will begin to question you—question your honesty in your materials budget, your associations . . . I'd heard that Lady Tolfee has decided against using you next Season."

"Unfortunately," I said. I held back tears but Wilhelm, who read actors all the time, knew how to read me, too.

He squeezed my hand. "I will see you next week for the final fittings for *A Sailor and His Lass* . . . and your young apprentices who make the lovely slippers, correct?"

I nodded. The girls were coming to the fittings. It would be their first time backstage not as performers, and I hoped to give them a happy glimpse of the life that could lie ahead for them.

"Till then," he said as he left.

I waited, alone in the box, and prayed. Then, certain that no one was about, I allowed myself the indulgence of a nearly silent cry.

I had badly misread Thomas and perhaps, somehow, my father and even mother with her desire to donate Winton. Was there anyone I truly knew?

I walked home. Now, in the yellow smoke–tainted dusk, the city closed around me and it made me claustrophobic. The early autumn was unusually warm, and my clothes felt as tightly wrapped as grave cloths. The heat seemed to melt the coal dust and mold it to the buildings, the lamp and carriage posts, and my clothing. It lined my lungs like a sticky golden syrup as I breathed in. I had developed a twitch under my left eye, and it presented itself more often when I was walking about town. I felt someone behind me though I could not see them through the heavy air. Footsteps. Who could be following me?

Jones, most likely.

My eye twitched again. I stopped and dramatically turned around, ready to confront my stalkers.

A young couple looked at me strangely and crossed the street to avoid further interaction. I supposed my eyes reflected my overwrought thoughts.

My eye would not stop twitching; it wriggled like a worm under my skin and I pressed my hand firmly upon it, which stopped the movement, but only until I let go.

I was going mad.

I walked on. I hadn't visited Sarah in some time, nor taken the girls to tea. I'd avoided the park, even, not knowing who would be lurking there for me. If someone were, could I turn to the police for protection and comfort, as Papa had always told me I might?

No longer. But . . . maybe.

I wanted nothing so much as to stay at home, but the more I yielded to that temptation, the more firmly entrenched it would become. I could not allow that.

When I arrived home, I quickly dashed off a note to Francis.

Dear Sergeant Collingsworth,

No, I must start over.

Dear Francis,

I *would* presume this time upon his Christian name, and pray he recalled our merry times together. Did I trust him? No.

*I hope that our conversation has not had the effect of
terminating our friendship. You had told me once that if I
were in need of anything to call on you. Your father had
mentioned that, too. I do find myself in a place where I
need some advice, especially as it regards the force. Would
you be able to call? Or perhaps I could meet you somewhere?*

   I await your reply and remain,
   Yours truly,
   Gillian

I posted it immediately. I must tell him about Jones, and ask
for his help. I had no one else to turn to.

"Louisa?" I asked. "Could you please pack a hamper for the
girls and me? I believe we'll take our dinner in the park, as there is
to be music tonight."

She smiled. "Certainly, miss."

The girls and I left to stroll in the late daylight; the breeze had
cleared the air a little, and I was grateful for that.

The river rolled on its muddy way, swans craning their long
necks this way and that in righteous indignation at being dis-
placed by scores of gliding rowers. Soon, the park would return to
its autumn slowdown and then winter hush. We chattered on
about the next week, when we'd be at Drury Lane every afternoon
for fittings, sewing circles, and meeting with the actors. I know
they were enthusiastic about getting out of Cheyne and I was enthusiastic for them. We walked home, three abreast, arm in arm,
safely.

No Jones. No foxes. The baker's cart remained, but the seller
manning it smiled kindly and did not look disreputable. Perhaps
things might turn out well.

•   •   •

The very next day, Saturday, the morning post brought a small package.

Thomas? My hopes soared, and I looked at the parcel. No, Francis. They fell again. The package had been posted from his home. The writing, however, was decidedly feminine. I opened the box and out tumbled the beautiful pincushion I had gifted to Francis's mother. It clattered to the floor and broke open at the hinge. I flinched.

Dear Miss Young,

The handwriting was spidery and difficult to read, as though written with a shaking hand. Shaking from anger? Or illness?

> *I have received your letter to Francis, and to spare him additional pain, opened it, read it, and am responding in his stead and without his knowledge.*
> *He has just told us not a day ago that he had made a proposal of intentions to you, but you firmly turned him down. And now you're asking for his help! Temerity!*
> *I think your family has caused just about enough trouble for ours. I've no doubt you find yourself in need of protection. But you shan't have it from us.*
> *I wish you well.*
> *Mrs. Emily Collingsworth*

What did she mean, she had no doubt I find myself in need of protection? A chill rolled through me, and I grew weak once more. I threw the pincushion into the wastebin, as though it had been sent to curse me. It might as well have.

CHAPTER TWENTY-NINE

The next day, Sunday afternoon, we returned from church to find a fine carriage waiting on the street outside our home. Thomas? My heart nearly burst. He had returned to me as I'd hoped he would! All would be well. He'd received my letter, finally, and had decided to respond in person . . . of course!

The girls looked at me, happily. We made our way up the steps without looking at him; I was not about to race to the carriage like a foolish schoolgirl; I would welcome him inside like the gracious lady I was.

Once inside the door, I turned my back to it and laughed. Yes, gracious lady, indeed. I smoothed out my skirt and glanced at the mirror, tucking a few unruly strands back into my pinned-up hair. I was happy that the day was light and my clothing and skin were not smudged by coal smoke. The brisk walk had brightened my skin. Good! I lightly bit my lips to bring some additional color to them.

The girls scurried upstairs with Mother Martha while Mrs. W remained with me, to chaperone. After a moment, Bidwell opened the door, and my hopes sank.

"Mr. Colmore Dunn." A cloud slid across the sun. "Please, come in."

"Miss Young." Colmore Dunn tipped his hat. He looked kind but reserved. I immediately changed my enthusiastic approach to match his.

"How nice to see you. How unexpected."

"Lord Lockwood had promised to look at your father's certificates," he said. "He would by no means break a promise and bid me come and review them, as they are an area of particular expertise for me, before he returns to town this week. I thought I may as well do it now."

Thomas would not break a promise, only my heart, which now collapsed inside me, causing crushing pain from chest bone to backbone. It was simply duty, then, the shackles he could not free himself from. That was fine. I would allow this unrestrained sense of duty to assist me. After procuring my home for his mother it was the least he could do. He had apparently replaced the plastron guarding his heart. I would adjust mine as well.

I turned toward Colmore Dunn and spoke a little sharply. "I understand you assisted in the sale of some acreage to Lord Lockwood from my father last year. I'm surprised you hadn't mentioned it to me."

"Confidential matter, Miss Young," he said. "I'm sure you understand. That being said, I found your father to be a fine man. I'm terribly sorry, but Matilda will be most upset if I'm late for our Sunday supper." It was clear he found the task not to his taste and had left it for the last minute.

"Lord Lockwood did not want to come himself?" I asked. I must know.

"He arrives in London tomorrow, has signings to conduct, and then is leaving again shortly after." He blushed once more, so I surmised there was more to it than that.

Without doubt he had told him of our recent estrangement. Maybe he believed Papa's suspected involvement with prostitution and fraud and had decided to distance himself from me. It would be understandable. Even Papa's own brothers on the police force had done so. Lord Tolfee felt he would be tainted by his wife's association with me.

I walked to Papa's desk and sat down at the chair, then reached into the drawer that held the certificates. I pulled out the thick handful and then handed them over.

Colmore Dunn looked through a few of them, glancing nonchalantly and humming an acceptance. Then he stopped and looked at one, then the next, very closely. His lip curled almost in revulsion. A sickly look crossed his face. He looked through several more.

"Is everything all right?" I asked anxiously.

Colmore Dunn looked at me. "No, I believe it is not. May I take these with me? I shall see them returned to you when I have fully investigated." He looked at me with hard eyes. "You do still want this fully investigated."

I understood him to mean that things did not look promising, rather, they looked potentially incriminatory. Mrs. Collingsworth's warning returned to me, and I shivered. *Did she know? Had her husband planted something damning?*

"Yes," I whispered. "Yes, I must know the truth."

Colmore Dunn nodded. "I'll return them within the week."

I showed him to the door, where he bid me a pleasant and perfunctory good-bye. I closed the door, but looked out of the window to the side of the door. The rat catcher, of all people, had stopped Colmore Dunn.

I sat down, heavily, in a chair.

Thomas, I thought. *What has come of us?*

Mrs. W came and put her arm round me, a very welcome gesture. "I did tell you about titled men, didn't I?" she asked, and I
nodded, silent.

"Even your mother knew that," she finished. "Being the daughter of one."

The next morning found us all preparing to go to the Drury. We
had promised to be in attendance and sew each afternoon from
noon to five, for final fittings for *A Sailor and His Lass*. We prepared ourselves early and then the girls and Mother Martha and I
began our stroll in the pleasant early-autumn air, carrying the
wardrobe bags with us.

"It's a fine day to be out," I said. I hoped no one was following
us. I hoped there would not be a public confrontation with Sergeant Jones. The thought of that brought my tic on, and I repri-
manded myself. It would do no good to worry; no one had been
following me for some time, and once I gave reign to the fancies
in my mind I may never again regain control.

I'd put the thoughts of the certificates out of my mind, for the
moment, by sheer will. If they were found to be fraudulent, I
would have no income from them, and I would need my work at
the theater more than ever.

Ruby was in a cheery mood; she was not the only member of
the household who eavesdropped. The night before, I'd heard her
tell Charlotte they might flirt with some of the younger actors.

She burst out in song, which she'd heard the week before at
the Theatrical Mission. "A sailor and his lass had met / At eve to
say farewell / For he was off to sea at morn / Leaving his love for a
spell. / 'Cheer up, my lass,' he whispered low, / In accents fond and
true . . ."

Charlotte jostled her friend. "Ruby," she hissed quietly.

Ruby did not seem to hear her. "'. . . Though wandering o'er the world I go, / I'll come back soon to you. / For I'll be true, ever true / Always true to thee!'"

Charlotte jostled her again and looked meaningfully in my direction.

"Oh," Ruby said. "Sorry, miss."

"There is nothing to be sorry about," I said. They both nodded glumly. We all knew I was lying.

We walked in through the back doors and down the stairs to the wardrobe room. There were other rooms that were used for dressing, and wigs, and preparations, but the wardrobe room was a central hive where costumes were finally fitted. There were long tables surrounded with women, heads down, sewing. There were daises scattered throughout the room, topped by sometimes preening, overwrought actors, insisting that something or another be immediately changed. Their dressers sought to soothe and cajole, mostly successfully. I smiled in remembrance. Even Mamma had been a prima donna from time to time. It was a part of their temperament.

On each wall were anchored wardrobe trunks and containers, labeled by gender and sometimes by performance; costumes for Juliet might be found next to a pantomime cow's skin. Some were to be found here, certainly, that my mother had once worn. They had probably been remade in years since; fitted for other actresses.

The girls and I worked till midafternoon; I told Ruby she might wander over to the wig room; she made quick friends with the milliner and returned donning a new creation every twenty minutes: first a milkmaid, then the Queen, and finally a scullery maid. She set the tables to laughter.

Yes, I would speak with Sarah about her, perhaps the following week. I might be able to find another seamstress at the Mission, as Mother Rachel had been using the new treadle to train another apprentice.

I didn't want Ruby to leave, though.

Toward late afternoon we returned home. *I hope Louisa prepared something nourishing for dinner,* I thought. We were all famished.

When we rounded the street to approach Cheyne Gardens, I sensed something was wrong. There was a police cart outside of the house, and I could see three or four uniformed officers standing outside of my house on the porch. How many more might be inside?

"What's happening, miss?" Charlotte asked me.

I shook my head. "I do not know." I looked up and down the street. No rat catcher, no neighbors. Toward the end, near where it turned to the Embankment, was the bakery cart pusher. He was speaking with one of the cops.

Ah. They'd planted him there.

Ruby slowed down. I stopped, several houses away from my door, out of sight, I hoped. I did not think that the girls should come with me. I turned to Mother Martha. "I think it best if you take the girls to the Mission."

She looked at me serenely; perhaps the day had tired her. "Will you join us?"

I inhaled. It was tempting. But I had Mrs. W, Louisa, and Bidwell to worry about. Not to mention the fact that it was my home.

Had this anything to do with the certificates that Lockwood and Colmore Dunn had taken just a day before? Could he have found something so seriously amiss that the police had been sent before informing me? It wasn't that they wanted to know when I'd be at the theater so they could meet me there. They wanted to know when I'd be away from my house.

"I shall join you later," I said. "I hope. Proceed with all speed and remain there until I come to collect you or send for you. Do not leave."

Mother Martha nodded, and the girls reached up and embraced me.

"You'll be all right, won't you, miss?" Charlotte asked. "They won't send you to jail, will they?"

"There is nothing to send me to jail for," I said. I hoped I was right.

"Now, go on with you." I urged Mother Martha back the way we had come. When they were out of sight, I walked down the street and marched up the steps. Two officers fell in place, blocking my path.

"This is my house," I said.

"The inspector said we should keep you here, miss, till he comes to fetch you."

"Then go fetch him!" I could hear my neighbors rustling, and saw some faces peeking from the curtains. The sheer indignity of it all. They'd all heard the rumors about my father, too, I knew.

Within a few minutes, Collingsworth appeared. "Well, well. Welcome home, Miss Young."

CHAPTER THIRTY

LONDON AND HAMPSHIRE
SEPTEMBER, 1883

I managed to keep my voice steady though I trembled inside. "What is the meaning of making free with my house?"

"The meaning of this, Miss Young, is that we've had some new information that this property might have been purchased with ill-gotten gains."

I tilted my head. "Purchased by whom with ill-gotten gains?"

"Your father, of course," he said. "The house had a large, and final, payment made on it last year, some months before his death, through a solicitor he was not known to deal with—secretive-like. Where an inspector might come by that kind of money, I'm sure I don't know. Buying property is an old trick to clean dirty money, one any policeman would know."

"He sold some land," I said. "That is easy enough to trace. You can ask my father's solicitor, Mr. Pilchuck. That is the most likely source."

"Ah, yes, the honorable Mr. Pilchuck. Well, maybe he did, maybe he didn't. Maybe that money went elsewhere. We can't be sure, now, can we? It will all unwind, and sort itself out, in time, and if ill-gotten gains were used, then the house will no longer be yours. Until then, this house and its contents are under my jurisdiction. I'll need to have it thoroughly searched, the items impounded, and have everything secured while the legalities are traced."

"You shan't find anything incriminating here," I insisted.

"Maybe, maybe not. Maybe something new shall appear since the last time I had it searched. Certificates, for example. I'm very interested in them. Where do you keep your father's investment certificates, Miss Young?"

I answered honestly. "In the desk drawer of his office."

"Nothing there," he said.

That's right, I thought. *Because Colmore Dunn has just taken them.* For better or worse, I did not know. But we would all soon find out.

A fresh and unwelcome thought: Could he plant evidence, here and now, divesting himself of anything that might prove his guilt, onto Papa, conveniently dead and unable to defend himself?

"I want those certificates, Miss Young." He drew menacingly near. "And I mean to have them—at any cost."

"Where are my staff?" I looked around. No Bidwell. No Louisa.

"I believe the maid said she was going to her mother's, and the man to live with a friend. They are long gone."

"And my chaperone, Mrs. W?"

"It was put to her that she might find somewhere to live for a time. Until all of this is sorted out one way or another."

"What did you do with her?" My voice was shrill now but I cared not.

"She'd take a train to stay with her sister, she said," Collingsworth answered. "About an hour or so ago. She was allowed to take a change of clothing or two and some pocket money. That's what you'll be allowed to take, too. Everything else will be kept here, under my guard, until further say-so."

My costumes! I would never, ever make the deadline for *Cinderella* if we all didn't work on them constantly. "I will need my costumes," I said.

"Terribly sorry, Miss Young," he drawled. "Everything in this house is seized for now."

"What could possibly be gained by keeping them?"

He smiled at me, his onion-skin teeth menacing in the waning daylight. *He knew exactly what was to gain. He's driving me out of my profession; that's what he'll do.*

I went to my room to gather some clothing. Collingsworth followed me. The door to my bed cubbyhole was opened.

"Just checking to see if anything has been added since the last time we looked," he said. "Neat trick. Smart man, your father. But not as smart as I."

I whirled on him. "He was your friend! He defended you against all comers."

A twitch of guilt passed his brow but left just as quickly. My letters and papers were spread on the bed. I went to scoop them up, but Collingsworth beat me to it.

"Allow me."

He looked at the love letters and passed them my way. "Of no use to me, or anyone. Take them if you like. Oh, and speaking of love letters, don't even think of running off to your viscount for help."

I shook my head. "What do you mean?"

"Francis told me all about him—you'll see him, but not Francis now, will ya? I have it on good account he hasn't been to see you since your falling out at Tolfee House. Well, the elite aren't going to help you, my dear, because it would mean turning on their own. That, they will never do."

"But you have turned on your own," I said. "And you are certainly not elite."

He moved toward me as though he were going to strike me and I flinched. That brought him pleasure, and he smiled. He flipped the King Street address card on the floor, like a playing card, and the train ticket, too. He opened the letter Papa had written. "Oh—here's something new."

Of course, he had not seen that one. I had received it from Roberts.

"'You shall be well provided for; our homes will hold both memories and treasures for you and, of course, you have your skills as an excellent seamstress,'" he read in a mocking tone. "Well, you have no home now, do you, Miss Young? Nor an engagement as a seamstress. Even if your house may, and I repeat, may, be returned to you after my boys search it, it surely will not be in enough time for you to finish sewing those pretty little frocks upstairs."

I gasped. He turned back to the letter.

"'Marry well, someone you trust and love without reserve, a man who can rescue you, my little "damsel in distress," should you need it.'" He laughed derisively. "You could have had Francis, a worthy suitor. But no. Damsel in distress. Perhaps Young had the gift of seeing the future, too, as this must be right distressing. What a quaint little phrase. Thought he was above himself, he did. Marrying a lord's daughter."

He tossed the paper to me. "'Fear not,'" he said, and then shook his head. "Poor advice indeed."

I reached down and took the letter. The photograph of the young lady was on the bed. "I'll take that, too, please," I said.

He leaned over and picked it up, looked at the girl, and then slid the photograph into his pocket. "No, I'll keep this. Pretty little thing. Reminds me of those two young apprentices you keep."

My bones went cold. I'd heard the threat. He could not reach them, not for now, anyway. "They know nothing. For goodness' sake, I know nothing!"

"Maybe the house knows something, then," he said, moving his arm around expansively. "I mean to find out if it does. You'd best gather your clothing and leave, Miss Young. It's getting dark outside. You don't want to be walking alone in the city, in the dark. Of course"—his eyebrows raised as if he'd just had a good idea—"I could ask Sergeant Jones to escort you wherever you might need to go!"

I didn't answer. He watched as I placed some clothing into a bag, praying silently as I did. I took all the money I had in the house, and after searching my bags, he let me go on my way.

I did not know where I would go, or what I could do. Should I speak with Wilhelm? Professional suicide, even as the seizing of the costumes was a certain death in any case. Perhaps I could find a sympathetic police officer. Francis had said that they were all working for his father in the Chelsea division—surely some were honorable, it's just that I did not know which ones those were, nor if the problems extended beyond Chelsea.

Collingsworth must have thought I had something that could do him great harm, and, after I'd told Francis I would not see him again, felt he could no longer contain that risk.

What could it be? Why now? The certificates. But he'd seen them already—he'd had them returned to me via Francis on the day we'd had our outing in the park. Or was he punishing me for turning Francis down?

Yes, he was.

I could not shake the buzzing from my head; nothing made sense. I was cold and hungry and did not know what to do.

First, I must go to the Mission and ensure the girls were safe.

I headed toward King Street and to the Mission, where I was warmly greeted by Mother Rachel. She took me into the sitting room and brought me a cup of tea in a plain white teacup with a tiny chip on the handle.

"Are you quite well?" she asked.

"I am," I said. "But then again, I am not."

I set my garment bag down and within a few minutes, Ruby and Charlotte came bounding up the stairs from the work-training area.

"Oh, miss, we were so worried!" Charlotte looked like she had been crying and even Ruby looked like she tottered on the edge of tears.

"Are you going to jail, then?" she asked.

I shook my head. In truth, I did not know where I could go.

"Maybe we can move to your big house," Charlotte said. Ah, she must mean Winton. Hadn't I told the girls it had been donated?

It was still free for my use for a few days, till the transaction was concluded on Friday, four days hence.

Wait.

I set my teacup down with some force, and the girls looked up at me with alacrity.

I held my hand up to silence them for a moment. I must think.

Papa must have brought something to Winton Park. Why else would he have been there just before his death? To hide something. And Collingsworth knew that and had gone after Papa had left, looking for it.

Whatever it was, though, it had not been found, or Collingsworth would not be desperate enough to seize Cheyne, thereby drawing attention to himself. Something plus . . . the certificates? Yes, there was something with the certificates, certainly. But there must be more. Notes. Incriminating investigation notes. It's what they'd all said the criminals were after.

But the notes weren't at Cheyne; they were at Winton, which, for the moment, was still owned by the Cause until it transferred to Thomas. They must be. I'd cleaned Cheyne top to bottom when the girls had moved in; Collingsworth had searched it twice before. Papa's letter referred to Winton, obliquely.

I'd tried and failed to find what was hidden at Winton. Collingsworth had, too. I must try again and not fail this time. I had so little time. I must find what Papa had intended me to find without anyone knowing I was going.

But how could I get to Winton without Inspector Collingsworth seeing me? I then mused aloud. "He'd follow me. Even if I availed myself of help, from Thomas or anyone, he'd immediately seize that house, too, in desperation. He still believes there is something to be found. Or is it only the certificates he's looking for?"

"Who would follow you, miss?" Ruby asked. "That bad man? Do you need me to make a wig for you?"

My eyes widened. I thought back on my orange-seller disguise. *No one sees me as "me" when I am dressed as a servant.* "Ruby! Yes, yes, I do. You have just given me the perfect idea. For a while, Cinderella must return to being a maid. Can you girls help me?"

"We can!" Charlotte said. "What should we do?"

Mother Martha could bustle Ruby back to Drury Lane to ask if she might borrow a wig—from her new milliner friend—and a maid's costume. I told her the name of a dresser I knew would help. "A brunette wig," I said. "With lots of curly hair to cover my face."

I knew maids were to have had hair pulled back, but in this case, I had to conceal myself, and that took precedence over propriety.

"Can the girls and Mother Martha stay with you? I know it is your policy to encourage people not to return so you may take on the newly needy, but . . ."

Mother Rachel sighed. "Yes. We are plum full. But I am reminded of the Scripture exhorting us to be not forgetful to entertain strangers."

"Thank you! It would only be for a day or two." I would either have to find what I needed to find by then or I would have to return to London and admit to Wilhelm that the costumes would not be completed in time, tell him that his very expensive fabrics and beading had been seized, and he'd have to find someone else to sew, quickly, in the midst of the busy Season.

No one would ever hire me again, were that to happen.

My society designing commissions had already ended.

Worse . . . where would my girls go? Ruby, perhaps to Sarah. But dear, quiet Charlotte, who did not stand out as Ruby did, but had a tender and strong heart. She could not be left alone.

"Go quickly, now!" Ruby and Mother Martha left for the theater, which was not far away.

Within the hour, Ruby and Mother Martha returned with a maid's costume and a billowing brunette wig. In spite of the solemnity of the task, and the difficulty of the day, we all broke out in laughter once I was dressed as an ill-mannered maid.

"They shan't recognize you, miss," Charlotte said. "I never would, and I'm used to seeing actresses." The rest of them agreed.

I asked Mother Rachel for a piece of paper and pen, so I might write a letter of introduction for myself as a hired maid come to pack the costumes for Miss Young, in case anyone stopped me. I had enough money for train fare there and back.

Once I was ready, Mother Rachel lent me a shawl and tucked a tin of biscuits into my bag along with some candles and matches. I was ready to take the day's last train to Hampshire. I would arrive in the dark, but that was perhaps best, as Collingsworth and his men would not be expecting this tonight, and were busy merrily picking through the bones of my home.

"Will you . . . Will you be able to sort out whatever this is?" Mother Rachel looked doubtful, but I could not allow her fears and doubts to daunt my courage at this moment.

I nodded.

I slipped out an hour later, hidden in a crowd of young women who had been listening to a rousing speech.

I thought back to what Thomas had said. *Every thrust has its parry and each parry its riposte. The parry is the main weapon. To be a good fencer, it is not just a show of good grace, vivacity, and to thrust with accuracy. The great point is to know how to defend and ward off the blows that the enemy gives.*

Do you have enemies, Lord Lockwood? I'd asked.

I do, Miss Young. He'd sat next to me. *So do you. We all do.*

I can parry. I shall.

I must.

CHAPTER THIRTY-ONE

I left the Mission, carrying not my bag but one that Mother Rachel had loaned me—it was frayed and patched and not at all fashionable; it had most probably been a donation some years past. I walked a few hundred yards, and then stood to the side, pretending to search the bag, but really, I was looking around to see if anyone was following me. I didn't see anyone.

Good. The disguise was working. That, or Collingsworth had not bothered to have me trailed, assuming he would find anything he needed at Cheyne, now that Winton Park had been long donated and was nearly sold. Perhaps he thought it had been packed and was owned by Thomas now. He'd not dare to trespass then. Would he?

I arrived at Victoria Station, a huge building made of Portland stone now green-washed with moss. I walked briskly through the stone archway and purchased a third class ticket. I could not ride in first, as a maid.

The platform was nearly empty. It was the last train out and by the time I arrived near Winton, it would be fully dark.

The train chugged to a stop and after the passengers had disembarked, I got on. I sat on a bench, which was plainly upholstered in a lightly stained wine-colored cloth. The arched ceilings were white and clean, but did not include any of the flourishes to be seen in the first class carriages; the benches were decidedly firmer, too.

I sat close to a window and pulled my bag close against my chest. A woman and a child had already boarded. Two men came in after me, saw I was alone, and sat on the bench directly across me. More and more people filtered in and soon the train chugged out of the station.

Night began to settle on London's shoulders like a dusky mantle; I counted the blinking streetlights as we pulled toward Hampshire. Once outside the city the lights grew farther apart till they finally disappeared. The low hum of chatter and a baby crying were the only sounds in my carriage. One of the men who had been sitting across from me came and sat to my left. Within a few seconds the other man came and sat to my right, trapping me between them.

"Fine night, but what's a young lass like you doin' out alone?" One of them leaned toward me, and I recoiled, but could not move too far in the other direction lest I bump into his accomplice.

The best answer was none, I decided. A fear, though: What would happen when I got off the train? Would there be a hired cab to take me to Winton?

Could these men be plants? Could the inspector have guessed my intentions?

They tried to speak with me for another minute or two, and I stood and moved up a few seats and across the aisle. They followed me and sat directly across me again.

"Yer goin' ta hurt our feelings, now," one said. "I don't think you want ta do that."

"Move away," I said firmly.

"Ooh, a saucy one," the other laughed. At that moment, a very large man, perhaps ten years older than me, came and sat down next to me.

He was much stronger, much larger, and certainly more intimidating than the two men I had just been trying to fend off.

"I don't think the lass appreciates your attentions," he spoke sternly to the men across from me.

"Who are you to tell us?" one man asked. "I don't remember us signing up to be working for you, my lord." He laughed.

The man next to me crossed his arms, flexing his considerable muscles in front of them. Even his hands were muscled.

"Shove off," the other man said, but he and his friend moved away.

I still did not know if this new man was menace or friend. "Thank you," I said.

He nodded. "My pleasure. I'm a local blacksmith, Erin Mackay. Where are you headed?"

"Winton Park," I answered. Should I have? There were only a few stops left. He'd know anyway.

"I'm getting off at that stop as well. Are you certain you're expected?"

"I've been sent to pack some personal belongings at the house for the woman who used to own it." The Cause had, after all, told me to pack my mother's belongings ahead of the sale, if I liked.

"Ah, Miss Young, then."

I ducked my head down. Did he know me?

"Yes," I said. He did not ask me for my name and I was glad.

"Is someone expecting you?" he pressed again.

"The estate manager." I certainly did not share that he was old, nearly blind, and perhaps demented.

I did not know how much to tell him, but I was now frighteningly aware that I had perhaps made a bad judgment call.

We arrived at the station, and it was, indeed, desolate and dark. A cold, early-autumn wind had blown in with the train and I pulled my borrowed shawl around me. The air smelt of smoke.

"Has there been a fire?" I asked.

The blacksmith nodded. "Some of the fields are being burnt this week. Field pests nesting in the rubble." He had a friend waiting for him, and after seeing me safely into the hired carriage, he went his way.

We drove through the rutted roads toward Winton Park. The approach looked different at night. Trees wept over the long drive, drooping branches that should have been trimmed in the summer, or the summer before, but hadn't. The drive had wheel ruts ground into it; dust flew up as the horses carried forth. There had not, apparently, been rain for some time.

The moon was at third quarter. I smiled, wistfully, thinking of Lady Mary's Sun and Moon gown. That life was gone now.

The house looming before me was black, not a light flickered anywhere within. It looked forbidding. The brick carriage house lurked to the left, the brick kitchens and laundry to the right.

Desolate. If I should scream for help, no one would hear me, once the driver pulled away.

"Are you certain you're expected?" he asked.

"Oh, yes. Miss Young sent me," I said. It was the truth.

He nodded warily.

I stepped out of the carriage and swallowed my fear. Davidson would be below stairs; that was some comfort.

"I can manage my own bag," I said, and paid him well.

He nodded and chucked the horses to turn around and return down the dusty drive.

I took my bag and crossed the bit of drive to the stone stairs that led to the front door. Collingsworth had let me keep my key chain; he had no need of them to enter Cheyne Gardens, had he?

Part of me wished I'd left this for the bright morrow. But the inspector might arrive at any time. I believed he'd dare to.

I had no choice but to press on.

Once inside the house I closed the door, locked it again, and let my eyes adjust to the darkness. I was glad to have been there recently, twice, so I had some sense of the layout of the rooms. I left my bag by the door and decided first to wake Davidson and find some oil lamps, which I knew were stored in the kitchens.

I lit a candle, then walked very slowly, so the wind caused by my movement didn't put it out. The flame was so small, but it cast monstrous, misshapen shadows on the walls and floor. They followed me. Of course they did.

I called out, "Mr. Davidson? Miss Young has sent me. Mr. Davidson?" I decided I could not do away with my costume yet in case I'd been followed. Davidson might speak up to Lady Lockwood or anyone else and that could filter back to Collingsworth.

The stairs creaked and moaned, and I kept one hand on the wall because the railing was loose and I didn't want to take a nasty tumble. Once downstairs, I walked all the way to the back, past the bells that would have summoned servants, and around the corner from the beer cellar. Davidson had taken over the steward's quarters, I knew, for his own. Water dripping from a leaky pipe, hitting concrete, and splattering was the only sound. Silence closed in around me.

The door to the Steward's Hall was closed. I knocked on it and heard nothing. "Mr. Davidson!" I called out again.

My voice echoed off the cold masonry walls. *Davidson . . .*

"I'm sorry to disturb!" I called out once more. Once more the faint echo. *Disturb* . . .

My skin prickled, and I pushed open his door, half wondering if I'd find the old man's corpse in there.

But no. The bed was neatly made, and the drawers, when I checked, were empty. He had moved out, no doubt, in advance of the imminent property transfer. I'd arranged for his pension; Lady Lockwood had likely told him he could leave early.

I was alone in Winton Park. No one knew I was here. No one could help.

I stood there for a moment, the weight of the four stories and tens of thousands of square feet closing in around me. In some ways, the darkness terrified me. But to the extent that it hid me to complete my task, I supposed I should be grateful.

Thomas—*my heart panged*—Lord Lockwood had mentioned that the house would need to be completely set up for gas lighting. Grandmamma, I knew, had not wanted that in her day; she worried that the vapors would kill her in her sleep or poison her guests while they ate. I had to look for the handheld lamps.

I walked the underground passage to the old kitchen; my movement threatened to snuff the candle once more; I wanted to walk quickly and find a lamp, but not so quickly as to put me in blackness.

Then again, if I'm lit up by candle, and someone is here in the dark, they can better see me, but I cannot see them.

The eerie silence followed me. There were no croaking frogs, whose rough hiccups usually came down through the overhead grate that let light and air into the underground passage. I hoped they had not been smoked to death. Once in the kitchen, I did not know which cupboards to look in.

I did not want to open any doors at all. *The beetles!* But I must.

I cracked one cupboard open and discovered dusty tea in tins and empty sweets containers.

A second door hid cleaning products—dangerously near the food storage. I should have to rectify that.

No, no, it is not my house any longer. I will not rectify anything. I pursed my lips in sorrow. In a way, I was glad to be here by myself. I could say good-bye to the house on my terms, floor by floor, room by room.

A third cabinet revealed a small cache of lamps, matches, and gallons upon gallons of lamp oil. I tried to light the first, and then the second, but the wicks were dry. The third, thankfully, lit. I took it, filled both it and the fourth one, and hurried back to the main house.

Once in the foyer, I wondered, *Where should I sleep? If someone should come, would they look for me in a servant's bed? Or my mother's? Perhaps it would be better if I did not sleep at all. I will start in on my task immediately.* I walked up the stairwell, round and round, like one of the nautilus seashell spirals I'd once seen on display in a museum. I stopped midway up and turned around, flooded with a memory.

Mamma told me to stay upstairs, that it would upset Grandfather if I attended. I was too young. But what was the sense of being here if I couldn't enjoy it all?

The music is lovely, and someone might ask me to dance if I look old enough to.

I decided. I slipped on my prettiest dress and then a pair of Mamma's jeweled slippers. Surely, they made me look of an age to attend a ball!

I stood at the top of the stairs, hiding just out of sight where I could see all but none could see me. The guests have nearly stopped coming.

I'll just walk, stately, down the stairway in mature, thoughtful steps. If only I can keep my toes pressed forward, the shoes will stay on!

But wait. Perhaps I won't be able to dance with these shoes on after all.

Oh dear. A stair tumble. Now Grandfather is glaring at me. Not Grandmamma, though. Dear Grandmamma.

In my mind's eye, I scanned the crowd for Thomas, but I just didn't remember seeing him. *More's the pity.*

I blinked to the present, and returned to my search, I reached the top floor, where the maids would have stayed. I held the lamp in front of me; there was a narrow hallway with a low ceiling, and several rooms off to each side. I walked, the floorboards creaking with each step, and stood in front of the first door.

I put my hand on the knob and held my breath. Why? I did not expect that anyone would be behind it, did I?

No. But I could not shake the foreboding that clung to me like a panicked child.

The room was empty—a stripped bed, an empty dresser. That was all, and it was repeated five times on that floor. There was frantic scurrying in the corner of the last room and I pushed my lamp in that direction. A mouse on his haunches stared at me, as frightened of me as I should have been of him. Instead, I was comforted that some other living being was here with me in this huge house. A fairy rhyme came to mind, and I changed it, just a bit, to suit the situation:

> *Three blind mice. Three blind mice.*
> *See how they run. See how they run.*
> *They all ran after the viscount's wife,*

Who cut off their tails with a carving knife,
Did you ever see such a sight in your life,
As three blind mice?

I laughed a little, which should have broken some tension, but again, my voice echoed strangely through the room, and it startled me instead. I moved to shut the door and the wind caused by the motion bothered the white curtains in the window; they shivered a ghostly dance.

I slammed the door behind me and quickly walked downstairs for the larger task, the family bedrooms. I began in Grandmother's wood-paneled room.

The room was still draped; I knew Lady Lockwood would order the furniture completely cleaned; her command to her maid to tidy everything in advance of my, and her, last visit let me know that she cared very much about a well-ordered home.

My pain relented a little. Better Winton goes to someone who thought her beautiful but neglected, and would properly care for her.

I looked through the empty wardrobe; there was nothing. I sat down on the stool in front of the desk. I'd looked through it on my last visit, but this time, I went more slowly.

There was some correspondence, a few sketches of her spaniels. I lifted a photograph. It was of my mother, in costume. And then, in a bottom drawer, playbills for plays in which my mother had appeared. Ticket stubs. Had she attended without Mamma knowing? It seemed so. Mamma had thought she'd never seen her act.

She clearly had, many times, secretly.

I gently stacked the playbills and set them in my bag. I would take these, too. Keep them with Mamma's costumes. I'd decided I would bring everything I wanted to keep to the costume room, and Lady Lockwood could simply have the contents of that room delivered to me.

While my bag was opened I noticed the tin of biscuits and prised it open. I ate one or two, but the crumbs stuck in my mouth. I did not even know where to find a cup in the house with which I might drink some water.

I finished searching that room. The very late hour plus the prompting of the biscuits made me hungry, but I pressed on. I visited each room in the hall, looking under the beds, shaking the blankets and sending swirls of dust into the air, which wreaked more havoc on my lungs than the London coal belch. The smoke from the neighbor's burning field was tickling them, too, as well as blinding me to any prying eyes outside of the property.

Were anyone to be looking for me, that is. Then, I couldn't see them, either.

By the time I made it to Mamma's adult room, the Tapestry Room, I was tired. I peered through the window. The sky had begun to tint lightly toward dawn, which would soon raise her head. I glanced to the west, toward the kitchens, laundry, and Mamma's costume room. Then, to the right, toward the carriage house.

Nothing. No light, no person. The silence in the house was deafening. I heard an occasional window shake. A few timbers creaked. But I was alone. Though it frightened me it was, perhaps, best for now.

I sat on the bed, thinking where to search next and, in spite of myself, fell asleep.

I awakened to a noise.

CHAPTER THIRTY-TWO

I looked at the watch pinned to my dress. I had nodded off to sleep and, exhausted by the week's events, had slept for hours; it was late morning the next day.

For a moment I thought I was in London. I peered out of the window, and the air was hazed with smoke—dreary and gray, thick and woody. I could see flames in the far distance to the east of the house; to the west, the view was clear and calm. I could see, barely, the outline of Darington.

The noise once more! A large metallic twist and then a push of oak. It was the front door—opening! What should I do? If I were to slide a piece of furniture in front of the door the intruder would hear me; I would mark my location and then I might be done for.

I leaned against the bedroom door, ear pressed to it, and tried to hear who might be coming in. I expected the thud of heavy footsteps, but instead, I heard a woman's light voice. And then a man's. They sounded familiar to me. I listened to the pitch, unable to discern actual words, and then realized with a startle, *I know who that is! It's Thomas's brother, Jamie, and his wife, Lisbeth.*

I quietly opened my door and their voices did not stop speaking so they must not have heard me. I tiptoed out the Tapestry bedroom and toward the staircase hall. I got as close to it as I could without actually placing a foot on the stairs.

If Ruby could see me now. I eavesdropped. Why were they here?

They must have settled in the Saloon—the largest, grandest, most beautiful of the reception rooms—because it was closest to the staircase hall. I could hear them.

"Your mother will have fits if she knows we are here!" Lisbeth said.

"She'll not know," Jamie answered. "No one will know, I promise you. How could she? I have Davidson's key; the old man is comfortably settled with his daughter in the village. There will be no others arriving till Thomas brings them from London after everything is properly transferred."

"I suppose so. I do not want to spoil his surprise. Jamie"—Lisbeth's voice grew soft, and I leaned over the railing to hear—"he will be so eager to see the pleasure on our faces. Will we have our own key? Is this really to be our home?"

I nearly fell over the rail and onto the stairs.

"Yes, my love," Jamie said. "Darington must be kept for Thomas's family. This way, he can still be of help to me, and you, my darling, with my . . . afflictions. We'll be close by but have our own home and family. And he will, too."

She squealed. "I feel so grand! Our home. And just ahead of the baby, too. But, Jamie . . . the stairs."

She got up, and I ducked back around the corner, hoping she wouldn't climb the stairs.

"Thomas knows someone at the London Hydraulic Power Company who will come to Winton and survey the possibility of having a lift installed. I overheard him talking to the hydraulic man, which is how I knew he'd intended it for us. Thomas said he could not bear to tear down the staircase, though. It had important memories for him."

My heart melted.

"Does Miss Young not want any of the furnishings?" Lisbeth asked. "I understood that she was to send someone along to pick up her mother's costumes and such, perhaps after the sale has closed. Perhaps she has made some arrangements with Thomas?"

They walked down the hall then, and I leaned over and listened. I did not think they would mount the stairs because of Captain Lockwood's injuries.

"He told me he'd hoped to hear from her after an unpleasant conversation they had at Lady Tolfee's ball, but Miss Young did not write. He sent a letter to her, which Miss Young did not respond to, and also sent several telegraphs. She'd left angry with him and did not move to reconcile."

I almost shouted. Where had my letter gone? And why had I not received his? A thought occurred. Why had Mrs. W's magazines been rumpled? Someone, most probably the police, had been leafing through them. And perhaps pinching my mail, isolating me further from anyone who might help, including Thomas.

Thomas had not heard from me and then let me have my way after I'd declined to eat supper with him. *I trust you know your mind, Miss Young,* he'd once said to me. *I would not seek to persuade you, or anyone, against your will and better judgment.*

"Does Miss Young want the art?" Captain Lockwood asked. "Even if she and Thomas have fallen out, we should ask her if there is anything else at all that she would like, or we could keep for her for as long as she'd like."

So kind.

"I shall write to her and ask," Lisbeth said. "I liked her very much indeed. It's too bad . . ."

"It is a pity, indeed," Jamie said. "I'd never seen Thomas so happy, ever, as he was when he was with Miss Young. He's done well by us and I hoped he would find happiness for himself, too. Alas."

"You're happy, then?" Lisbeth asked.

Jamie responded. "Knowing this is to be ours, now the papers are signed, well, last night was the first night I have had no nightmares since the war."

"I'm glad we shared this moment privately," Lisbeth said. "Just we two, our first day in our home. The happiest day of my life. I'm also glad Thomas will not know we breached his secret." A soft kiss.

They began to talk about their coming baby, and I slipped away, not wanting to intrude, even secretly, on their intimate thoughts and the happiest day of their lives.

I went back into the Tapestry bedroom and cried softly into my maid's apron.

Oh, Thomas, what a fool I have been. It's not that your mother wanted the house for herself, it's that she wanted it for her wounded child! Any good mother would want her child near her, especially a child, even a grown one, who needed help as Jamie did. It was not wrong that she prevailed upon her other child, Thomas, who would help her do what was best for them all.

Yes, Lady Lockwood had been cutting and sharp. But she had also truly appreciated the gift I'd sent, and I'd been so concerned with being treated badly that I did not see how I had made some very similar assumptions myself.

Lord, please let me be filled with grace from now on.

The mercy was this—it was not too late. Unless Thomas had eloped during his month's long journey to their other holdings, I could go to him and say what a fool I had been, and ask if he'd be willing to overlook that, this once.

I sneaked another biscuit out of my bag, hoping that Captain and Mrs. Lockwood would leave soon. There was another piece of my heart I needed to save before I could seek out Thomas. The part that had belonged to Papa. I could not rest until I knew.

Jamie and Lisbeth finally left, locking the door behind them, but as the carriage pulled away, it stopped midway down the drive. Jamie had the driver get out and look around for something, but he apparently saw nothing that concerned them because they soon were on their way once more.

I thought, *I must get directly to searching.* I did not know what I was looking for except some documentation from my thorough father. I pressed on in happy hope: the next day I would seek out Thomas and ask him and Colmore Dunn to help me with said finding.

I took another biscuit from my bag to quell the gnawing in my stomach. I spied the love letters from Mamma to Papa. An unwelcome memory summoned forth. Collingsworth, in my bedchamber, his voice sarcastic and sure.

Oh, and speaking of love letters, don't even think of running off to your viscount for help . . . Francis told me all about him—you'll see him, but not Francis now, will ya? . . . Well, the elite aren't going to help you, my dear, because it would mean turning on their own. That, they will never do.

What would Colmore Dunn find in the certificates? It had not looked good. Maybe they would not want to help me after all.

I must find what Papa had left here.

I finished looking in the Tapestry room and made a small pile of items I wanted to take with me. I went downstairs and through the passage to the laundry and the kitchens and continued to look for anything of Papa's, even risking the beetles. Nothing.

I looked longingly at the sink and the tap. I had no cup, but I could cup my hands. I turned the water on, and it spat brown liquid, and then ran yellow. Perhaps, given time, it would run clean. But I would not take that chance. I felt badly that I had not tended to this when Davidson had been here, neither I nor Papa. We had not known how to care for a house like this.

I pushed open the double doors into the old linen area, which now housed Mamma's things, and looked through the costumes once more, each trunk, one by one. Nothing in the pockets nor the false floors. Nothing in the sewing case. I peeked out of the small window in the room, but it was nearly dark and I could see nothing but a shadow of Thomas's house in the distance.

I hurried through the underground passage, and then upstairs into the main house. The oil lamp was flickering, and I did not want to be caught in the basement with no light.

I walked up the stairs and double-checked the lock. The house, which had seemed so cheerful with Jamie and Lisbeth and the autumn sun streaming in, menaced once more.

The cloths were pulled across the chairs in the Saloon. I heard the tiny squeak of mice. I looked at the gaping sockets in the chandeliers, then squeezed my eyes shut and remembered them lit and lovely, to change the mood. I ran up the staircase.

I should leave now. There is nothing here. I am at risk here at night. The house was ominous and seemed to have swallowed me whole, as Jonah had been, as I wrestled in its belly.

If I left now I would be walking, alone, in the dark. At least in the house I would be safe.

In fact, I decided I might remain locked inside by myself until someone came again. Perhaps Jamie and Lisbeth would come

with Lady Lockwood, very soon, as the transfer should be completed.

My tongue was dry; it had been an entire day since I had anything to drink. My stomach clenched with hunger, and I tied the
apron tighter around my middle to stave it off. I could wait a day
or two at most. No more.

I closed the door and looked out of the window. I opened up
my valise and pulled out the letters, to read for comfort with the
remainder of the lamplight.

First the love letters. Then, the letter indicating Mamma's
desire to donate Winton.

*I have donated it, Mamma, and the nicest people will move in.
You'd be so happy.*

I read the last letter, the one from Papa.

*Marry well, someone you trust and love without re-
serve, a man who can rescue you, my little 'damsel in distress,' should you need it.*

*I hope to, Papa. I just don't know about the certificates, you
see, and if Thomas . . .*

Wait.

I reread that.

Damsel in distress. I knew who that was. It was Rapunzel.

Rapunzel, Rapunzel, let down your hair.

My heart flooded with confidence. I had overlooked something! Whatever Papa had hidden was in the Rapunzel costume.
He had signaled me by tying the braids in an odd manner—
Mamma would never have allowed that, and Papa would have
seen them stored properly out of love for her. I wish I had noticed that my first visit—but then again, if I had, the evidence

might have been taken during the break-in at Cheyne that followed.

I would go to the costumes directly, in the morning, when there was light enough to see well. And, well, I did not want to traverse the house, and the underground passage, alone at night.

I pushed a heavy piece of furniture against the door, using much of my remaining strength, and then lay atop the made bed.

I was right. I knew I was right.

CHAPTER THIRTY-THREE

I didn't wake as early as I would have liked to, in spite of my excitement. The anxiety wrought by physical and emotional testing, and no water, had taken a toll. I coughed a little; the smoke had now oozed through the cracks in the house, surrounding the windows, and winnowed its way in through the mortar cracks. I looked at my watch pin.

Ten o'clock. I would go downstairs, look in the costume room, and leave. I could make it to the train and back to London by early afternoon. I would go to the police officer that I suspected had whispered through my door, warning me. Or . . . I could look up Colmore Dunn's office. Surely someone would know. I could ask Lady Lockwood where to find Thomas. I didn't want to see Lady Lockwood till my father's name was clear and I certainly didn't want anyone here to see me dressed as a maid.

I gathered my hair into a long blond knot, not bothering to replace the wig. It did not matter any longer. I looked out through the window; the entire green was fogged with smoke.

It seemed to me that the west fields, too, were blanketed with smoke. I did not think my fields, nor the Lockwoods', were to be fired. Thomas had said he intended to spray for Hessian fly. Hadn't he? Perhaps it had not been effective.

I had my bag packed and said a quiet good-bye to my mother's room. "With some luck, I shall return, to find you warmly loved by a new family," I said as I turned and pulled the door shut behind me.

I walked down the stairs, but felt, eerily, as if I was being watched. I stopped abruptly and listened. I heard nothing and walked round the next set of stairs. There were watching eyes, somewhere.

Gillian. You are imagining things. If someone had wanted to do you harm it could already have been easily accomplished.

Once on the main-floor hallway, I stopped. A tin rested on the floor. A biscuit tin. I had not noticed that the night before; it had been dark. I leaned down and picked it up; there was still a biscuit in it. I picked it up; it was soft and fresh.

Davidson? One would think the biscuit would have gone hard in a day or so, though, being exposed.

A cold sweat filmed my arms.

Someone else was here.

No, I reassured myself. *Gillian. You haven't heard or seen anyone else. Not a footstep, not a noise. The biscuit tin was left from another time. I would have seen or heard someone or Jamie and Lisbeth would have noticed. Wouldn't they have?*

Then again, they had stopped their carriage. Had they noticed something amiss?

I picked up my pace a little. Through the Servery, down the stairs, and through the passage toward the outbuilding that held the kitchens, the laundry, and the storage room.

I opened the door to the concealed servants' passage and was hit with a fresh blast of smoke. Why? Perhaps due to the overhead air grate open to the ground. I reached the bottom stair and a deposit of ash drew my attention. I bent to look at it; it was spent pipe ash, as if someone had tapped his pipe against the rail to clear the pipe, right there.

I knelt and leaned in closer. It was difficult to be certain because the air was already tainted with smoke from the field, but it did, to me, smell of that specific Turkish tobacco.

A shiver of fear ran through me. The biscuit tin. And now ash, expensive, exclusive ash, the kind of ash found in the Garrick Club, and also in the Collingsworths' pipes.

Surely not.

I picked up my bag again and began to walk purposefully toward the costume room. When I was nearly there, I passed the grate in the ceiling. Except that there was no longer a grate. It was a gaping hole. Someone had removed the grate, allowing for access into the house and the passage. The smoke poured in, too.

I would get to the costume room, and look quickly. I would find what I knew must be there and then I would run, not to London, but to Darington. I would love to have made a better impression on Lady Lockwood after Papa had been cleared. But this was no time for pride.

I did not want Jamie and Lisbeth to know I'd eavesdropped.

The blood rushed to my head and I clenched both of my fists, the one carrying the bag and the one that was not. I sensed risk racing toward me. I must reach the costume room with all haste and find what Papa had left.

I got to the room, slipped my free hand through the left door's handle, and pulled it open. Once inside the room, I set down the bag and closed the door behind me. I went directly to the case that held Rapunzel.

Was it my imagination? Did I hear footsteps? I stopped. I knew, when I was alone, that every sound was amplified. Perhaps it had been the pipes or men in the field.

I shook the dress, and there was nothing. I pulled it out of the case and ran my fingers over it. As I did, it seemed to me that a shadow went by the window. Had it been a shadow? Had I imagined it?

I returned to the costume and looked it over. At the waist, I recognized some very shoddy sewing. Someone had torn this and then sewn it back again. Someone who didn't know how to sew. I went to the mending table and pulled open a few drawers. Yes—there was the thread that had been used, loosely spooled.

I'm sorry, Mamma. I ripped the dress open along the poor seams. "Yes, yes, this is it!"

A notebook fell out between the layers of the gown. A small notebook, but as I opened the pages I read names and dates and places and companies. Officers with their division letters and personal warrant numbers.

Some were listed under the heading *Will Testify.* Some were listed under the heading *Compromised.* The names of some titled men appeared by the names of companies. A heading, *Seen Going into King Street*, was followed by names and dates. Then, *Fraudulent Companies.* An address on Berry Street was listed, and noted to have been paid with illegally gained income.

The Collingsworths' new house was on Berry Street. Inspector Collingsworth had said my house would be seized for having been purchased with ill-gotten gains.

No, it would not. But his would be.

Collingsworth was, in fact, listed next. Father? Son? Both? And Jones, among some others, under the *Compromised* column with details on their illegal activities.

I snapped it shut. "Papa. This will do!" I whispered in victory.

I heard footsteps, very clearly, then. I was not imagining this.

I opened the theater case and climbed into it, pulling the dress and the notebook in with me, and then pulled the door shut. If anyone looked into the room, they would see it all as it had been.

I breathed heavily, but quietly. My breath in the small space was heavy, hot, and moist. I didn't hear anything for a moment, but then I did. *Someone is standing outside the door.*

The door to the room opened. And then a voice. "Collingsworth said you'd lead me to it, you foolish, foolish girl. That disguise was clever, but I knew where to look."

Jones!

I nearly fainted with fear. My knees weakened, and I might have fallen had I not been so firmly propped within the trunk. I braced myself, expecting him to rush into the room and fling the doors open. I counted to ten. The door to the room slammed shut. Was he in the room with me, still?

The double doors were pushed open. He looked in each trunk and then opened the door to mine.

I screamed, and he yanked me out of the trunk. I clutched the notebook, but I was not strong enough to keep it in my hand. He wrenched it from me and opened it up, paging through it, before coughing.

"Ah, yes. The inspector will be very pleased indeed to get hold of this information. Thank you kindly, young miss."

"Give that to me!" I reached to snatch it, and he batted my hand away.

"It's mine, now, miss. Shame you went and read it, though, because now you'll have to join Sergeant Roberts, the other man who put his nose where it did not belong."

Was he going to knife me, too? I called for help.

"No one is going to help you, Miss Young. You made sure that no one was here, and I listened in on that nice young couple yesterday to see if they mentioned you. They did not. Bit of a boon—when they find the bones, they won't even know it's you. You'll just have disappeared, like this." He snapped his fingers. "Poof! A theater trick!"

"Someone will know," I said.

"No one will know. It seems it's your lucky day, however. The smoke is a much kinder way to die than committing self-murder by jumping from a high window of your former house due to your despair over your father having been found guilty and your viscount, the new owner of said house, having left you."

"I would never . . . ," I began, and then I realized he was saying he had been planning to stage my death to look like a suicide. My face wrenched, in spite of my efforts to keep my fear from it.

He laughed. "Anything else?" He picked up my bag. "I'll take this, just in case. He looked through the Rapunzel trunk. I tried to run for the door but he caught my arm and held it hard enough to bruise. When he found nothing of interest, he used a costume sash to tie my hands behind my back and then he shoved me back in, roughly. I tried to kick him, and he pushed me hard once more and then slammed the trunk door shut.

More noise—searching each trunk, I imagined—and then it went quiet.

"Sweet dreams, Miss Young!" he called, and then he laughed, and then he coughed.

Silence.

Sweat poured from me. The back of my throat ached from the smoke.

I counted to fifty and heard nothing. One hundred. Two hundred.

What should I do? Using my legs, I cracked open the door of the trunk. If he was in the room with me, it would not matter.

I pushed the trunk open, then walked to the sewing table, where I was able to find a scissors and maneuver to cut my way out of the binds.

The room suddenly filled with more smoke that had a bitter, acrid taste to it as it coated my mouth. I recognized the smell.

Lamp oil from the kitchens. The house was old and poorly sealed. The smoke had been pouring into the underground passage and was now seeping into the room. I did not know if I should break the window or if that would let in more smoke. I had no choice. I would open the door and run for it. I could leave by way of the passage, directly outside, and run to the west.

I tried to twist the knob and push the door open, but it would not push. The door was blocked from the outside! Something had been slid between the two handles to brace them shut. I pushed against it once more, and it budged but an inch—I did not have the strength to push through and break it.

The smoke was thick enough now that my eyes watered.

Jones had left me there. He'd set the fire to the west and then liberally poured lamp oil once I was stuck in the costume room. Nothing and no one would be left to clear Papa's name.

I felt weak. I had not eaten or had anything to drink in two days. I dragged one of the costume trunks to the door. Maybe I could tip it toward the door, and the heaviness of the trunk would crash against the door, forcing it open.

I tilted the trunk toward the door and pushed with all my might. It crashed with a mighty bang, and then merely leaned against the door. It did not open the door at all.

I sat on the floor.

What could I do? There *was* nothing left to do. The window was not big enough for me to fit through.

I took some pins and spelled out "Jones" as best I could. Perhaps they would survive the fire.

Papa, I'm sorry. Thomas, I wish . . .

I fell into a daze; my breathing came heavy and hard. I had to think through each breath now. My arms grew warm, but it wasn't the fire that would kill me, I knew. It was the smoke.

I curled into a ball on the floor. My mind felt hazy, and although my breathing was labored, I felt covered in a kind of filmy peace. I was glad of this—that I would die knowing that Papa had been true. It was a good way to die, except Thomas would never know about my letter and my love.

I closed my eyes, coughing, and then I thought I heard voices. Angels? Come, Lord Jesus.

No, I struggled to focus. Voices. Men's voices. I opened my eyes and then, yes, I did hear men's voices, closer and then farther away. Closer, then farther.

Perhaps someone was here. Would they know how to find me?

I struggled to stand up, and I inhaled deeply through a piece of a costume I held to my mouth.

I withdrew one of the drawers from the sewing cabinet and then I threw it with all my might at the window. The window shattered, and I fell backward with the effort.

I closed my eyes once more, and as I did, the case against the door jostled. Both doors were abruptly pulled open and the costume case, propped against one, spun on its edge, like a tipsy ballerina, from the force. I opened my eyes.

"Thomas!"

He ran in and pushed me out of its path; as the costume trunk lost its spinning balance it crashed heavily, noisily, directly upon him, where I'd stood only a moment before. He was pinned. He looked at me and then closed his eyes.

"Noooo!" I knew it was my voice, but it didn't seem to come from me. "Thomas!"

The blacksmith who had been with me on the train rushed in and pushed the case off of Thomas. He went to pick him up. Thomas's eyes opened. "Take her out of here," he said, pointing at me.

"No!" I protested.

"Take. Her!" Thomas insisted, and the blacksmith obeyed. He picked me up and ran me to the front of the house, where a stable boy held some horses that were clearly frightened by the fire, their eyes swiveling back and forth.

The blacksmith barked some orders to another stable boy who helped me onto the cart.

"There is a bad police officer, Sergeant Jones. He set the fire, and he's likely now racing to the train station," I coughed out. The blacksmith sent one lad on horseback to fetch the local constable and two others to ride ahead of the fire in the fields and look for Jones. Then he ran back for Thomas. A dozen or so men were in the fields pouring buckets of water—drawn, no doubt, from Winton—on the fire.

The driver was about to leave. "No!" I shouted. "I'll be fine. We'll wait for Thomas."

He nodded, but glanced at one of the other stable boys at my use of Lord Lockwood's Christian name.

In a moment, Thomas and the blacksmith came, Thomas walking but leaning against him. I tumbled out of the cart, still weak myself, and put my arm around his other side.

We got into the cart and with a supreme effort he held himself mostly up, wincing as the driver took off.

"Hello, Miss Young," he said. "You are most brave, and look lovely."

Tears began to stream down my face.

"It was not my intention to make you cry," he said. He reached out his forefinger, as we had when we had pretended to spar, and I reached mine out, too. He curled his around mine, gently, and then closed his eyes.

I did not trust myself to words. I leaned over and kissed him lightly on the left cheek, and then the right. He seemed to be lost in pain. I simply held him up while his eyes closed. The drive took much longer than I'd thought it would, but we had to go slowly, so as not to jostle him, and around the fires, so the horses didn't bolt.

Fifteen minutes later we arrived at Darington. This time, the blacksmith carried Thomas into the house.

CHAPTER THIRTY-FOUR

"Miss Young?" a voice called and a knock rapped the door at the same time. I struggled to sit up in the bed. I glanced out the window. It appeared to be dusk, but I could not be certain because of the smoke.

The four-poster bed was very comfortable, the linens soft, and I had to fight not to fall back into them.

And then I remembered. "Thomas!"

"Miss Young?" The voice was a little louder now.

"Yes?" I sat up and patted my hair down a little. I was in a dressing gown but had no memory of putting it on.

"It's Mrs. Lockwood," came the voice. "Lisbeth. May I come in?"

"Yes, yes, please do."

Lisbeth opened the door. I tried to read the expression on her face, to see if it would indicate anything about Thomas's condition.

She looked guarded. "How are you feeling?" she asked.

"A little tired, but otherwise well," I said. "Please, come in and sit down."

She sat in an armchair near the bed. The room was tastefully, elegantly decorated in claret-colored velvets, deep, well-polished woods, and had a small coal fire blazing to ward off the early-autumn chill.

I could wait no longer. "Thomas? I mean, Lord Lockwood? He is well? Tell me that he is."

She smiled at my use of his name, but then grew sober. "We are not sure. The doctor has been here to see him. His arm will be set. The rest we are unsure of. There were abdominal injuries. They may heal, or they may become infected and then heal, or not, in which case . . ." She looked somber. "Only time will tell."

I started crying and pulled the sheet up. Then I was shamed, weeping in front of a woman I barely knew. I dried my eyes. "I'm sorry. But it's all my fault. If I hadn't pushed the trunk against the door, it would not have fallen on him."

She came and sat on the bed with me. "Nonsense, Miss Young."

"Gillian," I said. "Please."

"You were trying to escape. Thomas was trying to help you. There is no blame."

I nodded. I did not believe her. "How did he know I was there?"

"Do you feel strong enough to talk?"

I nodded. "Yes." Oh! "My father's notebook!"

"The police officer has been caught at the train station, and a good and trusted local constable has it, and had it copied immediately, which he gave to Jamie. It will be brought to London," she said. "Fear not. It is in safekeeping."

I started to cry again, overwhelmed with it all. She handed me a handkerchief. "Thank you for your kindness. It means so much. How did all of this come about?"

She settled in. "Thomas just completed the purchase of Winton Park, as you no doubt already knew," she said.

I nodded.

"Then he traveled here from London. He was eager to give the keys . . . Well, that doesn't matter just yet. But he was eager to come home. He arrived, we had a lovely dinner together, and then, this morning, he went out to see the horses as they were being reshod after his travels to the Lockwoods' other holdings around the country."

I looked longingly at the jug of water on the bedside table. "Would you like some?" she asked.

I nodded. I was so thirsty. She poured the water into a crystal glass. It soothed my smoke-ragged throat as I swallowed. "I'm sorry, please continue."

"Once in the stables, he saw the fire between Darington and Winton Park. He knew the local fields were being fired, of course, with the harvest in. Our arable land abuts that which he purchased from your trust, but he had not ordered either field fired, though other local fields were being fired. He immediately knew something was wrong."

She stopped speaking, looked hesitant, as if concerned it was all too much for me to take in right then. "Please continue," I said.

"He mentioned it to the men in the stable, and the blacksmith commented offhand that he hoped the young maid who had been sent to pack up Miss Young's things had escaped before the fire was there."

She continued. "Thomas, of course, knew that he had sent no such maid, but he didn't know if *you* had, of course."

"Yes," I said. "I had told no one that I was going."

"He had set someone to watch you in London, to keep an eye on you whilst he was gone even though he thought you were no longer interested in . . ." She shrugged. "He wanted you cared for, no matter what."

Thomas. Thomas. My heart warmed. "What came of that man he'd set to watch me?"

"The police detained him the day they seized your townhouse, so he was not able to telegraph Thomas until Jones was captured at the train station. When word of that returned to the Metropolitan Police, they let him go, and he telegraphed today. Thomas did not know you were undergoing difficulties."

The man at the bakery cart and, no doubt, with several other disguises, had been his plant. Perhaps the rat catcher.

"In any case, Thomas asked what the name of this maid was, and the blacksmith said he did not know, but that he'd met her on the train on Monday night. She did not tell him her name, but she was a lovely lass with the prettiest silver blue eyes."

I smiled.

"Yes," Lisbeth said. "Then Thomas knew it was you. Then the smoke suddenly increased and was clearly gaining on the house and he hurried everyone out. The situation had clearly grown more dangerous for some reason."

"Jones poured lamp oil once he had me restrained," I said.

She nodded. "They gathered all the able-bodied men on the estate, and buckets, and set off. An accelerant of some sort had clearly been poured from the field toward the kitchens and laundry area, and the linen closet where you were found."

I sat up more firmly. "So it would look like burning the field stubble had set Winton on fire, but actually, it had been arson."

"Thomas rushed into the house looking for you. Several men looked in the carriage house, and one went toward the kitchens, which were on fire, but heard nothing. They regrouped, and when you did something to break the window the noise was heard, and

Thomas rushed to the storage room and then . . ." She looked at her hands. "You'll recall the rest."

"And Winton . . . ?" I almost didn't want to know.

She smiled. "It's fine. The men put out the fire before it got to the house. And your mother's things are safe as well. A little tidying up, a little rebuilding. It can be done when the house is modernized."

I laid back in the bed. Papa would be cleared; Mamma would be happy. If only . . . "Can I speak with Thomas?"

"Perhaps in a day or two," she said. "He's been given some medication to make him sleep. The doctor has said, in the case of internal damage, absolute rest and no movement or excitement is the best."

I nodded.

"That may be the best course of action for you, too," she said.

"Thank you." Once I could be reassured that Thomas was recovering well, we would return to London, perhaps together. My girls! *Cinderella!* Would I have time to finish the costumes?

What if Thomas did not recover?

No. Surely that would not come to pass. It must not.

"Gillian?" Lisbeth said.

"Oh, I'm sorry."

"I was saying that Lady Lockwood wanted to have dinner sent up to you. Do you feel up to eating something?"

"I'll try."

Lisbeth squeezed my hand. "Rest now. And pray."

"I shall pray with all fervency," I said.

Within an hour, a knock came at the door. It was growing dark by then, and I presumed it was a maid come to set the lamps and bring dinner.

"Please come in," I said.

A maid appeared, along with Lady Lockwood.

I struggled to sit upright. "Oh, I'm terribly sorry to have to greet you like this," I said.

"Don't get up, dear," she commanded, but gently. And I lay back again.

The tray was brought to me, with food and tea, and set on the bed. Yes, that Grey's tea, which Ruth had served to my father, likely when he'd sold the arable acreage to Thomas.

The maid turned around and curtseyed to her, and then to me.

"You!" I said with surprise. It was not Ruth!

The maid jumped. "I'm sorry, miss, do I know you?"

Lady Lockwood looked concerned, too, perhaps for my mental well-being.

The maid was the young girl whom I'd seen enter the carriage with Thomas, in London, outside of the Lyceum Theatre.

"I'm not sure," I said. "I thought perhaps I'd seen you in the theater district. I'm often there."

She smiled. "Perhaps. I was no longer able to act, and someone brought it to the attention of Lord Lockwood, who suggested I train as a maid under Lady Lockwood. It has been most purposeful." She glanced at Lady Lockwood.

Purposeful, I thought, and hid a smile. Then my heart broke again with the assumptions I had made and the fears I had tended, about Thomas and what I thought had been selfish intentions.

Would I ever be able to tell the man himself what he meant to me?

Lady Lockwood stood near me but did not sit down. She was not friendly, as Lisbeth had been, but I did not sense any rancor from her, either.

"I can have your . . . dress . . . cleaned if you like," she said. "Or

I'm sure we have something that can be quickly altered for you. Whichever you prefer, Miss Young, but you'll need to be suitably attired before you can be up and about."

I smiled. "I have no further need of my lady-in-disguise outfit," I said. "I can revert to being simply Miss Young. Suitably attired."

She smiled, lightly, her slightly doughy older-woman face breaking into soft wrinkles, even while her hair and outfit remained perfectly starched. "You have always been a lady, Miss Young, in or out of disguise."

My heart filled—unexpectedly—with affection. I did not let my welled tears fall, as I thought it would make her uncomfortable. I blinked them back. "Thank you, Lady Lockwood," I said. "I should like to speak with Lord Lockwood tomorrow, if possible."

"I will let you know if that is possible," she said. "Do try to eat something before you sleep. It will help you recover from your escapade."

I slept like the dead through Thursday. On Friday morning, the young maid brought me tea and breakfast, and I asked her if I might speak with Mrs. Lockwood. Soon, Lisbeth appeared in my room.

"Thomas?" I asked.

"The same," she answered. "No better, no worse."

"May I . . . May I visit him?"

"Yes," she said. "This afternoon. But first Mr. Colmore Dunn, Thomas's friend and barrister, has been here since yesterday. He is keen to meet with you whenever you are available."

"Oh, yes," I said. Now that I knew Papa was innocent I was

most eager to hear what he had learnt about the certificates. And then I could see Thomas!

Lisbeth's lady's maid came to help me dress in something borrowed, and afterward, she showed me to the library. Lisbeth tarried in the far corner, quietly chaperoning us.

"Mr. Colmore Dunn." I held out my hand. "It is good of you to see me." I sat down in a chair near the leaden cross-paned window where we could speak more privately. "You've heard . . . ," I began.

"About Lockwood, yes," he said. "I have not been able to see him. Have you?"

I shook my head.

"I believe he thought that your association had come to a conclusion?"

"He was mistaken, through no fault of his own," I said softly.

He nodded. "It did not take long, once I looked at the certificates, to investigate. The majority of the certificates were fine, legal, investments of long standing, intelligently chosen and would have increased in value if sold. The receipt signed by me, as you know, was for the sale of some land anticipating trustee duties, and I located the solicitor who had been instructed to pay off the house of Cheyne. I suspect your father had some concern that they may come after him, and wanted to prove the house had been paid for by directly traceable funds."

"So they cannot hold on to my home any longer?"

"No, Miss Young," Colmore Dunn said. "It has already been cleared of police presence, and the locks replaced. I received a telegraph this morning, and acted as your solicitor. I hope that was in order."

I could have kissed him, but of course I did not. "Yes, very much so. Thank you ever so much."

"There were, however, some documents which caused concern. Specifically, the certificates which were signed, but the ownership left blank; the companies they belonged to also matched investment certificates with Inspector Collingsworth's name on them."

I stood in shock. "What?" Lisbeth looked my way, and I looked at her reassuringly and sat back down. "There were no certificates with the owner's name left unfilled. They were all made out to Papa. There were no share certificates with Collingsworth's name on them amongst Papa's things. I'm certain of it. I reviewed them all."

Now Colmore Dunn looked shocked. "But yes. Both the blank ones and Collingsworth's are related to a tin mine scheme in Singapore, headquartered in London. In cases of fraud, these are sometimes handed out, *en masse*, and illegally, to the protector, to be filled in later as bribes or hush money. They increased in value so quickly they were more valuable, often, than cash."

"Collingsworth had been paid in this manner."

"Oh yes," Colmore Dunn said. "He was likely offering them to others doing his bidding, too. I'm certain once the lid is lifted the investigators will find many more means of payoff and protection money. Your father's notes will be a great asset for that investigation. They thoroughly documented the police he knew were involved, and those who were clean and would testify. He noted the names of both officers and titled men utilizing the underage King Street brothel, and they shall not bear up under the public shame which shall be heaped upon them. Many of them are likely involved in those illegal investments, too, and your father has documented it all. It's no wonder Collingsworth was desperate to get his hands on that notebook of your father's. It reveals all."

"They visited the King Street house to engage young women

of . . . ill repute. Is that right? Police and the titled, foreign investors, all of them?" My stomach clenched, and I closed my eyes for a moment to let a wave of nausea pass.

His face grew somber. "I will speak to you honestly, Miss Young, as Matilda would prefer I speak with her. Yes. I'm sorry to say that bad men often entertain potential clients and associates in a terrible manner and a few bad officers sometimes participate as a perquisite of the arrangement. Terrible business. Shameful. Knowing their names, though, will help trace their involvement both with, well, underage girls as well as fraudulent investment schemes. When Thomas is well enough, I am sure he will speak with Lord Shaftesbury and see that those men are brought to account as well."

Mrs. W was right. The highborn almost never answered for their actions. My face must have betrayed my lack of confidence.

"There are many ways to see justice wrought, Miss Young. It shall be done, I assure you."

"Did Collingsworth kill my father?"

"I do not know. Perhaps he did of his own accord, or was ordered to, or ordered someone to. As you've worked out by now, it's not likely that the cart accident was an accident at all."

"The angles weren't right," I agreed. "But I could not have known for certain."

"Without knowing the motivation behind it, it would have been difficult for anyone to ascribe his death to a murder with certainty. Now that we know what—and who—he knew was involved with criminal association and activities, and have notes to prove them, an investigation will certainly solidify the truth."

"Murdered," I said. I'd known it, I supposed, all along.

Colmore Dunn nodded. "It is most probable that your father was killed because he wanted to see justice brought in matters of fraud and the trafficking of those girls stopped. There will be an inquest, rest assured. The truth will out."

Papa. I love you. I admire you. I miss you. I'm so sorry.

"And the certificates?" I looked at a blank transfer share. "I am certain I have never seen this before. I looked through them all most carefully."

"Although Collingsworth's name was listed in your father's notebook, the proof of his involvement, and all the indictments that will follow, will be led by way of these transfers and attendant certificates."

"Sergeant Collingsworth—the inspector's son—returned them to me. I looked at them then and saw no blanks, nor certainly anything with his father's name on it. Is he—Francis, that is—under suspicion?"

"For the moment it is more than likely because of the level of his father's involvement. Everyone associated will be suspect until that suspicion is removed. He remains at his home, and in uniform, though."

"Could the fact that these certificates unaccountably appeared throw Papa's innocence into question?"

He thought for a moment. "Could possibly. The justices will want a clear accounting from whence everything came."

Perhaps Papa was not in the clear just yet. "I must visit Francis," I said. "Sergeant Collingsworth. He may know the truth of the certificates, as he had them delivered to me."

Colmore Dunn put his hand up in protest. "He may not have been involved. It may have been someone else," he said. "In any case, Lockwood would not hear of you calling on the man after what his father has put you through."

"But Lord Lockwood is too ill to accompany me." My heart crushed within me, under the very delicately beaded plastron of the dress Lady Lockwood had found for me.

I smiled, just a little. The crushed heart had provoked a sudden thought, another thought, a tenth or hundredth thought, of Thomas.

"Miss Young?" I'm sure Colmore Dunn found nothing to be cheered about at this juncture, other than the possibility of my father's innocence.

"I've just had an idea," I said. "Do you know where Lord Lockwood keeps his fencing equipment, here at Darington?"

He nodded. "Of course. There's an outbuilding we use for practice."

"I'd like your help with something, if you would. Then I shall ask him about London."

CHAPTER THIRTY-FIVE

HAMPSHIRE AND LONDON

I realized how contrary to etiquette it was, a lady visiting a gentleman's bedchamber. But Thomas could not be moved from his room and he had asked to see me. No one would contradict his instruction.

His valet whispered to me, "Do not stay long."

I agreed. "I shan't."

Then his valet went to the attached sitting room where Lisbeth waited for me.

I walked toward the bed and set down the item I had brought with me, quietly, on the floor.

"Thomas," I whispered. His eyes were closed, the lashes fanning out against his cheeks, which were pink with fever. I longed to caress the little sprinkle of freckles to the side of his eye, and this time, I did. His beard had been trimmed; his faithful valet had seen to it, I presumed. I could remain looking at him for a long while, drinking in the sight of him, a sight I had not expected to see, certainly not at close quarters, again.

And now, perhaps this would be the last time. I could not countenance the idea. I bent over and gently kissed his lips.

The lashes fluttered open, and he looked at me, his rusty-brown eyes clear in spite of the pain, and then he smiled. "I do believe, in the fairy tales, the prince is supposed to kiss the princess and then she awakens, not the other way round."

"If she had to wait for that, perhaps the princess would have gone unkissed."

He laughed, and then winced; it had clearly caused him some pain.

I silenced him and put my hand on his face. "You must get well."

He nodded, but we both knew he had little say over that now.

"Pray for me," he said.

"Constantly. I wrote to you immediately after Lady Tolfee's ball, but the letter was stolen. I'm sorry you did not know how I feel about you. It offered my apologies, and I said, well, I said you are all that I'd hoped for, which is still true, more than ever, true." I looked at the floor. "I've brought something for you. To take from you."

He looked at me wonderingly, and then I lifted up the plastron, which I'd had Colmore Dunn find. "What?"

I smiled. "You don't need to guard your heart any longer. I will do it for you."

He reached out and took my hand and brought it to his lips. They were very hot, and I tried to keep my fears from my face. I sought to further reassure him. "Has anyone explained to you the situation that occurred this week?"

"A little," he said. "Enough for me to know that you are safe and well, your father is likely innocent though it's not yet proved, and that Winton is not burnt."

"That is enough for now," I said. "May I send Colmore Dunn to question Sergeant Collingsworth? It may be that he has some information that will clear my father."

"Will Collingsworth speak honestly with him?"

"I don't know," I answered. "I hope so."

He took my hand. "You go. Colmore Dunn will accompany you."

I shook my head. "No. I will stay here with you till you are well."

He shook his head and when I could see it caused him pain, I laid my hand alongside his cheek. "Quiet, now. Do not move."

"You must go to London. It is likely that your father is not the only innocent man—it may be that Sergeant Collingsworth is also an innocent man, and I do not wish to see harm done by him. Nor do you, I know."

"Someone else can go."

He shook his head once more, but gently. "No one else can sew the *Cinderella* costumes. Finish the designs. Fuse the gowns with love and skill from within." He squeezed my hand. "Just you."

"No," I said.

"Yes, I insist. I do not want you to remain here, seeing me like this, being here if . . . I should rather have you think upon our best days."

I wiped away a tear. "Which lie ahead."

He smiled, the flush in his face rising. Fever. "Most certainly." He contradicted the fear he'd just spoken.

"Then you must stay in London," he said. "Until I come to fetch you."

"No. I shall return here until you are well."

He held my hand. "There is nothing you can do here. I will either heal or not. There are things you can do in London. You can collect your girls again. I assume you took them to stay at the Mission while you went on a mission of your own?"

I smiled. He knew me. No one could have told him that.

"Then there is *Cinderella*," he said.

"Someone else can sew it."

"Come, now, Miss Young. What of your calling? Where is the passion you so often spoke of?"

I leaned close. "My passion is here. At Darington."

He closed his eyes, and then looked at me once more. "Now, knowing that, I can be content whatever comes my way. Go, Gillian. Go, and sew, for me. Promise me. It means the world to me to know that I have encouraged you to do and be whom you are meant to be. Sew them for me. Please. I shall be there presently, in full health, and we shall watch the performance together and delight in your creations. I love you, Gillian."

"I love you, Thomas." I blinked but the tears fell anyway and he caught one on his hand. Then he closed his eyes, and his breathing slowed, and he fell back into his sleep again. I brushed his cheek with my hand and stood.

I will sew. I will sew for you. We shall have our happy ever after.

Lisbeth promised to keep me up to date, daily via telegraph, on Thomas's well-being. If he took a downward turn I should be back to Darington on the next train, or riding bareback or running barefoot if need be. I pulled a blue ribbon from my hair—a favor, for the swordsman—and left it wrapped round his fingers, whilst he slept, before I left.

Once in London, the first thing I did was hire a carriage and go toward the Theatrical Mission. Mother Rachel nearly cried when she saw me. "You've returned!"

"I have, indeed," I said. "I've come to collect my girls and Mother Martha. I do not know if there will be enough time to sew the costumes, all of them, and properly, as there are only two months before dress rehearsals. But we shall try."

"I have another woman I can send," she said. "If you have room. She's very experienced in the theater. Used to sew till she got married. Then her husband died, and she has nothing . . ."

"Send her along," I said. "Sooner the better!"

My girls raced up the stairs, and I gathered them into my arms and cried into Ruby's thick hair, holding Charlotte all the while. I let go of them and Mother Martha came to me, radiating peace and love.

"We've work to do, young lady," she said.

"We have!"

Once I got them settled and sewing, I thought I should find out how to contact Mrs. W. I did not know where her sister lived, but I should certainly send for her right away. I did not like to pry into her things but had no other means to find where her sister might live.

I went into her chamber, which was sparsely furnished. She rarely bought anything for herself, preferring to use the stipend from the account my mother had established for her for her charitable causes, and not for herself. I pulled open a bureau drawer. There was a Bible and some memorabilia from various speakers. There were some letters. I paged through them and found some with a postmark near the time her sister's husband had died. There was a return address on them: Oakley Manor. Her sister lived in Hampshire, not so far from Winton, perhaps twenty miles or so.

I opened the letter—yes, it was to her sister. I would send for her.

As I went to push the drawer shut, though, something caught my eye. It was round, and rolled forward as I pushed the drawer back. It looked familiar somehow. I picked it up. It was a wooden replica of my signet ring.

I held it and looked at it. Yes, it exactly matched the signet ring design, which was complex and unusual. It had red wax on it. It had been used to seal a letter at least once.

Any letter sealed with that signet would be understood to have been written by me. Or by Mamma.

Cold washed over me. I took a small handful of the letters that Mrs. W had written and returned to my bedroom. Once there, I fished out the letter that Mamma had written to Papa, telling him she wanted to donate Winton Park. I also opened up one of her love letters to Papa. I laid three documents side by side on the bed.

Mrs. W's handwriting on her own letters was different from Mamma's in almost every way. And the two letters from Mamma were nearly exact. But the manner in which Mrs. W hooked her letter *h* was very different from the way Mamma expressed it. It was expressed like Mrs. W's on the letter declaring Mamma's intent to donate Winton Park.

She'd tended to all of Mamma's correspondence; of course she could mimic her handwriting.

I recalled what Thomas had told me long ago, about fencing. *I repeat a stroke so many times that when I am fencing I can focus on tactic and strategy knowing my arm will do what it has been trained to do by repetition.*

She had forged the letter from my mother, stating her desire to give Winton Park to the Cause. She had lied to me. Duped me!

My fists balled and I could barely stand up straight as the anger coursed through me and forced the blood into my head. Then I thought back on her long life with us. She had always given, never taken. Or had she? Perhaps she had taken more that I was not aware of. Once trust is unresolvedly undermined, every-thing is shaded in question-mark gray.

I went to get the flower book that she had written in with Mamma. Yes, Mrs. W's *h* was hooked; Mamma's was not.

The light was going dim. Louisa had been found and Mother Martha came down the stairs. "Are you all right, Miss Young?"

I shook my head. "No, I do not think that I am. Someone I trusted seems to have done me a grave harm, and I do not know how to make sense of it."

"Have you asked them? Perhaps that would be best. Directly talking to one another solves many problems."

Yes. I wouldn't mail her, nor send for her. I would journey back to Hampshire, just for a day, and speak with her, directly and in person, there. I did write to Francis, at the Chelsea division, so his mother could not intercept my correspondence again. I asked if I might meet with him at his convenience and informed him I would be bringing my solicitor, Mr. Colmore Dunn. The next morning came his reply, a solitary word, *Yes.*

Mother Martha and the girls and new seamstress sewed all day, morning till night, though she did give me *Little Women* to read on the train, bookmarked. I would return and join them to sew shortly. I had to resolve two things first. Mrs. W and Francis.

I took Thomas's man for protection and boarded the train to Oakley.

Oakley Manor was large, as large as Winton Park. I do not know why that surprised me, except that given Mrs. W's abhorrence of wealth and titled people I had not expected to find her sister living on such a large estate. Thomas's man said he would wait in the carriage for me.

I walked up to the door, and a man opened it. "I am Miss Gillian Young, come to call on Mrs. Woodmore."

"Are you expected?" he asked. The rise of his eyebrows implied surprise.

"No," I said. "Certainly I am not."

He showed me into the sitting room, and within a few minutes, Mrs. W came to greet me. She looked into my eyes and I back at her and knew that she understood the reason for my visit.

"Gillian," she said. "I'm so glad you are well. I've worried and prayed, when they came to seize the house. Has it been returned to you?"

"Yes," I said. My tone was clipped. "Papa's name is cleared, and Collingsworth is in jail."

"Francis?" Her hand flew to her throat.

I shook my head. "No. Not yet, anyway." We locked eyes. She did not look haughty, but she did not look remorseful, either. She looked righteous. Self-righteous.

"Winton Park," she said simply. "You know."

"Yes. I . . . I am at an utter loss as to why you forged a letter in my mother's hand, or how it even came to pass."

She took a deep breath. "Can we walk in the garden?"

I nodded. She did not want the staff to overhear and I could not blame her. Once we'd arrived at the gardens, which were fading with the year, going brown with advancing age as a woman would go gray, Mrs. W began to speak.

"One of my responsibilities was responding to your mother's correspondence, as you know. She was often gone, and would not ever take the ring off her finger, having come from her own mother. Very much like you do not remove it now."

I twisted the ring on my finger. It would never leave my hand.

"We had a duplicate made so I could respond to her mail in a timely manner. When she died, I kept it."

"That all makes very good sense," I said. "I do not, however, understand why you forged a letter from her, indicating that she wanted to give Winton away. Did she ever tell you that, and you were simply carrying out her wishes?" I hoped. I truly hoped.

"Not directly," she said. The smell of mulch was pungent and earthy and stank of decay as we passed dormant flower beds.

"There is only a yes or a no," I insisted.

"Then no," she replied as firmly as I. "She was a bit frivolous, an actress, preoccupied. She was a lovely woman and my dearest friend. But right up till the end she needed me to ground her, to help her do what was best. She'd often told me that. Which is why she'd left your schooling to me."

"But that is a far cry from the letter and its implications, and how you misled me. I am crushed, honestly."

"I knew your father had paid off Cheyne Gardens; I'd heard him speak of it one day whilst you were at Drury Lane. So it was not as though I thought I'd leave you without a home. You had one home and I meant what I said in that letter. No one needs such a grand house."

"How dare you? You are living in a grand house now!"

A wave of realization crossed her face. "The cost that this house came with was not worth the gain," she insisted. "My sister would no doubt agree."

I shook my head. "If there was nothing wrong with you arranging to give my house away, why keep it a secret?"

"You are too young to be trusted with a decision of this magnitude." She stopped walking and turned indignantly toward me. "Perhaps somewhat frivolous, like your mother. It has always been my intention to do right by her, and by you. To guide you when guidance was required—and I believe it still is."

I faced her. "How dare you insult my mother—your friend and, I may point out, benefactress. What to do with Winton was not your decision, and I cannot understand why you think it should be. You didn't even pretend to guide me. You stole my property, because you knew that while I am now old enough that I would not necessarily 'obey' *you*, I would certainly honor my mother's wishes. Only they were not her wishes! I could have you charged with fraud! The property would have come to my mother if she'd lived longer than Grandmamma. But when Mamma perished first, my grandmother thought I would be a sound judge of what should happen with Winton Park. She'd left it to *me*, in trust. It was mine to decide what to do with."

Bowing under my unexpected fury she looked slightly shamed, fearful, and perhaps had realized a little the enormity of how she'd overstepped. Her voice was slightly softer, but not contrite. "In any case, you like the Cause, believe in it. I've seen it myself, with their Theatrical Mission outreach. The resources are being put to good use, *right now*, for those who need them, rather than being diverted to provide new pipes in an old house used only occasionally by the well-to-do."

I shook with anger. "When they came to look through the house the first time, for Papa's hidden items, you told them to return. You knew they, and I, would look through the cubbyhole in the bed and you placed the letter then, before their second visit." I had puzzled it out on the train.

"Yes," she said. "I placed the letter with the other letters. There was a picture there, of a young woman, among your father's things. I shouldn't have wanted to have thought he was involved in, well . . . But perhaps he was."

"He was not," I said firmly, though I did not know yet who the young woman was.

She sighed. "I'm so pleased. Your father was always such a good man, of good stock, hardworking and honest, and when I saw that picture, well, I worried. He was lovely to your mother. A direct contrast to"—she lowered her voice—"the titled," she whispered, and she oddly took on the tone of a young girl, though she was far from one. It frightened me a little.

"They do not account for their wrongs. Their women are mute—they cannot speak or act without the permission of their husbands. Look at Lady Tolfee, Lady Lockwood. This was not like your mother's situation—she married middle class and did what she wanted. Your grandfather made every visit to Winton Park a horror for her. She came to loathe it."

"Perhaps she had no love left for *him*. But the house . . ."

Her eyes looked toward the house. "This house belonged to my sister's husband," she said. "A viscount."

"The man who has just died?" I asked.

She nodded and lowered her voice. "He *took* me, when I was but a girl. Gave me fripperies and ribbons and told me how much prettier I was than my older sister. And then . . . And then he had me for the price of a penny cake, his final gift to lure me into his dark chamber."

Her eyes filled with tears. "It hurt for years, in my body. In my heart, forever. I would not wish that on anyone."

In spite of my anger, I recalled our many years together and softened for a moment. "Did you tell your sister?"

She nodded. "She said she was sorry. There was nothing she could do, and that he was unkind to her as well. That is not the kind of man your mother wanted for you. Now you'd come into your trust, Winton Park might have provided a dowry for just such a man. I knew I had to move quickly, and I did. I have helped you avoid marital misfortune and put the money to godly use."

Ah, yes. Godly use. I recalled the phrase she used in the letter: "The house is too big for one person, in truth. It is not necessary or even godly for anyone to have a home this size . . ."

I waited a moment, to calm myself, before continuing, and a familiar Bible passage came to me.

And he spake this parable unto certain which trusted in themselves that they were righteous, and despised others: Two men went up into the temple to pray; the one a Pharisee, and the other a publican. The Pharisee stood and prayed thus with himself, God, I thank thee, that I am not as other men are, extortioners, unjust, adulterers, or even as this publican. I fast twice in the week, I give tithes of all that I possess. And the publican, standing afar off, would not lift up so much as his eyes unto heaven, but smote upon his breast, saying, God be merciful to me a sinner.

I finally spoke. "Many titled men, like Lord Lockwood and Lord Shaftesbury, are kindly and work on the behalf of justice. There are good and bad men—and women—everywhere, in every class. I am a woman grown and can make my own decisions. I'm no longer a schoolgirl who must be directed."

"Will you not need me to return to London to further assist you, then?"

I answered firmly. "Perhaps your sister needs you here now."

She nodded. She knew that all was forgiven but all had irrevocably changed between us, too. "That is perhaps best. Will you . . . Will you tell the Cause?"

"Have you used my ring for any other purpose? Forged any other documents?" I asked.

Mrs. W shook her head.

"I shan't tell the Cause," I said. "But not to protect you. Because I do not want the gift, or those it helps, or my mother's memory, or my own work at their Theatrical Mission, tainted."

We stood and began walking back. As we did, she plucked a fading flower near the pathway. I thought of the flower book she'd shared with Mamma, which, in the end, had indicted Mrs. W. She brought the flower to her nose, but its petals, loose with age, fluttered to the ground as she did.

She loves me not. She loves me not.

When we reached the front, she coolly embraced me and I her before I turned to the carriage, which waited for me.

Nothing more needed to be said.

On the way back to the train station, I opened *Little Women* to the passage that Mother Martha had marked. I'd been too anxious on the journey out to read at all.

> *Don't laugh at the spinsters, dear girls, for often very tender, tragical romances are hidden away in the hearts that beat so quietly under the sober gowns, and many silent sacrifices of youth, health, ambition, love itself, make the faded faces beautiful in God's sight. Even the sad, sour sisters should be kindly dealt with, because they have missed the sweetest part of life.*

I closed the book and thought of my man, at Darington. He had told me not to come, but in this I would take my own counsel. It was but a stop or two ahead. I must go. I would arrive unannounced and uninvited, which would be most unusual, but I cared not. After the hired carriage delivered us to Darington, I asked the butler if I might see Lord Lockwood.

His mother came to greet me in the parlor. "Has he progressed?" I asked.

She shrugged. "It is difficult to know. The doctor has just today said to prepare ourselves for the worst."

My heart sank. "May I see him?"

She looked resolute, but as I held a soft and steady gaze, her face softened some. "It cannot do any more harm."

I didn't know if she meant that as a rebuke—if she blamed me as I, indeed, blamed myself for his injuries, but she led me upstairs to his bedchamber. After consulting with Thomas's valet, Lady Lockwood let me into the room. I went to his bed and sat on the nearby chair. His skin was pale and his breathing slow, perhaps too slow.

"Thomas?" I said softly. He did not stir. "Thomas?" I tried once more, but nothing changed.

I leaned over and kissed him, but he did not awaken.

I waited a few more minutes and Lady Lockwood reappeared. I understood; it was time for me to leave.

As the train moved forward back to London, I held my emotions in check, outwardly. Inside, I implored the Lord over and over again not to allow either Thomas or I to miss the sweetest part of life.

CHAPTER THIRTY-SIX

Soon after I returned to London, Louisa handed the delivered post to me. There was a note from Francis, asking if I could come and see him the following day at the Chelsea Metropolitan Police division.

Mr. Colmore Dunn was telegraphed and escorted me. The inspector's door was shut; the office dark behind it. I did not like to think how it was for him in jail but my own father was dead in Hampshire and I did not spare many moments of remorse for Collingsworth. He would have seen me dead, too.

We arrived at Francis's office and a constable opened it, announced us, and then locked eyes with Francis. He nodded at the constable and then the door was shut behind us.

"Sergeant Collingsworth, my solicitor, Mr. Colemore Dunn. Mr. Colemore Dunn, Sergeant Collingsworth."

"How do you do?" Colmore Dunn asked. Francis nodded and indicated that we should both sit down.

"I'd like to start by apologizing for my father," Francis said. "Turns out he was a wicked man."

I nodded. "I'd thought he and my father were like brothers."

He grimaced. "Perhaps Cain and Abel."

There wasn't much to contradict, but I appreciated his acknowledgment of it. "I'm sorry for you and for your mother," I offered, and he nodded.

"I'm here, primarily, about the investment certificates," I said. "When you handed them to me in the park there were only completely filled-out certificates with my father's name on them. By the time I handed them over to Mr. Colmore Dunn, there had been added to them some certificates to a fraudulent company with your father's name on them, and some signed but not filled out with an owner's name."

Francis nodded and sat back in his chair. "I'd believed all along that my father was correct in asserting that your father had been involved in prostitution and fraud. I was so disappointed; your father been a hero of mine, of sorts. I believed my own father, though, in spite of growing misgivings. Who wouldn't?"

I nodded.

"Father said I should watch you, and he put people out to watch you, too, and report back to him. I thought it was for your protection, but in truth, he wanted to see if you had found anything that would incriminate him."

"He had my house searched during the funeral?" I said.

Francis agreed. "Yes. That is probably when your father's certificates were taken."

"And then he had my house searched once more after I returned from Winton the first time."

He nodded once more. "To see if you had located anything there and brought it back with you. He told me. He said he was looking for evidence against your father and unethical officers. The items you found in your father's bedroom—the address and the photograph—they were things your father would not leave at the division because they *might* shed light on the fact that he was secretly investigating, if they'd been found, but could not in and of themselves bring about solid answers, as you yourself found out. No need to bury them in the country. The notebook, however, listed everything needed to bring about criminal convictions. It had to be guarded.

"Your father was on the trail of the true criminals, and had intended to turn them in, and at the end, I suspect he'd been tipped off that they'd come looking for that evidence. I don't suspect he knew he would be killed and then, after his death, framed for their crimes."

"So," Colmore Dunn asked, leaning forward toward Francis. "When did you know you were mistaken about your own father?"

"When Gillian dropped the picture of that young girl, I began to understand." Francis looked at me.

"You knew her. I knew you recognized her," I said.

"Yes. Because photos are rare, they are commissioned for affection or transaction—the latter, I'm afraid, in this case. She came to the division one day looking for 'Collingsworth,' and because she was young and I am unmarried, they thought she meant me. When I went to meet her, she said, 'No, not you, the older man.' I asked my father about it then, and he said he didn't know her."

"You believed him?" I breathed more heavily. Where was she? What had happened to her?

"I did at the time," he said. "But when you dropped the photograph, and I picked it up, I saw she was wearing one of my mother's brooches, a very distinctive piece of heirloom jewelry that had gone missing. I knew then—he was lying.

"As time went on and occasion allowed, I searched the house, including my parents' bedroom. I found more pictures of girls in a drawer—girls who would most likely be used or sold. I found evidence he had been seeing those young girls at the brothel on King Street. Then I found the share certificates, signed, but not filled out with an owner's name, which is illegal. Why was a Metropolitan Police inspector hiding illegal certificates? And money. Lots of it. More than an inspector might ever come by rightfully."

"And you knew for sure," I said softly.

"I knew. When you sent a letter to me asking me to come and help you, and Mother took it and handed it to Father, he grew nervous. He looked for the illegal certificates, which I had then taken. I had them on me when you recalled me to your house to turn me down the last time . . . You were being watched, remember, so we knew you were growing close with the viscount. When you went downstairs to get the tea, I slipped into your father's study and put them in with the others. You had told me where he'd stored them," he said pointedly.

"I did," I agreed. I leaned heavily back in my chair.

"I knew Lockwood would be able to help you find out who they belonged to. Your father"—he looked back at me—"had taught me that evidence was everything and hearsay nothing. I did not know there would be a notebook, which you found. The only evidence at hand were the certificates. I hoped they would clear things up. They did. My father is a criminal."

"I'm sorry, Francis. That must have been very difficult—but honest—for you to do."

His face went red and I thought, for a moment, he might cry. "Mother has still not forgiven me."

"You?" I said. "Your father was the wrongdoer!"

Francis grimaced. "And what would it be to her if she had stayed with such a man all these years? She will never admit it, though she's been fraught with nerves nigh on a year."

Yes, I recalled her rashes, her nerves, her needing to lie down in the midst of our visit.

"Father looked everywhere, and then took what Roberts had and thought that was the end of it. But when he discovered the illegal certificates missing from our house he knew he must act quickly, and he did. He seized your home to look for them. He knew you'd go to Winton or elsewhere to look once more—the letter from your father, which he'd then come upon, was oddly worded and he has a policeman's ear for oddly worded statements."

"Then he sent Jones to follow me."

"Yes." He turned to me and blushed. "I enjoy your company, and thought it would be nice to court you. But then that took on a pressing urgency once I knew Father had it in for you. I thought that if we, well, married, you would be protected."

I smiled once more. "I appreciate your concerns, Francis. Your heart was in the right place."

"I also sent you some Bible pages with words blocked out to warn you." He blushed more deeply. "Clumsy, I know, but well intentioned. I hoped to warn you away from those who would harm you. When I saw you wouldn't be frightened off, I knew you'd follow the certificates through to the end, too. You did. I was quite proud of you."

Francis stood and we did, too. "Gillian?"

He opened the door, and stood to the side. Colmore Dunn stood behind us. Lining the hallway were dozens of officers, all in uniform, standing at attention. The officer I'd met eyes with at the funeral, whose voice I'd recognized as the one at my door, caught my glance and held it. His eyes were filled with tears. Had he been Papa's friend, and perhaps tipped him off, in the end?

Francis took my arm. "They want to honor your father because they had been led astray regarding his actions and integrity.

As he is not here, and you are, they will honor you in his stead," he said. "We all took the oath to protect, and your father lived it."

Tears filled my eyes and began to slide down my face faster than I could brush or blink them away.

Francis recited the Metropolitan Police oath loud enough for every man to hear.

"I, Francis Collingsworth of London, do solemnly and sincerely declare and affirm that I will well and truly serve the Queen with fairness, integrity, diligence, and impartiality, upholding fundamental human rights and according equal respect to all people; and that I will, to the best of my power, cause the peace to be kept and preserved and prevent all offenses against people and property; and that while I continue to hold the said office I will, to the best of my skill and knowledge, discharge all the duties thereof faithfully according to law."

Papa. You kept your oath. I am here for you now as are all these men.

I walked down the hallway and every man stood at attention. I held my head up. My father would have wanted it so. The district superintendent himself offered his arm and led me to the carriage. Colmore Dunn said nothing as I sobbed all the way to Cheyne Gardens.

When I returned home, there was a telegraph from Lady Lockwood. "Thomas awakened, and suddenly progresses very well," it read, simply. "He shall be in touch soon."

My heart soared and I fell to my knees and cried. The girls were distressed by my tears until I told them they were tears of joy, and then they rejoiced with me.

The following week, I received a package, and a short note. I opened the note first.

It was in Thomas's hand! "Do not by any means sell or give this away! I shall see you as soon as I can travel once more. All will be well, so do not worry about the time from now till then—we shall have ever-after together. Sew! Sew! I remain, as ever, your loving and devoted Thomas."

I could barely contain myself and tore open the package like a child at Christmas. Yards and yards and yards of perfect white velvet: silky, the softest, most glistening fabric I'd ever seen, it cascaded in a shimmering froth over the hand and arm as it was held. So delicate, though, difficult to cut, easy to make a mistake. I would have to take my time and I would do it myself.

"Oooh, miss. For a wedding dress!" Ruby shouted from the stairway.

"Spying again, you naughty girls? No one has proposed marriage—at least not to *me!*" I pretended to be angry and then we all shouted with happiness and glee before racing upstairs to work till the wee small hours on *Cinderella.*

CHAPTER THIRTY-SEVEN

NOVEMBER, 1883

It was the one of the final nights of dress rehearsal for *Cinderella*, when the press would be present for the practice performance, ready to give what we all hoped would be stunning reviews of affirmation and appreciation. The costumes had been delivered, barely, the week earlier. Miss Vaughn, who was to play Cinderella, was thrilled with all of her outfits, and I was thrilled for her. "It is a triumph," Wilhelm had told me, and I sighed in relief. There had been no more visits from the police and my employer was happy. I could now, just barely, begin to rest.

The girls, of course, were most excited to see the forest fairies costumes onstage not only because those were the ones they had worked on, but because they themselves had been pantomime actresses.

"I shall see if I can acquire some tickets for you to attend a performance just after Christmas," I said, and they tittered like mice. "Why is that funny?" I shooed them upstairs to pack up the salon for the Season.

The next day Ruby would go to live with my friend Sarah Gordon, to apprentice with her as a wigmaker. She was excited, and

I was excited for her. But oh, how my heart would miss her. Charlotte would stay with me, not only to sew, but to help me arrange a new mission—I'd hoped to set up a dormitory for training young actresses to design and sew. Mother Rachel said she knew just the woman to be the housemother—someone from the Cause!

Later that afternoon a package was brought to me and I opened it.

I opened the box. It was filled with a dozen yellow long-stemmed roses tied together by a silver blue ribbon, and a card. "I would enjoy attending the dress rehearsal with you. Can you be ready by seven? With love, Thomas."

Thomas? He was in London? I'd had no idea! Why the dress rehearsal? Of course, well, *of course* I could be ready. Had he made arrangements? It would be most irregular for members of the public to attend if Mr. Harris had not been consulted.

I took a deep breath and then went through my wardrobe to find something suitable to wear.

Perhaps the blue crushed velvet. It set off my eyes and would look pretty with a snowy muff and fur hat. "Ruby!" She came running down the stairs. "Help me make a beautiful woven plait of my hair!"

"Yes, miss," she said. "Right away."

An hour later I looked in the mirror. Ready.

Ruby raced back up the stairs, and just before seven I heard a carriage roll up outside of my house. It was Thomas!

That day, I had no care for protocol. I flung the door open wide and raced down the steps, slightly slippery, and fell into his arms. The night was dark with autumn already, and the fog had crystallized into tiny jewels that hung in the air. He held me at arm's length for a moment, then pulled me to him, whispering my name and kissing my temples, my forehead, my lips. "I've come back for you, my love, my life. Let me look at you, keep you, never let go of you."

I nearly sobbed with relief and clutched him tightly, breathing deeply of his sandalwood and musk, but then, though, oh! Perhaps I might be hurting him. "You look so healthy, so well, but I do not want to hold too tight."

He laughed, loud and robust, strong. "You will never hold me too tight, my dearest love. I am well and your costumes are complete and we are together and shall never be parted again." His voice lowered to soft and soothing.

He ran his fingers over my face before pulling me near and kissing me. I closed my eyes and reveled in the moment, enmeshed in him, fully believing, now he was here, that all was well.

"You're back. You're recovered," I whispered once more, senselessly, thankfully. He kissed me once more and I heard a pair of giggles. Ruby and Charlotte stood on the porch steps.

"Come along, then," Thomas called out to them.

Why, yes, they, too, were dressed and ready to go out.

I turned to him. "They are accompanying us?"

He nodded. "Yes. I asked Mother Martha as well, but she declined."

We four got into the carriage and merrily made our way to the Theatre Royal. We walked through the beautiful doors and then into the foyer, which was filled with the press, some important patrons, and people in production—all of my lifelong friends! They looked at me and some waved. I had the idea that they were expecting us to be here somehow.

How wonderful. I had told Thomas I rarely attended as a guest, and he had arranged for me to do so on this most important night. A man strode toward me, purposefully. "Miss Young. I'm so pleased you could attend as an honored guest tonight."

I could barely stop myself stuttering. "Mr. Harris. Thank you, thank you very much. It's an honor, sir!" I was about to introduce him to Thomas, but they nodded toward one another so I assumed they had already made an acquaintance.

"My dearest," Wilhelm came close. "Here, take one of the front-row seats." He led us forward, and when we arrived at our seats I found that my friend Sarah was already there, and so were Francis, Colmore Dunn, and Matilda, who waved a friendly hello.

"You arranged for everyone to be here?" I could barely believe it.

"Yes," Thomas said. "You worked so hard. It only seemed right they celebrate with you."

We sat down in the middle of the row, just a few aisles back, and in a moment, someone tapped my shoulder. "Lisbeth!" I cried in delight.

She smiled. Jamie and Lady Lockwood sat on either side of her. "We all came from Hampshire for . . ." She stopped for a minute. "To ensure Thomas traveled well," she finished.

Well, yes, that made sense.

The lights dimmed and the curtains were pulled back. Act One.

The show was magnificent and the girls and I thrilled to see our work come to life on the stage. I sensed a change in the mood, though, from the stage and round me as we headed into the final acts. Thomas took my hand, directed me to stand, and then led me to stand in front of the stage.

"What . . . ?" I asked, but he did not answer.

The "prince" then walked to the front of the stage. What was happening? His lines, though, were correct, and he spoke directly to us.

"Why, who is this? I do declare I've seen that face before. It is—it is, I'm sure it is the girl that I adore."

Thomas turned toward me. "Yes," he said softly. "I am here with Gillian, the girl I adore."

Then Miss Vaughn, in her Cinderella gown, came forward and stood near the prince, speaking to Thomas. "There's some mistake about it, sir. Too humble I'm by far."

I smiled and said to Thomas. "Yes, she speaks the truth."

The prince spoke again. "Oh, no, you are the princess of the ball last night—you are!"

"Last night, and the night before, and the month before, and all the months ever after," Thomas said, drawing near to me. He partially withdrew something from inside his coat.

The prince spoke his line. "Now sit down, dear, and try it, it's a natty little shoe; but though the size is rather small, I'm sure it will fit you. 'Tis clear you are my darling of the forest and the ball, so prove it, Cinderella love, afore the gaze of all."

From the stage, the chorus struck up once more. "Such a nice little slipper, come try my plan. See now if you get it right on you can. If you are true, and your duty will do, you can get on the slipper, you can, you can."

Thomas went down on his knee, and undid one of my shoes, which felt intimate and right. Then he slipped on a perfectly fitted slipper—one that looked somewhat like my mother's but was, in fact, designed to my sensibilities and size.

"You are your own woman, wearing your own shoe," he whispered. It fit perfectly. He stood again. "Will you be my wife, Gillian?"

A tear slid down my face and he brushed it away. "I will, Thomas. Most eagerly."

He leaned over and kissed me, and the stage and audience burst out in applause and calls.

In a moment, the chorus broke out once more in song. "Cinderella, thy troubles are over! From thy side, Prince, no more she's a rover! And together you both are in clover!"

I spoke the next line after Miss Vaughn prompted me. "My life," I whispered to Thomas, remembering his words to me just an hour earlier. He'd read the script.

He answered after the prince. "My love."

"Me for you," I said.

"You for me." He wound his fingers through mine. "As we happy ever after shall be."

When the performance was over, Jamie and Lisbeth said they would see the girls home so Thomas and I could travel together. His driver took the long way. Thomas said to me, "I cannot wait any longer. Let's be married, in Hampshire, at Christmas."

Christmas! I could not tell him that there was no possibility that I could have my wedding dress sewn within a month. There would be other duties to tend to, arrangements to make.

He leaned over and cupped my face in his hands, looking at me without flinching, before kissing me softly, then searchingly, then deeply, once, twice, thrice. My head grew light and I leaned forward to respond by kissing him a fourth time before pulling away to steady myself.

"You're not marrying me for my land, are you?" he teased, and I grinned. I'd written to him about Mrs. W and the forged letter, which was no doubt why he had decided not to invite her this night. "If you'll wait till we are married, I can transfer Winton back to you, without duties owed."

"There is no need," I said. "Our children will inherit all."

"There is a need," he said. "It is yours. What would you like to do with it?"

I thought for a moment. "Jamie and Lisbeth should live there, I think. Perhaps your mother would like to join them. She's become so accustomed to their companionship."

He laughed aloud and put his hand on the back of my head, drawing me to him again, kissing me passionately before reluctantly pulling away. "I can wait no longer," he insisted softly. "Christmas cannot come soon enough."

We arrived at Cheyne Gardens and he said good-bye to me, reluctantly. The girls were not yet back; I assumed Jamie and Lisbeth had taken them on a scenic route as well to allow Thomas and me time alone. I went inside the house, quiet, a hush, and then proceeded upstairs to tell Mother Martha the wonderful news. But when I arrived on the third floor, I found her room empty, and her things gone. There was a note, and I picked it up and read it.

> *Dear Miss Young,*
>
> *With Ruby moving on to a wonderful situation with Miss Gordon, there is no need for me to remain here any longer. I thank you for your kindnesses; the Lord bless and keep you. I have left a token of appreciation for you in the salon. "He that diligently seeketh good procureth favour..."*
> *Mother Martha*

The light was on in the salon. Once there, I gasped. In the center of the room, beautifully arrayed on the dressmaker's dais, was a wedding dress.

"Oh my . . ." I ran over to it. It had been cut from the white velvet cloth Thomas had sent to me—cloth that had been rolled up in bolts that very morning. Not only had it been cut to fit me, perfectly, it had been delicately beaded throughout. It was a sophisticated design that draped perfectly; in fact, it was the most perfect dress I had ever seen, the work of several master seamstresses over six months or more.

Started and completed in one night. How? It was not humanly possible.

It had not been humanly achieved. Once more, the book of Saint Matthew. *Take heed that ye despise not one of these little ones; for I say unto you, That in heaven their angels do always behold the face of my Father which is in heaven.* Prickles ran up my arms and spine. I went weak in a holy awe at the realization.

Mother Martha had placed *Little Women* nearby and I picked it up. It was bookmarked; I had somehow expected that. I opened it and read.

Women work a good many miracles.

Yes. It all made sense. How could I have ever guessed? Expected? My heart beat faster as memories came forward. Mother Martha's frightening off the young man following Ruby. Her knowing the passage to mark when I spoke with Mrs. W. The perfectly cut gloves for Lady Lockwood!

And of course . . . protecting Ruby on the Embankment late at night.

I sank into a chair as I sought to fully understand. The protection our house had unknowingly been under during months of duress. My taking in the girls, to protect them, had brought me protection as well.

"It is not only women who work a good many miracles," I whispered. "Angels work a good many miracles as well. Thank you, Lord Jesus, for your constant care and attention, seen and unseen."

The front door opened and the girls ran upstairs. When they saw the dress, they screamed in delight. "Try it on, try it on!"

Charlotte insisted and I did right there by lamplight, which cast amber halos over us all. I looked in the dais mirror, and we were all struck into silence.

Ruby sighed. "Miss. You are prettier than Cinderella. You will be the most beautiful bride ever."

If love counted for beauty, I knew that would be true.

Thomas was right: Christmas could not come soon enough.

EPILOGUE

DARINGTON HALL, HAMPSHIRE
FOURTEEN YEARS LATER, 1897

The string quartet played quietly in the background; most of our guests had arrived and were merrily conversing with one another. A pleasant hum went through the room as the champagne was circulated. This year, every year, the charity ball at Darington was held in aid of the sewing homes I'd established in London some thirteen years earlier. Hundreds of girls were trained and sent into safe situations each year.

Thomas, his beard graying a little at the tips, but perhaps even more strikingly handsome as he'd aged, put his arm round me. "Are you happy, Lady Lockwood?" he asked.

"Indeed I am, Lord Lockwood."

Inspector Collingsworth—Francis—and his wife, Sarah, my dearest friend, Sarah Gordon, mingled comfortably with some local friends of ours. Lisbeth and Jamie were somewhere; I could not see them just then. All of a sudden, a certain silence descended on the room. Eyes were drawn to the stairway, where our daughter had begun to descend.

She was thirteen, just old enough to attend, although her siblings could not, a fact that they had protested loudly to little avail. My heart swelled in affection, and love for her coursed through me. Her hair was rusty brown like Thomas's, her eyes were mine—no, my mother's. No. They were blue shot with silver, but they were entirely her own.

She smiled at her father and me and then turned her glance toward someone in the room. I followed her gaze to a young man, perhaps four or five years older than she, who seemed transfixed by her.

Thomas saw him, too, and a dark look crossed his face.

"Come, now," I teased. "You should be sympathetic to the young man."

He shrugged a little. "In a decade, if he proves himself honorable and forthright, worthy, and has learnt how to fence, he can approach me. But no sooner."

"Dance?" I took his hand as the quartet struck up again.

"Willingly." He led me and we danced, and our friends joined us.

I leaned toward his ear and whispered. "I have been reading *Little Women* with our daughter. I came across a passage which my mother had read to and wished for me, and that I wish for our girl. 'To be loved and chosen by a good man is the best and sweetest thing which can happen to a woman; and I sincerely hope my girls may know this beautiful experience.'"

"Do you believe your mother's hope for you was realized?" For a moment, he looked apprehensive.

I smiled reassuringly. "How could you even wonder? Better than she'd hoped." I reached up and touched the beloved spray of freckles next to his eye, and then brushed his hair from where it had strayed on his collar. "Mother wouldn't have dared hope for Prince Charming for me, but I did, and here you are."

The music slowed a little.

"My life," he said softly.

I answered, "My love."

He kissed my forehead and then wound his fingers through mine. "As we happy ever after shall be."

AUTHOR'S NOTE

PANTOMIMES

Theater is a big part of London. The Red Lion was the first theater built in London, in 1567, during the Elizabethan era. As theatrical entertainment grew to be popular not only with the masses but with audiences from all walks of life, more and more theaters were built, and the West End sprouted its theater district.

Pantomimes grew to be increasingly popular and elaborate forms of theatrical entertainment in the Victorian era. The website Dictionary.com defines pantomime as "a theatrical entertainment, mainly for children, that involves music, topical jokes, and slapstick comedy and is based on a fairy tale or nursery story, usually produced around Christmas."

Because they were centered around Christmas and fairy tales, a visit to a pantomime around Christmastime became a popular form of entertainment for families with children. Often overlooked, though, were the children who performed in them.

In an article found at the Victoria and Albert Museum website, one can learn that there were sometimes over six hundred actors in a given pantomime—all needing costumes—and that during the Christmas holidays sometimes two performances a day would be put on. That is a lot of work, especially for children. The V and A tells us that "The most elaborate Victorian pantomimes were at Drury Lane Theatre in London."

The Christmas 1883 pantomime really was *Cinderella*, and my son was able to locate a copy of the actual script so, for the most part, the words drawn from that performance are the ones that were spoken.

About this same time, a woman named Ellen Barlee took up the cause of the Pantomime Waifs, as they were known, pointing out that they were often exploited as child laborers. She exposed that the children were not being educated, and given the negative public sentiment about actresses (who were thought to have low morals), the girls themselves had a difficult time finding employment when they were no longer children. Barlee worked tirelessly to help the girls develop wholesome domestic skills that they might use to find employment later, rather than being further exploited.

There was a theatrical mission on King Street, in the theater district, during that era, that reached out to actresses, actors, and pantomime waifs. Because prostitution, including child prostitution, was common during the Victorian era, too, people of good heart sought ways to protect the vulnerable from exploitation.

THE SALVATION ARMY AND CHILD TRAFFICKING

There were hundreds, perhaps thousands, of organizations intent on doing good for others in the Victorian era; it's heartening, and perhaps a little convicting, to see how many people were dedicated to lifting the misery of others. In this book, though, I focused not only on the Theatrical Mission but drew inspiration from the Salvation Army, a vibrant organization for good in London and, eventually, the entire world. All the best parts of the ministries of the Cause, in this book, were inspired by the work of the Salvation Army, a powerful tour de force for good in Victorian England. The news clippings I had Gillian read from her mother's scrapbooks were nearly exactly reproduced from actual clippings about the Salvation Army during the mid- to late-nineteenth century.

The Salvation Army was founded in 1865 by William Booth and his wife, Catherine. Both William and Catherine preached, though William generally reached out to the poor and undesirables they felt led to minister to, including prostitutes, alcoholics and morphine addicts, and the destitute, and Catherine raised funds from the wealthy. Their many children eventually joined them in ministry, and one son, Bramwell, was drawn to the cause of the exploitation of children. From the Salvation Army's website:

> "The law, as it stood in the early 1880s, said that a girl of thirteen was legally competent to consent to her own seduction. Girls under the age of eight were not allowed to give evidence against those who had abused them, as it was thought that they were too young to understand the oath.
>
> "Josephine Butler, a campaigner for women's rights, wrote a letter to Florence Booth, the wife of The Salvation Army's Chief of the Staff, Bramwell Booth, concerning the sale of young girls into prostitution. We have this letter and other correspondence relating to the case, including letters written by Catherine Booth, The Army Mother, to Queen Victoria.

"Florence Booth, as pioneer leader of the Army's Women's Social Work, had gained an insight into the lives of girls working as prostitutes. Through this work, the practice of trafficking girls to be used for immoral purposes, both in Britain and overseas, came to the attention of The Salvation Army.

"Bramwell Booth had walked the streets of London, seeing for himself the desperate situations that many of the young girls found themselves in. What he saw prompted him to speak with W. T. Stead, Editor of the Pall Mall Gazette.

"Stead was an admirer of The Salvation Army and was horrified to think that young girls were being bought and sold. He investigated the claims made by The Salvation Army and published his findings in the Pall Mall Gazette, 6–10 July 1885. The articles appeared under the title, 'The Maiden Tribute of Modern Babylon,' and Stead received much support. On 14 August 1885, the Criminal Law Amendment Act became law, raising the age of consent from thirteen to sixteen years."

Stead has been said to have been heavily influenced by his mother, an early crusader for the proper treatment of all women, including prostitutes. Sadly, after helping women and children into lifeboats and giving away his life jacket, Mr. Stead was among the victims of the sinking of the *Titanic*.

I wish the Criminal Law Amendment had been the end of it, that the good work these men and women did put a stop to child trafficking, but sadly, the practice continues. During the time I wrote this book, my friend Tina went to India to minister to rescued, formerly trafficked girls through the Catalyst Foundation, and our local Taproot Theatre Company sponsored a fund-raiser for Hetauda House, which helps such children in Nepal. England had its own large-scale scandal as recently as 1999–2013, involving the grooming of teenagers for sex trafficking and exploitation. And in Seattle, my hometown, the mother of a fifteen-year-old was interviewed by the *New York Times* in an article titled, "Every Parent's Nightmare," to discuss how her daughter had been trafficked into the sex industry.

There's more to do. If we each do for one what we cannot do for many, we can make a difference.

WINTON PARK

Winton Park was lightly based on Uppark, a country house in Hampshire, which suffered a catastrophic fire at one time. It's interesting to note that the writer H. G. Wells spent part of his boyhood at Uppark, where his mother was a housekeeper.

SPLICING FICTION AND FACT

It's such a pleasure for me to mix and mingle fictional characters (which I work hard to keep of the era) with people who actually lived. In this book, the most important "real" character has very little time on the page, but he had the most influence in history: Anthony Ashley-Cooper, Seventh Earl of Shaftesbury.

Lord Shaftesbury came from an old, storied, and moneyed family, but he took up the cause of the underdog at nearly every turn. He used his influence to help reform the lunacy laws, put in protection for child labor laws, and introduced laws protecting miners and especially climbing boys, better known as chimney sweeps. Those boys were often illegitimate children, or otherwise cast aside, and they suffered diseases of the lungs, eyes, and scrotum from being pressed up against sooty, hot chimneys so often.

Shaftesbury walked the talk. Georgina Battiscombe, in *Shaftesbury: A Biography of the Seventh Earl*, tells us that when Shaftesbury found a chimney sweep living behind his house in London, he rescued the child. He sent him to "the Union School at Norwood Hill, where, under God's blessing and special merciful grace, he will be trained in the knowledge and love and faith of our common Saviour." From this, I drew the inspiration for Thomas to take one wounded veteran and give him a warm home and employment as a driver.

Thomas's friend and barrister, H. A. Colmore-Dunn, was a real barrister practicing law at the time and was a fencing expert who went on to write books on the sport. His real wife was a progressive who was involved in suffrage—and writing novels.

Augustus Harris was the long-standing and famous manager of the Drury Lane Theatre, and was knighted in 1891. A gentleman of the era would belong to a club, and I find it amusing that Mr. Harris was the chairman of the Eccentric Club. The Garrick and the City of London Club, clubs to which Thomas, Lord Lockwood, belonged, are both still in existence. It's interesting to note that A. A. Milne of Winnie-the-Pooh fame bequeathed a large portion of his estate to the Garrick.

C. Wilhelm, the son of a shipbuilder, began work creating costumes at Drury Lane in 1877 and continued until 1897.

WHITE-COLLAR CRIME

The Victorian era was an age of expansion and capitalist fuel. Every decade brought new technological wonders. Because of the opportunities to make a lot of money, quickly, there was also an increase in white-collar crime and fraud. I was able to locate a court case involving a tin mine scheme upon which I based my false transfer shares crime. Then, as now, there were good investors and those willing to defraud, honest policemen and those who fell to their temptations.

This book is a tribute to all those who invest in the lives of others, whether it be by providing means for them to escape the human misery that is trafficking, by providing jobs and a future through employment, or by protecting the public well-being as police officers.

ACKNOWLEDGMENTS

I hardly know where to begin to thank the many people who sustain me with their love and affection, encouragement and exhortation, as well as bring their considerable talent and skills to assist me with the books.

Dr. Alex Naylor and Finni Golden are truly golden to me in the research, preparation, and editing of the books. They assist me as I research the dozens of threads that must be sounded out before being admitted into a book that I desire to be historically rich and accurate. Along the way they answer questions, prod me, and disallow me from putting a foot wrong, all with utmost intelligence and grace. When the manuscript is complete, these residents of Portsmouth, England, edit the work to ensure the characters sound English and not American, Victorian and not twenty-first century.

Jenny Q. of Historical Editorial is an amazing editor, friend, and sounding board. I would never write a historical novel without her assistance, and I offer my utmost gratitude and admiration for her skills, talent, and abilities. Plus, she is a wondrously smart, kind, and good person.

Sarah Gordon, Resident Costume Designer and Costume Shop Manager, or better known as Grand Empress of Costumeland, was a super help to me as I sought to understand theater costumers then and now. She showed me around her theater (Taproot) and her workshop, explained how costumers and dressmakers work, and answered my many pesky questions. You'll notice her little cameo—well-deserved!

I have so many friends willing to read the book and offer repeated professional insight: among them are Debbie Austin, Dawn Kinzer, Serena Chase, and Cindy Coloma. I am so grateful for their wisdom, friendship, and time.

My fabulous agent, Danielle Egan-Miller at Browne & Miller Literary Associates, along with fabulous co-agents Joanna MacKenzie and Abby Saul, did an amazing job not only offering editorial insight, but helping me navigate the complicated world of publishing. I'd be lost without them.

The final stop on this editorial journey is Beth Adams, senior editor at Howard Books. Her encouragement, plus on-point insightful edits, have made this book much stronger, cleaner, and engaging than it ever would have been without her, and I'm so grateful for her attentions.

Above all, I'm grateful for my husband, Michael, to whom I will have been married for thirty years when this book is published, and my amazing children, to whom I grow closer every year.

Thank you, God, for allowing me to join You in Your important work!

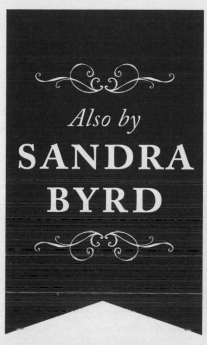
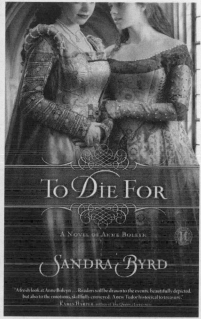

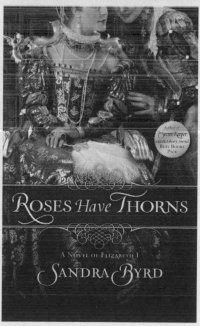

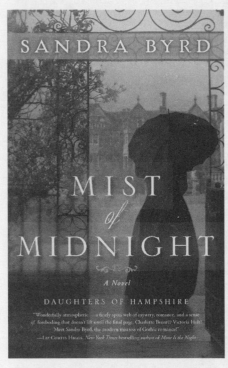
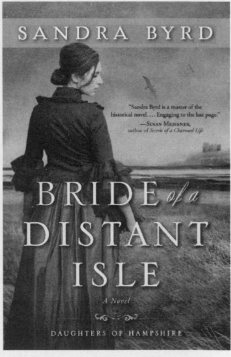